WHERE
ECHOES
LIE

ALSO BY SHANNON SCHUREN

The Virtue of Sin

WHERE ECHOES LIE

BY SHANNON SCHUREN

PHILOMEL

PHILOMEL BOOKS

An imprint of Penguin Random House LLC, New York

First published in the United States of America by Philomel Books,
an imprint of Penguin Random House LLC, 2021

Visit us online at penguinrandomhouse.com.

LIBRARY OF CONGRESS CATALOGING-IN-PUBLICATION DATA

Names: Schuren, Shannon, author.

Title: Where echoes lie / by Shannon Schuren.

Description: New York : Philomel, 2021. | Audience: Ages 12 and up. |
  Audience: Grades 7–9. | Summary: "A teenage girl must solve the mystery
  of the ghost bride to save her own future from the curse."—Provided by
  publisher.

Identifiers: LCCN 2021029274 (print) | LCCN 2021029275 (ebook) | ISBN
  9780525516576 (hardcover) | ISBN 9780525516583 (ebk)

Subjects: CYAC: Ghosts—Fiction. | Blessing and cursing—Fiction. | LCGFT:
  Novels.

Classification: LCC PZ7.1.S336555 Wh 2021 (print) | LCC PZ7.1.S336555
  (ebook) | DDC [Fic]—dc23

LC record available at https://lccn.loc.gov/2021029274

LC ebook record available at https://lccn.loc.gov/2021029275

Printed in the USA

10 9 8 7 6 5 4 3 2 1

CJKV

Edited by Liza Kaplan
Design by Monique Sterling
Text set in Adobe Caslon Pro, P22 1722 Pro, P22 Frenzy, Avenir, Mega LT, and Lake Informal LT Pro.

For Katie, who shares my own ghost story

THE LEGEND OF THE GHOST BRIDE

as told by Alice Slocum

Every town has its legends, and ours is no exception. In fact, Corbin is unique, because we've got two—the moonbow and the ghost bride. How they came to be intertwined, well, that's a story all its own.

It happened long ago, on a night much like this. Clear skies, aglow with the light of a full strawberry moon. The scent of honeysuckle so thick you could bathe in it. The air warm and heavy with the possibility of rain and the promise of summer. Nothing holds more promise than early June in Kentucky.

I reckon that's why our bride picked it. She was young, so young. And beautiful. All brides are beautiful, but this girl, there was something special about her. Radiant, some said, glowing with the kind of light that comes from pure happiness.

And why shouldn't she be happy? It was her wedding night.

But that part was a secret. She hadn't told her family about him—she was afraid they wouldn't approve. Which is a pity. If only someone had been there to help her. Or to warn her.

Really, it's a wonder no one guessed, what with the time she must have spent on that dress. Hand-stitched white lace, with a train long enough for its own caboose. She'd designed it to match the jewel-encrusted hair clip, which had been a gift from her lover—a sure sign his heart was pure. For a man doesn't give away a family heirloom if he doesn't have intentions. She wore it twisted into her hair just so, with a cluster of violets tucked in for luck. When she smiled, it put the sun to shame. How no one knew that girl was in love is one of life's great mysteries.

But she managed to keep her secret up until the wedding night. They were to be married, she and her lover, on the bluff overlooking the falls. They planned to meet at sunset, so they could say their vows as the sun slipped behind the mountains and the moonbow rose to bless their union.

Now, it wasn't as easy to get to the Leap back then. There was barely a path, let alone parking or pavement or cobblestone steps.

Certainly no safety railing.

But even then, it was the best view for miles.

The falls, churning and rolling beneath her. The sheer rock wall of mountain, rising behind her, moon-kissed and unbroken. Atwater Manor in the distance, lamplight flickering in the upper windows.

And so our bride was content to wait, surrounded by all this beauty.

As she did so, the air turned cool, and she shivered in her lace. The shadows grew long as the day faded into night. The perfume from the honeysuckle became cloying. Her radiant smile began to dim.

But somehow, the light from the manor grew brighter.

Only it wasn't lamplight flickering in those windows.

It was a fire.

Now, some say she should have gone for help. Had she run to the house and tried to help them escape, or even headed into town to alert someone, maybe the house could have been saved and the whole tragedy avoided.

But those people are fools.

For the girl knew how quickly fire can snatch away life.

As she watched, the flames grew ravenous, consuming everything in their path. Only seconds passed before the roof collapsed. Everyone inside—gone. Swallowed by a cloud of thick, dark smoke.

And only she was left, the full moon like a spotlight on the burning clearing that was now as charred and empty as her heart.

Just yesterday, he had held her in his arms, in this same spot beside the rainbow. But where a rainbow is a promise, a moonbow is the ghost of one—that wisp of colorless light really just a whisper of missed chances and loves lost. Of broken dreams and broken hearts.

Or so the girl thought as she stepped off the cliff.

To this day, when you see the moonbow rise? So faint it only shines from the corner of your eye?

That's a sign she's nearby. Wanting. Waiting. Wandering the river, searching for answers. Or for the love she lost, so long ago. Might be she's still hoping for a happy ending, for those promises at the end of her rainbow.

But since she only walks at night, she'll never find them.

CHAPTER 1

Anyone raised up around here has their own version of the ghost bride story. She's an urban legend, a spooky tale we pull out at slumber parties after the sleeping bags are rolled out, flashlight tucked under our chins, eyes wide and voices low. A clever trick used by our sweeties to get us to cuddle close in fear, or by our older brothers and sisters to scare us out of the woods and into our beds. It's a warning from our parents: a reminder to stay away from the falls, or boys, or both. Sometimes the story ends in screams, sometimes laughter, and occasionally even tears as we cry off all our mascara over the thought of that poor, sad bride and her dead lover.

My mawmaw, Alice—Malice to me, because I couldn't get my mouth around the rest of it when I was younger—tells it best. Malice is a genuine storyteller, by birth and by trade, and her story about that lovelorn bride will make you shiver so hard you'll shed your freckles. When I was little, I begged to hear it every chance I got, though after seventeen years and maybe a hundred tellings, I know the whole thing by heart. Every pause, every whisper, every gesture—from the finger Malice presses to her lips as she reveals the secret wedding to the tiny shiver and her slipping smile as the bride's happiness shatters.

The ending is my favorite part. The rise of the moonbow illuminating the ghost bride as she wanders, heartbroken, through the darkness. Ever searching for what she's lost.

Except, as it turns out, that's not the end of the story at all.

It's only the beginning.

It's the first day of break, the one between my junior and senior years, and we're having one of those slow-burn days we sometimes get in early summer, when the mountain fog and morning breeze trick you into wearing jeans, so that by the time the heat slaps you in the face, it's too late and you're stuck sweating it out in damp denim. As Malice finishes her story, I tuck the pearl and crystal clip into her long, gray braid and step back to snap a photo with my phone, bumping up against her cluttered bookshelves.

I show the photo to Malice, who studies the screen as she pats the back of her head. "That looks real nice," she says, and I can't argue. The hair clip itself has seen better days—the clusters of pearls nestled between the smaller stones have dulled to a creamy yellow, and the large center crystal has gone cloudy. But I love it all the same. And my braid work is on point. When I was younger, Malice used to do my hair just like this.

"The ghost bride always was your favorite."

"It's a good story," I say, taking the phone back and slapping her fingers away so I can comb some of the bumps smooth. "And you tell it best. Better than my English Lit teacher, that's for sure."

Malice twists in her chair to face me, yanking a clump of hair free. "Your English teacher knows about the ghost bride? Isn't he a *man*?"

If it had been Momma, I'd have rolled my eyes. But this is Malice, whom I adore despite her eccentricities, so I just smile and gently tilt her head back. "You don't have to have lady parts to have heard about the ghost bride," I say. "Everyone knows about her. She's famous. Like the escaped convict with the hook hand. Or the hitchhiking prom date who disappears from the back of your car after you pick her up."

"I'm not going to dignify that," Malice says, shifting in her chair and messing up my meticulous work again, "other than to remind you that those are urban legends. And a legend is different from a story."

I reach for her hair, but she's not finished. "Pure exploitation is what they are. Meant to scare kids and keep them in line. Don't make out in cars. Don't pick up hitchhikers." She waves her hands and I pull the comb out of the line of fire. "A story is different. It's a remembering. A history."

This time, I do roll my eyes. But it's as much for the messed-up braid as it is for her words. "Hold still, or you're going to be lopsided."

She folds her hands dutifully in her lap, but keeps talking. "The ghost bride is real, Rena Faye. Just because you've never seen her—and thank the stars above for that!—it doesn't mean she never existed. There's more to life than what you can see and touch," Malice continues. "I taught you better."

"Yes, but seeing is believing." I point the comb at her cluttered living room wall, where a half dozen of my framed photographs fight for space alongside deer antlers and the dull, black eyes of what I can only assume is a donkey with mange.

Her favorite has a place of prominence right in the middle, and I'm glad, because it's my favorite, too. Between waiting for the perfect moment, the setup, and the development in Momma's old darkroom, that shot of the moonbow took me almost twelve hours to capture and get right. It's the thing I'm most proud of.

"Who would believe in the moonbow if they'd never seen it?" I ask.

"Plenty of people travel here to see the moonbow," Malice argues. "Because they heard about it from someone else. It's the words that have magic. They make the story. *They* paint the picture. Although your photographs are real pretty," she adds, patting my hand.

From anyone else, that would come off condescending. But stories are Malice's thing, the way photography is mine. And I get what she's trying to say. When I'm taking pictures, it feels like magic. The way I can snap a shot of something completely ordinary, and only afterward find out that I've captured something else. The hint of sadness behind a frozen smile. The drop of honey tangled in the fuzz of a bumble bee. Or the bright colors hidden in the rainbow's echo. They were all invisible even to me before I took the photo. But those things were there. They were real.

Unlike Malice's ghost.

I love the story. But that's all it is—a story.

"Ma?" My own momma stands in the kitchen doorway, her

face a deep, scalded pink that matches the bright bandana tied around her ponytail. She holds out some kind of twisted sculpture with shaky hands and asks in a high, strained voice, "What is this?"

Malice squints at Momma, but then becomes preoccupied with the hem of her shirt. "Oh, that. It's nothing. You can just toss it in the trash."

My shock is reflected in Momma's expression. It's not unusual for Malice to have an unidentifiable piece of art in her house. But it's beyond weird that she'd tell Momma to throw it out.

I step across the room and take the thing from Momma, who bends over and rests her hands on her knees, like she's having trouble catching her breath.

Only the "thing" isn't a sculpture. It's a blob of melted plastic, scorch marks browning the sides of what may have once been a bowl.

Momma straightens and crosses her arms over her chest. "It was in the oven."

"I was boiling water," Malice says, jutting out her chin.

I jump as Momma screams, "With Tupperware?"

She puts an apologetic hand on my arm, takes another breath, and shakes her head. Then she walks slowly over to yank the curtains aside and open the window.

"I couldn't find a pan." Malice's voice is low.

"*That* I believe. All this junk . . ." Momma trails off as she presses the palms of her hands into her eye sockets and leans her forehead against the window frame.

Malice's wrinkles seem to fold into themselves as she shrinks back in her chair.

"That was the smell," Momma says, and I'm not sure if she's talking to me or herself. "When we first got here. That odd smell. I thought something had died under the porch. But it was melted plastic."

Momma turns, her watery gaze skimming past me, cutting through the dust-filled beam of sunlight to take in the piles of magazines and shelves overcrowded with picture frames and figurines.

"You can't live like this, Ma," she says, unaware of—or maybe just ignoring—the blistering glare I shoot back.

It was Momma's idea to spend the day cleaning Malice's tiny cabin, so she's hardly in a position to complain. Tiny and shotgun style, there are only four rooms—living room, kitchen, and bedroom stacked front to back, with a tiny bathroom tucked in beside the closet. I know what Momma's thinking, but she's wrong. Malice isn't a hoarder. Yes, the collecting has gotten worse over the past several years. But who can blame her? She'd been in demand for her gifts, once upon a time. She'd traveled the world, collecting stories, and people came from miles around to hear them. Now she's stuck here, with no one but me to listen. And as the words pile up inside her, so does the junk all around.

No. Not junk, and I hate myself for even thinking of it that way.

It's one of the things about Momma that irritates me most, the way she manages to twist everything around to her own point of view. The way she just keeps on picking and poking, until you can't help but see it, too.

I shake my head, trying to knock Momma loose. An impossible task, really. But Malice's collections don't bother me nearly as much as they bother Momma. Every piece must have a story, or Malice wouldn't bother keeping it.

When I was younger, she'd bring home something new after every trip. The taxidermy fox, who'd outwitted his brothers and sisters to become king of his den. The theater masks, tragedy and comedy, which must never be worn lest they become stuck and rob the wearer of the ability to laugh or cry—just as they had the last unfortunate young girl who put them on. The teaspoon that belonged to a grand duchess, who'd used it to poison her thieving husband.

Malice swore she wasn't making any of it up. It was the item that held the story, not the other way around. Once there'd only been a couple dozen items and I knew all their stories. Now she has hundreds of things—bottle caps and broken jewelry and wood carvings and, yes, far too many animal skulls—and I can't keep up. It must make her a little crazy, trying to find the time to listen to them all.

But time is what she has the most of now.

That's the reason I agreed to help Momma today, and also why I offered to do Malice's hair as soon as we arrived. Because I know how lonely she is. I also knew as soon as I picked up that hair clip, she'd start her story. Sure, my hand hovered over a pocket watch I hadn't seen before, wondering if it had belonged to a train conductor, or perhaps his widow, who'd worn it on a chain around her neck.

But I can never resist the ghost bride.

There's something so fascinating about her story—romantic,

yes, but at the same time horrifying. Her lover died, so she threw herself off a cliff. Is that really what love is supposed to feel like? So all-consuming? So destructive?

"Your opinion on my life ain't worth a hill of beans," Malice says to Momma as she struggles to get up out of her chair. She makes it, but bangs her knee hard on the coffee table.

"What are you doing, Ma? You'll hurt yourself."

"It's cooler in here if you keep the shades drawn," Malice says, waving one hand at the window and massaging her knee with the other.

I'm still holding the melted bowl, so I go into the kitchen to throw it in the garbage. My nose twitches at the overwhelming smell of bleach. Momma has successfully drowned out any notes of burnt plastic, that's for sure. I grab an ice pack from the freezer and take it to Malice as Momma slams the window shut.

"It'd be even cooler if you let me install that air conditioner."

Malice takes in a sharp breath as I help her sit back down and press the ice to her knee.

"Waste of money," she says once she's settled. "God invented breezes for a reason."

They've had this fight a thousand times. I adjust the ice bag and mouth Momma's retort along with her: "He also invented electricity." But for once, Momma only mutters it; her heart's not in it.

For a second, everyone seems to lose steam with the familiar argument. We all sit silently as the grandfather clock in the back room ticks relentlessly away. My palm starts to go numb from the cold and I switch hands.

"Rena Faye, when you're finished with that, I could use your help in the kitchen." Momma jerks her head toward the doorway, her eyes wide and lips pressed thin.

But the kitchen is already clean. Aggressively so. And I don't want to have whatever discussion she wants to have out of earshot of Malice.

"Cell phone game?" I say to Malice, forcing lightness into my voice. It's our favorite—Malice gives me a word and I find a photo from my gallery to match it. I can still cajole Malice into a good mood, and at the moment, I'll do anything to avoid talking about the melted plastic and the hoarding and whatever else is making Momma look even older than usual.

But I know I'm only ignoring Momma at my peril. She crosses her arms and raises one eyebrow, and the hair goes up on the back of my neck. I swear, that woman is some kind of witch.

"Rena Faye. Kitchen. Now."

"Leave her be, Tallulah," Malice says, taking the ice from me and closing her eyes. "Surely even you remember what it was like to be young, with a whole summer vacation spread out in front of you? It's no wonder she doesn't want to spend it cooped up in my kitchen. We have things to talk about. Plans to discuss." She flutters a hand in Momma's direction.

Momma winces, but I can't tell if it's from the "Tallulah" or because of Malice's literal brush-off. She hates being told what to do. And she loathes being called anything but Lou.

"Summer is not the start of any vacation," Momma says, not looking at either of us.

Most years, she's right. Usually, summer is only the start of vacation for the tourists who descend on our family-owned motel. From now until Labor Day, Momma and Daddy will be at their beck and call—Daddy doing more of the manual labor and general repairs, and Momma handling their demands with a plastered-on smile that wilts, along with her hair and makeup, with every screaming kid and petty complaint. Hospitality is not a glamorous business. And usually, I'm right behind them, picking up their soggy towels and cleaning their trashed motel rooms.

But not this year. For one glorious month this summer, I get to escape all that. Malice and I are going on what she calls our "Victory Tour." I'm not clear on how we're victorious exactly—especially given the monumental disappointment that led to the idea—but I'm also not about to argue about a break from Corbin.

Instead of stale muffins and coffee from the motel lobby, we'll be eating beignets in New Orleans, barbecue in St. Louis, and cheese curds in Wisconsin. While poor Momma will be soaking her feet in the river whenever she gets a free second, I'll be dipping my toes into all the Great Lakes. I can picture the photo series already. Clear water, pebbled sand, and a different toenail polish for each shot.

Four weeks, seventeen states, and—hopefully—a portfolio full of photos better than the ones I submitted to the Louisville arts committee, which failed to earn me an acceptance into their photography program this summer.

"She's just cranky because of the full moon," Malice whispers to me.

Momma groans, and I nearly join her. As much as I love full moon nights, for those of us with businesses built upon the tourism the moonbow attracts, the days before and after are pure hell. I saw the sunrise this morning—and not because I was trying to photograph it. Because I did eight loads of laundry and cleaned twelve bathrooms before we even got to Malice's cabin.

I so need this vacation.

"Or maybe she's jealous we didn't ask her to come," Malice says.

"The trip is off," Momma blurts, yanking her bandana and twisting it between her hands.

"Oh, for the love of god, Tallulah. Stop being such a party pooper. We'll send postcards. Won't we?"

But something in Momma's face tells me this isn't a joke. The coldness bleeds from my hands and up my arms, until my whole body is frozen. Unmoving.

Momma bites her lip. "Look. I didn't want to do this . . . now. But it's for the best. I'm sure you both can see that."

Rage surges through me, hot and fierce, freeing me from my shock. Instead of unmoving, now I'm shaking uncontrollably. "For the *best*? What does that even mean? The best *what*?"

"No. No no no." Malice's voice drowns out mine, head going back and forth. "No. We must go. Rena Faye is coming away with me this summer. You agreed. You know this, Tallulah. *You know.*"

"Quit with the ghost stories, Ma," Momma snaps. "That's part of the problem, don't you see? You two—you feed off each other. She doesn't need you filling her head with more nonsense and fairy tales." The edge in her voice is knife-sharp, her words cutting deep.

"It's not nonsense. She needs to hear about the . . . you know,"

Malice hisses, wide-eyed and wild. She tugs at her hair, pulling strands of my braid free. "She needs to be prepared."

For what? I wonder.

Momma's mouth trembles and her eyes are shiny, as if she can't choose between anger and sadness.

I am not so conflicted.

I grip the arm of Malice's chair, afraid of what I'll do without that anchor. "You know how much this trip means to me. To both of us. Are you trying to hurt us? To punish us? Malice is an adult, and I'm practically one. You can't keep us from going."

Momma raises weary eyes to mine. "She set a plastic bowl on fire. In her oven. Trying to boil water." Her chest hitches. "She could have died."

Denial lodges in my throat like a stone, and I bark a laugh to knock it free.

"I'm serious, Rena Faye."

"Oh, come on, you're exaggerating. Besides, we'll be eating out. No one will be cooking."

I watch Momma's mouth as if in slow motion, opening, forming objections, and I talk over them, faster and louder, trying to drown out her protests. Scrambling for some magical combination of words that will wash that determined expression off her face.

"I'll drive. And take care of all the details. Keep track of everything. I can do this. You have to let me try. You know this is my last chance."

Momma turns her face from my desperation and gives a slow shake of her head. "I'm sorry. This trip is not happening."

My righteous anger is gone as quickly as it came, leaving

behind a cold emptiness that is not enough to hold me upright. I sink to my knees and Malice places a hand on my shoulder.

"Rena Faye, take me to my room."

I expect Momma to argue, but she slips wordlessly into the kitchen to bang some pots around.

"Ignore her. She's just a scaredy-cat," Malice says over the din. "Can't stand to face her fears, so she hides behind her work."

Momma bangs louder. I haven't seen much that can make Momma back off. *Piss* her off, sure. But scared? She doesn't have the imagination for it.

I didn't want to do this now, she said. Which means she was thinking about canceling our trip even before she found the plastic in the oven.

I shove down the disturbing thought for the moment and help Malice into the bedroom.

She's perfectly capable of walking on her own. Usually. Sure, she threw her hip out in a fall last year. But she lives alone and gets around just fine. It's Momma's cruel words that have weakened her somehow, and she leans on me for support.

I push the bedroom door ajar and am hit with a wave of hot dust and the citrusy scent of Jean Nate body spray. I take a breath and hold it as Malice slips off her shoes and sags down onto the bed.

"Listen, Rena Faye." Malice leans forward, a gleam in her red-rimmed eyes. "I need to tell you something. The truth. It's time you heard it. I don't know how long I'll be around to protect you."

Gooseflesh rises on my arms, despite the stifling heat. "Don't talk like that."

"She's real," Malice whispers as I shove aside some stacks of old *National Geographic*s to sit on the bed beside her. "And she's angry."

I blink. Whatever truth I expected her to impart, it wasn't this. "Who—Momma?"

"The ghost bride." She grabs my hand. "There's more to the story than I've told you. A curse."

I rub Malice's shoulder, trying to calm her down. "I'm not afraid of the ghost bride," I tell her, which is true. "I'll be fine," I add, which is a lie.

My resentment of Momma and her arbitrary, life-ruining directives is so all-consuming I may burst into flames or spew lava from my mouth. But Malice doesn't need to hear about it. She and Momma have their own source of conflict. And anyway, Malice seems less disturbed by our canceled trip and more preoccupied with her silly ghost bride.

"We are tied to her, the bride," she says. "The curse is both our burden and our responsibility. I thought I would be the one to break it, but I've failed. It's up to you now. You need to find the answers. It's the only way."

"What answers?" I ask. "And what do you mean by 'curse'?" Malice is more befuddled than usual. Damn Momma and her ultimatums. Malice is wrong—Momma's not scared. She just hates the thought of me being too far away to control.

"She walks because she has unfinished business. And as long as she walks, the curse will continue. There's no other way to stop it. It's up to us."

"Us who?"

"The women in our family."

"So Momma's cursed too?"

"It's passed from mother to daughter."

"So why isn't Momma the one telling me all this?"

"Your momma shirked her responsibility. I had hoped to pass this on while we were on the trip. To buy you some time." She fumbles at the back of her head, loosening the clip, which she then presses into my hand.

I rub a thumb across one of the pearls. "I don't understand."

"We are the keepers of her story."

"Everyone knows her story," I say gently.

"But only *we* know the truth. And until she finds peace, you are in danger." She squeezes my hand so hard the blood flow slows. "I wish it weren't this way," she whispers. "But there's nothing I can do to stop it. Your momma thinks ignoring it will make it go away, but she's wrong. Promise me you'll be careful. Promise you'll help her. It's the only way."

It isn't me Malice should be worried about. But she's so small and frail, hunched over as if trying to avoid a blow. I disentangle my hand from hers and ease her back onto her pillows.

"I'll try," I promise, snapping the hair clip into my messy bun.

This seems to appease her, and she nods. But even as she closes her eyes, I'm wondering, for the first time, if maybe Momma was right. Malice does seem . . . confused. And I have no clue what she expects me to do.

How can I possibly help someone who doesn't exist?

CHAPTER 2

Malice's cabin is only a few miles from our motel, but "few" is a relative term, and mountains don't make for straight roads. I hear there are places where you can drive in the same direction for miles and stare off into the distance without finding a tree of any kind, but I have a hard time believing in magic like that without seeing it for myself. I guess maybe now I never will.

"Don't start," Momma says, holding up a finger before pulling off her bandana and cranking the AC. She angles the vent so the air is blowing directly in her face. Then she pulls a pack of cigarettes from the glove compartment. The drive home from Malice's is the only time she smokes. Our visits always leave her frayed, like a fuse has been lit, deep within, then quickly snuffed. But each time, the strand grows a little shorter. Eventually, something is going to ignite.

Today might be the day and I may light the match.

I side-eye Momma from the passenger seat, picturing her exploding, a huge *kaboom* of confetti and glitter.

No, not glitter. More like thumbtacks. Or nails.

I fiddle with the radio dial to give myself time to think. I need to choose my timing and my words carefully. The drive isn't long, and once we're home, she and Daddy will be a united front, impervious to any of my arguments.

I stop on a Christian Lopez song I think she might like, but as soon as I remove my hand, Momma slaps the radio off.

"You know how much this trip means to me," I say, cracking my window and angling my face into the fresh air. It feels like hot soup, but it's still loads better than nicotine-laced air conditioning. "I need it. Like you keep reminding me, there's no money for college. A scholarship is my only shot."

She clenches her cigarette between her teeth, squinting against the smoke. "I'm sorry, baby. But you heard her. She's not lucid."

There's a curse. I shiver and brush aside the memory. "Of course she's lucid. She knows who we are. She knows what day it is. You're taking one silly mistake and blowing it way out of proportion."

I angle my body against the door so I can search her face for some sign as to why she's reacted so drastically. "Were you looking for an excuse to stop us? You said you didn't plan to tell us 'now.' Does that mean you'd already planned to cancel the trip?" My voice gets higher with each, more impossible question.

Momma sighs.

"When??" I can barely keep myself in check.

"Don't be ridiculous. That trip was never going to happen. It was just another one of Malice's stories." She snorts, smoke streaming from her nostrils. "You were just the only one who believed it."

Her lie is like a slap. "That trip was my graduation present, and you know it." I'm breathless with rage. Her glib dismissal of everything I've been working toward, everything I've dreamed of, is not the trivial matter she thinks it is. It's a betrayal, pure and simple.

But before I can gather my thoughts enough to tell her how badly she's hurt me, she says, "Look, Rena Faye," and points the tip of her burning cigarette at me. "You get what you want out of life through hard work. And determination. And maybe, just maybe, a little bit of luck. Not by running off on some wild vacation at your first taste of disappointment. While the rest of us sit home and sweat our asses off."

"But . . ." I stutter, and stall out, way too many past arguments loaded into that one word. "I *will* be working. I'll be building my portfolio. That's the whole point."

"You can take photos here. People travel from miles around to photograph the moonbow. Be grateful for what you have for once. Instead of pining over what you don't."

We're almost home, and there are so many things left unsaid. I can't lose sight of the goal, no matter how much I'd rather scream and cry and throw a fit, or better yet, freeze Momma out with icy silence. A part of me thinks this is what she's hoping for.

So instead, I point out the obvious. "Malice gave me this trip. It was a gift. You can't just take it away. It's not your decision. And people take vacations all the time. We run a motel! Clearly you understand the concept."

"Maybe so. But Malice is old. And broke."

"She's not that old," I argue. "And we aren't going to spend a ton of money. Besides, what matters is what's in her heart."

"Her heart is full of red meat and corn liquor," Momma says.

"And there's a reason she calls me her 'retirement surplus.' She was over forty when she had me."

Before I can respond to the cheap shot at her own mother, she apologizes. "Sorry, baby. That was low. Today's visit put me on edge. I had no idea she was so far . . ." She shakes her head and reaches to ash out the window.

"So far what?" I glare at her profile.

People say we look alike, but I don't see it. Sure, my pointy nose is undeniably hers. And we both have the same lank, dishwater-blonde hair and the same colorless, thick eyebrows that make it appear as though we're always confused. No sepia filters for us—we'd disappear.

But Momma is lean and muscled, as if fat can't find her sitting still long enough to settle. I'm just flat, except for my face, which is round from what Daddy calls "baby dough," as if it's only age that wears hard lines into a woman's face. Momma sure agrees; she likes to say that women age faster the longer they live. Whatever that means.

"It doesn't matter. What matters is she still has family to care for her. You've always had a special bond," Momma says. "Lord knows I can't talk to her. Spend as much time with her this summer as you can. But a trip is out of the question. And you have to stop encouraging her to tell those stories."

"She's a storyteller. That's what she does." I clench my hands into fists.

"*Was* a storyteller." Her dismissive tone makes me want to scream. Or slap her.

"She's just lonely," I say through gritted teeth. I shouldn't be surprised Momma can't see that. She's never been good at understanding other people. She doesn't have the patience for it. "She's used to being surrounded by people who love her, who want to hear her talk. Now she's only got us."

"And whose fault is that?" she mutters out her window.

I can't answer around the lump in my throat. None of this is Malice's fault. My first and only chance to see the world—to walk on a real, honest-to-god beach and eat gobs of Chicago-style pizza and ride to the top of the arch in St. Louis and float in the Great Salt Lake like a human bobber—all of that has been stolen from me, and not by Malice.

This is all Momma.

We're both silent, her smoking, me taking ragged breaths and trying not to give her the satisfaction of my tears. Instead, I hold my phone steady and wait for breaks in the dense tree line for a glimpse of Atwater Lodge, high on the ridge on the other side of the river. I'd thought it was Sleeping Beauty's castle when I was younger, the kudzu-covered fields surrounding it like magical fairylands guarded by the lush, green vines. Even now, the sight of it still calms me.

"What did Malice mean?" I ask as the top of the lodge crests into view. I hold the button, raising my voice over the *click click click* of the shutter. "About a curse?"

"How the hell am I supposed to know?"

Do I imagine it, or does Momma's hand tremble as she grinds out her cigarette?

"But she said you know."

"She says a lot of things."

I can't argue with that. "She told me I was in danger, and that I need to be careful. Is that true?"

Momma rolls her eyes. "Listen to yourself. Of course it's true. But not because you're cursed." She grips the steering wheel so tightly, her knuckles go white. "I've been telling you this your whole life. Look at how many kids drown in the river every year, or get lost in the woods. Why do you think I worry so much about you?"

Because you're a control freak?

"Look, whatever Malice said to you, I don't want you messing around with it. Forget it, okay? It's not your responsibility."

"But that's exactly what she said. That it was my responsibility. She said I have to try to help her—the bride." *Because you refused.*

"She's dead. She doesn't need your help. What she needs is to rest in peace. Poor girl."

"Wait a minute. Are *you* saying she's real, too?"

Momma hesitates. "Of course not. It's just a story. There's no dead bride wandering the woods, hell-bent on revenge."

My skin prickles and my throat goes dry. Malice mentioned a curse, yes. And the responsibility of our family to help. But she didn't say anything about the woods. Or revenge.

So what does Momma know that I don't?

CHAPTER 3

Most of Corbin earns a living from tourism, one way or another. Used to be the coal mine, until it closed, and whether life had been better back then depends on who you ask. It's been twenty years, give or take, since Jackson Dunlap Sr. boarded up the mine and his son opened up their stately home as a commercial venture, inviting guests from all corners to come and vacation in style. But he didn't invent the moonbow—that was all Mother Nature or God or whoever you believe is responsible for the river and the waterfall and the rainbow that appears above it on the night of the full moon. Mr. Dunlap wasn't even the first to exploit the phenomenon for cash. But he made it classy, and that made all the difference.

Before that, our Moonbow Motel was the premier stop for moonbow viewing. A quiet roadside attraction, made popular mostly by word of mouth. But while we were almost directly across the river from Atwater Lodge, we didn't have direct access to the falls like Dunlap did. So when he decided to get in on the action and tried to nudge us out with his advantages of location and luxury, we chose to focus on our own strengths—affordability and kitsch.

The Whitakers have been in the hospitality business longer than the Dunlaps. Daddy's grandpa built the motel three generations back, in the late 1940s. Daddy took over from his mom and dad, my G-mom and G-pop, after G-pop went to be with Jesus. G-mom lived with us until this past winter, when she moved to her own version of paradise, also known as Boca. Daddy's sister, my aunt Ellie, also works here, but she doesn't have what you would call a controlling interest in the business. She's an employee, same as me and Graham and all my cousins.

Momma pulls into the Moonbow Motel at the far end of the horseshoe-shaped parking lot, but instead of turning down our driveway, which runs behind the business and up the hill toward our house, she steers left, slowing to a crawl as we pass between the two-story, mid-century motel with the jutting lobby on our right and the fenced and gated outdoor pool to our left.

This is what summer smells like for me—baked asphalt and the sharp tang of chlorine. No use wondering anymore if that's true for the rest of the country. I'm not going to find out.

I've already popped my seat belt, so when Momma slams on the brakes, I fly forward on the leather seat. "What the . . . ?"

"Please tell me your brother is not first cleaning the pool"— she glances at the clock on her dashboard—"at four-thirty in the afternoon."

I lean over to peer around her shoulder. As much as Graham getting his butt chewed might soothe my tattered soul, in all fairness, Momma's wrong this time. "No, it looks like he's done cleaning. He's just taking selfies with those girls in bikinis."

My older brother is perched on the tiled half-wall that separates the pool from the parking lot, his arms wrapped around the shoulders of a girl in a metallic swimsuit that burns my retinas. Those photos will be overexposed for sure.

Momma closes her eyes and pinches the bridge of her nose. "Jesus, help me. At least tell me they're older than they look."

I open my mouth to ask, but she beats me to it. "Twelve, Rena Faye. They look twelve."

I study them critically. "Nah, they're older than twelve. Fifteen, at least."

This is not what she wants to hear. Probably because Graham is just shy of his nineteenth birthday. She makes a whimpering sound in the back of her throat, then steers the truck toward the corner at the far end of the lot where the diner and motel run perpendicular but don't quite meet. Daddy built a trellis wall to hide the dumpsters in the corner, mimicking the geometric design on the railings that line our balcony, and Momma parks the truck in front of it.

"Where is your father?" she mutters, tossing aside her seat belt and yanking the keys from the ignition.

Daddy strolls out the front door of the diner as if we've summoned him, hands in the pockets of his khaki work pants and a smile on his sun-lined face. "There's my girls," he calls.

He looks absurdly happy, given the events of the afternoon. I find it hard to believe that Momma wasn't texting him immediately upon finding the Tupperware in the oven. And surely she conferred with him before calling off our trip. Momma may be the brains behind our whole operation, but Daddy's word is law.

As he gets closer, he holds out his hands, and I hold my breath. But he doesn't say anything about the trip. Instead he asks, "How's Mawmaw? What new treasures has she unearthed this week? Bat wings? Insects with little pins through their carcasses?"

But Momma is as tightly wound as he is relaxed. "I am not in the mood, Harlan," she says, ducking his embrace to grab the garbage bags she filled at Malice's out of the truck bed. "Do me a favor," she says, tilting her chin toward the pool, "and go over there and try to keep your son from racking up a child pornography charge."

Daddy follows her gaze, his gray eyes narrowing, though his smile remains in place. "Relax, Lou." He rubs at the stubble on his jaw. His five-o'clock shadow accentuates the puckered scar running along his jawline. He turns that cheek away from my camera, every time.

"He's just keeping the customers happy. We live and die by social media reviews these days," he says. "You know that."

"Uh-huh. And while he's busy keeping up with customer relations, who's manning the front desk?"

We all pivot to stare at the family piling out of the SUV in front of the lobby.

Poor Daddy. He hesitates a fraction too long, and Momma shoves the garbage bags at his chest. "That's what I thought."

"Rena Faye can handle it," Daddy says, winking at me. "It's about time we give her some more responsibility around here."

I raise one eyebrow, wondering what I've done to elicit this kind of glowing encouragement. Is this some kind of good cop/bad cop game they're playing?

Momma's not buying it, either. She smooths her denim shirt, runs a hand through her sweaty, tangled hair, and strides over to the lobby, muttering something under her breath about ignoring paying customers and jailbait.

Daddy hides his disappointment with a shrug. Then he hands me the bags. "Guess that puts you on garbage duty, baby girl." He turns to go, then stops. "Is that what you left the house in this morning?"

I look down at the gray lace tank, then back at him. "Um. Yes?" My stomach turns over, and not just from the rank smell of Malice's trash. "I haven't been anywhere but—"

He's already shaking his head. "God can see you everywhere."

God probably never had to clean a house in ninety-degree heat, but I don't say that out loud. That would be sass. And Daddy doesn't care for sass.

"I know, Daddy. But it's hot." I wave the garbage bag in the general direction of the pool. "It's not like I'm running around in a bathing suit, like Graham."

His eyes narrow slightly. "That's different. You're a lady. I expect you to act like one. Now take care of the trash. And then go change."

I hold back a sigh and nod. I should have known his newfound faith in my abilities wasn't going to stick. The only thing he trusts me with is the garbage.

• • • •

We eat dinner at the motel, not unusual for a moonbow night. I throw a couple of pizzas into the toaster oven we keep behind the front desk while Momma wipes down the table in the dining alcove off the lobby. No continental breakfast here—that would detract from our diner business—but we do have a coffee station, a couple of vending machines, and frozen pizza. Since G-mom's exodus to Florida last January, we've been struggling to find enough help to keep the diner open. Right now, we only serve breakfast and lunch and then close midafternoon so Momma and Aunt Ellie can still attend to motel business. Whenever guests complain, we offer them a free pizza, delivered to their room. It's a big hit, at least according to our Yelp reviews.

Daddy joins us at the last possible second, keeping the door ajar so that we can hear any customers who come in. He checks that I've changed my shirt, gives me a satisfied nod, and sits. We join hands as he leads the dinner prayer, and our collective "Amen" is barely finished before Graham has his phone out, head bent over the screen and shaggy hair hanging in his face. He stopped cutting it last year in the hopes that it would make people take him more seriously as a musician, but it just looks like he can't afford to shower.

We used to be close when we were younger. That was before I realized there were two sets of rules: one for Graham and one for me. I think I'd resent him less if he acknowledged the unfairness of it all, or at least pretended to feel bad about it. But he's either too smart to rock the boat, or too dumb to notice he's the only one with a life jacket. I'm guessing it's the latter.

Daddy wipes his mouth with a napkin and tosses it on one of the empty cardboard platters. "So. Your mother and I have been discussing some . . . restructuring for the summer. In light of Mawmaw and Rena Faye's"—his eyes shift in my direction and then slide away, like a snake escaping danger—"change of plans."

Change of plans. Like any of this had been our idea. I knew he was in on it. And I knew he'd back Momma. I bite my lip.

"Graham, you'll be taking over some of the managerial duties. Reservations, billing, scheduling. All you, buddy."

Graham glances up from his phone, the screen turning his face an eerie shade of blue. "What? What'd I miss?"

"You're putting *Graham* in charge?" My voice climbs three octaves. It's not that how Graham spends his summer affects my life; there's just a tiny part of me, deep down, that really would have liked to see him scrubbing toilets for a change.

"Is there a problem?" Daddy is all wide-eyed innocence, but I know better.

"Problem?" I ball my napkin and shrug. "No. Why should I care? It has nothing to do with me. I've got the month off, remember?"

Graham interrupts me, clearing his throat. "Hey, thanks, man, I appreciate that. But I'm going to pa—"

Daddy doesn't give him a chance to finish what was clearly going to be a refusal. "No need to thank me. You've earned it."

Earned it? Graham's hardest tasks are leaf blowing in the fall, snow blowing in the winter, and blowing off work the rest of the year. And I could've told Daddy, if he'd asked, that Graham has no real interest in this motel. No, my brother's grand plan is to become a famous musician. How he'll accomplish that minus any talent or ambition is anyone's guess, but again, not my problem.

Daddy shifts his focus to me. "As for you, young lady, you seem to be misinformed about some things. No trip means no vacation."

I shove my last slice of half-eaten sausage and mushroom aside, my appetite gone. "That's not fair. I still need—"

"What you need is to pitch in. You think we make so much money we can just afford to let you gallivant around all summer, with no responsibilities? We are a family, Rena Faye. With a family business at the height of tourist season. If you're home under our roof this summer, you're helping out."

I slouch in my chair. "Maybe there is a curse," I mutter.

"What did you say?" Daddy slams his hand down on the table, making us all jump.

Momma's face goes pale and she sets down her own half-eaten slice.

"Nothing."

"It doesn't sound like nothing. It sounds like Mawmaw has been filling your head with nonsense."

"Her stories aren't nonsense. They're . . . stories," I say. We've had this argument before. I've never been able to convince him of the benefit to Malice's gift.

"Stories about demons?"

"No!" But I know "a ghost bride's curse" isn't going to go over any better. "It was just a story about Corbin. A legend."

"I will not tolerate any of that kind of talk." He leans across the table. "Do you understand me?"

I swallow hard and nod. "Yes, sir."

He exchanges a look with Momma. "Did you know about this?" When Momma doesn't answer, he adds, "Clearly, you should have intervened."

But I'm not interested in hearing all the ways we've disappointed him. "I'm not asking for the whole summer off," I say. I know that arguing is not going to help my cause. But at this point, it's all I have. "And I won't be lollygagging, or whatever it is you said. I'll be working on my photography." I look from Momma to him and back, hoping she'll support me on this. "That's what the vacation was for. We agreed on that."

"Photography is a hobby," Daddy finally says, the way he'd say "lying is a sin." "An expensive one. And I'm just going to say it—money is tight. If you want to keep taking your little photos, you'll need to do it on your own time."

And just like that, he's reduced the thing I love most, my passion, to something inconsequential.

"Without the trip, this is just a regular summer. And like every summer, we're going to need you here," Daddy says.

"Doing what?" I ask. It's a legitimate question, and one I honestly want him to answer. During a regular summer, I'd be doing housekeeping. But Aunt Ellie and her oldest daughter, my cousin, Hazel, had agreed to pitch in extra for the month I was supposed to be gone.

Daddy's gaze flicks to Graham.

"Dear lord, no."

Daddy slaps the table again.

"What? That was an honest-to-goodness prayer." I hold up my hands. I'm not lying. If Graham gets put in charge of me, I'll have no choice but to appeal to Jesus, because my summer will be pure hell.

"Name one thing Graham has done around here to justify

getting to boss me around. One improvement. Whose idea was the pizzas? Mine. And the moonbow hikes? Me again. If it weren't for me, Atwater Lodge would be getting all our business."

Not the smartest move, mentioning our biggest rival, but I'm tired of holding back. It's bad enough I'm facing yet another summer of nothing but cleaning up after demanding, stuck-up tourists. There's no way I'm doing it under Graham's supervision. I need time to work on my portfolio—which was supposed to be based on my cross-country adventures. Without that, not only do I still need to take the photos, I need a whole new concept. It makes my head hurt just thinking about it.

But even that pain sounds positively heavenly compared to the summer they're suggesting.

"I'm still the boss," Daddy says, hedging. "But we need someone to be the face of the motel. Graham is good at customer relations."

I think about the girls at the pool this afternoon and almost laugh, but it's more sad than funny.

"And if something goes wrong," Daddy continues, tilting his head toward Graham, "guests need to feel they're in capable hands."

"And you think *he* has capable hands?"

Graham holds up his hands and flips them over. "These babies are gold."

"You once got one of 'those babies' stuck in the vending machine!"

He scowls. "That was a long time ago."

"It was last summer! You were trying to fish out a free Snickers."

"I was hungry."

"We have a key to the machine!"

"Enough!" Daddy yells. "Rena Faye, we're not belittling your contributions. And sure, maybe this isn't what you had planned for the summer. But let's try to treat it as the blessing it is."

It's a good thing I've lost my appetite, because there's no way I can swallow this BS.

My phone chirps, but as my hand drifts toward it, Daddy says, "Don't even think about it."

"We're in the middle of a conversation," Momma adds.

"Graham has been practically glued to his phone this entire time!" I say.

Momma and Daddy give each other a look. I know I've gone too far, but I can't help it. The double standard is just too much.

"Fine. May I be excused, then? I'm done."

"We're not finished with our discussion," Daddy says.

"What's left to say? I'm working this summer—I'm assuming without pay as usual?"

Momma's face is all the answer I need.

"Got it. So, the trip is off. Graham is in charge. I'm back to cleaning toilets. You think photography is a stupid little hobby." I tick them off on my fingers, one by one. "Have I missed anything?"

"We didn't say—" Momma begins, then closes her mouth and drops her gaze to the table.

"Now that you mention it . . ." Daddy says.

"Oh my go—sh. What now?" My phone beeps with another text notification. This time I grab it. "It's Daisy. She's back." But I don't want to let Daddy off the hook that easy. "Now that I mention what?"

Momma stands. "We're getting off track here. Graham"—she jerks a thumb at the door—"you're leading the hike tonight. Get moving. Rena Faye, you can catch up with Daisy on whatever is so important after you clear the table." Her tone does not invite discussion, even from Daddy. "We'll talk about the rest later."

"The rest" being unimportant, apparently, because it only involves me.

CHAPTER 4

Our house sits on a ledge above the motel, accessible by a walking path behind the storage garage or through a security gate at the far end of the motel parking lot. My friends all say it looks haunted, but really it's just old. It was here long before my great-grandpa even had the idea to go into the tourism business, and it shows. If you squint, the tall, narrow structure lists to one side, like the rocks behind it are the only thing holding it up. The gray paint is peeling, the gingerbread detailing is broken, and since we never use the front door, the walkway leading to the sagging porch is overgrown with weeds. Momma keeps saying we need to do something about it, mainly because she's worried about scaring off customers, but there never seems to be the time or the money, and anyway, it's not too bad unless you get up close.

Summers, we don't get much chance to get up close. Most of our daylight hours are spent at the motel. Momma and Daddy only come home to sleep, and even then, Momma's been known not to make it past the couch before she collapses in exhaustion.

But that could also be because their room doesn't get much of a cross-breeze and our window air conditioners are almost as old as the house itself.

By some miracle, I got the big front bedroom when G-mom left for Florida. I want to think it was meant to make up for a lifetime of living in Graham's shadow, but I suspect it has more to do with the fact that the window overlooks the motel, and Momma likes the idea of being able to keep tabs on me even when she's working.

I love my bedroom, but today, I only stop long enough to grab my key before heading back downstairs to my sanctuary—the tiny darkroom off the laundry room. Daddy set it up for Momma right after they got married, turning the old linen closet into a workspace for her art. I can only assume that at one point, he took *her* photography seriously. Or had a more generous view of hobbies. Which makes it all the more frustrating that he's so dismissive of my dreams.

Momma had talent. We still use all her old shots for the website and brochures for the motel, and some of them are truly breathtaking. She's never given me a clear reason for why she gave it up, other than the usual vague "no time" excuses. Lucky for me, she at least made time to show me how to use her old camera, and how to hand-develop the photos.

Those memories—her helping me light up a shot, the two of us bent over a developing photo—are some of the best I have. But something changed between us when I started talking about art school a couple years ago. That was when Momma put her foot down. College was too expensive to waste on what she called a "throwaway" degree. If I wanted her and Daddy's help, it was business school or nothing.

But not everyone dreams of running a crappy roadside motel all their lives.

There are people who make careers out of their art. Professional photographers. And I'm going to be one.

I'm not working on anything currently, but I flip the sign on the door to NO ENTRY anyway. My family knows better than to bother me when I might be in the middle of a project. Even if they don't support photography as a career, they wouldn't dare interrupt and risk ruining whatever I might be developing.

Besides my phone, I have two cameras. The film one belonged to Momma, which is what I use the darkroom for. The other is a Polaroid Instamatic I bought myself last year with birthday money. Those photos are never great, and the film is crazy expensive—not something I'd ever admit to Daddy. But I love the anticipation of waiting for that picture to fill in. It captures a little of the thrill of the darkroom, but in real time. I never get tired of that feeling. Sometimes I like to imagine it was the same for people back when photography was first invented—that heady blend of magic and belief. It sounds impossible, the ability to capture someone in a still frame. But once the photo is developed, there you are. Staring back at yourself. Forever frozen in time.

But as much as I adore my Instamatic, my true love is film. There's a recklessness to it, like a gambler trying to hit the next big score. Because, sure, you can take multiple shots. Open up the shutter and let rip. But you don't actually know what you have until you get into the darkroom. The flutter of my heart when

I've gotten a good shot more than makes up for the sick burn of disappointment in my belly when a shot gets blurred, or my subject moves out of frame. As Daddy is fond of saying, the harder the work, the sweeter the payoff. Of course, he's talking about the motel when he says that. But the sentiment applies even better to photography. I've never found any sweetness in a well-made bed.

I haven't been in here in at least a week, what with the rush of finals and the scramble that comes with the last few days of school. Copies of my latest photos of the moonbow still hang from plastic clips on the line above the developer baths. A series of shots that had been damn hard to get. And which the application committee at the Governor's School of the Arts had dubbed "mediocre."

I tug one of the photos free and look at it.

While the composition is well done, it is hard to see anything beyond surface-level beauty here. The committee would advise the applicant to dig deeper. Show us what the subject means to you.

It still stings.

I'd applied for this year's GSA, a three-week intensive arts program in Louisville. The application process was rigorous, but the payoff would've been totally worth it—an all-expenses-paid opportunity to study photography with a bunch of like-minded students. A month without cleaning up after tourists. A month away from Corbin and the suffocating togetherness of my family. Not to mention, GSA opens doors. Colleges, scholarships, internship opportunities.

But I'd been rejected. *Surface-level. Mediocre.*

That was when Malice suggested the Victory Tour. After all, she reminded me, clearly I had talent—it just needed to be developed. Like a photo. Why not travel and, as she said, "fill my bucket"? It would be just her and me—an early graduation present. It wasn't GSA, but it was something to look forward to.

Daddy keeps hammering home my canceled "vacation," but the Victory Tour was more than that. It was a chance to hone my skills and build my portfolio. With no income and no financial help from my parents, applying for a scholarship is my only shot at art school. And no one's handing those out for surface-level work.

Someone bangs on the door, so loud and insistent I nearly fall elbow-first into the pan of developer.

"Rena Faye Whitaker! Open this door, or so help me, I will kick it down!"

I open it. My cousin and best friend, Daisy Renfro, is barely five feet tall, so I'm not overly concerned about what kind of damage she could do to the door. But I am thrilled to see her.

Her grin is at least as wide as mine.

"Sister cousin!" she squeals as we throw our arms around each other.

"Sister cousin!" I echo our familiar greeting, but don't even try to match her decibel level. Technically we're cousins, but we might as well be sisters. We grew up real close, and I trust Daisy more than pretty much anyone else in the world.

She's been away this year as a freshman at the University of Kentucky—UK—and talking to and seeing her less frequently has felt like having a limb amputated.

"I missed you," I tell her, downplaying the drama. It's more her thing anyway.

"Of course you did! I'm surprised to see you standing here,

frankly. How did you not die of boredom?" She grabs my wrist and drags me out of the darkroom. "It stinks in here. Come into the kitchen and tell me everything I missed since Easter break."

Daisy rummages in our cupboards for snack food while I sit at the table and try to come up with something interesting to tell her. But the only gossip I know is that a bunch of the graduating seniors got drunk after the ceremony, stole a golf cart, and drove it into the river. Luckily, far enough away from the falls that they could get out and walk to safety. Too bad for the golf cart they left behind, though; it stalled in the muddy water.

"Nothing ever happens here," I say. "You know that."

"What about Wade Dawson?" she asks, digging a pretzel into a container of peanut butter. "Is he over me yet?"

I flick the salt off one of the twists. "Please. Wade will never stop pining. It's about time you put him out of his misery."

"Now what would be the fun in that?"

"What about you?" I ask. "Any good college stories?"

She licks the peanut butter off her fingers and screws the lid back on. "None you haven't heard already. Finals sucked, but I survived and am thrilled to be back home where I don't have to constantly worry about whether the guy hitting on me is just trying to get in my pants or trying to murder me."

"Because you already know?"

"Yup. Turns out there's some benefit to growing up in a small town. Now get dressed. We've got plans." She shoves me toward the stairs.

"You've been home like thirty seconds. How can you possibly have plans?"

"One, I'm me. Two, it's moonbow night! So go change." She bats her lashes as she studies my jeans and T-shirt, flashing sparkly eye shadow the same blue as her eyes. "You're not wearing that." It isn't a question, because Daisy doesn't ask. She tells.

"Why not?" I say, falling back easily into our familiar routine, where I pretend to argue but ultimately do what she says. It's always been like this, as long as I can remember, both because she's older and she's bossy. Besides, even when she steers us straight into trouble, I know she's always got my back. "You're wearing a fur coat," I say, taking in the curly pink mohair as Daisy fans herself. "How is that any better? It's eighty degrees out."

She grabs the lapels, which barely close over her curves, and spins in a half circle. "Like it? I got it at the thrift store. Besides, I'm sure it will cool off sooner or later."

I'd forgotten how much I missed that relentless optimism. "It's definitely you."

As we climb the narrow stairs to my bedroom, I tell her all about the canceled trip and the news about Graham getting promoted.

"Could be worse," she says.

I stop on the landing. "In what possible way?"

She links arms with me and pulls me along. "Look, Graham's a slacker. It's not like he's going to be breathing down your neck. He doesn't give a shit about the guests unless they're young and cute. He's going to pay zero attention to housekeeping. I'm assuming you'll still be doing the bulk of that?"

I give her a look, and she coughs to cover a laugh.

"No thanks to you. Aunt Ellie said you got another job this

summer, but she didn't say where," I say, heading straight to my closet as she goes over to the window to pull the shades.

"I'm working at Atwater."

I hold a shirt up to my chin. "You're kidding."

Daisy gives me a look. "You know I love Aunt Lou and Uncle Harlan. But they pay for shit."

I have always secretly wanted to work at the castle on the hill, but of course it's out of the question. My parents would disown me for an act of betrayal like that. I'm not so sure they won't do the same to Daisy. "How'd you manage that?"

"I answered their ad. And you can't wear white. Grass stains." Daisy sinks down in my desk chair and swings in a circle.

"Grass stains? What exactly are we doing?"

"We're going to party," she says. "Preferably in clothing that is not going to broadcast that fact." At my puzzled expression, she rolls her eyes, then grabs the shirt I'm holding and hands me a denim jumper from the pile beside my bed instead. "Here. Put this on. No grass stains. No beer stains. Denim hides a plethora of sins."

"Plethora?"

"Yes. I'm a college girl now, remember?"

"Right. You've learned big words *and* how to party. I just didn't think we'd be committing a plethora of sins."

"This is your last summer of freedom and I'm going to make sure you enjoy it!"

I frown at the back of her head in the mirror, watching my eyebrows wink together and wishing for the eleven billionth time they weren't so thick. I haven't trimmed or plucked in a week and already I look like a Muppet. "Isn't next summer my last summer?"

"No," Daisy says. "Trust me on this. It'll be all, 'You're an adult now,' and 'You better start thinking about what you're going to do for the rest of your life.' This summer, no one expects anything of you."

The last part isn't exactly true, but I take her point.

"And anyway, you've got the perfect schedule." Daisy throws herself down on my bed and cups her chin in her hands. "You're done every day by, what—three? That leaves us all afternoon and night to hang out. Thank God or baby Jesus or whoever that your trip got canceled."

"Hey!"

"It's not personal," she says. "I would have missed you."

"Same. Obviously. But . . ." I struggle to find the words to let her know how much the trip meant to me. "Have you ever tried to picture life outside this town and gotten totally freaked out? Because instead of your future, you saw . . . nothing?"

"First of all, no," she says. Only she says it so quickly I know she hasn't given any thought to what I've said. Which shouldn't surprise me. After all, she's just spent a year away from Corbin. I'm the one who can't break free.

"Second," she continues, "the big city is not that great, either. It's dirty, it's loud. People are rude. My roommate had her car parked in the overflow lot and it got broken into, like, three times. Trust me on this—you do not know how good you have it here. Luckily, I have the perfect way to remind you. A visit to the woods for a moonbow make-out session with some hot boys." She flips over onto her back, throwing her arms wide. "That is the only future I want to think about right now."

I sigh. It must be nice to be able to just focus on what's right in front of you. And I wasn't lying. Of course I would have missed Daisy terribly on my trip—so much so I thought about asking Malice to invite her along. But as much as I love Daisy, I wasn't sure she'd get it. Sometimes, I can't help but want something . . . more. Something different. Something I don't even know how to put into words, much less say out loud. Even to Daisy.

So I drop the subject and pull on the denim jumper. "I know who my hot boy is. But who exactly did you have in mind?"

"Hello, Whitakers!" Daisy throws open the lobby door, sending it crashing into the window behind it. "Sorry, Aunt Lou." She pulls her sunglasses down her nose and makes a frowny face at my mom as she tries to untangle the door from the long, slatted shades that cover the wide front windows.

Momma throws dagger eyes and I tense, but she isn't pissed at Daisy.

"Damn it, Graham. That broken spring was on your maintenance list this morning."

He slouches behind the front desk. "Relax, Ma. Hakuna whatever. Our customers are on vacation. They just want to chill. They don't care about things like springs and doors."

Ladies and gentlemen, your "capable" motel manager.

Even if customers don't care about broken doors, what Graham fails to realize is that leaving home means they can rely on someone else to do the fixing. Otherwise, why bother packing your belongings and leaving exciting places like Chicago and

Nashville to drive into the middle of the Kentucky mountains? People are trying to get away from their own worries and inconveniences, not be saddled with ours.

Daisy goes over to link her arm through Momma's, her grin revealing the gap in her front teeth that four years of orthodontia have been unable to correct. "How y'all been?"

Momma wraps her in a hug. "We've been good. Great. How was the end of your first year?"

"Spectacular!"

"Dean's list, I'm assuming?" Daddy asks, leaning in the doorway to his office.

Daisy wrinkles her nose and waggles a hand back and forth. "Ish."

I happen to know she barely squeaked out a 2.5, but there's no way I'm telling Daddy.

"And what're you studying again? Lady history?"

Daisy narrows her eyes ever so slightly as she tells Daddy, "It's women's studies, Uncle Harlan. And anthropology."

"Ah. Women's studies. Is that where they teach you you're too good to work for family?" Daddy asks, keeping his tone light.

"Not too good," Daisy counters with a brittle smile. "Just too broke."

After an uncomfortable silence, Momma asks, "How're your mom and dad?" Even though she sees her in-laws more often than Daisy. Aunt Ellie is here every day, after all. "I bet they're so happy to have you home for the summer."

Daisy manages a grin. "I think Momma might already be counting down the days until I leave again."

"I'm sure that's not true!"

"Well, my closet is now her craft room. So." Daisy shrugs.
"You know how laid-back my momma is when it comes to her
crafting. Or . . . anything."

Momma actually giggles, because Daisy has that effect on
people.

"We'll have to catch up for real sometime soon," Daisy says,
sliding her sunglasses back on. "Right now, Rena Faye and I have
plans."

In an instant, Momma's focus shifts to me with laser precision.
"Where are you girls off to?"

Graham is smart enough to recognize this moment for the
gift it is; he's out the door before I even have a chance to blink,
much less formulate a reply.

"Moonbow." Daisy beats me to it, tilting her head just a bit,
so that her blonde head bumps Momma's shoulder. "We're meetin'
some boys at the overlook."

I force myself not to grimace. The overlook is owned by
Atwater Lodge. Momma has never expressly forbidden us from
going over there, but I know how much she hates it. Still, she al-
lows it because she thinks it will keep us out of the woods. Where
I *am* forbidden to go. To hear Momma tell it, there's all kinds of
dangers lurking out there. It's a wonder I'm still alive.

"Uh-huh." It's obvious that in addition to being irritated,
Momma also doesn't believe her. Not that she has any reason to;
Daisy is clearly lying. The overlook is for tourists. On a warm,
clear night like this, it's bound to be packed. And not by anyone
we know.

She probably thinks we're headed to Lover's Leap, but she'd be wrong about that, too.

"So kitsch, right? But I guess Chance thought it sounded romantic." Daisy rolls her eyes. Her superpower is looking innocent. Maybe it's the tooth gap, maybe it's that she's barely five feet tall in heels. For whatever reason, she can lie like nobody's business, and people usually just smile and let it go. Even, sometimes, Momma.

Momma tucks a stray lock of hair behind her ear. "How about instead of heading across the river, you hang out with us tonight? Help out with the tour? I'm sure Chance would understand."

Chance Caudell is my boyfriend, and he works for his family's horse farm, same as I do here at the motel. It's one of the many things we have in common. So I'm sure if I told him I had to work, he wouldn't bat an eye. In fact, he'd probably offer to help. But I'm not going to give him the option.

Instead, I grit my teeth and say, for what I'm sure will be the one and only time I'll get away with it this summer, "Sorry, Momma. Tonight's my night off. It's Graham's turn."

Then I grab Daisy and drag her out the front door, pulling it shut behind us as the humid night gulps us up and swallows us whole.

Daisy stumbles in her wedge sandals and yanks her arm free to fan her face. "Slow up. I think I'm going to have to ditch the coat."

She casts a backward glance, probably to make sure Daddy isn't watching, then slips it off to reveal a glittery tank with spaghetti straps. She does a little shimmy to make the wide silver dots sparkle. "What do you think?"

"I think you overdressed for drinking in the woods."

She rolls her eyes. "Every occasion is an *occasion*, Rena Faye. Have I taught you nothing? Better to be the best dressed than the worst. Besides, it's moonbow night!"

Malice's warning comes back to me suddenly. "Right. Moonbow night. Speaking of, so you know the story about the ghost bride?"

She widens her eyes comically. "Duh. I love that story! *Soooo* romantic and tragic, amirite?"

"Right. But I don't mean that. Today, Malice told me something strange about it. Something about a curse." I try to remember her exact words. "She said I have to break it. That it's my responsibility."

Daisy wrinkles her nose. "Weird. Why you?"

Before I can answer, we're interrupted by a shout from somewhere behind us. We turn toward the motel, where two girls are goofing off on the upper balcony. One is climbing the iron trellis with an ice bucket while the other backs away, hands held high, oblivious to the patio chairs behind her.

"Hey. Be careful!" I call, several dozen scenarios fighting for attention in my head, most ending in death. Or a lawsuit.

They both freeze, then lean over the railing for a better look. It's the girls from the pool, the ones Graham flirted with earlier. A blonde and a brunette, in matching cut-offs and tank tops. Daddy would not approve.

"What's it to you?" one of them calls, while the other giggles. She's on vacation in Kentucky. What the hell does she have to be so cheerful about?

"I work here," I say, because I know from experience that "I live here" makes me sound like some kind of Norman Bates wannabe.

"We don't want to have to mop up the blood after you fall down the stairs," Daisy adds, her voice louder.

The second girl's face turns white, then red.

Uh-oh. I've dealt with plenty of bored tourist kids before and I can hear the complaint already—*they threatened to push us down the stairs!*

I say, "If you're bored, we've got some retro video games in the lobby."

We use the term "retro" a lot. G-Pop never bothered to update, and by the time Daddy took over, our mid-century modern motel had become retro-chic. But to these two it probably just looks old. "Or you could try the night hike," I say, forcing an upbeat tone into my voice that is the exact opposite of the disgust on their faces. "It's a lot of fun."

"What the hell's a moonbow, anyway?"

"It's kind of like a rainbow, but formed by the moon instead of the sun. So it's spookier."

It's the tactic I usually take with younger kids. Teenagers typically don't ask or care. And these girls are having none of it; I can tell by their vacant expressions. Or maybe that's how they always look.

"It's haunted," Daisy adds. "By the ghost of a demon bride, who jumped to her death after her lovah betrayed her." She makes her voice go deep and spooky.

The blonde rolls her eyes. "Please. What are we, twelve?"

Older than twelve. Excellent. I shoot Momma a mental apology and add, "Graham leads the hike." After all, how much trouble can he get into with a dozen other guests watching?

Bingo. Their faces light up. I jerk a thumb toward the front of the building. "Meet him in the lobby in twenty minutes. If you don't have flashlights, let him know and he'll lend you one. And don't forget bug spray."

Daisy and I watch as they scamper off, hopefully to put on more clothes.

"Demon bride?" I ask, raising an eyebrow.

"Yeah, that's right." She rolls her eyes at my expression. "Oh, please. Don't tell me you prefer Malice's kiddie version to the real one? Besides, you're the one who said there's a curse."

"*Malice* said there's a curse," I correct her.

"Whatever. Get your butt in the car and I'll tell you the *real* legend of the ghost bride. And then you can tell me all about this so-called curse."

"I'd really rather not." But I'm talking to the night air. Daisy's already in the car.

She and Malice might put stock in that old urban legend, but I'm not that gullible. I believe in what I can see.

Unfortunately, right now I can see that Daisy isn't going to let this go.

THE LEGEND OF THE GHOST BRIDE

as told by Daisy Renfro

A long time ago, a girl loved a boy. And like so many girls, before and after, she believed he loved her too. He promised her the moon and stars, but like the sky they lay under all those winter nights, his promises were cold and empty. Still, she loved him, and so she did what lots of girls do when they love a boy—she pretended not to see his imperfections.

Before long, she was pregnant. And though she knew theirs was a child born of love, she also knew no one else would see it that way. She'd be labeled a whore, or worse, even if they married immediately. She decided the thing to do—the only option she had, really—was to tell him. Then they would leave Corbin together, go somewhere far away where they could raise their baby in secret.

But before she got up the courage, she heard he was engaged to another woman. It might have been a rumor. There was no real evidence of him courting anyone. But the whispers were enough for her.

She should have just asked him! Sat him down and told him of the life they'd created together. Reminded him of their passion, and their love. But she was scared. So she did what a lot of scared and confused girls do. She made a stupid mistake.

One that would haunt her for the rest of eternity.

No one actually knows if she meant to start the fire that night. Or why she dressed herself in a wedding gown. Maybe it was an accident. Or maybe she thought if she put herself in peril, he would save her. It could be as simple as that—her just trying to get his attention.

Whatever the reason, she was wrong. He died in that fire.

So she threw herself off the cliff, taking their unborn baby with her.

And now she's doomed to walk the riverbank beneath the moonbow forever—a grave reminder to the young women of Corbin.

She shows mercy to those who are smart, those who don't pin all their hopes and dreams on one lousy boy. As for those who don't heed her warning . . . Let's just say they aren't here to tell their stories.

CHAPTER 5

We all learned the science of the moonbow, way back in grade school. When the night is clear and the moon is full, the light reflects off the water droplets in the mist produced by the falls, creating a moonbow. With extended exposure, it can be photographed in full color. But human eyes can't perceive color in such low light. So instead of a rainbow, what we see is more like her dark, brooding sister. Her shadow self. Or her ghost.

The position of the moon in relation to the waterfall, the angle of the falls, the force of the water—all of these are factors, and they can all be explained by science—except for the parts that can't. Because nothing explains the *magic* of it. That flutter of wonder when the moon clears the treetops, and that arc of pale light suddenly appears. And it is sudden: One second, darkness. The next, light. But it's somehow also gradual, not so much an appearance as it is a revealing. As if the moonbow has been there all along, and the only change is that we've finally been deemed worthy to perceive it.

There are a few other places in the world where you can see

one, and most of those are by chance. Cumberland Falls is the only waterfall in the northern hemisphere that consistently produces a moonbow, on every clear night from two days before until two days after the full moon. If that sounds rehearsed, it's because it's straight off our motel website. What's harder to express to our guests is how incredibly lucky we all are—both those of us who live here and those able to visit—that such a place exists, where magic happens on a regular basis.

So much of my childhood is tied to that moonbow. My first clear memory is from the summer I was four. The whole evening had a feeling of anticipation. My daddy standing on the front porch, studying the sky with absolute seriousness. Graham and I "resting" in the afternoon to prepare for the long and late evening, but instead wiggling and giggling beneath our covers. A picnic dinner of cold fried chicken and potato salad, eaten in the twilight of our kitchen. The ride to the falls in the back of the pickup, the summer wind whipping our hair, our mouths pressed shut to avoid swallowing bugs. And finally, that hushed walk out to the falls, clutching my brother's hand as we stepped over the throngs of tourists lying with pillows and blankets on the rocks, fearful of the dark but thrilled to be out in it for such a momentous occasion. Graham led me carefully to the edge of the cliff, and there it was. An arc of light and dark, emerging like magic out of the spray. And my daddy's quiet voice, his breath tickling my ear as he leaned down to explain to me how it came to be that we were here in the middle of the night, viewing a rainbow in the moonlight. We were blessed, he told me, to witness a vision that most of the world would never see.

There were so many nights like that, so many quiet afternoons and late suppers. Once I got old enough, Daddy shared his own special place for viewing, far from the crowds and the noise. Then it was just the three of us—me and Graham giggling wildly as we trailed Daddy through the woods in the dead of night, shrieking at the snap of a branch or the hoot of an owl.

As we got older, Graham and I both chanced Momma's wrath at least a time or two to join our friends at the overlook, which was exciting as a kid and then deemed tacky as a teenager when we realized most of the people there were tourists. Or adults. After that, we took dates to Lover's Leap—the Leap, for short—to park and make out in seclusion, at the very spot where the bride jumped. Now part of Cumberland Falls Park, it's one of the favorite places for locals to view the moonbow. Further from the falls than the overlook, but much less crowded. Eventually, though, we found our own spot, like everyone in Corbin ultimately does, hopping the safety railings to climb down the rocks and closer to the water. Or, in our case, heading into the woods through a hidden trail. It's possibly illegal, probably dangerous. But we all take the risk for the chance to be alone.

I've seen the moonbow so many times that most of the visits have all blended together in my mind into one big, fuzzy clump of memories. Like a quilt, made up of the fabric of time, stitched tightly with the thread of tradition, and stuffed with the love of my family, they've brought me comfort and warmth over the years. But as time goes on, they've gotten heavier. Smothering.

Sometimes, I dream that I'm standing out on the ledge—just like the bride. Rocky and uneven, with only a thin metal cable separating me from the eighty-foot drop to the water below. I always wake up before I have the chance to climb back to safety.

Or to jump.

Tonight, Daisy and I head to that same secret spot, the one we found when we were deemed old enough to be let loose by ourselves. Daisy, being the oldest, was always in charge, and the only rule back then was to stay out of the woods. But of course, we plunged fearlessly into the forest, giddy with that first taste of freedom, and ventured way farther than our parents ever would have guessed.

She tells me her version of the legend as we drive the twisting mountain highway, past the brightly lit lodge, down a steeply pitched road, and turn off onto a dirt track that, as far as anyone else knows, leads to the water treatment plant and not much else.

Before we get that far, Daisy steers her Chevy Tracker off the road, nearly bottoming out as she pulls onto a grassy patch beneath a willow tree with trailing branches long enough to hide us. As she cuts her engine and the headlights fade, a thick darkness settles over us, along with a sense of uneasiness that hangs heavy in the air.

"So, what do you think?" Daisy asks. "Am I as talented as your mawmaw?"

"As dramatic, maybe. But your story is way different from Malice's. Where did you even hear it? Or did you make it up?"

"Of course not! It's the one our babysitter used to tell us when she wanted us to stop whining about nightlights and monsters and go to bed."

Daisy climbs out of the car and pats her pockets for her keys before she locks up. Once, years ago, we got stuck out here and had to call Graham to come and bail us out with a slim jim. It was a costly mistake, because it gave away our secret location. Around here, we guard our moonbow spots as closely as our mommas beg us to guard our virginity. But better Graham than our parents, we'd figured. He might use it—and he did—but at least he couldn't stop us from going back.

"It's not that different from Malice's," she says. "The bride still offs herself. Mine just has more pizzazz."

"Hey!" I'm offended on Malice's behalf. "Her story has pizzazz! And no demons," I add. Thank goodness. If it had, Daddy would've forbidden me from ever hearing it.

"Okay, so maybe I exaggerated a bit," Daisy says as we pick our way down the slope. We step carefully through the grass and vines and toward a tree blanketed with kudzu. In the dark, it takes the shape of a giant swelling up out of the forest, his massive arms beckoning us forward.

Or warning us away.

I follow Daisy through a small break in the tree line, ducking to avoid hitting my head.

"Maybe she's not a demon. But she's definitely pissed off and out for revenge. Wouldn't you be?" Daisy asks.

"I guess." The shadows of night give way to the full dark of the forest, and I'm absurdly grateful for the metallic glint of Daisy's tank top, which shines like a beacon whenever a beam of moonlight pierces the foliage above. "Wait. What? I didn't say anything about revenge. You sound like Momma," I say.

"So what's the curse, then?"

I try to recall Malice's exact words. "Malice made it sound like the bride's story was part of the curse. And she told me that to break it, I have to help her find peace. Or someone from my family does, anyway."

"Like me!" Daisy stops so suddenly I nearly plow her over. "This is getting better and better!"

"Not you," I say, flinching under the weight of her glare. "Sorry. But Malice said the responsibility is passed on her side, from mother to daughter."

My cousin puts her hands on her hips. "Doesn't matter. I'm still going to help you. And if that pisses the bride off, too bad. She should be grateful."

"Um, no. She isn't pissed off, or grateful. She isn't anything. Because she's not real."

Daisy trips on something and swears. "Shit. Don't say that. Of course she's real. The story wouldn't exist otherwise."

I swing my phone around for light, trying to avoid whatever tripped her up. This story is a touchstone of my childhood, as much a part of me as the falls and my family. But that doesn't mean I ever believed it was true. "It's an urban legend."

"And where do you think urban legends come from? They all have to start somewhere." Daisy points her phone at me. "What's more likely? A bunch of people randomly decided to make up stories about dead brides?" She pauses. "Or. A girl died on her wedding day, tragically, and the people who witnessed it kept talking about it. Better yet, the people who saw her *ghost* kept talking about it."

Before I can answer, something crashes through the bushes in the distance and Daisy stops. So does my heart.

"Possum," she says unconvincingly.

"Or bear."

After several long seconds during which neither of us breathes, the noises move farther away and then fade. Whatever it was, it's running from us, not at us. It's not that I'm scared, exactly. I've been on plenty of night hikes. But I wouldn't hang out here alone, either. The forest can be dangerous after dark.

"What witnesses?" I ask once my heart rate returns to normal.

But Daisy is moving through the brush and doesn't answer.

She ducks under one last branch and I follow, and then we're both standing in a small clearing in front of a pile of crumbled stone and mortar. With Daisy away at college, we haven't been back here since last summer, and as my eyes adjust, I see that the year has not been kind, at least not to the old building. There used to be a partial roof, but that's completely collapsed now, as has the doorway. There were bad storms this past spring. It's amazing that two of the walls are still standing, one corner somewhat intact. Moonlight beams through a round hole that once held a window.

When we were younger, we pretended this was the church where the bride was going to take her vows—an act destined to never happen. It wasn't, of course. This was some kind of mill, using the river to generate power, though the section of building that held the wheel is long gone. But Daisy and I have always been good at making up stories.

I turn slowly, soaking it all in. The sweet scent of honeysuckle, with a minerally undertone of wet rock. The faint whisper of running water. The puddles of moonlight that bleed into the shadows.

"It's just like I remember," Daisy says, kicking at a pile of dead leaves. "Totally haunted."

Haunted. My breath hitches in my throat, which is ridiculous. Ghosts aren't real. There's no one else here, living or dead.

At least not that we can see.

I swat away the random thought. The women in our family sure do know how to get inside each other's heads.

Daisy runs her hand along the back wall and pulls out an old, brittle roll of paper from one of the cracks, releasing a flood of memories. We used to leave wishes for the bride and pretend they'd come true. How much simpler would everything be if I could just leave it all in the hands of that poor, dead girl?

Let Momma change her mind.

Let Malice be okay.

Daisy unrolls the paper. "'I wish Chance would kiss me,'" she reads aloud, and hoots with laughter. "I guess we know how that one turned out."

My cheeks get hot. "She did come through for me on that one." I step over and pull a handful of papers from the wall. "But what about you? What did fair Daisy wish for? A passing grade in English?" I hold one out of reach as I unfurl it, which is easy because she's so short.

"Or maybe for Officer Scott to let her off with a warning the next time he pulled her over?"

"If I'd been smart enough to wish for that, I wouldn't have had to forfeit my car senior year."

"BETRAYAL HAS LEGS. LOYALTY HAS ROOTS," I read. "Weird. What is that supposed to mean?"

"You tell me. I didn't write it."

I crumple the papers and tuck them in my pocket. She's clearly lying, but I refuse to take the bait. I'm not going to get pulled into the whole ghost-bride-curse thing again. Instead, I head toward the riverbed. Two large blue ash trees bend over what years of our foot traffic has worn down into a walkway. From here—or even from perched in the arms of one of the trees—we'll have a perfect view of the moonbow.

"Remember the game?" Daisy asks, breathing into my ear, and I jump.

Wasn't she standing near the ruins? I peer into the darkness. But that's just a shadow. Not Daisy. Not a . . . figure.

Just shadows.

"How could I forget?" I say, shuddering a little. Between the shade and the flowing water, it's cooler here. And buggier. I slap away a mosquito as an owl hoots somewhere above me.

I debate taking off my shoes and wading in. The river always calms me. Sometimes I like to pretend it's washing away all my hurt and disappointments, carrying them somewhere far downstream where they'll never find me. Tonight, I need that more than ever. But I can't quite latch on to the wishful thinking of my childhood.

"You okay?" Daisy asks.

"I'm fine." I try to shake off her probing gaze, as well as the sudden sense of loss pressing down on me and stealing my breath.

"Good. 'Cause we've got work to do." Daisy hands me something. Malice's hair clip.

I turn it over in my hand, trying to brush aside the sense of wrongness at seeing it here, out in the open, instead of safe at home where it belongs. This is an heirloom, one of Malice's cherished possessions. "Where did you get this?"

She rolls her eyes. "Relax, sister cuz. I took it off your dresser." She turns me by the shoulders and pulls my hair back with a rubber band. Then she pulls my T-shirt from her backpack and drapes it over my head, using the clip to hold it in place. "Perfect."

"Daisy." I reach for the back of my head, but she slaps my hand away. "I'm not in the mood," I say. "What were we thinking, anyway? A wedding that ends with us throwing ourselves in the river?" On hot days, that was our favorite part. But now . . . "Isn't it all a little—"

"Disrespectful? No. And anyway, we're not going to play make-believe this time. We're going to conjure her spirit. How else are we supposed to help her move toward the light?"

"Conjure . . ." I break off, shaking my head. "I was going to say 'melodramatic.' But I think you've proven my point. This is even stupider."

The wind picks up and Daisy pinches my arm. Hard.

"Ow—"

"Don't say that," she hisses, her normal exuberance replaced by dead seriousness. "Not where she might hear you. What if you make her angry?"

Daisy's insistence unnerves me, and for a moment, the echo of Malice's words is almost audible. *She's real. And she's angry.*

Between the two of them, I've had enough of this curse talk.

"Look," I say. "Suppose she is—was . . . a real girl. Once."

Daisy arches an eyebrow at this small admission on my part, and I hurry on. "That was years ago. What could we possibly do to help her now? She's long dead."

I regret the words the moment they're out. Though I don't believe in any of this hooey, they sound like an invitation, a calling forth of someone—or some*thing*—that I have absolutely no desire to meet in this isolated patch of woods in the dead of night.

The wind rustles, and leaves kick up around us, and for a second, everything Daisy fears seems possible—the ghost bride could be real. And here. Standing behind us. Watching us.

"Malice has given us a real, live ghost story! The least we can do is—"

"We're not having a séance," I say, trying to ignore the prickling on the back of my neck. "I can't believe I'm going to say this, but maybe my momma had the right idea. I've got enough on my plate this summer without having to worry about conjuring ghosts or breaking curses or whatever."

"You realize you're taking all the fun out of this." Daisy throws up her arms, and her angry exasperation feels so normal, so Daisy, that I laugh out loud.

Of course there are no ghosts. Being in the forest at night is enough to make anyone jumpy, what with the moving shadows and night sounds that amplify and sharpen in the dark.

"Will you at least play the game?" she asks, pulling a bottle of champagne from her backpack.

When I nod in defeat, she whoops with joy. "We need more time to set up a real séance, anyway. Instead, how about you take your vows like a dutiful little bride? Then"—she waves the bottle back and forth—"we celebrate!"

She runs back toward the ruins and I have to hurry to catch up, careful to keep my gaze on my feet so I don't fall.

Not that there's any real need to hurry. We're alone.

And I don't need to look behind myself to prove it.

CHAPTER 6

Our bride game was never about marriage. There were never any boys involved, and the vows we took were always for whatever one of us deemed important on any given day. Over the years, we have pledged ourselves, among other things, sister cousins, unofficial members of the Baby-Sitters Club, and honorary wives of Zac Efron. Okay, so sometimes there were pretend boys involved.

Tonight's ceremony is no different. Daisy wants me to commit to the Summer of Me.

"This sounds a little too much like hippie shit," I say. "Even for you."

"You're the one who said you've got too much on your plate. You're not taking your trip, and you're stuck at the motel, and I know that all sucks. But I for one am not going to listen to you whine about it all summer." Daisy shoves a handful of dead branches into my arms, draping them like a bouquet. "So shut up and repeat after me. I, Rena Faye Whitaker, do solemnly vow . . ."

She waits for me to echo her words. "I, Rena Faye Whitaker, do solemnly vow . . ."

"To embrace life. And myself. I will love myself, honor myself, cherish myself."

I repeat the lines, and Daisy finishes with, "By the power vested in me by the ghost bride, I now pronounce you Keeper of Your Own Fate!"

She pops the cork on the champagne and presses her thumb over the bottle as she points it at me, the bubbles showering me along with her laughter.

Despite the corniness of the situation, I join in. Because it's hard not to love Daisy. Even when I want to strangle her. I wipe champagne from my cheeks. "Is this why you told me to wear denim?"

She shrugs and hands me the bottle. "To sister cousins."

"To sister cousins." I raise it before taking a long drink.

We sit together on a cement slab that used to be a portion of the wall, sharing the bottle and letting the night breeze dry my wine-soaked hair. She rests her head on my shoulder, and for the first time all day, some of the choking disappointment I've been carrying lets loose. Maybe Daisy is smarter than I give her credit for.

I drain the bottle and wiggle it at her. "All gone."

"No worries. I took two from my daddy's cellar."

"Won't he notice?"

She sits up and wrinkles her nose. "Are you kidding? Every year, he drives up to Louisville to get a bottle from the same year—1998. The year him and Momma were married. But they never drink it. There's like twenty bottles down there."

"That's really depressing."

Daisy pops open the next bottle. "Tell me about it." She lets the champagne spill for a second before shoving her mouth over the top. When she's done, she wipes her mouth, eyes watering. "What I can't figure out is why he keeps wasting the money."

I think about it for a moment, picturing Uncle Ford making the same lonely drive two hours north to buy a bottle he knows he'll never drink. "Maybe stopping feels like giving up."

A branch snaps somewhere close by, and we both freeze. Daisy shoves the bottle behind her, while I struggle to my feet, a slew of possibilities running through my head. A bear. A cop. An escaped convict with a hook hand. The last seems only remotely plausible, but we're in the middle of nowhere, alone, so I leave it on the list.

Daisy grips my hand as a shadow detaches itself from the tree line.

Then another.

My heart pounds at a dizzying rate.

Daisy lets out a blood-chilling scream, but I can't speak at all.

Until I recognize the silhouette.

"Chance?"

"Oh, thank god!" Daisy sags against me, almost knocking me over, then rushes forward to slap the other guy in the arm. "You scared the living daylights out of us!"

"Sorry." Chance shoves his hands into his pockets, a sandy curl flopping over his right eye in a way that I find as adorable as it is predictable. He scuffs at the ground with a cowboy boot, waiting patiently for the forgiveness he knows is coming.

His friend—who on closer inspection I recognize as Graham's

buddy Knox Barnett—does not look the slightest bit sorry. He just looks bored, ambling into the clearing and slouching against the tree trunk, legs spread out in front of him, long hair slicked back from his face. His work shirt is unbuttoned, the sleeves rolled up to his shoulders to show off his tattoos. His latest is a big guitar on his left shoulder with a banner wrapped around it that reads *bluegrass never needs cutting*.

His shirt logo says ATWATER LODGE, and his presence here tonight solves the mystery of which cute boy Daisy is planning to hook up with this summer.

"So, ladies. What's the plan?" Knox gives my cousin a lazy grin as she drinks directly from the wine bottle. "Care to share?"

Daisy gives him a critical look. "Maybe. For a price."

He reaches for her, but she ducks under his arm and behind a branch. She's no easy catch, and I'm not sure who to feel sorry for. Daisy has never wanted a serious boyfriend. She prefers to keep things casual, or as she puts it, share the wealth. Why should all the other men miss out?

But Knox might be even better than her at avoiding commitment. The guy would flirt with a garden hose if he thought he might get lucky. Actually, some of his girlfriends have had the IQ of yard tools. But maybe I'm being unfair. Charming and sleazy aren't *always* trademark qualities of a douchebag. I sometimes have a hard time separating my feelings for my idiot brother from my feelings for his friends. But isn't it their fault for hanging out with an idiot in the first place?

Then Chance gets tired of waiting and pulls me close, and I forget all about Daisy and her string of broken hearts.

When we've thoroughly said our hellos, I pull back and press my hand to his cheek. I've had a crush on this boy since I was old enough to know what that was, and even after three years together, I still can't believe we're a couple. In the real world of Corbin, Kentucky, Chance Caudell is the closest we're ever going to get to a prince. And I'm not the only one who thinks so. Half the girls in Corbin would push me off a cliff if given the opportunity to date our star quarterback.

I've learned to watch my back.

He tugs on the T-shirt veil. "What's with the getup?"

My smile hardens on my face, and not just because I sense a hint of judgment in his tone. Chance isn't jealous, exactly. He's too confident for that. He just doesn't like it when I do things without him. Especially if it involves other boys.

We've never told anyone else about our game. So I don't need Daisy's hard stare—which she manages without detaching her lips from Knox's—to remind me not to spill our secret.

I touch my hair and then wave my hand. "Oh, we were just drinking and being silly. I'm a bride."

The corners of Chance's eyes crinkle when he smiles. Also when he's pissed. Sometimes it's hard to tell the difference. "So who's the groom?"

"It's not like that."

He reaches over me and snaps the clip open, letting the shirt fall to my shoulders. "I like your hair better down."

Daisy slides in between us before I can protest. "Enough chit-chat. It's moonbow time, bitches."

She leads the way, pulling me forward, and Chance takes my

other hand as we make our way down to the rocky bank of the river.

We find a strategic spot where we can see the overlook but no one can see us, our backs tucked up against the wide trunk of a shingle oak. Knox drains the second wine bottle, then opens his backpack to drop our empties inside and pull out a couple of longnecks.

Daisy makes a face and shakes her head, but Chance and I each take one.

Chance clinks his bottle with mine and lines up his leg so we're touching. "Happy first day of summer."

"Happy first . . . moonbow. This summer . . ." I trail off as Daisy bursts into loud laughter.

Chance graduated last week, so technically his summer has already started. And it isn't just his summer. It's adulthood, college, the rest of his life. Why does that all sound so depressing and sad?

"Happy summer," I say, forcing aside the thought. I clink his bottle back and then Knox's.

Knox is Graham's age, so he's been out of school two years already. Summer for him means more of the same—working at Atwater Lodge.

"Happy summer?" His voice drips sarcasm. "I've been demoted. So more like crappy fucking summer."

"Demoted to what? Bellhop?" I'm joking, but I swallow my laugh when he says, "Maintenance."

"Seriously? Why?"

"The prodigal son is back. Home from boarding school." He swirls the last dregs of his bottle and downs them before tossing it back into the pack and pulling out a fresh one.

"Really? Dunlap is home?" I ask. I hadn't heard, but it makes sense. Jackson Jr. passed away suddenly this past winter, an event that plunged the entire city into mourning for weeks. It was in one of these full-page photo spreads that I saw my first glimpse of the boy Daisy and I went to school with back in grade school, when private and out-of-town was not an option. "What was his name again? Asher?"

"Arden." Knox drags it out, making it sound like the noise a dying cat might make. "And Arden"—he does it again—"needs managerial experience. Which means I need to step aside so he can get it."

In all honesty, I'm not so sure Knox would be the best choice for front desk manager to begin with, but he cleans up nice and he knows how to schmooze a customer, which is more than I remember about Arden. "Wasn't he that sad kid who was always getting bloody noses? Am I thinking of the right guy?"

"Oh, don't play Miss Innocent," Daisy says. "You know exactly who he is. You kissed him on the playground, underneath the monkey bars. Remember?"

"I did not." I deny it automatically.

Chance narrows his eyes. "You and Arden Dunlap were a thing?"

"We weren't a thing," I say. "I just felt sorry for him. He was so sad all the time. I wanted to make him feel better."

"Uh-huh. Sure," Chance says.

Daisy points a triumphant finger in my direction. "I knew you remembered!"

"Did it work?" Knox asks.

"What do you think?" Daisy asks at the same time I say, "I don't think so."

"Was that the time he would not stop crying at snack break? And his mom had to come and get him?" she asks.

I have a vague recollection of him as a pale kid with freckles, crumbling his cookies into his milk, tears streaming down his face. "Yep. Our romance was doomed from the start."

"Well, apparently he's our boss now," Daisy says. "So wish us luck."

"Oh, come on, he was five. He probably doesn't cry as much anymore. Or bleed," I add, though, who knows? "I mean, you used to eat glue."

"Glue sticks," Daisy corrects. "They looked like grape Push Pops."

"*Mmmm.* Push Pops." Knox nuzzles the top of Daisy's head, and they both look so happy, I feel guilty for my earlier doubts. Maybe all those country songs are right and love really does find a way. Or whatever the cornball message is supposed to be.

Our conversation dwindles as the moon rises. The breeze from the river cools us, and as I breathe in the faint scent of pine and wet rock, the river and the beer start to work their magic and the tension eases from my body. I blink to bring the moonbow into focus as the soft arc of gray and white light flickers in front of us like a feature film. The faint sound of clapping and cheering carries on the wind, drowning out the roar of the water. Flashes go off as the tourists try to take pictures, and I have to laugh.

Flash photography is a mistake on moonbow night.

Chance and I each have another beer, and I lay my head against his chest and listen to his heartbeat. It's a perfect moment—the water, the moonbow, my boyfriend, my best friend. Maybe this summer won't be so terrible. What else do I think I need?

I look over at Daisy, snuggled up against Knox. She smiles contentedly, then grabs his beer and holds it up in a toast.

"To us," she says, echoing my thoughts. "I say we stay here, just like this, forever. The future can suck it. Who's with me?" she asks, taking a sip of the beer and shuddering. "Gah. It's warm." She shoves the bottle back at Knox.

"Maybe that's what we should—" I almost say "ask the bride for," but stop myself. No more bride talk. Instead, I point at the water frothing at the base of the falls. "We should start our own rafting business."

Chance laughs, then goes quiet when he sees my face.

"I'm serious," I say, annoyed at his quick dismissal. "Midnight moonbow rides. Get people as close to the falls as possible. There's still a beach down here somewhere, right?" Access to the swimming beach was closed when I was young, after someone drowned. But there must still be a way down.

"Tourists would go crazy for that. Moonbow overhead. Spray on their faces. We'd rake in cash." I point my beer bottle at the rest of them.

Knox tips his head to the side and stares at the river thoughtfully, while Daisy rolls her eyes in my direction. "Aren't *you* just the entrepreneur?"

Chance asks, "What's so bad about our real future?"

And just like that, the moment is lost.

"We don't need to start a business. We already have one." He shifts to look down at me. "Didn't your daddy talk to you about coming to work at the ranch? Since your trip was canceled?"

I stiffen. Is this what Daddy was hinting at earlier? As if there were a chance in hell I would spend the summer working with horses. I'm allergic. Plus, I hate them. Just the thought makes me break out in hives.

My cheeks heat, the beer loosening my tongue. "How did you know my trip was canceled?"

"We're off to a good year," Chance says, ignoring my question and my discomfort. "We've got some big groups booked in, and I talked one of the state parks into adding us as a stop on their regular trail ride." He bumps his knee against mine and I pull my leg away.

He looks confused, then hurt. "I just thought . . ." He trails off. "I mean, we've got to start thinking about this sometime, right? After all, the ranch will be mine one day."

Coldwater isn't really a ranch. It's a horse camp, which is a fancy way of saying they have stables where horseback riders can stop off to feed and groom their rides. They also offer trail rides and boarding, as well as birthday parties and a whole slew of other horse-related activities that I'm sure someone with interest in horses would find terribly exciting.

I am not that someone.

Chance and I have talked about the future, but only ever in an abstract, far-off fantasy kind of way. Mostly because deep down, I know our visions might not match. In mine, I'm a world-traveling photographer, stopping home now and then to regale my family with tales of my exotic travels while we page through glossy magazine spreads of my photos. Chance is there, too, of course. Doing what, though, I'm not sure.

I probably should have asked him, since apparently in his scenario, I'm some kind of horse lady.

But my guilt over not asking evaporates when he adds, "Your daddy agrees with me."

I may have been hazy on the details, but so was he. And the fact that he talked to my daddy without me—made decisions *for* me—without so much as asking me a question? It makes me so furious that for a moment, I can't breathe. When I do finally inhale, I choke on my beer, yeast burning my nostrils and my throat.

Daisy leans over to whack me on the back.

"You talked to my daddy?" I croak when I've recovered. I wipe my burning eyes with the neck of my shirt. "When?"

He doesn't answer.

"When did you find out about my trip?" I ask again. "Because I just found out today. And you weren't at the motel after that, at least not that I saw."

He still doesn't want to answer, but this time, I wait him out. "Yesterday," he finally says.

Yesterday. While I was at school, finishing up my English final, Chance was at my house. Talking to my daddy. About me. "Yesterday," I repeat. "You knew how much that trip meant to me. And you've known about it since yesterday. But you didn't think to tell me?"

No one speaks for what feels like a full minute. Even in the dusky light, I can tell Chance is trying to calculate his options, choose the words that will hurt me least. Hurt *him* least.

"I didn't think it was my place," he finally says. "I knew it would upset you."

"Of course it upsets me! But you lying to me upsets me more!"

"Hey! I never lied."

"No, but you kept it from me. That's practically the same thing."

"Come on, Rena Faye—"

"And worse than that," I keep going, "you knew it would upset me. But you didn't even try to comfort me. No 'How are you doing?' texts?" I wiggle my phone at him. "Not even a 'Hey, what's up?' Instead, you were all, 'How can I make this work to my advantage?'"

"It wasn't like that," Chance says, his eyes narrowing. "We were just talking, and it came out. It's not really me you're mad at anyway. I was just trying to help. If you calm down and think about it, you'll see this is for the best."

"Best for who?"

Chance refuses to look me in the eye, so I glare at his cowardly profile as all of the disappointments from the last few weeks—from today—weigh me down, and for a moment I can't get the words out.

Does he think it's *for the best* that I was rejected from the Governor's School? Is it *for the best* that Malice and I can't take a trip because what Momma says goes? Is it *for the best* that everyone has decided I will just keep cleaning up after tourists for no pay and without complaint? And am I supposed to think it's *for the best* that my daddy and my boyfriend are talking about my future—a future that doesn't seem to take into consideration any of what *I* want—behind my back? When neither of them has even bothered to tell me they're sorry about my dreams getting crushed?

I struggle to my feet, shoving Chance's hand away as he reaches to help me.

"Maybe we should take a break," I say, trying to hold back the tears. "I think *that* would be for the best." My beer bottle tumbles and shatters on the rocks beneath my feet and somehow the broken glass makes everything worse.

"And for the record, it *is* you I'm mad at."

I gather my things and head into the woods before he has a chance to respond.

CHAPTER 7

Chance wants to "talk things through," but I refuse to let him speak, so while Daisy and I walk ahead, he and Knox follow in silence. The moan of the wind through the trees is drowned out by the words screaming inside my head.

Betrayal. Disloyalty. Doubt.

He tries to kiss me when we reach the car, but I turn my head and refuse to look at him, even in the mirror as we drive away, though I know he watches us until we're out of sight.

Daisy hasn't uttered a word since I demanded she take me home, but I can tell it bothers her to have to leave early.

"You can go back and screw him later." It's a bitchy thing to say, but I'm in the mood to burn everything down, and even she isn't safe from my rage. We've said worse to each other over the years, but that's the benefit of love—you expect the best and tolerate the worst.

To her credit, she just shrugs and says, "If he's lucky," and then keeps her mouth shut the rest of the drive.

"Do you need me to come in?" she asks as she pulls into my driveway, where she waits for me to change into my spare T-shirt. "Help you throw things? Torch his jacket? Erase his photos on Insta?"

I toss my dirty top into her back seat and manage a tiny smile. "I don't think I have the energy. I just want to go to bed. But thanks."

"Sure. He's being a dick."

"He is. Isn't he?" I turn in my seat. I need her to back me up, need to know she agrees with me. Already I'm second-guessing myself and my outburst. "I mean, right?"

"Absolutely." Daisy nods vigorously, her hoop earrings bobbing. "Talking to your daddy behind your back and not telling you about the trip? Not cool."

"And working at his camp? That's just absurd, right? He knows I'm allergic."

This time, her nod is less enthusiastic.

"What?"

She shrugs one shoulder, her furry jacket slipping down.

"No, tell me. You think I overreacted?"

"I mean, I get why you're pissed. And you've got every right. It's just . . . you hate working here. I thought you'd jump at the chance for something new. And an excuse to hang out with Chance all summer? Seems like a no-brainer."

My face goes hot. I hate that she doesn't see that this is so clearly not going to work. "That's not the point."

She shrugs. "From where I'm sitting, it looks like an out."

"Look, I appreciate the advice. But for once in my life, I want to make a decision based on what I want. Rather than just avoiding what I don't."

It sounds good. Right, even. The only problem is, it's hard to break yourself of a habit you've kept up for, well, basically your whole life. Because what *I* want never seems to be one of the options. It's like my life is just one long, crappy buffet of unappetizing choices.

"But . . . isn't that basically what you're doing now?" She gives me her best "Daisy doesn't take bullshit" look—eyebrow raised, head tilted to the side.

"Ouch." And I don't mean the sting as I peel my legs from the leather seat.

"Truth is a brutal bitch." She flashes a grin that goes from silly to sinister as I close the car door and the interior light shuts off. "And so am I," she adds through the open window.

I watch her taillights as she rounds the curve down the hill and turns onto the highway below. Is she right? I balked at Chance's suggestion at least partly because this has been one long day of everyone else deciding what's best for me. But this isn't a "lesser of two evils" situation—it can't be—because if that's the case, I've clearly miscalculated somewhere. There's no way letting Graham bark orders at me is the lesser evil. In *any* scenario.

The house is dark, which probably means the night hike is over and my parents are in bed. Who the hell knows what Graham's doing. Everything looks quiet at the motel, so at least he isn't partying with minors.

I lock the door behind me and leave my shoes on the mat, tiptoeing through the kitchen and down the hallway toward the stairs. One of the old floorboards in the foyer creaks, and I freeze as a lamp switches on.

Momma is curled up in a chair in the far corner of the front room, her feet tucked under her. She's in dark leggings, an oversized T-shirt, and big fuzzy socks, despite the heat. Her feet are always cold.

"You scared the crap out of me," I say. "I thought once I'm a senior, you'd stop waiting up."

"I can't sleep if you're not home. Besides, how else will I know when you miss curfew?"

I check my phone. "I'm early."

"For once."

I resist the urge to roll my eyes, though barely. I've missed curfew once in my life, when Chance's car slid off the road into a culvert and we had to wait for his daddy to come pull us out. I'd called, though. Graham, on the other hand, has always treated his curfew like an amusing suggestion. But as far as I know, he's never once gotten in trouble. And Momma never bothers to wait up for him, either.

She rubs her eyes and squints blearily toward me. "What happened to your hair?"

I touch my head, then pull my fingers through the tangled mess as I realize I don't know where Malice's hair clip is. Hopefully, Chance still has it. "Oh. I . . . let it down. Because, you know . . ." I don't know how to tell her without explaining about the bride. "Can we talk about this tomorrow? I'm tired. I've had a sh—a rough night." I grab the railing and put one foot on the stairs, as if daring her to stop me.

She doesn't, but her gaze burns pinholes in the back of my shoulder blades.

"Chance and I broke up," I blurt, hating her a little for making me say it out loud.

"Sorry, baby." Her voice sounds deeper tonight, throaty, like she's swallowed all the other unspoken words between us.

"Don't—" I turn toward her, but don't finish the thought. What would I say, anyway? *Don't call me baby. Don't apologize for something you don't mean. Don't act like you care.*

She sits up and stretches her legs out in front of her. "I know you were . . . upset by my announcement earlier. And I wanted to explain—"

"Upset!" I don't want to have this conversation, don't want to talk to her at all, but the word bursts out of me like a cannonball. "You mean because you let me get my hopes up for a trip that was never going to happen?"

I march into the room and stop in front of her.

She winces and rubs the space between her eyes, as if my anger is a visible thing, and it pains her. I hope it is. At least that would mean she isn't completely oblivious to my feelings.

"Maybe my timing could have been better." She rolls her eyes toward the stairs, and I take this to mean that she didn't okay it with Daddy before she did it. "But I had to tell you sometime. The oven thing made it obvious it had to be sooner rather than later. Malice is . . . she isn't well, all right?" Momma says, her voice sharp enough that it leaves us both momentarily speechless.

In the ensuing silence, I hear a soft ripping noise. She's clutching the armrest of her chair so hard she's torn the fabric.

"You're exaggerat—"

"You saw her. She's . . . fading. She needs care. More than I can provide. Maybe more than we can afford."

The air is heavy, weighed down with a tension that isn't just about the two of us. "And when exactly did you come to this conclusion?"

"It's been evident for a while. I think I just didn't want to see it."

"A while," I repeat. "Long enough for Daddy to come up with a plan. One that sucks for me and benefits Graham. Even if he is an idiot. So typical."

She ignores the insult to her firstborn, maybe because she knows it's true. "It's what's best for everyone. Graham's good with people. And he's got his associate's degree now."

"And what about me? All I'm good for is scrubbing floors?"

"Oh, please. Is that really what you're so pissed off about? That our real-life struggles are getting in the way of your fantasies? You think somehow by helping us out, you're being denied the chance to live your life?"

Yes! I want to scream it, but I know it will only make me sound petty. "I just want to know why I'm always the one being asked to give up what I want."

"How about you dial back the drama a notch? Or five? You think you're the only one who's ever sacrificed anything?"

I think about the darkroom, empty and abandoned until I took it over. Is that what she sacrificed? Well, who asked her to? I certainly never asked her to give up anything.

"What is it that you want?" Momma asks. "What great

plans"—she holds up a hand—"besides the trip, what is it that you think we're holding you back from?"

Her features are sunken and gray, distorted in the lamplight and the shadows from the bookshelves behind her as she studies my face. I can see she's looking for clues to some empty promise she can make that will shut me up fastest. I hate these mind games she plays, hate the urgency with which she whispers the question.

"You're my mother. Isn't it your job to know?"

She sags back in her chair, as if my words have loosened something, while my resolve to make her hear me—see me—only tightens. "At the very least, you should know I hate working here. I hate the tourists, with their clogged toilets and their moldy towels and the cigarette stench in the nonsmoking rooms and the sheer amount of filth they generate! And now Graham is going to be in charge of all my shifts? I will never get a break!"

"Your daddy is the boss, and he thinks this is for the best."

For the best. Did he and Chance rehearse that?

"And what do *you* think?"

Pause. ". . . I agree with him." But she hesitates just long enough that I know she's lying.

"Then I guess neither of you know me very well."

I turn away, toward the darkened windows beside her, where the NO VACANCY sign flashes on the road below, red and defiant. Beyond that, my own watery shadow wavers in the old glass. "I want to go to art school. More than anything. I want to take pictures for a living. I don't want to work at the motel for the rest of my life. Or for Chance's family."

I regret saying it as soon as the words are out, even more so when I catch her reflection in the narrow pane as she rears back in her chair. As if the idea is so preposterous, she can't ponder it without flinching.

"You don't know what I'm capable of!" I cry, stung by her total lack of faith in me, her disbelief that I could do any more than this. "What if I won't work here this summer? What if I refuse?"

"Oh, don't be ridiculous." She sounds tired, bored even, which angers me even more. She's the one who brought up this stupid topic in the first place. "You live here, you work here. That's just how it is."

"It doesn't have to be. And I'm not being ridiculous. What's ridiculous is you suggesting the only choice I have is the one that benefits everyone else."

"That isn't true."

My hurt is a physical thing, boiling beneath the surface of my skin, like lava. And with her final denial, it all comes out.

"I know about Daddy and Chance, okay? Somehow, Chance already knew about the trip being canceled. Before me! He told me all about your little plan. How you ruined my summer so you can pimp me out to shovel manure for the Caudells. This was never about Malice at all, was it?"

"Rena Faye, please." She's practically begging, her tired voice holding the hint of a tremor. "I wasn't a part of that conversation."

"How convenient."

"Oh, for the love of God!" She throws up her hands. "Would you quit with the exaggerating? This isn't some grand conspiracy! Malice is old! Money is tight! It just makes logical sense to keep you home this summer. If Daddy happened to mention that to the Caudells, is it any wonder Chance asked you about it?"

There is always an excuse. Always a reason I'm the one who's overreacting. I'm the one who's too dramatic, too ridiculous, who wants too much. Just once, I want her to take my side.

Just once.

"Crying isn't going to change anything," Momma says.

I swipe at my cheeks. "I'm not crying."

She clicks off the lamp, as if the sight of my weakness disgusts her.

Maybe it's the darkness that gives me the courage to ask, "Why do you hate me so much?"

"How can you even ask me that?" For the first time, she sounds truly angry.

I should have left when I had the chance. This is always how it is with us—I bare my soul, with the fervent hope something will change between us. That for even one moment, we might share something important, the way I imagine other mothers and daughters do. And sometimes we get so close, our toes right up to the edge of some kind of understanding. And then she turns around and proves she doesn't understand me at all.

"This is what you always do," I say. "You dismiss everything I care about, anything you don't agree with. I'm good at photography. Maybe not as good as you were, but I will be. And I'm going to get that scholarship. Just because you gave up on your dreams doesn't mean I have to give up on mine."

I take a cruel satisfaction in her quick flash of anger. "Watch it, young lady. You have no idea—" She pauses. "You know what? It's not worth the argument. It's late, and I'm done. We're stretched thin this summer, and this family is going to pitch in wherever we need to," she says, "and that includes you. Because we live in the real world, and it's high time you grow up and join us."

The words hang in the stillness long after she leaves the room, fading slowly, until all that's left is the ticking of the clock on the mantel, and this gulf between us that is so much deeper and wider than I thought.

CHAPTER 8

After my argument with Momma, I barely sleep. The last thing I want is to roll out of bed at 5:00 a.m. to serve pancakes to cranky tourists. But when she knocks on my door to tell me in a clipped voice that she doesn't have a waitress and she needs my help, I do it. Not because I want to, but because the tip money and guilt are both great motivators.

Somehow, Momma and I make it through the entire shift without speaking—other than in breakfast terms: *Order up. Side of bacon. Hold the onion. We're out of syrup.*

Honestly, this is how we usually communicate. Surface level, palpable tension hovering below. If it weren't for our argument and my seething anger, this would be just another Saturday.

Except today the motel is at capacity, which means I have to run over and start cleaning rooms immediately after cashing out my last table. I toss my tray on the counter and leave, letting the door slap defiantly so Momma knows I've gone.

I'm one of two housekeepers on today, and so we split up

and work our way down each corridor, starting at the far end and meeting in the middle, first at the suites on the second floor, and finally the lobby, where we finish for the day. Our thirty-two regular rooms are divided evenly by floor—sixteen on each—and then by wing. The suites are directly above the lobby and have jetted tubs as well as sleeper sofas and mini fridges. They're also a pain to clean. I swear, the more people spend on a room, the worse they treat it. I have a theory that if we lower the price on the suites, it will cut our workload in half.

Momma disagrees with me. Of course.

But at least she'll be doing the suites today, in between breakfast and lunch, so I won't have to worry about that. Sixteen rooms each is nearly impossible as it is, but moonbow weekends have a two-night minimum, which means a quicker spray and polish and no bed stripping on the first overnight. Plus, we can usually count on at least a couple of guests having their DO NOT DISTURB sign on the door handle. I have a love/hate relationship with those signs. A reprieve today means a filthier room tomorrow. Still, a break is a break. And I could really use one.

"How bad is it?" I ask, tying my apron as I join Daisy's older sister, Hazel, in the upper corridor. The one benefit—and I use the term loosely—to working the breakfast shift is I'd gotten to skip loading the supply cart and picking up the daily assignment sheet, which lists the rooms being vacated.

Hazel got stuck with that duty. And Hazel is not a morning person. She shoves a cart toward me and rolls her eyes.

My phone buzzes.

I pull it out and stick it between a pile of towels. "I'm here.

Working. Promise." I flash what I assume is the Girl Scout sign of honor but might just be a wave.

My cousin yawns so hard her jaw cracks, then shuffles off with her cart, while I shove mine down the corridor in the opposite direction.

When the phone buzzes again, I lift the towels to peek. Chance. Again.

Still. Working.

I hit send, then knock on the first room. "Housekeeping." When no one answers, I let myself in with the master key. On a scale of sparkling to filthy, this ranks somewhere in the messy middle, which, honestly, is the best I can usually hope for. It still sucks.

Chance tries to call while I'm gathering the dirty towels, and I turn on the vacuum cleaner to drown out the sound. When I've sucked up as much dirt and hostility as I can stomach, I key in the passcode to my voicemail. So far, he's left seven messages. I'd listened to the first on the way over: "Rena Faye, call me." He sounded desperate. "Please. This is all just a misunderstanding."

I put the phone on speaker and leave it to play the rest as I make the beds. The messages are all a variation of the same: He deserves a second chance, he wants to apologize, he wants me to apologize for blowing things out of proportion.

After that one, I delete them all and turn off the phone. Better to fume and disinfect in silence than to have to listen to his justifications. What worries me most is I know I'm going to end up forgiving him. Or worse, letting this slide. I mean, we've known each other since we were toddlers. He's been a part of my life as far back as I can remember. I can't imagine a day without him in it.

But I can't imagine a scenario where I end up apologizing to him either.

I scrub the toilet furiously, then flush, wishing the rest of my problems were so easily disposed of.

He deserves a second chance, he says. There's always a second chance for guys, isn't there? What about us? What happens when a woman makes a mistake? Says something she regrets? Makes a scene? Takes one crappy photo, or forgets how to boil water for a second?

Where's *her* second chance?

It's after three by the time I finish throwing the final load of bedding and towels into our industrial dryer. I've been on my feet all day, without a break. So much for the Summer of Me. The only benefit to being this exhausted is I'm too tired to think much about anything—Chance, Momma, Malice, art school. They're all just words floating through my fatigued brain.

I stumble into the lobby and grab a cold bottle of water. Then I collapse into one of the upholstered club chairs in the corner and hold the bottle to my sweaty forehead.

Knox is hanging out at the front counter, his lanky form sprawled across most of the space. "There she is. Breaking hearts and pushing brooms. Up top, RF!" he calls, holding up a hand.

I salute him with my middle finger. "Where's Daisy?"

He spreads his arms in a "How should I know?" gesture, and I take the hint. One date does not a couple make.

I turn to Graham. "Make me a pizza," I beg, but he ignores me.

"I was just telling Graham—" Knox breaks off as I narrow my eyes, daring him to mention my fight with Chance, but he rallies and finishes with "about my new gig" instead. "You are looking at the new official rafting guide of Atwater Lodge."

"Rafting guide?" I tilt my head. "Sounds impressive. Do go on."

"Daisy accused me of feeling sorry for myself," Knox says. "And I thought, that will never do. I'm too pretty to be sad. So I marched in there this morning and asked Arden Dunlap for a raise." He slicks back his shiny blond locks. "Suggested we start offering rafting tours. Up close and personal. To the falls. And at first he was all, I'm not authorized to do that. And I was like, Dude. Man up. Show some management initiative."

"You told your new boss to man up?"

Knox throws me a wink. "Actually, I told him if all it worked out, he could take the credit. As long as I got to keep my tips. And he agreed. Thought it was a great idea."

"Wow. Knox. That *is* a great idea. Wherever did you come up with it?" I lay on the sarcasm thick as butter, although my heart isn't totally in it.

Knox gives me a lazy grin, the one that turns most girls to mush. Honestly, I can't blame them. He's hard to resist when he's trying this hard.

"Relax, RF. That's why I'm here. To say thank you." He bows low and gestures to me with a flourish. "You should come on over and check it out," he says. "Free rides for gorgeous ladies."

Graham makes a gagging noise deep in the back of his throat.

"Thanks. I'll do that." I feel a pang of something then that could be hunger, but might be closer to longing. It's almost strong enough that I pick up my phone to text Chance, before I remember I'm not speaking to him.

It's hard to tell if I miss him, or if he's just a habit that's going to be hard to kick.

I take a long drink from my water bottle and let my head flop back against the chair. Where are these thoughts coming from? This is Chance. Things have always been so easy with us. Clearly, the heat is getting to me. And this is only my first day of hell summer. How am I going to survive?

"Man, you're going to have your work cut out," Knox says, rolling around to slap the desk in front of Graham. "I'll be nabbing all your customers. What are you gonna do then?"

Graham shrugs indifferently. If my parents are counting on him to bring in enough money to keep the motel going, he's going to have to start paying closer attention. Or we'll start losing even more customers to Atwater.

"Whatever," Graham says, completely unconcerned about customers or profit. "As long as you're still free to play gigs. I just got off the phone with a club owner over in Whitley City. They had a cancellation tonight and they want us to fill in."

"Sweet!"

"You're on desk duty tonight," I remind him, staring at the ceiling.

"Not anymore." Graham says. "I'm in charge of scheduling, remember? Which means, dear sis, you're pulling a double tonight."

I sit up, dumping half my water in my lap. "I worked the breakfast shift *and* cleaned about a thousand hotel rooms. No way am I—"

"Isn't this what you were whining about to Mom and Dad last night? Something other than housekeeping?" He smirks and holds out his hands. "Here you go. Desk duty. You're welcome."

"Screw you. I *knew* you were going to pull this crap." I turn to Knox. "What do they pay housekeepers over at Atwater?"

He shrugs. "Dunno. I was getting twelve dollars for front desk, so I'm assuming around that?"

"Twelve dollars an hour?" I turn to Graham. "You want me to work double shifts? I want a paycheck."

Graham wiggles his fingers at me. "Don't let the door hit you in the ass."

"Fat chance," I say. "It was your job to fix it, so I'm guessing it's still broken."

I retreat to my darkroom, where I can brood in silence and where the urge to smash things won't be quite so strong.

Though I have nothing to develop, I turn on the red light because it soothes me. Then I call Daisy.

"I'd let him sit in it for a day or so," she says as soon as she picks up, as if no time has passed since she dropped me off last night. "But any more than that and it's going to be hard to pick up where you left off."

Is she this ready with advice for everyone, or just me?

I pull an old photo of Chance and me off the counter. Prom,

last year. It's an okay picture. They hired a professional to take photos in a booth, but I'd wanted one with my own camera, so I'd asked the couple behind us in line to snap it. As a result, Chance looks like he's staring off vacantly into the distance. I grab an X-Acto knife from the shelf, my hand hovering about the picture. "Who says I want to pick up where we left off?"

She's quiet for a second, either because I've shocked her or she's busy with a customer. "Are you seriously considering . . ." She muffles the phone for a second to thank someone, her voice full of false cheer. "Are we talking *over*-over?" she asks, once she's back. "Or are you just trying to make a point?"

In all honesty, I'm not sure.

I turn the photo sideways and scrape away at the lopsided curl hanging over Chance's eye, shaping it into an upside-down question mark. Or maybe a fishhook. "Whose side are you on, anyway?"

"Life is a circle. A circle has no sides."

I groan. "Don't give me any of that philosophy bullshit."

"If there were sides, yours. Of course. But . . . this is you and Chance. You know how I feel about mo-nog-a-my." She drags out all the syllables so long, even I'm bored by the time she's done. "But you guys—you just go together. Like peanut butter and chocolate. So the right side—*solution*," she corrects herself quickly, "is the two of you, together. In the same circle. See what I did there?"

I hold up the photo to the light, a red glow shining through the pinhole. I've scratched too hard and poked out his eye. "Oh, I see all right."

"If you want him to squirm a little, I get that. But my advice? Cut the guy a little slack. Send him a text to let him know there's at least a chance at reconciliation. Even if you don't mean it yet."

I toss the photo into the trash. "I don't want to talk about Chance. That's not even why I called. I had an epic fight with my mom."

Daisy lets out a heavy sigh. "Deconstructing Aunt Lou is going to take more time than I have right now."

"Sorry. When are you off?"

"Soon." She covers the phone again briefly. "Five at the latest. Come pick me up and you can complain about whoever you want."

"Hey!" I half laugh. "It's not my fault Momma has it out for me. I swear, she hates me. Or Malice. Maybe both of us." I pause and Daisy doesn't say anything. "Fine. Maybe I do complain too much. I'll come get you and you can lecture me in person."

"In the meantime, you might want to think about whether you care more about being right than about doing the right thing. Bye-ee."

I stare at my phone as she clicks off. Daisy loves to give advice. And usually—or at least, more than half the time—I listen. But this time, I'm not so sure. Because it isn't that I can't see the difference she's talking about. It's just that, to me, this argument with Chance isn't so much a choice between being right and doing right as it is a choice between doing the right thing and doing the easy thing.

The door swings open, the natural light so bright and sudden that for a moment I'm stunned.

"Graham tells me you're too busy to do your job." I recognize Daddy's voice, dangerously low, though all I see is the outline of his body in the doorway, his arms crossed over his chest. "But you have time to hide out in here and mess around?"

"Mess around?" It never pays to argue with Daddy, but sometimes I can't help myself. "I'm not sure what you mean. I did the breakfast shift at the diner and my housekeeping shift. Now I'm—"

"Refusing to take desk duty, is what I heard."

I jump to my feet, my face burning, though I'm not sure why I'm explaining myself. It isn't like I've been caught goofing off. I've already worked nine hours today, without a break. Where I am or what I'm doing isn't the point. "I've been up since five. I've already worked a double. Isn't this bordering on child labor? There are laws against this kind of treatment."

He hesitates.

"Why can't Graham do it?" I ask.

His jaw tightens. As usual, I've said the wrong thing.

"Graham has plans," he says. "Unlike you, hiding out in here and disrespecting your mother."

My face burns hotter. How long was he been standing outside the door, listening to my conversation?

"We talked about this," he continues, "and I thought I made myself clear. There is no money, nor do you have the time, for your little hobby this summer."

"You said on my own time," I say. "This is my own time. It won't interfere with work."

"It already has. Besides, what is the point? You gave it a shot and they rejected you. Not everyone is destined for glory. Sometimes you have to cut your losses and move on."

He glances at the photos hanging on the line and shakes

his head as he shifts his body away from me. As if my failure is contagious.

He waves me out of the darkroom, and when I step through the door, he snaps his fingers at me until I hand over the key. When I finally do, he twists in in the lock and slips it into his shirt pocket.

"Hey!" My heart pulses in my throat, so hard I almost throw up. "You can't do that."

It's not enough that my trip is off? That I'm working my butt off for nothing but tip money? While he and my boyfriend casually plan out my future?

Now he's taking away the thing I love most?

No way in hell.

"My work is in there."

"No. Your work is down there." Daddy points toward the hill.

What if I won't work here? I asked Momma last night. *What if I refuse?*

Don't be ridiculous, she said. As if she couldn't even contemplate the possibility.

"You can't do this," I repeat.

"Actually, I can. I'm the boss."

It's a good thing I haven't bothered to change out of my uniform, because it's easier to illustrate my point. I reach behind me and untie my apron, letting it fall to the floor.

"Not anymore, you're not. I quit."

CHAPTER 9

Lucky for me, Daddy's left the truck parked by the gate with the keys in the ignition. I've already done the unthinkable. What's one more broken rule?

Right now, I need to get away—from this place and everyone in it.

I roll down the windows and crank the radio up so loud I can't hear myself scream. They'll all be sorry. Eventually.

Angry tears mix with the sweat on my face, and I drive until they both dry, which leads me to downtown Corbin. Our motel isn't in the city proper; it's more like city-adjacent. Like the falls and Atwater Lodge and all the other moonbow destinations, we're a couple miles west of the interstate, while Corbin itself lies to the east, the reality to our fantasy.

Where we offer a chance to relax, to reconnect with nature and leave all your problems to someone else for a time, downtown Corbin is where people do real-life stuff for themselves. Grocery shopping, car repairs, worship, education. Not to say my life isn't real. But there's a certain amount of varnishing that goes into selling tourists our version of paradise.

I spend more time in town during the school year, but over the summer I can go weeks at a time without making it past the interstate. Today, I find myself driving toward the high school more from habit than desire.

It's still too early to pick up Daisy, so I park alongside the football field and stare out across the empty expanse. How many hours have I spent—wasted?—in those bleachers, waiting for Chance to finish practice, or cheering him on during a game? My hands chapped from the wind, throat raw from screaming, all for a sport I really don't care about.

When did his life become mine?

I swipe more tears with the back of my hand. Beyond the school building, far up on the mountain on the other side of town, I can just make out one of the guard towers of the federal prison where Daisy's dad works. Uncle Ford, of the tired marriage and champagne dreams. Maybe it's not just Momma. Maybe none of the adults in my life are living the lives they wanted. Maybe they all wish they could quit.

Somehow, I doubt Momma will see that as a valid argument when she hears about my showdown with Daddy. I chew my lip and turn the volume way up, pounding the steering wheel along to Daughtry, so I can't hear her judgment in my head as I swing a U-turn at the end of the block.

I don't know where else to go, so I drive toward Atwater Lodge. The sight of it always makes me feel better. As much as Momma and Daddy hate the place, I've always been fascinated by the sprawling manor high on the hill, within spitting distance of the falls. Some early Dunlap ancestor had clearly felt the magic pull of the water and been smart enough to follow it long before anyone else. Building his mansion so close only cemented his already good fortune.

When I was little, I liked to pretend I was a princess and Atwater was my castle. My bedroom would be on the top floor, so I could lean out my window and pat my dragon's nose. As I got older, whenever I was sad or mad or frustrated or bored, it calmed me to imagine what it would be like to have enough money to live there. Fresh-squeezed orange juice at dawn on the wide stone terrace. Croquet on the lush front lawn, followed by a nap in one of the hammocks stretched between the tall pitch pine trees.

Never mind that I hate orange juice and have never played croquet, or that everything I know about rich people I learned from watching TV. All that mattered was that in my fantasies, I belonged at Atwater as much as I wanted it to belong to me.

I turn in at the entrance, grateful to have an excuse to get closer. From afar, the four-story limestone structure is both gorgeous and imposing, with a history and permanence our motel can only dream of. Up close, it's breathtaking. Flags wave from the top of the building, while a green-and-white-striped awning welcomes guests into the lobby. The driveway is designed to lead guests to the front door and then deposit them into the parking lot around the corner.

I slow to a crawl, admiring the postcard-perfect pictures I could take here: the hand-in-hand couple wandering the manicured lawn, framed perfectly between two willow trees. The family picnicking beneath the maple tree on the side lawn, the light dappling the blanket beneath their basket with splashes of red gold. The picture is so clear I can almost taste the peanut butter in their sandwiches and the sunshine on my face.

They'd be gorgeous photos, no question, but they wouldn't be life-changing. They still wouldn't tell *my* story.

On the corner of the wide veranda, a tour guide dressed in khakis and a polo shirt stands talking to a small group gathered in the shadow of the lodge. He looks about my age, or close enough, and though he keeps talking to the crowd, his gaze follows me as I drive past.

It has to be Arden Dunlap. But there's no trace of the weepy, pale boy I remember; he's all grown up. Not a tear nor a bloody nose in sight.

I pull into a parking space, cut the engine, and peel my sweaty palms off the steering wheel. I text Daisy.

I'm early. Long story.

She texts back almost immediately. **Can't wait to hear. Stuck though. Need another hour.**

Super. The truck is heating up. I drum my fingers on the wheel and glance back out the window at Arden. His gaze meets mine across the parking lot and I jerk my head around, feeling like an idiot. I don't want him to think I'm staring.

I text Daisy again. **Did you grab my hair clip last night??**
No, sorry!

That's what I should be looking for. Instead of sitting here, staring at this poor guy and drooling over his hotel like some kind of creepy stalker. Still, how amazing must it be to live here?

One last look. Then I'll go find my hair clip.

I lean out the window.

Arden Dunlap is standing directly next to my truck.

I let out a yelp that I'm sure sounds like a dying beaver and jerk back, banging my head on the frame.

"Oh, gosh. I'm sorry. I didn't mean to startle you. Are you all right?"

I rub the lump on my head and then try to straighten the tangles in my hair. "Um . . . no? I mean, I'm fine. I mean . . ."

"Did you need something? I saw you drive in. You looked . . . lost."

Lost. The word echoes in my head as he finally names the feeling I've been struggling with the last few days. I stare at him, speechless.

"Is there something I can help you with?" he asks again, slower this time.

I close my mouth and shake my head. I've heard of customer service before, but this is ridiculous. "I'm just, you know," I raise a palm. "Looking. Around."

"For anything in particular, or . . . ?" He rocks back on his heels, the smile on his face professional but not uninviting.

"A . . . friend. Works here," I add quickly. I sound like I'm some loner cruising for random strangers to befriend. "She's on duty, though. And I'm early."

"So your friend works here. And you work for the Moonbow Motel?"

How the hell does he know that? "Actually, I'm unemployed," I say, the word unfamiliar on my tongue.

An expression ripples across his face, disbelief, maybe, or distaste, and I bristle. Okay, so maybe it's obvious I've been doing grunt work. I haven't showered and probably smell like a toilet and look like something I scraped off a bathroom floor. But what right does he have to judge me?

"I get it. The lot is for guests, right? I'll just wait out on the road."

"No, it's not that. It's . . ." He trails off, running a hand through his hair. "I'm trying to be polite, but I'll just say it. You guys are kind of our rivals." He points at the side of the truck. "So I'm . . . surprised, is all."

I face-palm. The truck. The motel logo. Good lord, I'm an idiot. "Yeah, no," I say, my voice muffled by my hand. "I get that. But I really am waiting for a friend. As for my job, it's a long story."

When I finally look up, he's fighting back a grin. "I didn't say it was a bad surprise. And I'm the one who's sorry. That was incredibly rude." He finally breaks down and smiles, his dimples deepening. "Besides, I love a good story."

"Me too." I'm suddenly aware of how good-looking he is, polished and clean, like he's never worked for a living except to play someone who works for a living. No wonder Knox hates him.

He stares at me so long I start to fidget. "I should go."

"You said it was a long story," he reminds me. "About your job."

"Oh. Yeah. Well, my—" I stumble over the words. "It's true. We—my parents, I mean—own the Moonbow Motel. And I sort of, well, quit. Today."

He gives a low whistle. "You quit your family business? That's either really gutsy, or . . ."

"Really stupid?" I finish. "Yeah, probably that. You have no idea."

"Oh, I think I have some idea. I mean . . ." He gestures toward the lodge behind him. "Has the thought crossed my mind a time or two? Sure." He shakes his head. "But my mom would flip out."

How long has he been working? Ten minutes? I've been tied to the motel my whole life.

But then I feel guilty. Of course he can't quit, even if he wanted to. His daddy just passed away and his momma is depending on him. But my situation is totally different.

"So what now?" he asks, leaning against the door. "Are you looking for another job? Or is this just some ploy to make them sweat?"

It was an impulse, I want to say. A stupid, spur-of-the-moment thing. Making them sweat sounds good. Begging me back even better. But what if I could do something to show them—Daddy and Chance and Momma—that I'm perfectly capable of living my own life? Of making my own decisions.

So I say, "I'm looking," instead.

"I see. And what kind of skills do you have?"

I laugh, then sober when he frowns. "Are you actually interviewing me? In the parking lot?"

"Sorry. I just assumed you were interested. You were staring before. At the sign." He points to where he was standing earlier, to the WE'RE HIRING poster in the window of the lodge.

His lodge. My dream. Our competition.

Correction. Momma and Daddy's competition.

"No, you're right. I'm interested," I say, and he holds the door as I climb out of the truck.

"I'm Rena Faye, by the way."

"I know," he says, giving me another smile. "I remember."

Less than twenty minutes later, I am in possession of both the uniforms and paperwork I'll need as an Atwater Lodge employee. Daisy and I are co-workers. She is going to lose her mind.

She isn't the only one.

I can't believe I did it. Without asking anyone else's permission. Without stopping to think about how it was going to affect my family, or the motel, or Chance's ego.

I made this decision all on my own, and it feels pretty damn good.

Right now, I am powerful. Unstoppable.

I take a left out of the parking lot, steering down the mountain toward the dirt service road.

I still have time to kill, and I'd rather walk in the sun than sit in the truck. Besides, I still need to find Malice's hair clip.

I pull my hair into a twist on top of my head with a band I find in the glove box, pocket my phone, and climb from the truck. The giant tree, the sentinel, is no less imposing in daylight. I trail my fingers along the leaves as I duck around it and into the woods, a talisman for luck.

The hike takes far less time in the daylight, which makes me question whether we got turned around last night. Still, it's no wonder we've been able to keep this place our secret for so long. This is the heart of the forest, far from any of the marked hiking trails.

In the tree-dappled sunshine, it's apparent the ruins are in even worse shape than I thought. Piles of broken stones litter the ground, while those still standing are in grave danger of a similar fate. A strong wind could topple them. I suspect the only reason it hasn't are the moss and vines, wound so tightly they function as a kind of supportive brace. Oddly enough, this is one area the kudzu hasn't taken over completely.

And it's my lucky day—I find Malice's hair clip lying on top of the stone Daisy and I use as an altar.

Which is strange. Did Chance drop it here? We were standing down near the river when he took it from me.

I shake off the question and check my phone. I should head back. To get Daisy, not to go home. If I go home, I have to face Momma and her judgment and her disappointment. I have to *live in the real world*, which probably means apologizing to Daddy, letting Graham walk all over me while my parents use me for cheap labor, and dropping the fantasy of working at Atwater Lodge.

I decide to hold on to that dream a few minutes longer. I tuck the clip into my bun, then walk over to the wall and run my fingers over the bricks before sliding one of the papers from the crack. We really did ask the bride for a lot, didn't we? Poor girl. We should've let her rest in peace.

BETRAYAL HAS LEGS. LOYALTY HAS ROOTS.

This is the one I read last night. But I'm almost positive I put that one in my pocket, not back in the wall. I slide out another one, slower this time, an uneasiness prickling at the back of my neck.

BETRAYAL HAS LEGS. LOYALTY HAS ROOTS.

Cool wind tickles my face, much colder than any Kentucky June breeze. Goose bumps pucker the skin on my arms as another half dozen papers blow toward my feet, mixed in with a tumble of dried leaves.

I kneel to dig through the leaves and dirt. With each slip of paper, my heart pounds harder and my vision goes blurry.

Every one is the same. None of them in my handwriting. Or Daisy's.

So who wrote them?

The wind rips through the trees with a howl, grit stinging my face.

And then I see her.

A girl. Standing less than ten feet away, her hand resting lightly against the trunk of a tree. She looks my age, maybe a little older, but blurry around the edges and drained of color, like an old photograph. Her long, dark, wet hair clings to her pale cheeks and drips onto the bodice of her tattered gown.

The ghost bride.

I can't breathe. Can't speak, much less call for help. The taste of blood fills my mouth, and there's a roaring in my ears, as loud as if I am standing at the top of the falls.

She grimaces and reaches a bony hand toward me.

This can't be happening.

Ghosts aren't real.

I fall back against the ruins, the unearthly sounds coming from my mouth almost scarier than this vision, though not by much.

"Please," I whisper. Or try to.

She keeps her arm outstretched as she moves slowly, sound-lessly toward me, her empty, cavernous mouth like an open gateway straight to hell. The wind pummels me, scattering the leaves and blowing the papers out of reach. She points to the dirt at my feet, and a word appears there in the earth as if scratched by an invisible hand.

ROOTS

"I . . . I don't know what that means." My lips are numb, and I can't focus. Clearly, she's angry. But I don't know how to appease her. "Please," I try again.

She moves her mouth wide, as if to scream. But no sound comes out.

Instead, a branch snaps somewhere in the woods, and she vanishes. No puff of smoke or vaporization. No soft fading. Just—gone.

The roaring stops, and now all I hear is my own heartbeat as it tries to escape my chest. I roll over onto my hands and knees and heave once, twice, into a pile of molding leaves.

Nothing comes up. I lay my cheek against cold stone, my body shaking too badly to move, though I know I need to run, need to get away from this awful place.

Did that really happen?

I'm under a lot of stress. I haven't eaten all day. Maybe I hallucinated the whole thing.

But her image is burned into my memory, and no matter how hard I try to convince myself otherwise, it's hard to shake the thought that the ghost bride might be more than just a story.

And if she's real, the curse could be, too.

CHAPTER 10

I make it back to the truck without seeing her again, but I'm not sure if that's because I run full tilt with my head down, ignoring every sound but the battle cry pounding of my heart, or if she's really and truly gone. Tree branches tear at my skin, sharp and stinging, trying their best to hold me, while their slippery roots twist beneath my feet.

ROOTS.

That's what she wrote in the dirt. And all those papers—they said BETRAYAL HAS LEGS. LOYALTY HAS ROOTS.

I don't know what that means, but these roots aren't taking me today.

I throw myself into the truck and take off down the road, making it home in record time and without killing anyone, by some miracle. I nearly drive off the side of the road twice and narrowly avoid running over someone's dog only because he's smart enough to get out of the way. I've been lectured a thousand times on the dangers of drinking and driving. But it turns out being scared shitless by a ghost and driving is infinitely more dangerous.

A ghost.

No.

Yes?

I leave the truck at the bottom of the gate and run up the hill to the house; my only goal is getting to the safety of my room.

She can't touch me there.

I slam the door. Lock it. Think about climbing under the bed, but I'm too keyed up. Instead I pace, texting Daisy with shaking fingers.

I saw hee.

Smthe ghost bride!!!

WHERE R U??? CALL ME!

Pounding on the door nearly brings my heart out of my throat and onto the floor.

"Rena Faye, we need to talk. Open this door."

I collapse onto the floor and lean forward, pressing my head between my knees.

Breathe. Don't throw up. Don't pass out.

"Not now, Momma," I call weakly, swiping tears and snot with the back of my hand.

"Oh, is this an inconvenient time?" She rattles the door handle. "I'm not kidding, missy. I heard about your little stunt this afternoon."

My stunt? My mind is blank. Was that what it was? Please let it be a stunt or a prank. That would at least make sense.

But she was so real. So terrifying. So . . . sad.

"You're not quitting."

Oh. My. God. I am having an honest-to-god panic attack here—because I think I've just seen an honest-to-god *dead* woman—one who might have tried to *kill* me. And Momma's carrying on about me quitting?

My phone chirps and I snatch it up.

WTF are you talking about???

"Are you texting in there?" Momma's voice is piercing, but I ignore her.

The ghost is REAL I saw her
Where?
At the clearing

Three bangs on the door, loud enough to rattle the doorframe. Great. Now Daddy is out there too. The phone slips from my hands and lands on the wood floor with an ominous crack. I flip it over. The screen is dark, the glass shattered into a spiderweb pattern.

"Damn it!" He pounds once more on the door before Momma interrupts him, talking in a whisper so I can't hear.

I shove the phone under the bed and press my hands between my knees to stop them shaking.

"I know you're upset," Daddy says, his voice calmer than I expect. "But you can't just run off every time you're upset. You want me to take you seriously? Come out here and talk to me like an adult."

They think this is about the darkroom and my job. My rage

from those few hours before feels remote, like it happened ages ago, to someone else. I have more serious concerns now. But maybe if I tell them what happened, maybe if they see how upset I am . . . maybe they can help me. Protect me.

"You aren't helping yourself with this childish behavior," Momma says. "We're family. You can't quit family."

"You're a Whitaker," Daddy adds. "And Whitakers aren't quitters."

Who am I kidding? Momma doesn't believe in ghosts. And Daddy will just think I made it up to avoid getting into trouble. I fling open the door so quickly, Daddy takes half a step back. Momma stands behind his shoulder, arms crossed over her chest. Seeing them there, looking so normal—so alive—makes me burst into tears.

"Who said I was quitting the family?" I ask. "Is that what you think? That I'm *betraying* you?" I gulp down a sob. "That I'm not *loyal*? I've always been loyal. Maybe you're the ones who need reminding. Because I'm family, too. Betrayal has legs, but loyalty has roots!"

Daddy's face goes slack and his mouth falls open. "Wha—"

I slam the door on Momma's shocked expression.

"What the hell is that supposed to mean?" he asks Momma.

"You tell me!" I holler through the door.

Dead silence follows, which Momma finally breaks by saying, "Why don't we all just take a few minutes? Calm down."

She lowers her voice and I press my ear to the door. "She's had a long day. Let's give her some space."

This is unexpected. Shocking, actually. Momma is not usually one for granting me personal space. Or personal anything.

I wait for them to leave, listening long after their creaking footsteps descend the stairs before I retrieve my phone. I'm hoping for another text from Daisy, but the screen is too damaged to read. It was a cheap phone to begin with, but that doesn't mean Momma will be inclined to buy me a new one.

I toss it on the bed and circle the room, less like a wild animal and more like a creature of habit. Everything here is familiar—my Himalayan salt lamp, my throw pillows made from old T-shirts Malice brought back from her travels, the Swiss chalet music box she gave me for my twelfth birthday. These touchstones ground me, reassure me. I am home. This is real.

Not like the ghost. That was just a figment of my imagination. Wasn't it?

I press my hand against the cool, solid glass of the mirrored closet door. I barely recognize the pale, frightened face reflected back at me. I'm as much a mess as she was. Crazy eyes. Wild hair.

What the hell happened to my hair?

I yank the clip out and let it fall to my shoulders, running a hand through the tangles.

I saw a ghost. A real, live—no, that's stupid. A real, dead ghost. Only I don't believe in ghosts.

The closet door is slightly open, and I shove it closed with a tingle of fear. If ghosts are real, can they travel wherever they want? Could she be hiding in my closet? Right now?

I back up slowly, until my legs hit the bed and I sink down.

No, damn it.

I jump up. I will not live in fear like this. I yank the closet door open, my hangers swinging from the force. Just clothes and shoes. Of course.

Ghosts don't exist.

So what did I see? And who wrote those notes? And the word in the dirt?

BETRAYAL HAS LEGS. LOYALTY HAS ROOTS.

Is that a curse? Does she think I betrayed someone? What have I done that would count as a betrayal? There's no way she could know about me quitting my job. Or working at Atwater. Besides, the note was already there last night.

What was it Malice said—that I need to help her? So maybe it isn't a message about me at all. Maybe it's about her. Her lover and his betrayal. Maybe she's asking me for help.

Ughhhhhh.

I cover my face with my hands. This is ridiculous. I'm over-thinking this and making shit up. She isn't real. I need to talk to someone else. Someone who isn't potentially insane or hallucinating.

Where the hell is Daisy?

I flop onto my back and turn my head to the photo board above my desk, where I've tucked dozens of pictures into the satin ribbons over the years. Most of them are selfies—me and Daisy, or me and Chance. A photo from a formal my sophomore year, Daisy and I standing back to back, her head resting against my shoulder blades, arms entwined. Me in my fitted navy tank gown, with the sparkly overlay like thousands of stars against the night sky, and Daisy looking like she was poured into a strapless yellow tulle ball gown with a bow bigger than her head.

That memory feels more real than whatever happened to me in the clearing. Maybe I'm losing it. Maybe I imagined the whole thing.

There's another photo from when we were younger, taken in the motel pool—me, Graham, Knox, and Daisy, our faces tanned dark as leather as we cling to the side of the pool and smile up at the camera, like nothing in the world would ever make us stop. And my favorite photo of me and Chance, the night he won the game that would take them to state. They'd lose the championship, but we didn't know that yet when he ran off the field and scooped me up to kiss me, his hair wet with sweat, his body warm with the heat of victory.

Chance.

I wonder what he'd think about all this. Would he believe me? Or tell me I need to pull myself together?

A noise at the door nearly sends me out of my skin, until I recognize Daisy's rapid, impatient knock. I unlock the door and sneak a quick glance into the hallway as she slips in. It's empty.

"Did you see my mom?"

"Who cares about your mom? Tell me about the ghost!" Daisy jumps onto my bed on her knees and grabs my hands, pulling me down with her. "What was she like? What did she want? What did she say? Tell me everything!"

My throat is dry and I swallow convulsively.

"She was . . . wet. And scary." My voice breaks. "Haunted."

"Your powers of observation are astonishing," Daisy says dryly.

"No. I mean, she looked haunted. Angry, maybe. Or sad? And

I keep remembering what Malice said about my family being cursed."

"Mmhmm."

"I know it sounds ridiculous, but it felt like she wanted to tell me something. Or maybe hurt me. I don't know. She wrote something." I shove my hands in my pockets, but come up empty. Damn. I never picked up any of the papers. "'Betrayal has legs. Loyalty has roots.'"

Daisy raises an eyebrow. "You read that last night. Are you sure you didn't dream this?"

"No! I mean, yes, it was on the paper last night. But today, too. A half dozen, at least. All the same. And she traced one of the words into the dirt, too. *Roots*."

"*Roots*?" Daisy wrinkles her nose. "What the hell does that mean?"

"I don't know," I whisper. "A threat, maybe? To be loyal to my family. Or else?" I hold my breath, anxious for Daisy's practical advice for once.

"A threat?" She shakes her head, her topknot flopping side to side. "No. I don't buy it."

I'm both relieved and annoyed. "So you don't think I'm cursed, then?"

"I didn't say that." She leans back against a pile of throw pillows, picking up one and playing with the tassels absentmindedly. "But that saying is just so vague . . . like fortune-cookie wisdom. You'd think if a ghost wanted to curse you, she'd be clear. 'You will die!' Something like that."

"I'm not making it up," I say, although it's already starting to seem less real and more like a story. The longer we talk, the more my fear dissipates. Just like the ghost bride did.

"I'm not accusing you. I'm just trying to get an accurate picture. Ooh, picture!" She sits up straight and grabs my hands. "Tell me you got a picture!"

I shake my head. "I didn't think of it. I was so freaked out."

"Okay, then." She sounds a little less convinced than she did mere seconds ago. "So we're back to your eyewitness account. What did she look like, physically? What was she wearing?"

"Are you kidding me? She was wearing a wedding dress! It was dirty. Gray. Old. She looked like a dead, wet bride."

Daisy narrows her eyes and taps her lips with a manicured finger.

"What?"

"I'm thinking." She hesitates, then says, "It's too bad you didn't get a photo. I mean, you photograph everything."

"Not everything." I hate how defensive I sound, especially because I know she's right. It's unlikely—impossible, really—that I actually saw a ghost. I don't blame her for not believing me.

"You said she threatened you. Could it have been a warning?"

"A warning to what?" I stand and pace the room again. "This is what I hate about ghost stories. Suppose she is trying to warn me. Or curse me. Why not just say so? Clearly she can write! And"—I pivot and point at Daisy—"if that's what it was, why warn me right before attacking me? Doesn't that defeat the purpose?"

"It depends on the purpose." She cocks her head to the side, apparently more interested now that I might have been in mortal danger. "Back up, though. Did she actually touch you? Like, physical contact?"

I shake my head. "She just . . . it was windy. Like, she made it that way. And cold." I rub my arms. "And then there was a noise and she was gone."

"What kind of noise?"

"Something in the woods. A snap, like a branch or something."

"Like someone was in the woods? Running from the scene of the crime?"

It's not that I haven't thought of any of this. If I'm starting to see things that aren't there, I need someone to snap me out of it. But of all people, I thought I could count on Daisy to believe me. "You think this is some kind of Scooby-Doo situation? I'm telling you—I saw her!"

"You saw *something*," she corrects, going back to braiding the tassel on the pillow.

I stare out the window. She's right. I don't know what I saw. Or who.

"Thanks for remembering to pick me up, by the way." She tosses the pillow at me.

I grab it and whack her in the head as I sit down next to her and lean back against the headboard. "Sorry. I wasn't thinking. At all. I just had to get out of there." The memory of the dead girl's face swims to the surface of my brain and I shake it away.

"Anyway, I've got other news," I say.

"Right. The fight with Aunt Lou. What's that about?"

"Not just Momma. Daddy too. In fact, I quit."

Daisy's eyes widen comically, then she laughs. "Get outta here."

"No, I did. Real dramatic-like, too. You would've been proud. I threw my apron on the floor and marched out."

A smile hovers at the corner of her mouth.

"What? I'm tired of everyone else making my decisions for me. I want to have my own adventures. The Summer of Me, remember?"

"And how did they take it?"

I lift a shoulder. "About like you'd imagine."

"So what are you going to do instead?"

We both jump as the door bangs open, Daddy looming in the doorway.

"What the hell is the meaning of this?" he calls.

In his fist is my Atwater Lodge shirt.

THE LEGEND OF THE GHOST BRIDE

as advertised in the Atwater Lodge welcome packet

When was Atwater Lodge built?

Businessman, entrepreneur, and nature-lover Franklin Dunlap wasn't looking for property when he stumbled across the breathtaking Cumberland Falls back in 1850. He was merely on a nature hike with his young bride. But once he'd found his own unique piece of paradise, he wasted no time purchasing the land. Franklin and his descendants built and refurbished their mansion several times over the years, but the building we know today was finished in 1920, after a devastating fire claimed the previous family home.

Who are the current owners?

Atwater Lodge has been in the Dunlap family for nearly a century, serving as a private residence for eighty years before Kezia and

Jackson Dunlap Jr. had a vision to renovate the property, turning it into the stunning vacation destination it is today.

Is the lodge haunted?

Since the lodge first opened its doors to the public in 2002, there have been whispers of a ghostly figure who appears during the full moon. Some see her as merely a form in the mist; others claim to see the figure of a woman in a white gown (commonly referred to as the ghost bride) who rises out of the water at the base of the falls.

Who is this ghost bride?

Popular lore suggests our apparition is a local bride who snuck onto the grounds to take some post-wedding photos—always a popular activity here at the lodge, what with our stunning views! As the story goes, she was insistent that her new husband get a photo of her in her gown with the falls in the background. Though he warned her to be careful, she continued to move closer and closer to the edge of the cliff, until in her excitement, she slipped and fell—a tragic yet avoidable accident.

Is the viewing area safe?

Absolutely! We've taken great care to ensure the safety of our guests. And if you're lucky enough to catch a glimpse of our ghost bride, please heed her warning—stay behind the safety rails and obey the posted signs!

CHAPTER 11

I flip the new employee folder shut, glancing once more at the watercolor print of the falls on the cover before tossing it onto the empty patio chair beside me. My orientation is supposed to begin at ten, but since Momma refused to let me drive the truck, I had to catch a ride with Daisy this morning. Which means I have been sitting here for an hour and a half, sweating buckets in my new Atwater Lodge uniform. Malice used to tell me that women don't sweat, they glisten, but if this is glistening, then I must look like a disco ball. They can probably see me glisten from space.

The veranda in front of the lodge is wide and uncovered, the area to the right of the main building dotted with metal tables and umbrellas offering questionable shade. The other side is framed by a pair of weeping willows lining the path toward the swimming pool, as evidenced by the sound of splashing and whiff of chlorine when I'm gifted with the occasional breeze. I fight off the strong urge to jump in.

I shuffle my white tennis shoes against the stone patio, the varying shades of beige and gray polished smooth by wear and weather. I've already gone through the welcome packet material Arden gave me. Twice. It's all BS, of course, at least the part about the bride.

It's not that I haven't heard this version of the story before—it's the same watered-down one you'll find on most websites and tour brochures. A generic, sanitized tale of romance and tragedy. The kind of story Malice calls "pure poppycock." I'm not surprised the lodge has adopted it; they're clearly using the legend as a precautionary tale. "Be careful, or it might happen to you!"

Maybe it's some sort of legal disclaimer that absolves them of responsibility. Because there have been accidents over the years.

There is a curse.

Nope. Sorry, Malice. I've got to go with Momma on this one. People are just stupid. Especially tourists.

Every time I hear about someone climbing out over the railing at the top of the falls and falling, I experience an odd mixture of pity and understanding. Because I've felt that pull: that secret longing, deep inside. I want to face the danger. Walk out onto the cliff, leap into the roaring water of the falls. Not to die, but to conquer it. To prove I'm stronger and more powerful than Mother Nature herself. Maybe then people will take me and my dreams seriously.

Like Daddy. He was so filled with rage yesterday after he found out about my new job, he went from raving lunacy and back to white-faced calm in the space of minutes, until the only color on his face had been his purpled, puckered scar. It seemed to roil beneath his skin as I kept repeating myself: *I quit. I won't work for free anymore. I have another job.*

In the end, he'd turned and walked away while I was mid-sentence, leaving me alone with Daisy. Who was thrilled, of course. And maybe even a tad impressed.

Not Daddy. And definitely not Momma. What I see as independence, they see as betrayal.

BETRAYAL HAS LEGS.

I squeeze my eyes shut. I've gone over it and over it in my head—the sighting, the ghost, the vision, the whatever-it-was—worrying the memory thin. It must have been a hallucination. Stress-induced, most likely.

It couldn't have been real.

"Rena Faye!"

I open my eyes. Arden is waving at me from the front door.

He jogs over, breathless and smiling. "Thanks for coming. Sorry you had to wait. I hope it wasn't too long."

"You don't have to thank me. You're paying me to be here," I remind him, and then mentally slap myself. I may as well have said, "I'm only in this for the money." Which isn't even entirely true.

"So we are." He smiles, and my stomach flutters with first-day jitters. But I did the right thing, coming here. I just have to keep reminding myself.

After a strained pause, Arden offers me a reprieve.

"So, how about we start with a tour?" He leads me away from the lodge, and though I ache for the coolness of an air-conditioned building, I follow him toward the pool and try to think cold thoughts.

"So we've got the standard outdoor pool and hot tub." As I trail him past the willow trees, though, it's clear this pool is a few steps above standard. Expensive lounge chairs surround the zero-depth entry, and the water is a light, shimmering turquoise, thanks to the expensive tiling rimming the pool as well as the walkway between pool and hot tub.

The painted concrete of the Moonbow Motel pool is sad and cheap by comparison.

"Guests of both the lodge and the cabins can use them, but not the general public." Arden taps the tall fence and cocks an eyebrow at me. "You'd be surprised how many people try to sneak in."

"Actually, I wouldn't. We have the same problem. Had. I mean, my parents do." I sweat harder. Is it weird to talk about the motel? My family's business isn't a secret or anything. But it feels wrong, somehow. Like I'm giving away intel to the enemy. Even if we did go to school together, once. A long time ago.

If Arden notices my discomfort, he doesn't say anything. "I keep forgetting how much we have in common. The worst are the skinny-dippers. So awkward. Am I right?"

"Yes! Sooo awkward. Do you wait for them to get dressed? Or chase them out naked and toss their clothes over the fence?"

"Actually, I prefer tossing the clothes first, then chasing them out."

Our eyes meet and we both burst out laughing.

"We keep it lit at night! Anyone can see them from the second floor," I say.

"Same!" He shakes his head. "Doesn't make a bit of difference."

I like the way his forehead wrinkles, like he can't quite fathom it. Most everyone else, when I complain about the business, acts bored and begs me to shut up.

Arden touches my arm as he guides me gently past the pool. "Back here are the tennis courts," he says. "We keep them locked so the equipment doesn't walk off. It's touchpad entry and guests get a code when they reserve a court. Staff can play, too, but only during off-season if the courts aren't booked." He glances down at my shoes. "Do you play?"

I laugh, then realize he's serious. "I'm not really into sports," I say, which is a gross understatement. But he has no way of knowing that. Unlike the rest of the population of Corbin, Arden doesn't know I once tripped and broke my ankle while walking the mile—yes, walking—for our Presidential Physical Fitness Award. And he wasn't in the crowd at the pep rally last fall when I was the first junior to go headfirst into the mud pit during the class tug-of-war. I don't know his secrets, and he doesn't know mine. It's an odd feeling, being a mystery to someone.

"No sports," he says. "So what do you do for fun?"

"I'm a photographer."

His eyes light up. "Digital or film?"

"Both. But mostly film. I have a darkroom. It used to be my mom's." And now it's locked. But I don't want to think about that.

"Wow. Very cool."

He sounds sincere. "Are you into photography?"

"Sort of. I shoot mostly digital, primarily to capture color and light. I'm really a painter." He points to the folder in my hand. "That's one of mine."

I hold up the watercolor print of the falls. "Seriously? You did this?" I study it closely. "It's really good."

He shrugs and his cheeks go pink. "Thanks. I'm hoping to go

to art school next year. Maybe study in Europe. They say the light in the south of France is different from anywhere else on Earth." He grimaces. "Sorry. That sounded cooler in my head."

I smile. "So you've never been?" I assume with all his money, Arden can vacation wherever he wants.

"Nope. The farthest I've been from Kentucky is a ski trip to Colorado. Unless you count the 'It's a Small World' ride at Disney."

"I mean, how can you not?"

"Someday, though. Maybe." He flings an arm toward the lodge. "Of course, that's assuming my someday doesn't include *this*. Which, you know, it does. So . . ." He lifts a shoulder.

"And are you okay with that?" I'm not sure why I ask. It's none of my business, and besides, who am I to judge? Quitting on my parents and taking this job out of spite doesn't mean I don't still know firsthand the pull of family obligation and loyalty.

LOYALTY HAS ROOTS.

"At least I never had to work the mine," he says. "Mom keeps reminding me how grateful I should be for that."

I press my lips together and try to focus on his words. Everyone in Corbin knows the story of the Black River Mining Company. After Arden's grandfather racked up a mound of debt, he declared bankruptcy and closed the mine, leaving a lot of people without jobs and without pay they were already owed.

Jackson Jr. opened Atwater Lodge to the public shortly after his father's suicide.

"Sorry," he says.

It's the third time he's apologized to me this morning. I'm

not used to people worrying about whether they've offended me. I kind of like it.

"For what?" I ask.

"I'm not supposed to talk about that in public. People hate us for what Grandad did."

"I don't hate you," I say. The mine closed before I was born, so while I know the basics, I don't have any strong opinion about it. My parents do hate him—or at least his family—but it's because of the lodge, not the mine. But I don't tell him that.

"I'm glad." He flashes his dimples, then leads me down a narrow path behind the tennis courts and onto a cement pad with a rusted metal table and chairs that are clearly a smoking patio for the staff. The lodge is built into the mountain. So far, all the amenities have been on the same level as the parking lot, but beyond the railing, there's an abrupt drop of about fifteen feet to another patio below.

Arden uses a key to let us in the side door. "That's one of our wedding venues down there. We use it for outdoor services, or as a dance floor for receptions. It's got a great view of the falls. Come on, I'll show you."

The building juts out in a way that blocks our view, so I follow him inside, through the kitchen, which is bustling with activity. Arden points out the stairwell in the corner which leads to the guest rooms above—"for room service"—and down to the banquet rooms below. But instead of taking the stairs, we walk past the kitchen staff and through the swinging doors into the dining room.

The only room I've ever seen bigger than this is our school gymnasium. And this is a tight second. Chandeliers glitter overhead. Ornate French doors stand open to the pool area, and through them a few guests sit eating and drinking at an outdoor bar. The opposite wall is painted with a mural of the falls, larger and more impressionistic than the scene on my orientation folder.

It's like I've wandered onto the set of *Downton Abbey: The Hotel Years*.

Arden leads me into the grand hallway of the lodge proper, and it's all I can do not to gasp. Forget Downton Abbey. This is like a real-life version of Clue Manor.

"I can't believe you live here," I say.

"Not *here*." He sounds defensive. "This floor is all hotel." He points toward the towering carved staircase in the central hallway, which curves at a landing halfway up and leads to the second-floor balcony that wraps around the hall above our heads.

"Second floor is guest rooms. My mom and I have a private apartment on the third. So basically, I live in the attic." He gestures to my right, toward the towering double doors. "That's the front entrance. Library and offices to the right; parlor, coat room, and restrooms to the left."

We turn around and I finally see the front desk, massive and ornate, tucked in behind the staircase. "Guest services and concierge. Beyond that is the bar. It used to be Grandad's parlor. He was notoriously stingy with his liquor. Joke's on him now."

Arden smiles, urging me to share the joke. But I'm too distracted by the view beyond the desk. The hallway opens into a large seating area, with comfy sofas and chairs arranged in front of a massive stone fireplace—and a huge painting that hangs above the mantel.

A painting of a woman in white.

"Who is that?" I ask, drawn toward it.

"That's the ghost bride." He grins. "What do you think? I found it in storage. It looks like it belongs there, right?"

I stare up at the life-size painting.

The ceilings are tall, and her face is far enough above me and partially hidden behind a birdcage veil, so I can't make out her features. But the dress and the hair are all wrong. This bride wears a simple tea-length gown of cream-colored silk, with exposed shoulders and a sweetheart neckline. Her hair is long and falls freely to her shoulders, pinned back on one side by a clip.

Malice's hair clip.

For a second, I am back there in the woods. That cold, cold wind pushing me back. The pale woman in her tattered gown, with her dripping hair and her howling, hungry mouth. Her long, grasping fingers reaching out. For me.

But she isn't the woman in the painting.

So if this is the bride, then who—or what—did I see?

I stumble back a few steps, then out onto the balcony through the glass doors that flank the fireplace. The sunlight warms my chilled skin, and the roar of the water drowns my racing thoughts as I move toward the railing.

I need to pull it together. So maybe I'm crazy. So what? Isn't that more likely than ghosts? Either way, do I really want Arden to find out?

He comes out and stands beside me. "Everything okay?"

I force a smile. "Sure. Just needed some air." This is completely illogical, since the lodge was a comfortable temperature and out here it feels like we stepped into a sauna fully clothed, but he doesn't press the point. Instead, he leans on the railing next to me. "Best view in miles. Besides the Leap." He points to a cliff at the bend of the riverbank, jutting out from the trees.

The balcony hangs out over the falls, a roof to the dance floor patio I'd seen earlier. To my right, the stone walkway runs along the river and back up toward the public parking lot. While Atwater is built as close to the river as safety allowed, the Dunlaps have always allowed the public onto the overlook itself. Maybe as a gesture of goodwill. After all, what kind of monsters would keep all this beauty to themselves? But really, it was probably too much trouble trying to keep them out.

I have to admit, this view is almost worth the Atwater Lodge price tag. I've been to the overlook below. And I've climbed the rocks underneath it. But both of those pale in comparison to this.

I open my mouth to tell Arden this. Instead, I ask, "Have you ever seen her? The ghost bride?"

Arden stares out at the water. "My mom isn't a fan," he finally says, which doesn't answer my question.

"And yet you've got a gigantic painting of her."

"I mean, she's a great promotional tool, right? But for some reason, Mom hates the painting."

"And what do you think?"

"I think it's a good composition," he says. "It's harder than you think to capture people on that scale and make them look natural. And the colors are a great match for the lobby. It's almost like she was painted to hang there."

"I'm not talking about the painting. I mean the actual story. The ghost."

"Some people say ghosts are merely projections of your own fears," he finally says. "Or wishes, maybe."

It takes me a second to puzzle out his meaning. "So you're saying you don't believe in them?" Which makes him a normal, rational human being. So why doesn't that make me feel better?

He tilts his head. "It's not so much a question of belief as it is a lack of evidence. Trust me, I'd love to believe." He grips the railing and leans back. "I just haven't had the opportunity."

I wonder if he'd consider my experience "evidence."

"But it's a nice thought, isn't it?" he continues. "That the people we've lost still exist out there, somewhere. In some form. And that they can communicate with us, even? Instead of just being, you know, gone."

Of course. His dad.

"Maybe it's better to think of them at peace," I say. "Instead of wandering and restless, trying to get out one last message."

"Maybe." But Arden doesn't sound convinced. "Honestly, I think most people probably leave things unsaid when they die. Unfinished business and all that. And if there were some way you could get a message across, wouldn't you want to try?"

The thought reminds me of Malice's insistence, and it unsettles me. *It's up to you now. You need to find the answers. It's the only way.*

But if she's really a dead girl who's found a way to communicate with the living, why be so vague? And why choose my family? Why *me*?

"There's one more thing I want to show you," Arden says, breaking into my thoughts. "I think you're going to like this."

He leads me back inside, past the reception desk and down a corridor at the front of the building. It takes a minute for my eyes to adjust to the darkness after the brightness outside. When they do, I'm standing in another room from the game Clue. Wood paneling and gleaming wood floors. Red leather chairs clustered cozily in front of a stone fireplace. Twelve-foot ceilings, the walls papered with a forest green floral print. All that's missing is a detective in a trench coat.

But what I'm more interested in are the photos. Dozens of them, scattered across all four walls. Some framed, others tucked discreetly behind plate glass and individually lit.

"This is the photographic history of Atwater Lodge," Arden says. "Everything that's happened, it's all here. Cool, right?"

"Cool as hell," I say. I step closer to inspect some of the photos, careful not to smudge the glass. The oldest begin to the right of the door, and by *old*, I mean from the beginning of the medium. There are some tiny shots of an earlier version of Atwater Manor, perched precariously close to the water. And a few photos of people standing on the Atwater lawn, stiff and unsmiling. Judging by their clothing, this was probably the staff for the original home. Those early photos took forever to develop, and I appreciate the dedication to documenting this moment. I follow the photos around the perimeter of the room; it's almost as if I'm looking at the history of photography itself, as the photos shift from black and white to sepia, and then washed-out color prints.

From behind us, a woman clears her throat, and I turn.

"Kezia Dunlap," she says, holding out her hand.

I resist the urge to wipe the glass where I breathed on it. My own hands are sweaty, but I shake anyway. "Hi. I'm Rena Faye."

"So I'm told." She eyes me as if I'm a stain that needs eradicating.

Arden's mom is movie-star gorgeous and model tall, her auburn hair a mass of tight curls that resembles some kind of sculpture while also looking completely effortless. She has a thin scarf knotted once around her neck, dangly earrings, two arms full of silver and white-gold bangle bracelets, and sage green eyes that pierce and hold me in place.

"What do you think of our little library?" she asks.

"Impressive."

Kezia's smile softens.

"Mom organized all of this," Arden says, sounding proud.

"Well, that's my job, isn't it? Preserving the Atwater legacy." She rests a possessive hand on Arden's shoulder, and I have no doubt what the real Atwater legacy is.

"These photos have to be some of the earliest I've ever seen," I say, turning back to the wall.

Kezia taps one of the staff photos behind the glass. "This is the oldest photo we have. It was taken in 1875."

"That predates the handheld camera by at least ten years," I say, and I know I'm showing off. But something about the way Arden's mother looks at me makes me want to prove I don't belong in whatever category she's already slotted me into.

"Rena Faye is a photographer," Arden says. "She's also interested in our ghost bride." There's something in his voice I can't decipher—a hint of pride, or maybe defiance.

Kezia makes a face. "Those hobbies are contradictory, no?" she asks. "Unless—are you interested in spirit photography?" She says the last two words the same way my history teacher says "Black Death."

"No," I say quickly. "I mostly shoot landscapes. Sometimes animals. I'd love to get into travel photography. You know, real stuff."

"So you don't believe in ghosts, then? Smart girl," she says, twisting the ring on her finger.

Arden's eyes narrow. "Mom. Can we not . . . ?"

She presses her lips together. "I'm afraid my son and I have a difference of opinion when it comes to our local legend. While he adores those kinds of stories, I'm afraid I find them gauche. Still, I've promised to give him the reins this summer, so I suppose we'll see what kind of clientele his new advertising might attract."

Arden's face turns red, and I make a mental note to ask him about what taking "the reins" entails once his mom has left. For now, I frantically try to come up with a way to change the subject. But Kezia beats me to it.

"Tell me, Rena Faye," she asks. "What do your parents think about you working here?"

Oh, shit. Did Daddy call her and say something? Am I about to be fired? "Um. They . . . well. I mean, I suppose they'd rather I were helping out at home. With the motel. But they . . . they understand." The lie is so enormous I can barely force it out.

"I went to school with your mother, you know," Kezia says. "Has she ever mentioned me?"

Of course. She's talked about "that Atwater bitch" a handful of times over the years. "Uh, no. Mm-mm. I don't think so."

"You remind me of her a little. It's the eyes, I think."

"I get that a lot."

"She was also very interested in the ghost bride."

"Momma?" I pause. "I don't think so."

"Oh, yes. Obsessed, I'd even say. Some ridiculous story about a curse, as I recall. That didn't end well for her, did it? I do hope you've got more common sense than she did."

"Mom!" Arden hisses the word like a leaking balloon. "You can't say things like that. I'm so sorry." Another apology.

"I think Rena Faye and I understand each other. Don't we?" Kezia arches one perfect eyebrow before turning back to her son.

My breath catches, and all I can do is nod.

"Now then. It's nearly noon. Peggy's most likely already started on the cabins. Let's not keep her waiting any longer."

She steps through a door beside the fireplace I'd missed upon first glance and closes it behind her, leaving Arden and me alone.

How is it that Kezia knows about the curse?

And what else does she know?

CHAPTER 12

"I'm so sorry." Arden keeps apologizing long after his mother is gone.

"What? No, it's fine." I wave him off. "But what do you think she meant about my mother? Being obsessed? Because my mother is *not* obsessed with the ghost bride. She's whatever the opposite of obsessed is."

"She's probably got her confused with someone else."

Sure. Because there are probably plenty of Lou Whitakers around Corbin who look like me.

"Why don't I show you to the housekeeping cottage?" Arden says.

I let him lead me away; I'm supposed to be working, after all. Not worrying about Kezia or Momma or the ghost bride. Or the curse.

When Arden says "housekeeping cottage,'" I picture a laundry room like we have back at the motel. But here, the housekeeping staff has its own building—a fairly large one, situated behind the tennis courts and painted brown to blend in with the trees.

"Lodge housekeeping is separate," he explains. "Only cabin staff work out here. It's easier than lugging everything back and forth." He pulls open the door and waves me in. From the outside, it looks homey. Inside, it's basically a laundromat with a giant storage closet. Three women stand sorting tiny amenity bottles at a long table that separates the washing machines and dryers from the aisles of shelving.

"The cabins are weekly rentals," Arden says. "Monday to Sunday. So Sundays they all need to be turned over. It's sort of an all-hands-on-deck situation. Peggy is in charge out here. She'll let you know where you're needed and what to do. That's pretty much it." He shoves his hands in his pockets. "I've got to get back inside. Are you okay?"

Am I okay? Somehow, whenever Arden asks me a question, it's like he actually cares about the answer. No, I'm not okay, but I'm also not an idiot. I know he means with this, the job, the cleaning. No matter that his gaze is probing and concerned, or that the question feels more like he's reaching deep inside of me, uncovering dark truths I'm afraid to face rather than just being polite.

"I'm good," I lie.

I turn to the employees folding laundry. The oldest is shorter than me, but solid muscle, her white hair cut short and spiky. Her eye makeup behind her purple glasses is flawless. "Rena Faye," I say, giving her a little wave.

"I'm Peggy," she says, giving me a once-over. "Done this kind of work before?"

I nod. "Since I was old enough to fold a bedsheet."

She narrows her eyes, so I add, "My parents own a motel."

"But you don't want to work for them." It's a statement, not a question, and somehow I like her more for this.

"Hell no."

She snorts a laugh, and the other two women giggle. "My momma used to tell me, family does for family," Peggy says. "But I say, family does *to* family. The kind of shit you'd never do to your neighbor. Or your dog."

The stranglehold of guilt releases, just a little, and I take a deep breath. "You've got that right." I take the piles she's sorted and start to package them into the containers on the counter, nodding hello to the two women across from me.

"I'm Jen," says one, snapping her gum.

I know her, or at least of her. She was a few years ahead of me in school: a cheerleader whose crowning glory was marrying her high school sweetheart. She's still cute, but in a sad kind of way—her black hair dried out and pulled into a tired bun. Even her freckles are faded.

Peggy points to the other. "That's Sadie."

Sadie has earbuds in and isn't paying any attention to any of us.

"Hope you're okay with overtime," Peggy says, swapping out my full box for a new one. "Sundays are a bitch. Don't get me wrong; it's heaven out here compared to in the big house." She jerks a thumb. "Tuesday through Saturday are a breeze. Making beds, swapping towels. Those days, you might get asked to help out inside after. But Sundays"—she gives a low whistle under her breath—"almost make up for that."

"How late is overtime?" I ask. I'd planned to bum another ride with Daisy after work. Without my phone to check in with her, I'm lost. I can try and find her on my break, but I don't know when that is and asking about it two minutes into my shift will only make me sound like a slacker.

"Past dinner," Jen says. "It's usually a ten-hour day, by the time we finish with the laundry and whatnot."

Wow. Well, this is what I wanted, after all. Freedom. This is the first day I can ever remember not being involved with the motel in some way. Even when I'm not working, there's usually breakfast at the diner or making coffee for the lobby, or searching out Momma in one of the rooms to get the truck keys for school, which usually leads to running something somewhere—trash to the bins, or sheets to the laundry room. I feel light and free, but also like I gnawed off one of my own limbs. I no longer have to worry about it weighing me down, but the phantom pain still haunts me.

"Checkout is noon," Peggy says, "but you always get stragglers. Twelve cabins, and they take about an hour each to clean. Mopping, scrubbing, dishes. The whole nine yards. These people know how to trash a vacation rental, let me tell you. They pay a cleaning fee, and by god do they use it."

"I had a theory, back at the motel, that the more we charged for a room, the worse shape guests would leave it in. I used to say we should let them stay for free and we'd never have any cleaning to do."

Peggy nods appreciatively. "You're onto something. Maybe not free, though. People take advantage of free. An incredible deal. One time only."

"See? You should be in charge!" Jen says.

"Don't I know it."

Peggy hefts one of the bins and gestures to me to do the same. I follow her outside, where she loads her bin into the back of a golf cart.

"Do I get to drive this?"

"The novelty wears off quick. But yes. It's easier than carrying supplies to the farthest cabins. Kinda peaceful, too."

She's right. It's quiet back here. The cabins were designed for privacy, and none of them are visible from the road or the lodge. In fact, the paved path leading from the laundry shed seems to vanish into a darkened canopy of trees. Where it ends is anyone's guess. We're miles from the ruins, but it's similar enough to my secret forest clearing that I'm getting serious flashbacks.

A cool wind blows and I shiver.

"You ever hear any ghost stories about this place?" I ask Peggy, keeping one eye on the trees behind her.

She slows in her packing of the cart, suddenly very interested in the number of towels per pile. "You grow up here? Corbin, I mean."

"Never been anywhere else." Thanks to Momma.

She side-eyes me. "So you must know about the bride."

I glance around, then feel foolish. Who would be listening? Arden? "Of course. My mawmaw was telling me that story before I could walk." I lower my voice. "Have you ever seen her? The bride?"

"Who's your mawmaw?" she asks, avoiding the question.

"Alice Slocum."

"So you're Tallulah's girl. A Whitaker."

I nod. The sun is hot on my neck and I feel it blistering as I wait for Peggy to go on.

"I'm surprised, actually. That you'd be working here." She rocks back on her heels. "Your mom and Kezia, they used to be tight back in the day. But not anymore."

She slaps at a bug near her ankle, and I jump. Tight? Kezia had said they'd gone to school together, but she certainly hadn't been complimentary. And Momma has never talked about Kezia at all aside from general grumbling about the Dunlaps and their lodge.

"I don't think—"

"I'm what you might call a local historian. I know everything that goes on in this town. Had my DNA done, too. I'm related to St. Patrick." She puts her hands on her hips, waiting for my reply.

I know I'm supposed to be impressed by the saint thing, but I'm more interested in the local historian part. "So you must know all the stories."

"Oh, I know 'em. Know where the bodies are buried, too."

"You mean, the bride—"

"I'm just messing with you!" Peggy slaps the cart and hoots with laughter. "Look, it's a fun legend. But I volunteer at the historical society, part time. And there's no record of her anywhere, honey. No birth, no death. No wedding. No grave. And believe me, I've looked."

This is what I've been saying all along—it's just a story. So why do I feel deflated?

"Oh, come on. You look like I just peed in your Cheerios.

Don't get upset. It's a dumb story, anyway. A ghost who's so mad about killing her own self, she haunts everyone else?"

Peggy sounds like my mother. "I'm not upset," I say. "I . . . I thought I saw her."

But she's not listening. "I'll tell you this, though. Damn smart of Mr. Arden to capitalize on the story. Our little bride is going to generate a nice amount of publicity for the hotel, you mark my words. I'm actually surprised Kezia never thought of it. She's always been the real brains behind the operation."

Peggy heads over to Cabin 2, leaving me with a map and instructions to Cabin 8. Jen and Sadie head out on their own cart, Jen waving and tooting the horn, Sadie leaning back with her eyes closed.

Suddenly I'm alone.

I assume the hotel is full—it's a moonbow weekend, after all. But there's no one around. No wandering guests, no kids playing in the woods.

But why would there be? This is the staff area. The paths for the tourists are out in front of the tennis courts. They're also wider, and well lit. Still, it's weird that I don't even see any other staff.

I used to have this fantasy, when I was younger, that everyone else in the world would vanish, all at once. And I'd be left alone. More like a nightmare, really, although sometimes it was fun to imagine the motel rooms empty and quiet, the pool calm and devoid of screaming kids doing cannonballs off the side. But even in my own make-believe story, I always knew that after a few hours of solitude, I'd be too terrified to enjoy it. What would I do when night came, and there was no one to help keep the monsters away?

This feels like that.

I shake off the heebie-jeebies and get into the golf cart. At least if I find any monsters—or ghosts—I have a better chance of outrunning them on this thing. According to the map, Cabin 8 is nestled into the trees a few hundred feet down the path from the laundry shed.

These guests appear to have checked out on time, because the cabin is dark and deserted and I'm creeped out all over again. I didn't realize I'd be working alone in the middle of the forest. I half hope Peggy shows up to check on me. Even if she doesn't believe in the ghost bride. Her or anyone else around here. Which should be comforting. It's like I keep telling myself—the bride is just a figment of my imagination.

And not a vengeful spirit who could be lurking behind any of these trees.

I heft my tub and head up the stone walkway, key in hand. The door creaks open, revealing a cabin that is probably homey when it isn't trashed. A living area with a big-screen TV and fold-out couch, the latter unmade, the cushions scattered across the floor. Dining nook complete with full kitchen, dishes piled in the sink and across the breakfast bar. A stairway leads to a loft above, which is presumably where at least one of the beds is located.

I set down my cleaning supplies and get to work. First task— strip the beds.

I'm standing in the darkened loft when the door opens below.

"I'm up here. Started on the beds," I holler down to Peggy.

No answer.

"Peggy?" I step over to the loft balcony, where I have a clear view of the room below. The door is ajar, but I don't see anyone in the living or kitchen area.

Probably I didn't pull the door tight and the wind caught it.

There's another creak behind me. This one like the sound of a footstep on the stairs.

I'm afraid to turn around. My mouth feels like it's stuffed with cotton. I clutch a pillow to my chest, which is the least effective weapon ever, but also the only thing I have.

"Hello? Is someone there?"

Another creak. Another footstep.

Then Daisy's head appears at the top of the stairs.

I lob the pillow at her as hard as I can, but she ducks and it crashes into a painting on the far wall. "You scared the shit out of me!" I yell. "What are you doing here?"

"You thought I was the ghost, didn't you?" My cousin is way too pleased with herself. "In the car this morning you were all, 'I don't want to talk about it. She isn't real.' But she is and you believe in her!" She hops from one foot to the other and claps her hands.

"Oh, please." I go back to stripping the bed, much more aggressively than before. "I didn't think you were the ghost. I thought you were a rapist. Or a murderer. I'm clearly going to have to lock the doors behind me when I'm out here by myself."

"I thought I'd come by and see how your first day is going." She watches as I grab a fresh set of sheets and spread them across the bed. "And I had an idea. About your ghost bride."

"She's not *my* ghost bride. She's not anything except a figment of my imagination."

"Come on. You don't have that good of an imagination," Daisy says.

"Shouldn't you be working?" I ask.

"I am. Guest relations." Daisy taps her nametag. "Housekeeping is in direct relation to our guests."

"I think you're reaching," I say. "And anyway, haven't you ever heard of passing the buck?"

"I never understood that phrase. If I had a buck, I'd keep it."

"I think it's a different kind of buck." I pull the coverlet back over the bed, fluff the pillows, and wave her toward the stairs.

When Daisy doesn't take the hint, I grab the errant pillow and reach out to straighten the picture on the wall. It's another painting of the falls, similar to the watercolor in the main dining room.

"There's one in every room," she says. "Overkill, if you ask me. People are here to look at nature, not a facsimile."

"Same artist?" I lean forward, squinting to pick out the faint signature hidden within the rocks. *Dunlap.* Arden?

"I have to work late," I say as I head down the stairs. "Any chance you can pick me up after?"

Daisy follows me down. "As a matter of fact, that's what I've been trying to talk to you about. How about I pick you up and we go back? To see the ghost bride?"

"Um, what?"

"You heard me."

"Yeah, well, I pass," I say.

"Okay, I'll admit, I reacted badly when you told me yesterday. I needed time to think. Today, the answer is so obvious. We need evidence."

I groan. "Why does everyone keep talking about evidence?"

"Who's everyone?" She narrows her eyes. "Who else have you told about this?"

"I haven't told anyone." Except Peggy. But she didn't hear me. Or pretended to ignore me.

"Good. Because, no offense, dear cuz, but if this gets out, people are going to say you're . . ." She whistles and twirls her finger by her ear.

I slap it.

"See? That's why we need evidence," she continues. "But it's better if no one knows we're working on it. At least not until we have something concrete."

"Working on what?"

"Malice's curse, of course!"

"I already told you, I don't have time for that. I have a real job now. One I'm going to lose if you keep distracting me."

"Pull up your big-girl pants. We are going ghost hunting!"

"Ghost hunting? And *I'm* the loopy one?"

"I'm talking real paranormal investigation. There are studies being done to prove paranormal phenomena as we speak. By real scientists."

"And what do these real scientists do, exactly?" I ask. "I'd love to know what it is you think we could possibly accomplish that they haven't."

She just shrugs. "Look, it's not exactly my area of expertise. But what I do know is that if you, Rena Faye Whitaker, were the first person to obtain photographic evidence of the spiritual realm? You could write your own ticket to art school."

Daisy knows how to tempt me, that's for sure. "Either that, or they'd label me a fraud and I wouldn't even be able to get a job at the Walgreens photo counter."

She holds up a finger and turns away, pressing the other hand to the headset tucked behind her ear. "Hold on. It's the front desk. This is Daisy." A pause. "Yes." She squints at me, then at the cabin door. "Cabin 8. Okay, thanks."

She drops her hand and stares at me. "Uh-oh."

"Uh-oh what? Am I getting fired? On my first day?"

"It's not that."

The roar of an engine interrupts her, and we both run out onto the tiny porch.

"Too fast," she mutters, marching over to the road. Tires squeal as the driver throws the truck into reverse.

Chance's truck.

By the time I reach them, Daisy is kneeling beside a small, broken pine and giving him an earful. "—dead. You ran right over it! What the hell were you thinking?"

"It's just a plant. They're everywhere." This is as close as Chance gets to apologetic, and his expression changes to relief when he sees me. Which maybe proves he isn't as smart as he thinks he is.

"Help me out, Rena Faye," Chance pleads, and now *he* sounds like a child.

Daisy puts her hands on her hips. "I take back my earlier advice. Dump his ass."

The thought doesn't sound as unbelievable as it did a few hours ago. And that shakes me. "Why are you here?" I ask him.

Chance looks from me to Daisy and back, maybe surprised I

didn't defend him. "You weren't answering. What did you expect me to do?"

Daisy throws up her hands.

"I've been looking all over for you," he says, stepping forward and lowering his voice. "Why haven't you answered any of my calls or texts? I was worried something had happened to you."

"My phone is broken," I say, crossing my arms over my chest.

He sighs with relief and wraps his arms above his head. As his T-shirt rides up, exposing his tight stomach, I have a sudden urge to punch him. Right in his bare belly. "Oh, thank god. I thought . . ." He steps forward, as if to embrace me or kiss me or something.

I don't wait to find out what. "I'm still mad at you," I say, holding out a hand to stop him. "We're not good."

"What is going on with you?" He looks at my shirt. "You work here now? That wasn't just some kind of dumb stunt?"

"I do."

He pulls off his baseball cap and runs a hand through his curls. "Come on, Rena Faye. This isn't for you. What's this gonna do, except hurt your daddy?"

I wince. I don't want to hurt Daddy. But he hurt me. And I'm so tired of everyone telling me what to do. "Is it really my daddy you're worried about? Are you sure you aren't just pissed that I'm working here instead of at your camp?"

He works his jaw. "There's got to be a better place to talk about this." He takes my elbow. "Get in the truck and we'll go somewhere private."

I yank my arm free. "I told you, I'm working. I can't just leave."

"Haven't you proved your point? You stood your ground. You didn't blink. You win."

"You think this is a game?"

"No! But I've known you my whole life. And I honestly don't understand what you're trying to do here."

I don't either, but I'll be damned if I'm going to tell him that. "I'm hoping to make some money. And I'm hoping to do it out from under my family's thumb." *And yours.*

The list is never-ending.

He sighs and holds up his hands. "Fine. Suit yourself. We don't have to talk about the job."

The way he says it sets off a warning bell in my head. "Wait. Did Daddy ask you to come here?"

"I went over there to talk to you. Like I said, I was worried. Your daddy told me about your new job. And . . . he did . . . *suggest* that maybe I could talk some sense into you"—he hurries through the sentence when my face goes hard—"but I don't care about any of that. I care about you. I care about us."

The way he looks at me, like I'm all he's ever wanted . . . like the only thing he wants is to set things right . . .

I feel myself weakening. We've never fought this long before. Even before we were dating, Chance was a constant in my life. One of my best friends. Easygoing. Easy to talk to.

Plus, I love him.

"Fine," I say. "Pick me up after work and we can talk."

"Sweet!" His whole face lights up. He's like a puppy, and I feel guilty all over again. Because I can't guarantee I won't kick him.

"Seven o'clock," I tell him, without any real idea of what time

I'll be done. But it doesn't matter; he can wait. "In the front lot," I add. "Don't come back here again."

He pops his hat on and manages to land a quick kiss on my cheek before I can react.

I touch it as I watch him drive away.

Daisy comes to stand next to me. "I'm guessing this means ghost hunting is off the table?"

"It was never on the table," I say.

Then again, yesterday I might have said the same about reconciling with Chance. It's funny how quickly the unimaginable becomes reality.

CHAPTER 13

Chance is waiting at the front entrance when I finally clock out and head to the parking lot. The whole facade is lit up like daylight—spotlights shining up the stone walls of the building, strategically placed to avoid windows, while the grounds and walkways have lower, softer lights on posts. But it's nearly 8:00 p.m. and I'm exhausted. Between the rush to turn over all the cabins and the emotional toll of learning new routines, new names, and new faces, I can barely keep my eyes open, let alone form a coherent sentence.

He's showered and changed since he was here earlier, smelling like soap and AXE body spray—not even a whiff of horses. His jeans are clean, and even his shirt is a step up from his usual tee; he's wearing a checkered button-down he usually saves for church and weddings.

"I brought you these," he says, handing me a bouquet as I climb into his F-150. One look and I can tell the flowers are from the gas station near his house. I'm not sure if I should be annoyed or touched. It's a sweet gesture, but the wilting petals and baby's breath take me right back to the cheap, eager dates of middle school. Why don't we braid friendship bracelets and write each other's names on our shoes while we're at it?

"Thanks," I say, laying them across my lap. "So. You wanted to talk?"

"Not here." He pulls out onto the highway, turning in the opposite direction of our houses.

"Where are we going?"

"You'll see."

It isn't until he takes the turn for the public park that I understand where. And why.

The Leap has the best view of the falls outside the Atwater property. It's where Chance and I spent our first date. Even the flowers make sense now. He'd handed me a bouquet just like it in the back seat of his daddy's truck, many moons ago.

"Surprise," he says softly, and his face is so sweet and hopeful, lit by the moonlight streaming through the windshield. It almost makes me want to kiss him. But I don't.

He parks the truck in the corner of the lot, beside a group of white pine trees. "You look like you had a long day," he continues, reaching behind us and pulling out a small cooler from the back seat, "so I brought sustenance. A moonbow picnic."

"MoonPies and Coke?" I ask.

"What else?"

He jumps out and runs around to open my door for me. "It's the last night of the moonbow, so I figured we shouldn't waste it."

The moonbow is visible up to two days before and two days

after the full moon, but the best viewing time gets later on each night. Tonight—the fifth night—there is zero chance of seeing it before midnight, and I don't plan on our talk lasting nearly that long. After all, what do we have to say to each other that hasn't already been said at least a dozen times?

He pulls a blanket from the back and as his hand brushes mine, my heart clenches. He's as much a part of me as this place. Loving him is easy, as automatic as breathing, and I've done it for as long as I can remember.

So why does it suddenly feel like I can't catch my breath?

As Chance spreads the blanket on a boulder, I step out onto the concrete platform.

Where Atwater's overlook is perched nearly on top of the falls, the Leap is higher and farther downriver. What you lose in proximity, you gain in a view that is all-encompassing. This is where the best photos come from, the ones that put Cumberland Falls in nature calendars and end up framed on someone's wall after their vacation.

This is where I took *my* photos, the shots rejected by the application board as "lacking depth."

And this is where the stories say the bride stood that night, waiting for her lover.

I turn toward the lodge, which is lit up like a Christmas tree. This is the view she would've seen. If she were real.

Except this didn't become a park until the 1930s. Before that, it was basically wilderness. And the Atwater mansion would have been lit by candlelight, not electricity. No pavement, no cobblestone steps.

No wall to hold her back.

I stare down at the churning water and jagged rocks below.

"Penny for your thoughts," Chance says, handing me a bottle of Coke.

I take it and chug the cold, sweet liquid until my eyes water. "I was thinking about the legend of the ghost bride," I say, wiping my mouth.

"What about it?"

"This is supposedly where she jumped," I say, pointing my bottle toward the river.

"Jumped? Or fell?"

"Jumped," I say. "She was waiting for her lover when she saw the fire. She waited, but he never came. So she knew he must be dead." I take another sip from the bottle. "She was heartbroken, so she jumped. And now she haunts this place. Always searching for him."

But that can't be the whole truth, can it? Because what about the curse? It won't bring her lover back.

So what *does* she want? What is she looking for?

I think about asking Chance what he thinks. Telling him everything that has happened over the past few days. I can picture his reaction as clear as if it's a movie playing out in my head. *I saw her. The ghost*, I'd say. And he'd shake his head with a little smile. An exaggerated eye roll, maybe. And I almost tell him then, if only for the familiarity of those gestures, for that smile I know so well. The reassurance that the ghost was all in my imagination, and that Chance and I, we are what's real.

But something holds me back.

"Seems extreme," Chance says. "Jumping off a cliff."

"What do you mean?"

"Well, why didn't she go see if he was okay? Maybe he wasn't dead after all. Maybe he was helping put out the fire or something."

He ducks his head under the weight of my stare. "I'm just saying, flinging herself off a cliff was a stupid thing to do, especially before she'd even given him a chance to explain himself. Most problems can be worked through without so much drama."

He isn't talking about the ghost bride anymore.

"Are you saying I'm being dramatic?" I ask, hearing my voice go up. I take another drink of Coke, trying to calm down. "Because you'll notice I haven't threatened to jump to my death. In fact, I'm doing just fine—" I stop before saying "without you" because it sounds too permanent.

"Just fine," I repeat. "No drama, no suicide."

"No explanation," he shoots back.

"No explanation? Have you hit your head and suffered some kind of trauma? Or are you just choosing not to remember what you and Daddy did behind my back?"

"It wasn't like that!"

"How was it, then?"

"That's what I've been trying to tell you. I was waiting for you in the lobby the other day and we just got to talking. It's not like we made some kind of deal. I didn't buy you for forty pieces of silver and a goat."

He always mixes his metaphors. I used to tease him about it. Now I just want to slap him.

"If you're looking for some kind of medal for acknowledging me as a human being, rather than a piece of property," I say, "just keep walking."

He breathes in sharp through his nose. "I told him we were shorthanded. I wasn't even hinting or anything—just making conversation. And he suggested you might be interested. Since he knew your trip was getting called off."

I can't picture it the way he's laid it out, I suspect because it's all fiction. "So you were all, 'We really can use some help,' and Daddy was like, 'You know who you should ask?'" I raise an eyebrow.

Chance rubs a hand across his face. "I don't remember our exact words. The point is, nobody was trying to hurt you. And honestly, I don't know why you're so upset. You're going to come work with me eventually. Right?" There's a tremor in his voice I haven't heard before. An uncertainty at odds with his confident, crown prince image.

"I don't know," I say, tripping over the words. "It isn't something I've ever thought about."

"But you've thought about us. You . . . and . . . and me," he stutters. "The future, I mean."

But it's that vague talk again. The way we always tiptoe around the specifics, but never touch them directly, thus avoiding any discomfort. And any commitment.

"What does that mean, exactly? The future. Tomorrow? Next year? The rest of our lives?"

He blinks, a deer in the headlights of my questions. I'm not sure why I'm pushing him, why I'm trying to back him into making a promise clearly neither of us is ready for. But I'm also tired of playing this game. Of pretending our future holds all this wonder and mystery. That there's something shiny and magical about settling down with your childhood sweetheart right out of high school, without ever leaving home or seeing what else might be out there. Is that romantic? Or just sad?

"What I wanted to tell you is I never meant to hurt you," he says. "And if you don't want to work at the ranch, fine. But don't tell me you're happy over there." He gestures to the lodge. "Working for them?"

"Why wouldn't I be?"

"They're the enemy."

"They're good people." I don't tell him about Kezia and her talk about Momma. "Just trying to make a living. Like we are."

"A living by stealing your daddy's business."

"You sound like Momma," I say. "But there's room for all of us." I don't know if I fully believe this, but he also doesn't know my parents as well as he thinks he does. "Besides," I add, "Momma and Daddy aren't saints, either."

They canceled my trip. And they want me to give up the one thing I'm good at. But I don't tell Chance this. A week ago, I wouldn't have hesitated. Now I wonder if he'd agree with them. Just how close is he to my daddy? Not only that, just how much is he *like* my daddy?

The thought unsettles me. I tell myself I'm nothing like Momma. But she married her high school boyfriend and now she runs his business. She's never left Corbin. It's a pattern I'm dangerously close to repeating. Taking the job at the lodge may have felt like breaking free, but here I am with Chance, right back where we started. Maybe we're all just destined to become our parents. Or make their mistakes.

"I love you," Chance says, stepping closer.

"I love you, too," I say. Because it's true. But also because I've uttered those words a thousand times, and they come automatically.

He takes my hand. "Can we start again? Not over," he says. "But from where we were happy."

I swallow around a sudden lump in my throat as I think about the thousands of versions of us that exist. Swimming, riding bikes, exploring the forest, skinned knees and red popsicles and catching tadpoles and kissing under the bleachers and prom and homecoming and the moonbow. We *were* happy. I'm just not sure anymore when all of that ended.

He tugs me gently, and I let him pull me into his arms. There's a certain comfort in knowing where you fit. But when he leans in to kiss me, I put a hand on his chest. "There's something I need you to do," I say. "You need to promise you won't make any more decisions for me."

"I promise," he says, pressing his lips to mine.

I pull back once more. "And no more talking to Daddy. Not about us. You come to me first. Got it?"

"Got it." He kisses me then, for real, and I kiss him back, and for at least this moment, my world makes sense again.

We stay like that a while, though not long enough to see the moonbow.

When he drops me off, he grabs my hand again before I can get out of the truck and pulls me close, kissing me, hard, like he's sealing the deal. Or stamping me. "Don't forget your flowers," he reminds me, handing them over.

His headlights warm my back until I'm inside, the door shut and locked behind me. Only then does he back out and drive away.

I tiptoe into the living room, pausing by Momma's darkened chair. "Chance and I made up," I whisper. But she doesn't answer or switch on the light, and when I finally do, she isn't there.

For the first time in my life, she hasn't waited up.

CHAPTER 14

The next morning, Momma and Daddy are both already at the diner by the time I'm up and moving. The last thing I want to do is argue with them, but I need my camera back. I've never been this long without it, and I have to start working on my portfolio. Plus, there's the matter of a new phone. There are also questions I need to ask Momma. I may not be working at the motel anymore, but I'm still their daughter. And after Kezia's odd mention of Momma's "obsession" and with Peggy's comment about them being "tight," I'm more curious than ever. And I'm betting Momma is, too, now that I'm working with her old BFF. Even if she won't admit it.

The bell over the front door announces my arrival to everyone in the place: a half dozen tourists as well as Daddy, who turns his back quickly, hunching over his newspaper when he sees me. The rest of them go back to eating their bacon and drinking their coffee. The smell of both gets my stomach rumbling.

"Morning," I say, sliding onto the stool beside him.

He ignores me.

I fiddle with the salt and pepper shakers, lining them up on the checkered linoleum counter. Daddy doesn't make small talk, and I'm not sure how to begin a conversation without him choosing the topic and then dominating it.

"So I was wondering when I can get into my darkroom," I say, brushing aside a few errant salt crystals.

He rattles the paper but doesn't respond.

I sigh. "At least let me grab my camera out of there?"

Nothing.

"Fine." I spin my stool away from him and his childish cold shoulder tactics. "I thought we could discuss this like adults. But I guess not."

I lift the counter flap and duck into the kitchen, where Momma stands over the stove. "I'm working," she says without looking up.

"I know." I lean a hip on the counter. I've stood in this same spot a thousand times, answering her questions about homework and chores, or telling her about my day. But it's never been this awkward. I long to say something about Atwater, or ask her about Kezia, but it's clearly not the time. "I'm sure Daddy told you about the darkroom," I say instead.

"That's between you and him."

"All I want is my camera back," I say. "I really need to be taking photos this summer if I'm going to put together a portfolio in time to apply for scholarships this fall."

"That's up to your Daddy."

"O-kay. And when do you think he might be speaking to me again?"

Momma shakes her head once, hard.

"How about my phone, then? Are you allowed to make a decision about that? Or that's up to Daddy, too?"

"Damn it!" She slaps down her spatula and turns to me, eyes narrowed. "What about your phone?"

I pull it from my front sweatshirt pocket. "It broke."

She glances down at the screen. "You'll have to use it like it is."

"It doesn't work."

"Well, I don't have the time or the money to shop for a new one."

I shove it back in my pocket. "Fine. But don't get upset when you can't get ahold of me," I tell her. I know it's breakfast and she's busy, but would it kill her to listen to me? Look at me, for once? "Can I at least borrow the truck?"

She slams the plate she's holding to the counter and takes a ragged breath before finally turning in my direction. "What did you just ask me?" But she doesn't wait for my answer. Instead, she takes the plate out to Daddy, forcing me to follow her to the counter.

"I can't find the keys," I repeat. "They weren't on the hook or in the truck." We all share the beat-up old pickup. As long as Momma doesn't have errands, I've always been allowed to drive it. But her fury forces me to reevaluate.

"Is she seriously asking if she can drive the truck?" Daddy addresses this question to his plate, as if his scrambled eggs are an oracle. "Maybe she should've thought about that before she quit."

My whole body gets hot. "I should have known you'd find a way to punish me for trying to live my own life."

Daddy dumps a glob of ketchup onto his hash browns and raises his eyes to Momma. "Tell her my truck is not going near any Dunlap property."

"Actually," I say, turning to Momma as I struggle to keep my voice even, "I have the morning off. I want to check in on Malice."

"Tell her—"

"I'm right here," I say, stepping around Momma and waving a hand in Daddy's face. "I can hear you."

"Go, then. Live your own life," Daddy says. "And while you're at it, use some of that fancy Atwater cash to buy your own car."

I duck under the counter and make it out of the diner without giving him the satisfaction of my tears, but I only make it as far as the lattice fence by the dumpster before I start to cry. I press myself up against the side of the building and stare up at the impossible blue of the sky, letting the sunlight scorch my tearstained face. I want to scream—at Daddy, at the world—and holding it back is like holding poison in my belly. But what choice do I have? If I let it out, it will burn us all.

The back door squeaks open and I let my head fall to the left. Momma is on the other side, watching me through the screen. "Here," she says, her arm snaking around the frame, holding out her keys. "Have it back by the time the lunch shift is over."

I don't know why Momma chose to defy Daddy and let me use the truck, but I suspect it has more to do with Malice than with me. Our argument from the other night is still festering in me as I drive the deserted highway to Malice's house, Momma's words worming their way under my skin so that I half expect them to push up and appear like some kind of puckered scar. *Don't be ridiculous* on one arm and *Grow up* on the other.

The truck sputters, the steering wheel jerking beneath my hands. I manage to steer it over to the side of the road, coasting the last couple of feet as the engine coughs and then quits.

This can't be good.

I shift into park and turn the ignition key, but nothing happens. The cracked screen on my phone is a reminder I am on my own.

Crap. Crap crap crap. Daddy is going to blame me for this somehow, I just know it.

I get out and walk around to the front. Press my hand on the hood and jerk it back. It's hot. Great. Maybe it overheated?

I stare up and down the road, willing a Good Samaritan to stop and help. But as I haven't recently acquired the powers of telepathy, nothing happens. Which means I can either wait here for someone to come along or the engine to cool off. Or I can leave the truck where it is and walk the mile and a half to Malice's house.

Both options sound hot and tiring, but at least Malice has water and a phone, so I opt for door number two. The gravel crunches sharply under my flip-flops, while the sun is like a torch at my back. I pull my hair off the back of my neck in hopes of a cool breeze, but I'm probably just hastening the inevitable sunburn.

I move to the far side of the road, so oncoming cars will hopefully see me before they run me down. The air is filled with the scent of hot asphalt and the occasional cloud of insects, but otherwise nothing moves. Without the distraction of the radio, I'm left with only my thoughts for company, and those are a jumbled mess. Between Momma and Daddy, and Arden and Atwater, and Chance and his ranch, my head is buzzing louder than the annoying bee keeping pace with my ear.

I swat around my head and run, hoping it will lose interest.

The loudest thoughts, the ones I can't outrun, are of the ghost bride.

No matter how many times I tell myself I imagined it all, every time I close my eyes, I see her. I don't want to admit it, even to myself, but she looked real. As real as the sun burning my neck. As real as the blisters forming between my toes.

I saw her.

And worse, I felt her.

This is the thing I haven't told anyone, not even Daisy.

I felt her sadness, like it was my own. And even if I can find a way to explain away the rest of it, I don't know how to shake that feeling. Her grief and anguish were so overwhelming it just about makes me weep every time I think of it.

I know it isn't possible. Ghosts don't exist. I know this the way I know the earth is round and the sky is blue.

But if what I saw and felt was true, everything I've always put my faith in—science, physical evidence, rational thought—might be wrong.

So where does that leave me?

It takes me a little under an hour to reach Malice's house, and by then I'm dehydrated and cranky.

She greets me at the door in typical Malice fashion. "It's hotter than blue blazes out there. Only a fool would be out walking in this weather!"

"The truck overheated. And my phone is busted."

"The truck, my aunt Fanny. You're the one who's overheated. Let's get you inside before you let all the heat in." She pulls me into the relative coolness of the cabin, shaking her head and muttering. I've never felt more loved.

After I borrow her phone to call home for a ride, she hands me an ice pack for my neck, and seats me in front of her fan while she makes lemonade.

Momma's voice fills my head, and I have a fleeting thought about Malice mistaking salt for sugar as I take my first, tentative sip, but the drink is delicious. Sweet and tart and cold. I chug down a full glass, which earns me another scolding.

"Slow down before you give yourself a stomachache."

I smile and hold out my glass for a refill. Then I rip off the Band-Aid. "I quit the motel."

Malice pours from the pitcher and sits down opposite me with her own glass, already wet with condensation. "Your daddy's motel?"

I nod, holding my breath as I wait for her response. She's always supported me, but this may be a bridge too far, even for her.

Malice sighs. "I figured one of these days they were going to push you over the edge. I told Tallulah as much. Canceling the trip was one thing." She shakes her head. "But making you work for Graham all summer? When you need to be focusing on your pictures? I knew that wouldn't fly."

I nearly dump my lemonade. "You knew? About Graham? And didn't tell me?"

She lifts one shoulder. "She's my daughter. And they need the money. They're between a rock and a hard place, you ask me. Which they didn't." She gives me a pointed look. "But don't you go feeling guilty about it. I don't know that free labor is the answer to their problems."

"I do feel a little guilty," I admit. "But we had a big fight and Daddy locked me out of my darkroom and it just felt like the last straw, you know? Like if I was willing to put up with that, I might as well roll over and give up. Let him control every decision I make."

"You're much too smart for that," she says, and I wonder where her confidence in me comes from. Because even now, I'm not sure I made the right decision. What would that certainty feel like, knowing you've done the right thing? I've never had it.

"So what are you going to do instead? Focus on your pictures?" She pronounces it like "pitchers."

I hesitate, moving the ice pack around to my chest, which is sunburnt as well. "Actually, I got another job. At Atwater Lodge."

A long moment of silence passes before Malice bursts into peals of laughter. "Oh, honey. You did not!" She slaps herself on the thigh. "Your momma must be fit to be tied!"

"She's not happy." This might be the understatement of my life.

"Oh, lord." Malice snorts and wipes a tear from her cheek. "Thank you. I needed a laugh like that."

"What's Momma's problem with Atwater, anyway? I mean, besides that they're our competitor. Someone told me she and Kezia actually used to be friends."

Malice's gaze sharpens. "You've been talking to Peggy

Vanover," she says, setting down her cup. "Busybody if ever I met one. But the woman knows her history."

"So it's true?"

Malice braces herself against the couch with both arms, wincing as she stands and moves slowly to the bookshelves in the corner. She pulls one out and hands it to me: the *Corbin High Yearbook, 1998.*

"Kezia McCreary." Her voice has a dreamy quality. "She and your momma were inseparable, once upon a time." She leans over the back of my chair and pulls her sweater close around her, though it's easily pushing eighty degrees in here. "Course that was a long time ago. Things change."

I flip open the cover. The pages are yellowed, jumbled with old, grainy photos, and loopy signatures in colored ink stain the pages. Malice leans over to tap a photo of Momma and Kezia, Momma with her hair in pigtails and Kezia's curls a wild, untamed mass. They're both dressed in red and white, hound dog faces painted on their cheeks. They were so young. So happy. I don't know if I've ever seen Momma grin like that.

"What happened?" I ask.

"The curse is what happened," Malice says.

I choke on my lemonade, the citrus burning my throat and nostrils. Why does everything keep coming back to that stupid curse?

"They got into a big fight," she continues. "The summer before senior year. Tallulah said Kezia owed her an apology. And Kezia wouldn't budge. Both of 'em stubborn as tree stumps."

How is it I've never heard this story? I touch the smiling

photo. As if I can absorb the magic of their happiness through my fingertips. "You're saying they fought about the curse?"

She leans forward and lowers her voice. "They fought about the ghost bride."

"But Momma doesn't believe in the bride."

"Of course she does. My daughter is many things, but she's not a fool. Scared, yes. Stupid? No."

So did Momma lie to me? Because that's two people now who have contradicted her.

There's no dead bride wandering the woods, hell-bent on revenge.

Wasn't that what Momma said?

"Okay, you say she's scared. Kezia called her obsessed. But I'm sorry. None of that sounds like Momma."

"People change, Rena Faye."

Do they, though? To me, Momma has always been, well, Momma. And she's never believed in the ghost bride. Unless . . . "How has she changed? Why?"

"Life, I s'pose. Changes all of us."

"But how do you make sure it doesn't change you wrong?" I struggle for the words. "That you don't let it make you angry and bitter?" I swallow. "Like the bride?"

"That's the question, isn't it? Faith, I suppose. Or luck. Or maybe it's not up to us at all." Her gaze narrows on me, suddenly clear and focused. "Why are you so curious about the bride all of a sudden?"

This is my opening. If I'm being totally honest with myself, it's the real reason I came here today. Because I need to hear what Malice thinks about my encounter.

"I saw her," I say. "I saw the ghost bride."

Malice sinks down onto the coffee table, almost falling off the edge, and I jump up to help her.

"You saw her," she breathes. "I knew it. I knew you were the one. All these years, all my research. And I never once saw her. What was she like?"

"She was just like you'd imagine from the story. Bridal gown. Long hair. Dripping wet. And furious."

"Furious? How do you know that?" she asks sharply. "Did she speak to you?"

"No-o." I draw out the word. It's not a lie, exactly.

But Malice knows me too well. "What aren't you telling me?"

I've never told anyone this before. If I can trust anyone, though, it's Malice. "Daisy and I used to leave these notes for her," I say. "It's a silly game we used to play. Just, like, wishes we'd write down. And we used to pretend she'd grant them."

Malice narrows her eyes; her mouth moves but no sound comes out. She doesn't interrupt, so I keep going, the words coming faster. "And they were all still there, all our old notes. Except, something else was written on them. A . . . threat. Kind of."

"What kind of threat? Tell me exactly what happened."

"I was there alone. Reading the notes. And suddenly, it got cold. There was this big gust of wind, and there she was. Holding out her hand." I do the same, although now mine is trembling. "And her mouth was open, like she was going to speak. Or maybe scream. She wrote a word in the dirt. *Roots.*" I pull in a ragged breath. "And then she was gone. Vanished." I snap my fingers. "Just like that."

Malice finally blinks. "Well now. That's a story."

I seize on this explanation. "It must be, right? Just a story? My subconscious lizard brain dredging up the story from my childhood? Because I've heard it so many times?"

"Nothing is ever 'just a story,' Rena Faye," she says. "It's always a vessel of something deeper—a shared knowledge. A search for meaning. Oral tradition goes back further than any other kind of history. That's why it's so important to share. We all have stories to tell. It's how we make sense of the world, how we get to the heart of our own truth."

"How is this my truth if I don't even believe in her?"

"Don't." Malice holds up a hand and shuts her eyes. "Don't say that." She begins to rock back and forth. "Our family has been tasked with carrying on her story. Curse or no, we must take that responsibility seriously." Her eyes snap open. "The note. What did it say?"

As I tell her, her face goes slack.

"It's starting already. The curse," she whispers. "I know it as well as I know the back of my hand." She holds up her fingers. "Your phone. Your daddy's truck. Don't you see? It's a pattern." She grabs my wrist. "Did you anger her?"

"No!" My hand shakes and lemonade splashes the tabletop. I set it down so I can gently pull Malice's fingers free. "No," I say again, softer this time. "It's just my bad luck. You said the curse happens to all of the women in our family, but you seem fine. And Momma's not cursed."

She shakes her head slowly. "It was my sister. Helen. She drowned, in that very river. When she was around your age."

I remember hearing this story when I was younger. Once. It wasn't something Malice ever liked to talk about, and I feel like a jerk for bringing it up now.

"I'm sorry," I whisper. "We don't have to—"

"After that," Malice says, her voice trembling, "I knew it was up to me to save the rest of us. And I tried to find the bride, I did. Since I couldn't, I did the next best thing—I made sure I carried on her story. Faithfully. If I couldn't help her, at least I could make sure she wasn't forgotten. For the next generation. And for Helen."

"I still don't understand. Momma was the next generation. But she refused, and nothing bad happened to her. So what if I refuse, too? What if I just say to hell with it?"

But Malice shakes her head. "It doesn't work like that. The curse will find a way. It destroys people. Your momma, she got scared. After the curse took Kezia from her."

"You said they had a fight."

"That's what she does. Don't you see? She takes what you value most. For your momma, it was Kezia. For me, it was Helen."

As creepy and tragic as *that* sounds, this is all just fantasy. I force myself to smile and pat Malice's hand. "I know how much you must miss Helen, but I don't think that's what's happening to me," I say gently. "Do I wish I had a phone and some wheels? Yes. But I can live without them."

Malice holds up a finger. "Perhaps. But what do those things represent?" Her gaze holds mine as I swallow around a sudden lump in my throat.

"Freedom."

"You see? You can refuse, but you can't avoid it. The curse is there, whether you believe or not. And you've already made contact. There's no going back now."

When the front door swings open, we both jump. I drop my glass and it shatters, while Malice knocks the pitcher over, lemonade spreading in a sticky puddle across the table and onto the floor.

"What kind of mess are you two making?" Daisy asks, surveying the damage with hands on hips.

"You startled us." I step carefully around the broken glass. "Stay," I tell Malice. "I'll clean it up. I don't want you to cut yourself."

Daisy wiggles her fingers. "Hey, Malice. How you doing?"

"I've been better," Malice says, sounding weary.

I head to the kitchen for a bucket of soapy water, and when I return, Daisy is kneeling on Malice's other side, away from the spill.

". . . and then the truck breaks down? It's not a coincidence. It's the curse!" Malice says, gripping Daisy's hand.

Daisy squeezes back. "No worries. We're going to take care of it." She winks at me and I nearly drop the bucket.

"What do you mean, 'take care of it'?"

"What I told you yesterday. We're going to lift the curse."

CHAPTER 15

Once we've cleaned up the mess and said our goodbyes to Malice, I don't waste a minute.

"What did you mean just now, we're going to lift the curse?"

Daisy slips on her oversized sunglasses and starts the Jeep. "Exactly what I said. We're going back there. To the clearing. We're going to A, get evidence, and B, tell that scary bitch to stop messing with you!"

My stomach sinks. "She's not messing with me," I say. "But if she were, wouldn't going there be dangerous? Like, life-threatening, maybe? I'm not saying I believe any of this curse stuff," I add quickly. "But if she can break my phone *and* my truck without even being present, think of what she could do in person."

"I'm not leaving there without a photo. So unless she kills us . . ." Daisy trails off and shrugs. "Think of it like this. Either way, we'll be famous."

She slows the Jeep as we approach the truck, stopping in the middle of the road and pressing the window down as Uncle Ford wanders over to us.

"Hey, Daddy. Uncle Harlan," she calls.

I lean forward to look at my daddy, who is leaning against the side of the truck, arms crossed. He glares back at me but doesn't say anything. Thank goodness Momma sent Daisy to pick me up. I can feel the heat of his anger from here. In a car together, it would've scorched me.

Daisy drops my keys into Uncle Ford's hand and he ducks his head into the window.

"Hey, Rena Faye. You all right?"

"Hi, Uncle Ford. I'm good. A little sunburnt is all. Malice took care of me." I nod at the truck. "Sorry you had to come out. I don't know what happened. It just quit on me."

"Happens," he says, although it never has before. "Where're you girls off to?"

"We're stopping at Rena Faye's so she can change. Then we're going ghost hunting," Daisy says.

I close my eyes and mentally slap her, but Uncle Ford seems unfazed. "Ghost hunting, huh? Have fun." He slaps the side of the Jeep and backs away as Daisy pulls out.

"Why on earth would you tell him that?"

"Why not?"

I'm still struggling for an answer as she pulls into the motel parking lot and slams on the brakes. "What the hell is he doing here?" Daisy asks.

Chance's truck is parked in front of the lobby.

"Um," I say, remembering that we haven't talked about my getting back together with Chance.

I can't see her eyes behind her shades, but I can feel her glare.

"Hey, you're the one who told me not to drag the fight out," I say.

"Yeah, that was before I realized he turned into a dick while I was gone. Besides, I kind of like the idea of us both being single this summer. You know, sister cousins. Wild and free."

"We're still sister cousins," I tell her. "How about I be wild and you be free?"

She sniffs. "As if you could pull off wild alone."

I shove her in the shoulder and get out, holding a hand above my eyes to try to block the sun. Chance waves at me from the lobby window and I lift my hand half-heartedly. He comes bounding out the door, then slows, maybe still feeling the residual awkwardness of our recent big fight.

"Hey." He waves again and stuffs his hands in his jeans pockets.

I lean over and kiss him on the cheek, which makes him blush and Daisy gag.

"Can we move this little reunion along?" she asks. "Rena Faye, go change. And grab whatever you need—camera, lightsaber. Whatever you think will help."

"Lightsaber?" I echo, at the same time Chance asks, "What's going on?"

"I'll fill you in while she's getting ready," Daisy says, waving us both into the Jeep. She drives us up the hill and I jump out and run inside, stopping at the darkroom to check the door. Still locked.

But when I go upstairs, I find my camera lying in the middle of my bed.

I can't imagine Daddy relenting, so Momma must have put it there. As some kind of apology?

But trying to puzzle Momma out could take days, and I don't

have the time. I change out of my sweat-stained clothes and pin up my hair. The jumper I wore the other night is still in the hamper and I dig through the pockets, then shove the bride's note into my jeans.

Daisy and Chance are waiting outside, leaning against the Jeep. She straightens as I come around the side of the house.

"I don't understand why you would go back there by yourself," Chance says by way of greeting.

Daisy peers at him over the top of her sunglasses. "*That's* what you don't understand?"

Because you were being a jerk and you dropped my hair clip when you took off my veil, I think, but instead I say, "I wanted to make sure we hadn't left any trash behind. We left kind of quickly."

"Who cares why she went back?" Daisy asks impatiently. "The important thing is the spot is haunted. And we can be the first to record the encounter! Gather some EVPs and whatnot."

"We're not ghost hunters," I say. "The truth is, there's a family story about her, okay? Supposedly, she's put a curse on me. Or something."

"Jee-zus, Rena Faye!" Daisy shoves away from the car and grabs my arm. "Just get in the freakin' car, please. If you insist on telling him everything, at least do it out of earshot of your guests." She jerks a thumb at Chance. "You, too, Skeptic Sue."

Chance shrugs and gets into the back seat while we take the front, scooting forward so his head is in between ours. Daisy blasts the AC, turning the radio down a notch when Lady Gaga's voice screams out of the speakers.

"So what's the curse?" Chance asks, raising his voice over the music.

Daisy and I exchange a look.

"What? Did she threaten to kill you? Steal your firstborn if you can't guess her name? What is it?"

I'm mildly impressed he knows the plot to "Rumpelstiltskin," but Daisy isn't. "No, dumbass. She wrote a note."

He just stares. "A note?"

I catch his eye in the rearview mirror, and he quickly hides his smirk.

"It was a scary note," I say, though I don't know why I'm defending her. I'm with Chance on this one. Right?

"And what did this mysterious note say?"

I hand him the scrap of paper.

He reads, "'Please let Wade Dawson invite me to the dance.'"

"Flip it over!" Daisy yells.

I raise an eyebrow. "Wade Dawson? I always thought that was one-sided."

"Shut up and focus," she snaps.

"The back is blank," Chance says.

"What? No." I grab it back from him and turn it over, and over again. Willing the words to appear. But they don't. "It was here, I swear. And not just here. At the clearing, too."

I can feel their doubt as if it's a physical presence in the car. "She wrote it. In the dirt." I hold the paper with trembling hands. This is the proof I wanted, isn't it? Proof that I imagined it—out of stress or guilt or whatever I was feeling that day, from my fight with Daddy and my jumping ship to Atwater.

It was all my imagination.

I should be relieved. I don't even believe in ghosts or curses. I believe in things that are real. Things I can see.

Except I did see her. Even now, I can't let go of her image. Her overwhelming pain and grief. Her palpable, wordless anger as she reached for me, tracing that one word in the dirt.

ROOTS.

"You obviously grabbed the wrong paper," Daisy says. She meets Chance's gaze in the mirror and makes her voice go low. "It said 'Betrayal has legs. Loyalty has roots.' Ominous, no?"

"No," Chance says, while I say, "Yes."

"Ominous how? It's a meaningless bunch of words."

I pinch my lips together and turn my face to the window. I don't have an answer he'll accept. A bunch of words, yes. Made up, maybe. But not meaningless. Whether they came from a dead girl or my own subconscious, they're important. I'm just not sure how.

"Oh, screw this," Daisy says, throwing the car into reverse. "Let's go see for ourselves."

Chance scoots back and scrambles for his seat belt while I do the same.

"Wait," I say.

"Man up, Whitaker. This time, you'll have backup," Daisy says. "Corroboration."

"I don't need anything corroborated, thank you very much. I'm fine with not knowing what I saw. As long as I don't have to see it again."

Daisy shoots me her "no bullshit" look.

"What you saw was clearly an illusion," Chance says. "Or a hallucination, maybe. Were you drinking?"

I half turn in my seat. "Was I drinking? At four in the afternoon? No, I wasn't."

"But you were hungover. Knox brought beer," he reminds us. "And you had quite a bit of champagne before we got there."

Sure I was drinking the night before. I'd also barely slept and I was almost certainly dehydrated. These are all excuses I've made myself. But there's something about him insinuating that I've imagined it—in that patronizing tone—that just pisses me off.

"Who are you, my father?" Daisy snaps. "None of us had enough to be that hungover, certainly not by midafternoon the next day."

"All I'm saying is there must be a logical explanation. I'm sure Rena Faye agrees with me."

The only thing I'm sure of right now is that I don't want Chance speaking for me.

"I get it," he continues. "You guys liked to play these little games in the woods. And sure, the ghost story is always fun. But come on. We're all practically adults now. You've got to let some of this childish stuff go."

Daisy swerves the car suddenly, and Chance is jerked backward as his seat belt tightens.

"Sorry. Skunk," she calls out cheerfully through gritted teeth.

Part of me knows he's right. He's just trying to look out for me. Even if he's being a total jerk.

But there's another part, buried deep inside—a part that says to trust myself, trust my eyes. After all, I did see . . . something. And that part of me desperately wants to believe.

I think of what Arden said—his wistful hope that our loved ones are still with us. Is it really such an outrageous thought? That grief or love or a need for closure might somehow bind a spirit to someone on earth in a way we can't explain?

Malice doesn't seem to think so. Daisy either. And they are my constants, my family, my past.

But Chance does. And he has always been my voice of reason, my heart, my future.

As I look back and forth between them, my chest goes tight. Like I'm bound into a sweater that no longer fits, like I'm tied up and tied to this place and tied to this impossibility where everything and nothing is true. And choosing what I believe may unravel something I won't be able to knit back together.

Daisy parks in the usual spot. I stay in the car as they both climb out, watching through the windshield as my cousin points her phone toward the break in the tree line and Chance nods at whatever she says.

I don't want to go back. For all my insistence on the ghost being a figment of my imagination, what if she's not? The terror of that day is still fresh, as if it lives in the air, and each breath brings it back.

Suppose the unimaginable is true: ghosts are real, and I've been cursed. If Malice is right, and our messing around is what called the ghost bride forth in the first place, what will she do to me this time, when I come back with reinforcements? The same thing she did to Helen?

Daisy waves me over, her gesture overly exaggerated. Chance stands beside her, staring at the sky and looking bored.

I shake my head firmly. "No," I say out loud, though they can't hear me with the doors shut. But even if there isn't a murderous, vengeful ghost out there just waiting to attack, am I really going to let them go without me? While I sit here in the car? Alone?

I open the door.

"This is a terrible idea," I say. The full heat of the day smacks me in the face, and I swat away the sudden swarm of mosquitos and gnats. "I never should have told you about any of it."

Daisy snorts. "Like you've ever been able to keep your mouth shut. I'm going to record everything," she continues, holding her phone above her head as she heads into the woods.

Chance falls into step beside me.

"That way," Daisy continues, "hopefully we'll either have audio or visual evidence. Although it would be helpful to have a second recording." She looks at me hopefully, and I hold up my empty hands, working hard to keep them from shaking.

"No phone, remember?"

She untangles my camera strap from her shoulder and hands it to me. "You're in charge of still photography, then. Shoot everything. You never know what might be lurking in the background."

Chance looks like he is having serious second thoughts about coming with us. As Daisy marches ahead, he puts a hand on my arm. "You don't have to do this, you know."

"I know I don't."

But he's wrong. I *do* have to know, one way or the other. Either she's real and I'm cursed. Or she's not and I'm nuts.

Why isn't there a third option?

"I know you're scared," he says. "But there's nothing to be frightened of. I'm here."

I shake off his hand, then make a show of swatting at a bug. I know he's trying to comfort me, but it's irritating. Like everyone else in my life, he keeps urging me to grow up, but doesn't actually have any confidence in my ability to do anything without him.

But if he's right and there's nothing to be scared of, his presence makes no difference. And if he's wrong, he'll be just as dead as I am.

"I'm not scared," I lie, aiming my camera and taking a photo of his face. "We should catch up. Don't want to miss anything."

I force a smile and pick up my pace.

The last time I was here, I was running for my life, and it takes everything I have not to turn around and do it again. I stare straight ahead as I point the camera and snap the air around me, not brave enough to look beyond our path.

What's that shadow behind the tree? *Click.*

Something's moving behind that rock. *Click.*

There's no breeze, so any movement is suspect, and I take photos as if my life depends on it. Daisy can't fault me for this, at least. If we end up with no evidence, it won't be for lack of trying.

We reach the clearing without incident, Daisy first. She stands motionless as she holds out her phone and pans across the ruins. They look the same. Everything looks the same. I search for a sign, some evidence that everything I said happened actually happened. But there's nothing. No disturbance. No discarded papers.

No ghost.

Did I really imagine the whole thing?

"Can you breathe any quieter?" Daisy whispers. "It's interfering with the audio."

Chance ignores us as he picks his way carefully over the broken rocks to the wall, where there are still a few rolled-up papers stuck into the cracks. Apparently, we left more wishes than I remember.

Some of those are going to be embarrassing if he reads them.

He raises his head and grins at me. Too late.

We're almost there. A few more minutes, and we'll be done. No evidence. No ghost. Unless . . .

"Where are you?" Daisy calls into the trees, her voice almost a song. She is done being patient. "Come out, come out, whoever you are."

My heart pounds—too fast—and the skin on my face is tight and hot. My temples and fingers pulse and swell like overinflated balloons about to pop. I stumble and catch myself on a low-hanging branch.

"Show yourself!" Daisy turns, arms held wide, pointing the camera in all directions.

"Stop it!" I hiss, and take a tentative step forward. "You don't know what—"

A branch cracks, the sound like a shotgun in the silence of the forest.

We stand like that for what feels like hours—Daisy, with her hands outstretched, inviting god knows what. Chance, frozen against the wall. And me, a sweating, blubbering mess, cowering behind the tree. I close my eyes and pray—nonsensical phrases from my childhood. *The Lord is my shepherd.* And *Now I lay me down to sleep.* Why is it I only remember the first line of any prayer? Probably because I started daydreaming the minute the preacher started talking.

Sweat trickles down my back and stings my eyes, but I still don't move.

The forest is silent, too, as if holding its breath. No birds in the trees, no buzzing of insects. Maybe they were all chased off by Daisy.

Or something else.

"This is ridiculous," Chance finally says, breaking the spell. "This was all a colossal waste of time. Can we go?"

Daisy turns the recording on him, and he holds his hand over the screen as he shoves it away. "Get that thing out of my face."

His dismissal stings. "I didn't make it up," I say. "I'm not a liar. Something happened to me here."

He won't meet my gaze. "Come on, Rena Faye. It's obvious, isn't it? There's nothing here. No curse." He waves a scrap of paper. "No ghost."

I swallow around the lump in my throat as I push away from the tree and head down the path. "Fine. You're right. Let's go."

"Rena Faye." Daisy's voice is hoarse.

I turn back. She's pointing at the tree with a shaky hand, at the spot where I was just standing.

At the letters carved deep into the tree, as if someone dug in a knife, over and over and over again.

Two letters.

One word.

GO.

CHAPTER 16

And we do.

Over pizza back at the motel, the three of us are seated around one of the breakfast tables. And for the tenth time, Daisy asks, "Did you get it? Did you get a shot?"

"Yes." I pick at the crust. "I think so." I tried, anyway, before panic overtook me and I ran. Daisy and Chance were right on my heels.

Daisy can barely keep her mouth shut, but Chance has been unusually quiet since the drive back. Quiet, but not still. He gets up and paces, then sits down for a few seconds, until he's back up to feed a dollar into the vending machine. When the Coke drops down, he offers it to me.

"Thanks." I take it but don't open it.

"I'm just going to say it." He slides into the chair in front of me and folds his hands on the table. "Nothing actually happened out there. You know that, right?" His gaze darts from me to Daisy. "We didn't see anything supernatural."

"We didn't see anything supernatural *yet*," she corrects him. She tears off a bite of pizza and chews with her mouth open. "We'll know more once Rena Faye develops the film and I have a chance to go over the video."

"That carving could have been there for months. Years, even."

Daisy shakes her head. "Uh-uh. We've spent tons of time there. We would've noticed."

She could be right, but I'm just not sure. "It was on the back side of that tree. We wouldn't even have seen it if I hadn't . . ." I can't bring myself to finish the thought: *been cowering behind it.* "Maybe Chance is right and it's just a coincidence."

"Or. Maybe the ghost bride is trying to send us a message," Daisy says.

"So what's the message?" Chance asks.

"'Go,'" says Daisy. The look she gives him is so disgusted, I almost laugh out loud. "Get out. Leave me alone."

"But you won't do that," he says.

"Of course not."

He nods and bumps his fists softly against the table a couple times before looking up at me. "I'm sorry, but I have to ask. Are you messing with me?"

"What do you mean, messing with you?" The realization dawns slowly. "You think I carved that word myself? That I made this whole thing up, for what—attention? And then dragged you out into the woods to be my witness?"

"That's not what I—

"No." I don't let him finish. I shoot Daisy a look and she knows this is between me and Chance.

She jumps up, grabs her keys and a final slice of pizza, and is out the door.

Chance reaches for my hands, but I move them to my lap.

"Come on, Rena Faye. You have to understand why I'd ask."

"Really? 'Cause it seems like the only reason you'd ask is if you think I'm a conniving bitch."

He winces at the profanity. "Look. We both know Daisy's not my biggest fan. And you've been . . . different this summer. Since she's been back."

"No. I've been different since my summer went to shit," I correct him. "I've been different since my trip got canceled and you and my daddy started talking behind my back."

"This again? I thought we agreed to put that behind us."

Did we? Or was that another decision he made without me?

"I don't want to fight," he says. "Not about something this dumb. I didn't mean to accuse you of anything. Whatever happened to you in the woods, as scary as it was, it was clearly a one-time thing. There's nothing there now, right? And even if we assume some ghostly bride left us that message, we did what she asked." He opens his hands on the table, palms up. "We left. So it's over. Agreed?"

I shake my head, then nod. I don't want to fight, either. And he did apologize. Sort of.

Just because he doesn't believe in ghosts doesn't mean he doesn't believe in me.

On Tuesdays, Daisy doesn't work until noon. Chance is off lead-ing some trail ride, and Daddy's not speaking to me or Momma now, because of the truck incident. Which means Momma isn't speaking to me either.

So I have no choice but to call Arden for a ride.

"Thanks for picking me up," I say as I climb into his gleaming white SUV.

Arden's eyes are hidden by his sunglasses, but his dimples aren't. "No problem. Glad I could help." He glances at the pickup as we turn out of the lot, which Daddy and Uncle Ford towed back here yesterday. "I suppose your parents don't want you leaving that parked by us all day."

"Actually, I broke it," I tell him. "It overheated yesterday and cracked something or other. Which I'm still not sure how I was supposed to know or prevent. But at any rate, my daddy is pissed off and I'm out of wheels for the rest of the summer."

"I hope that doesn't mean you'll be quitting."

What does he mean by "hope"? I have a boyfriend. Should I tell him? It's not like he's asked. It would be stupid to bring Chance up now, out of the blue. Even stupider that I haven't mentioned it before. He's probably just being nice and making small talk. Who wants to end up short-staffed?

"He'll get over it," Arden says, and I jerk my head toward him. "Your daddy, I mean. In the meantime, I don't mind playing chauffeur."

"Thanks. I can give you gas money."

"*Pfft.* It's like six miles. I'm glad we get to spend some time together. It'll give us a chance to talk photography. I want to hear all about your darkroom."

Why the question makes me nervous, I have no idea. "Um,

sure. It's not super fancy or anything. It used to be a closet, I think. My momma set it up when they first got married. And now I use it. Or I did, anyway."

"Not anymore?"

I don't want to bore him with all of my domestic drama. "I'm super busy right now," I say. "Plus, I've been kinda bummed about this summer program I applied for. I didn't get in."

"You mean the Governor's School?" he asks. I'm so surprised I bang my knee on the dashboard as I turn.

"You've heard of it?"

He shrugs one shoulder. "I went last summer, actually. It wasn't that big of a deal. And it's very competitive, so don't feel bad."

"No big deal," I echo. "But you made it."

He blushes. "Yeah. It was my second time applying, but I finally made it. Honestly, I think it might be the one thing my dad was genuinely proud of me for."

The sight of his pink cheeks is like a Band-Aid over my raw feelings and I'm immediately ashamed of my jealousy. It's not like his application beat out mine or something. They liked his art, which is great. Awesome. He's awesome. At art.

"I'm sorry about your dad." And I am genuinely sorry I haven't said so yet; I should have. As frustrated as I am with my own parents right now, I can't imagine losing one of them. "Were you close?" I ask.

"In some ways. We had a lot in common. But we didn't see much of each other, especially in the months before he died. He was busy with work, and I was away at school. I always thought after graduation, maybe . . . Once I came back here. Now it's too late."

I swallow around the lump in my throat and blink furiously.

"Sorry." He glances over at me. "Way too depressing, way too early."

"No, it's okay. I'm glad . . ." I start to echo his earlier words, but swallow the rest of my sentence. *Glad you could talk to me* sounds like I'm hinting at something. But I certainly don't want him to think I meant *glad your dad died.* "I'm here, I mean. If you ever need to talk," I finish awkwardly.

"Thanks. Same. I mean, if you ever want to talk art. Or photography." He slows for the turn into the lot. "I'd love to see your photos sometime."

"You probably don't," I say. "The scholarship committee called them surface-level and mediocre."

He winces. "Ouch. But, you know, any feedback from them is good. My first year, they didn't give me anything to work with. Just 'not good enough.' So you must have some talent. If they're encouraging you to go deeper."

I stare at him, open-mouthed. I hadn't thought about it as encouragement, because I hadn't been able to get past the sting of rejection.

"Sorry. I didn't mean to make light of it. I know it sucks."

"No, it's fine. I mean, it's not. But it will be. I'm not giving up," I say, the words taking on new meaning as I voice them. Because I have given up, at least a little. I've neglected my art lately, and while I have a whole bunch of excuses, the truth is I miss taking photos and being creative. I've been letting this rejection and my non–road-trip summer stop me.

But no more.

"I'm trying to build a portfolio," I tell Arden. "So I can apply to art school."

"Yeah?" He beams. "That's great! Let me know if you need another eye on anything," he says.

"I will. Thanks."

He pulls up behind the housekeeping cottage and I grab the door handle.

"You know, I was worried about coming back to Corbin, after being away so long."

"Worried about everyone being up in your business all the time?" I ask.

"That, yes. But it's kind of comforting, to know someone always has your back. My old school was hyper-competitive. Lots of backstabbing. Not so much back-having." His grimace melts into a smile. "So I'm glad I came back. And now I get to reconnect with my old friends. Like you."

I think about our moonbow gossip session, where Daisy and I made fun of his tears and nosebleeds. While I'm glad he considers me a friend, I haven't been much of one to him. Yet.

But I can do better. "I'm glad you came back, too," I say, and his smile is so genuine, it melts away some of my guilt.

CHAPTER 17

The work at Atwater is much the same as the motel, except on a bigger scale and with no daily checkouts. Instead, it's bed-making and toilet-cleaning and towel-folding and trying to ignore the voice in my head insisting I've made a terrible mistake.

Luckily, the voice is vague, and I've made many mistakes. It's hardly fair to focus on just one.

When we finish with the cabins, it's afternoon. Peggy informs me I have an hour before I'm due back at the shed to help with laundry.

"You look like hell," is what she actually says. "Your eyes are all puffy and bloodshot. I hope you're not having an allergic reaction to the cleaner. Go grab some lunch from the kitchen and get some fresh air."

"I'm out of cash," I say. "Can I run a tab?"

She hands me an envelope. "Here."

"I didn't mean . . . I don't want any charity. I'll just figure something out."

"Charity?" She snorts. "That ain't charity. It's your share of the tips from last week."

I thumb through the ten- and twenty-dollar bills. "This is my share?"

"We split it," she says, sounding defensive. "And you started on Sunday, so I had to give Jen and Sadie a bigger cut. Next week'll be more."

There is at least sixty dollars here. And next week will be more? On top of the paycheck I'm receiving? I do a quick mental calculation. At this rate, I'll be able to replace my phone within a few weeks. And after that, everything can be banked for college.

"Thank you!" I crush the envelope in my fist and fight off the urge to kiss her.

Peggy waves me away. "Go. Eat."

I use my newly earned tip money to buy a box lunch from the café window outside the pool, but instead of following my first instinct and heading for the falls, I take the hiking trail that veers down toward the river. It's creepily empty, but no wonder. The temperature has been inching closer to ninety all day, and now, with the sun directly overhead, the last thing any sane person wants to do is hike. I bet not even a ghost would be caught dead out here.

"Wait up." I flinch at the sound of another voice, but it's only Daisy. I need to get a grip.

She raises her lunch bag. "I thought we could eat together."

I can't think of a reason to say no, although I want to. Seeing her squashes some of my fortune-induced euphoria and brings back the awful memories I've been trying to push aside all day.

"My break's almost over," I say.

"No, it isn't. You get an hour. It's barely quarter after."

I don't even ask how she knows my schedule.

"Besides, we need to talk ghosts."

I groan. "That's the last thing we need to talk about."

"Just because yesterday was a bust—"

"A bust?" Did she forget the ominous warning?

"Don't look at me like that," she says. "I mean in terms of actually seeing her. Clearly, we've done something to provoke her. Otherwise how do you explain the notes and the tree?"

"I can't explain it. Any of it. Which is why we need to forget—"

"Which is why we can't give up yet," she says loudly, overriding me. "You know Malice. She wouldn't scare you for no reason. You saw her yesterday—she's afraid of something. She looked more haunted than you do."

I catch my apple before it rolls onto the ground. "I look haunted?"

She snorts. "Duh. Aren't you?"

I rub the apple on my shorts and press my thumb against a brownish bruise. "Haunted sounds so dramatic. Just because I *might* have seen a ghost"—saying the words out loud still chills me, but I try to hide my shiver—"one time, does not qualify as haunted."

Daisy takes a bite of her own apple and chews quietly for a moment. "It's an interesting question, though," she finally says. "Is haunted a state of being? Or a measure of degree?" When I don't answer, she continues, "Can you be a little bit haunted? Or is it an all-or-nothing situation?"

"I . . . I have no idea." I wave a fly away, then take a bite of my sandwich. All-or-nothing is a terrifying thought. As if once I admit I've seen her, she'll never go away. On the other hand, I can't *stop* seeing her. And at least Daisy has stopped using the word "cursed." For the time being.

"It's your experience," Daisy says. "You get to say."

"It's not like I'm an expert. It's just my word against everyone else. And I don't even know if I believe in her."

"And why is that?" She leans over the table, her blonde hair flopping forward. "Why can't you just trust yourself and what you saw?"

I poke a finger into the soggy bread. "Because I don't *know* what I saw."

"I notice you didn't tell Chance about the ghost," she says, tossing the apple core into her bag.

"What? Of course I told him. You were there."

"Only after I did," she shoots back. "He didn't know anything about it until he showed up at the motel yesterday."

I look away from her and into the trees.

"Was it because you were afraid he wouldn't believe you? Make fun of you, or call you crazy?"

"I don't know," I say softly.

"You need to stop bending over backward to make yourself worthy of other people. Make them worry about whether or not they deserve *you* for a change."

I shove aside the rest of my lunch, my appetite gone. "I don't want to talk about Chance," I say.

"Good. Me neither." She grabs my bag of chips and rips it open with her teeth. "Look at it this way. People believe in all kinds of things that can never be scientifically proven. Love. God. Life after death. Do you think those people are crazy?"

"Love, God, ghosts?" I say. "No, no, and . . . I don't know." A few days ago, number three would have been a solid yes. Believing in ghosts is not something sane people admit to. And yet . . .

Daisy points at me. "No! But did you know that even more people believe in ghosts than in a higher being?" she asks. "I looked it up."

"And your point is?"

"My point is you say you only believe in things you can see or feel. But clearly, there are exceptions." She takes a chip from the bag. "I'm just trying to establish where your boundaries lie."

"So you can push them?"

She grins and spreads her arms wide. "Why am I here, if not to help open the doorway to possibilities?"

"I prefer some doors stay firmly shut, thank you very much."

"Too late." Her singsong reply sends tiny fingers of unease trailing along my neck.

"Cut it out," I say, standing and shoving trash into my lunch bag. "We have not opened some portal to the underworld. I refuse to accept that."

Daisy snatches the chips out of reach. "Maybe, maybe not. Could be what you saw was just some kind of radio frequency, or interdimensional time rip. Or maybe your ghost is a soul in purgatory. Unfinished business to attend to before she can ascend to wherever. That's what we need to figure out."

Unfinished business. It's similar to what Arden said the other day.

I glance up and down the empty path. "So. Speaking of un-finished business." I try to make my voice light. "Did you have a chance to look at your video?"

"Yep," she sighs. "There's nothing there."

Nothing there. It's so heavy, so final. But of course there's nothing there.

You can't film something that isn't real.

I should be relieved. Instead, I'm strangely disappointed.

"We're going to need a new tactic. Done?" Daisy asks. Barely pausing between topics, she takes the trash out of my hands and stuffs it into her brown bag. "Let's keep going. Down to the beach."

Until she mentions it, I hadn't realized where this trail ended. The swimming beach is located downriver from the falls, tucked in between the cliffside and the woods at the foot of the Leap. It used to be open to the public, and Daisy and I would go every summer, either with my parents or hers, until it flooded badly one year and never reopened. That was also the year a high school girl drowned in the river.

I push aside that dark memory and follow Daisy down the set of wide wooden steps that leads to the sand. They're broken in some places, and the beach—or what used to be the beach—is covered in debris. Decaying trees and fish carcasses, along with lit-ter washed up on shore. As I duck under the branch of a low tree, I'm surprised to see a makeshift wooden shed leaning against the rock wall that forms the park above.

The last few steps are missing, so we have to jump onto the sand below. I blink and try to orient myself. I haven't been down here in years, but something about it is familiar. I look up at the cliff beside me to my left, then off to the thick forest beyond the beach to my right. Something more recent is niggling in the back of my brain. But what?

Finally, I shake it off and head toward the shack. Knox is leaning against the side, rolling a cigarette between his fingers.

"Where'd you come from?" I ask.

"This is where we keep our rafting gear. Hey, Daisy," he adds, raising a hand. "You ladies want a ride?" He gestures at himself, and I'm not exactly clear what he's offering. "On the house."

"No thanks. My break's almost over." I give my cousin a side-eye. At least now I know why she wanted to stroll on the hottest day of the summer so far.

"We were just eating lunch and telling ghost stories," Daisy says.

"Oh, yeah? Know any good ones?"

"I know the best one," Daisy says. "But I should let Rena Faye tell it. She's the one who had the actual sighting."

Shit, no. I turn my back to Knox and slice my hand across my neck. I never should have told Daisy about the ghost. The last thing I need is for her to mention any of this in front of Knox. He'll tell Graham, Graham will tell Daddy, and then god only knows what'll happen next. Baptism? Exorcism? Whatever it is, it won't be good.

"A ghost sighting?" Knox asks.

I widen my eyes in warning at Daisy and pinch my lips together before turning back to him. "Nothing. She's teasing, obviously."

But Daisy says, "Yep. Rena Faye saw the ghost bride. And I'm jealous."

"Really?" But Knox is more interested in Daisy's pouty lips than our ghost story.

I laugh nervously, and it comes out sounding like a hyena. "That's ridiculous. Who would be jealous of a ghost?"

"I'm jealous because I want to see her, too. We tried yesterday, but no dice."

"Do you ever stop talking?" I ask.

"I bet I know a way to make you stop," Knox says, lighting his cigarette.

"Ewww." I mime gagging.

He grins so wide I think his face might crack. "Easy there, sweetheart. What do they say about girls who protest too much?"

"That they're better off than the girls who never learn to speak up?" I say.

Daisy laughs and covers it with a cough.

"We should get back," I say, ignoring Knox's glare.

"You know," he calls as we're walking away, "if you want to see a ghost, I know a place."

"No thanks."

But Daisy isn't so quick to dismiss his offer. She turns back, one hand on her cocked hip. "What did you have in mind?"

My stomach clenches. I don't know what he's going to suggest, but somehow I know I won't like it.

"You want to see ghosts, you've got to go where the bodies are buried."

He's probably right. But I have no desire to spend the night in Hillcrest Cemetery.

CHAPTER 18

The rest of the week passes quickly. My parents and I have entered an uneasy truce where we aren't fighting, but we haven't made up, either. It's more like awkward small talk that seems to shrink the longer we go on. They don't ask about my job at Atwater, or Chance, or the mysterious other boy who picks me up every morning, and in return, I refrain from mentioning that they managed to find the money to add another maid to the payroll.

Instead of going home most afternoons, I pick up extra shifts in the laundry room, staying late every day after we finish with the cabins. Even with the addition of my tips, I still need all the extra zeroes on my paycheck I can get. Art school isn't cheap.

I pull my hair into a topknot, relishing the cool breeze on the back of my neck as I wait for Arden on the veranda. The temperature has dropped tonight with the sunset, and the chill in the air is as welcome as it is unusual.

"Ready?" he asks, strolling out the front door, tossing his keys and catching them. He's swapped his uniform for jeans and a light jacket.

"You changed." It's the first time I've seen him dressed in anything else, and my brain does a weird short circuit. He looks good in jeans—less like a hotel manager and more like a regular guy.

Does he have more in mind than driving me home?

Do I *want* him to have more in mind than driving me home?

But we're just friends. He's never been anything but polite to me. And I have a boyfriend. Even if I've never told Arden so. And even if things have felt off between Chance and me lately.

Arden looks down at his clothes. "Oh, crap. Were you waiting long?" He goes to slap himself in the forehead and hits himself in the face with his keys.

"Ow."

"Are you all right?" I ask, wincing and trying not to laugh at the same time.

He groans and holds his eye. "I'm fine. Just feeling like an idiot." He hands me the keys. "Why don't you drive? You know where we're going anyway."

I stare down at his moonbow key chain as he strolls to the side lot.

"You know where my house is," I say, hurrying after him.

He's picked me up and taken me home every day this week, and if I stop to think too long about what that means or why he's doing it, it would probably freak me out. So I don't. I've gotten pretty good at avoiding the things I don't want to think about. By the end of the summer, I'll have had enough practice that I might even be able to go back to working for my parents and pretending it's what I want.

Arden leans against the driver's-side door, and I stop in front of him and hold out the keys. "Would you rather—"

"No." He's holding his arm at an odd angle.

"Did you hurt your arm, too?" I ask.

"No," he says again, his cheeks pink. "I made you something." He reaches in and pulls out a piece of paper from inside his jacket.

It's a drawing. Of me. Or at least my profile. I'm staring off into the distance, my chin cupped in my hand, a dreamy look on my face. It's a gesture so familiar, I wonder how often he's been watching me. A camera hangs around my neck. And beyond, in the background, is the faint outline of the Eiffel Tower.

My hand trembles as I hold the paper. He's taken me out of Corbin—to Paris.

Suddenly, I have a hard time catching my breath.

"Do you not like it?"

"No," I say. "I love it." My voice is thick. "I think this is the nicest thing anyone's ever given me."

"Oh, that can't be true," he says, but I can tell I've made him happy.

"You're good," I say, finally tearing my gaze away from the drawing. "I'm not surprised they picked you for the Governor's School."

He looks away quickly, down at the asphalt. "Thanks. I learned a lot there, honestly. Enough to know that I wish I were better. But you're an easy subject."

I want to ask what that means, but I don't have the nerve. It

sounds like a compliment, but a loaded one I'm not ready to un-
pack. As it is, the sketch proves he really sees me. And not just the
Rena Faye who works for him. Somehow, he's managed to capture
how I view the world. The person I am in his eyes is the person I
want to be, and the idea that that might be possible sets off fireworks beneath my skin.

"Ready?" he asks. He opens the driver's-side door for me, and
as I slip past him, I notice his eyes. Sea green, and deep enough to
drown in.

I'm in so much trouble.

"So. It's finally Friday," he says, going around to the passenger
side. "I've been waiting for this."

"TGIF," I say, my voice uneven. Waiting for what? Where is
he going with this? Weekends don't usually hold the same excitement for those of us in the hospitality business—they just mean
longer hours. But he's looking at me like he's waiting for me to say
something.

When I don't, he says, "We're meeting Daisy? At the cemetery?"

What.

"Unless . . . did I get that wrong?" He pulls out his phone. "I
put it in my calendar when she told me."

I turn on the ignition and grip the steering wheel. Too shocked
to speak.

"It's fine," I say. "I just . . . forgot." I haven't forgotten. I didn't
know she invited him.

This will be the first time we've hung out, besides work or
driving to and from. The thought makes my stomach flutter in a
way that's not entirely unpleasant.

"Who else is coming?" I ask as I shift into gear and back out of the space.

I've been worried all week that Knox might invite my brother. Graham being there now would make this even more awkward. But Arden says, "I think it's just us, plus Daisy and Knox."

Us. Which makes it a foursome. Or what is sometimes referred to as a double date.

In spite of the coolness of the evening, I can feel myself sweating as I steer the car up the winding road toward Hillcrest Cemetery.

The gravel parking circle is more of a turnoff on the side of the highway, separated from the cemetery proper by a ring of stones. Beyond, the hill climbs at a faint incline, the headstones tilting and twisting like bodies in the dark. It's old but well tended—the grass is clipped short and many of the stones in the newer section bordering the pine forest to the west even have fresh flowers.

Daisy and Knox are already here, waiting for us beside Daisy's Jeep.

"Did you bring your camera?" Daisy asks, after Arden and I have parked the car and we all stand facing each other, couple to couple.

Only we're not a couple. Are they?

"Why would I bring my camera?" I ask. "I came right from work."

Arden reaches out to shake Knox's hand. "Hey, Knox. How're the boat rides going?"

"Smooth. Real smooth. Thanks, man."

"No, thank you. Great idea."

"The guests sure love it," Daisy says.

"Right. It's definitely lucrative, which makes my—Mrs. Dunlap happy," Arden says.

Knox juts his chin at me. "Single tonight? Where's Chance?"

My face goes hot and I'm grateful for the darkness. "Not coming," I say quietly. "I didn't . . . I didn't think he'd be interested. Plus, he's probably working."

A stilted silence follows what is clearly a lie. Arden finally breaks it by asking, "So. Why the cemetery?" He looks around expectantly. "Are we going to play Bloody Mary? Or try to speak to some spirits?"

Knox shrugs off his backpack. "Ask Rena Faye. I'm just here for the scenery." He leers at Daisy as he offers her a beer. "Anyone else?"

We all take one.

Daisy twists her cap and says, "Hillcrest is the closest cemetery to the falls. I checked."

We all pivot toward her voice as she moves back farther into the darkness, stepping carefully around the gravestones. "It's likely this is where they buried her."

"Where they buried who?" Arden asks.

"No one," I say, at the same time Daisy says, "The ghost bride."

"Ah. And why does it matter how close we are to the falls?"

Knox finishes his beer and swaps it out for another, watching us like we're a movie. "It was much harder to transport bodies back in the day," he finally says. "Before the roads went in."

I shiver.

Arden sets down his beer. "Here. Take my coat."

"Thanks. I didn't realize it was going to be so cool tonight." Then I turn to Daisy. "Can I speak to you for a second? In private?" Before she can object, I take her elbow and steer her behind a tall stone bearing the name Price.

"Why did you invite Arden?"

She lifts one shoulder. "I don't know. You guys have been hanging out, and he seems fun. And it would've been weird for it to be just you, me, and Knox. He'd think you were crashing our date or something."

"This is a date?"

She looks at me, deadpan. "In a cemetery?"

"Okay. Fine." Maybe I'm making a bigger deal than I need to. "But I'm with Chance."

"Jeez, it's not like you're married. Lighten up." Her phone buzzes. Her frown is bathed in blue light as she checks the screen. "Speak of the devil. Chance wants to know if I've seen you," she says, already tapping out a reply.

"What are you telling him?"

She pockets the phone. "Relax. I told him you had to work late and you'd see him tomorrow."

"Can we get this show on the road?" Knox yells so loudly I jump. I haven't been whispering, exactly, but this isn't the kind of place conducive to being obnoxious, either.

"Did you hear that?" Daisy asks, her hand on my arm. She's straining back toward the darkest corner, and my flesh puckers.

"Knox?" I ask. But my mouth is dry; I know that's not what she meant.

"No. It sounded like—"

"Before you go all creepy, I'd rather we didn't tell the boys about her. It."

"How else are they going to help us?"

"They know about the ghost bride. Everyone does. And I'll tell them about what I saw. But they don't need to know about the curse. Agreed?"

I force her to look at me, to promise, though she seems unconvinced. Or maybe she's just distracted. She's still got one ear cocked toward the graveyard. Listening.

Maybe for a soft whisper, so low it had to be the wind.

Not someone telling us to *GO*.

That can't be what we heard.

The four of us sit in a circle in the clearing between the old part of the cemetery and the new, on the sharp incline that delineates the two. And I tell them what happened to me in the clearing.

"So that's it?" Knox asks as soon as I'm done.

"Pretty much," I say.

But it's not. I haven't told them everything. I've left out the curse, and abbreviated most of the details, like what she looked like. And what I felt. I half expect Daisy to chime in to tell them about Malice, or the warning on the tree, but she seems distracted tonight, alternating between holding out her phone to record the night and turning away from us to face the darkness.

Then she stands up and wanders off. Knox trails behind her, leaving Arden and me alone. Together.

"Were you scared?" he asks.

I keep my eyes on my cousin and her guy until the darkness swallows them up. "I was at the time," I say, getting to my feet. "But the more I think about it, I'm not sure what I actually saw."

Something moves in the tree above us, and I instinctively duck.

"And how about now?" Arden asks, and I can hear the smile in his voice.

"Maybe I'm a little jumpy," I admit, "but cemeteries don't generally scare me. I think they're more sad than anything. All these people. All these lives. Over."

"I know what you mean," he says. "Like, did they accomplish everything they set out to do? Did they achieve their dreams?"

I lean down to pull some weeds at the foot of the grave we're standing over. "Unless their dream was to end up in the ground in Corbin, we'll never know," I say. "Each stone tells a story. But only the end of it. Look at Oren here. We know he was married." I gesture at the heart-shaped double stone. "And he outlived his wife. Which is kind of heartbreaking. But who knows? Maybe he found happiness with the rest of his family. Maybe he had a dozen grandchildren, who will all someday lie here with him."

Arden moves closer. "That's kind of lovely," he says.

Is he . . . leaning toward me? I step back, flustered, and trip over one of the gravestones. Arden reaches out to steady me.

I look down at his hand on my arm, and he moves it.

"Or maybe he died miserable and alone," I say. "And now he's stuck here. Trapped. He'll never leave Corbin." I wave a hand toward the other graves. "None of them will."

Arden looks around for a moment. "I don't think of it as stuck. I think of it more like giving them roots."

I turn to look at him so quickly, I wonder if he can hear my neck crack. "Roots? Why would you say that?" Why would he pick that particular word?

"Everyone needs a place they belong," he says. "Maybe not for them," he adds, gesturing at the gravestone. "But their families still need a place to go. To mourn." And then I see the pain in his eyes, and I feel like a stupid, heartless jerk. What the hell is wrong with me? Here I am, yammering on about dead people being stuck in the ground, and his dad is probably buried somewhere in this very cemetery.

"Arden, I'm sorry," I say. "I didn't mean . . ."

"Don't apologize," he says. "Though I have to admit, I liked your first story about Oren better." His soft voice breaks some of the tension between us.

Then he says, "I have to confess something," and my heart starts beating double-time.

Confess what? I somehow desperately want to know and also need him to never voice the words he's about to say out loud. I open my mouth, to tell him to keep whatever it is to himself, but he's faster.

"I saw her."

"What?" I ask loudly.

Somewhere in the darkness beyond us, Knox chuckles, low and sexy.

"I lied to you. That first day, on the balcony? When you asked about the ghost bride? I avoided your question, but I knew what you were talking about. Because I've seen her." He rubs a hand over his mouth. "I was afraid to tell you because I didn't want you to think I was some creepy nerd. 'I see dead people.'"

"I . . . don't know what to say."

"You don't have to say anything," he says. "I know it sounds crazy." He closes his eyes and shakes his head. "Sometimes I think maybe it was a dream. But then I remember how scared I was." He shudders.

"When was this?" I whisper. "Where?"

"I was about five or six?" he says, scrunching up his forehead. "I was with my mom. We'd been swimming at the beach all day. I remember it was the Fourth of July, because I wanted to do sparklers, and instead, my mom took me on this hike along the bottom of the cliff. To this place she used to go when she was younger. There was an old mill or something—"

I don't let him finish because I have to know. "What exactly did you see?"

"It was this girl, all wet and dripping, with her mouth open. Like she was screaming. But no sound came out."

"Stop," I whisper hoarsely, and I can barely get the word out. I'm paralyzed, stuck to the ground by fear. And something else.

Recognition.

Because what Arden saw is the same thing I saw.

All this time, I've been doubting myself. Refusing to let myself really believe.

"Guys, check this out! Over here!" Daisy's call snaps me out of my frozen state. My hand is outstretched, reaching for Arden's, and I snatch it back and shove it in my jacket pocket—*Arden's* jacket pocket—so none of them can see how badly I'm shaking.

I'm not crazy.

And I'm not alone.

The ghost bride is real.

"What is it?" Arden calls back, and I'm grateful because I don't trust my voice right now.

He uses his phone flashlight to guide us down the rows of gravestones, past a crumbling mausoleum and around a pair of stone angels to where Daisy stands near the top of the hill. She's found a fenced area, separated from the rest of the nearby graves by waist-high black iron spikes. But before I can get a decent look at what's inside, Arden turns off his phone.

Which is why I don't see the marble angel, teetering on its base behind me, until it's too late.

CHAPTER 19

"Watch out!" Daisy cries.

Arden shoves me out of the way, just in time, wrapping his arms around me and landing beside me with a soft *oof*.

The statue hits the ground right where I was standing.

We stare at each other for a second, nose to nose, until Daisy yells.

"Oh my god, Rena Faye!"

She holds her flashlight out, first illuminating me, before swinging it over to the marble angel. The three feet of solid marble fell from a base nearly as tall as I am. Had it hit me, I would have been seriously injured. Or worse.

"You could have been killed!" she says. "The curse doesn't seem so stupid now, does it?"

"What curse?" Arden asks, and we're so close I can feel his breath on my face.

I blush and roll away from him, taking the hand Knox extends to help me up.

"You okay?" he asks, training his phone light on me.

I brush myself off. "Yeah. I'm fine." But my heart is hammering and my head is pounding and my nose is filled with the smell of charred ash.

The ghost bride is real.

Does that mean the curse is real too?

"Is something burning?" I ask, and Knox frowns down at me.

"Maybe you should sit for a minute."

Daisy is still shrieking. "This thing must weigh a ton. And it just . . . falls over? Are you fucking kidding me? She's *trying* to kill you. It's gotta be the curse."

"It's not the curse," I say quickly. It can't be. I have enough to worry about. There cannot be a dead bride trying to kill me. "It could've happened to anyone. These things are old. And the ground is so uneven. Right?" I look at the others for confirmation.

"The stone is cracked back here," Arden says, but his voice trails off as he makes his way carefully around the base. "There's a lot of rubble on the ground here. I think it's probably been loose for a while."

"Loose? How does marble come loose, exactly?" Daisy asks.

Knox is still staring at me. "I'm fine," I repeat. "But something is on fire. Seriously. Can't you smell that?" The smell of burning wood clogs my nostrils and my throat, hot and smoky and thick.

Only there isn't any smoke.

Knox glances over at Arden and lowers his voice. "Chance is my dude," he says. "Is there something he should know?"

My stomach does a somersault as I struggle to breathe. "That's none of your business." My face is hot, burning. "I mean, go ahead.

Tell him about tonight. There's nothing going on. We're just friends, hanging out."

"Right." Knox's teeth gleam white and wolfish in the muted blue light from his phone. "He'll believe that. Lucky for you, we both know he's not the jealous type." He leans closer, and I can smell the beer on his breath and I'm almost grateful, because it drowns out the smell of fire.

"I'm not cheating on Chance." I push Knox away and stumble, trying to get fresh air into my lungs.

"Are you okay?" Arden asks, suddenly beside us again. "You scared me back there."

"Yeah. I . . . Do *you* smell that? Something burning?"

Arden shakes his head. "No. Are you sure you're all right?"

I sink down to my knees, and he kneels down beside me and catches my hand in his, holding it for a beat and squeezing lightly before he lets go to pick up the beer bottle I dropped.

My heart soars and then nosedives. This is all just too much.

Daisy kneels on top of the angel, using one hand to brush away the dirt from the inscription and the other to snap photos with her phone.

"That has to be some kind of sacrilege," I say.

She ignores me.

"Check this out. Nell Whitley Dunlap. Born 1856. Died 1947." She looks up at me, her eyes shining in the blue light of her camera. "What if it's her?"

"It's not her."

"How do you know?"

"For starters, she's young. Not . . ." I do the math in my head,

"Ninety-one. Besides—" I break off as my gaze travels down the statue's extended arm, her finger pointing toward Knox. "That's a headstone, dumbass. You can't sit on it!"

He gets to his feet slowly, kicking at a pile of ash on the ground beside the grave.

"There's your fire," Arden says. "Looks like some kids were fooling around, ignoring the burn ban. Maybe we scared them off. This is cold, though. Nothing to worry about now."

"I thought . . ." *I thought I could smell it.* The fire. I shake my head and push Knox to the side to sweep back the tangle of vines and find a tiny stone marker with a single name etched into it: Georgianne.

Whoever she was, she apparently doesn't warrant a LOVING MOTHER or DEVOTED WIFE inscription. She doesn't even get dates.

Her small gravestone looks out of place here, in the newer section. No wonder her grave is the one some reckless kids decided to vandalize.

But Daisy is still fixated on the toppled angel. "Who's Nell?" she asks, showing Arden the inscription.

"Some ancestor. Why does it matter?"

"This is the Dunlap section, right?"

When Arden doesn't answer, she uses her light to show us the graves, one Dunlap after another, all tucked up against the hill.

"Here's a thought," she says, pausing long enough to glance at each of us in turn, though she lingers longest on Arden. "What if she was a Dunlap? The ghost bride, I mean."

Arden jerks his attention away from one of the stones at the end of the line. "What? No. That's impossible."

But what Daisy says makes sense. For once. I walk over and look down at Nell's stone. She was a Devoted Wife *and* Mother.

"Actually, it's not impossible," I say. "Someone clearly cared enough to display her portrait in the Atwater lobby. And the story mentions the lodge. Even if the bride isn't Nell and was much younger than she was when she died, it doesn't mean the bride isn't some other Dunlap."

Arden is shaking his head before I even finish. "I think I would know if I were related to the ghost bride," he says. But he doesn't sound sure.

Knox, who has been abnormally quiet since accusing me of cheating, finally speaks up.

"Arden's right," he says. "The ghost bride wasn't a Dunlap. And I can prove it."

THE LEGEND OF THE GHOST BRIDE

*as told by **Knox Barnett***

She was crazy.

That's the way my grandma tells the story, and how else do you explain it?

It was a warm summer night in the beginning of June, and up at Atwater Manor, they were preparing for a wedding. One of my great-great—I don't know how many greats, but something-great—grandmas worked at the big house, back in the day, and she was out in the yard setting up the chairs and tables. When this . . . woman . . . appeared. Just showed up, out of nowhere. She was crying—hysterical—claiming she loved the groom and they were meant to be together and he had betrayed her.

But Mr. Dunlap, he didn't even know her. Said she was just some local girl. That she'd probably seen him, in town or whatever, and had somehow decided since he was a Dunlap, he was the answer to her problems. Things were tough back then, my grandma says. Not quite the Depression, but close. She was probably the daughter of a miner, and we all know how tough that life can be.

But get this—the girl was wearing a wedding gown.

Can you believe it? This crazy stalker had made herself a wedding dress, then showed up to the scene of Mr. Dunlap's actual wedding, wearing it.

Like maybe he was going to just get rid of his real bride and marry her instead?

My grandma says he was a decent guy. He tried to talk to her. He was worried about her sanity, of course. I'm sure he was also worried about her making a scene, and he didn't want his new wife hearing any of this, not right before her own wedding. I mean, even if the chick was crazy, women have a tendency to believe this stuff.

But the woman wouldn't be calmed. She screamed and cried and carried on for what felt like hours, my grandma said. And they fought—she physically attacked Mr. Dunlap, while he tried to hold her back. He waved off the help, told the servants to go back inside.

That was his second-biggest mistake.

His biggest was what he did next—head back inside the house and leave her alone on the lawn.

Because the bitch set the house on fire.

Someone smelled smoke and sounded the alarm. Luckily, my great-whatever grandma managed to get out, along with the rest of the staff. They all survived.

Except for the crazy bride.

She managed to set her dress on fire while trying to throw more kerosene onto the flames.

And then, half-mad and burning, she ran to the edge of the falls and threw herself off the cliff.

And now they say she walks, on summer nights when the moon is full. Personally, I've never seen her. But if she does? If she's restless or haunted or doomed or cursed?

It's her own damn fault.

CHAPTER 20

"That's your proof?" Daisy says. "A dumb urban legend? You're not even telling it right."

Is Knox smart enough to detect the death of their summer romance from the disgust in her voice? My cousin will tolerate many things, but bad storytelling is not one of them.

"Your grandma says the bride wasn't a Dunlap, so she wasn't a Dunlap?" Daisy continues.

"Well . . . yeah. Story's pretty clear."

"I have to agree with Knox," Arden says, and Daisy rolls her eyes.

"What a surprise."

"You said 'story's pretty clear.' That's the key word, though. *Story.* As in made up." Malice's voice whispers in my head. *Nothing is ever 'just a story.' It's how we get to the heart of our own truth.*

The only truth Knox is searching for with this tale is that women are crazy, and woe to the poor men who have to put up with them.

Or maybe he meant it as a warning to me? *Stay away from the Dunlaps, you crazy bitch.*

"Come on, Rena Faye. We're out of here." Daisy grabs her empty beer bottles and pockets her phone.

"Hey, slow down," Knox protests. "What's the rush? You wanted a ghost story, right? That's why we're here."

"Thanks, but I've heard enough," she calls back over her shoulder.

I look at both the guys. "Sorry. It's been . . . interesting?" I take off Arden's jacket and give it back to him.

"What an idiot," Daisy says when we're seated in the Jeep.

I know she means Knox, but I can't stop thinking about what Arden said—the vision of the bride he saw.

"Not that you ever want to hear that misogynistic drivel again, but I took a recording back there of the ghost story and whatever," Daisy says.

"You did?"

She nods.

I want to talk more about this, but first, I need to tell her about Arden.

"When you and Knox went ahead of us before, Arden told me something about the ghost bride." I pause. "He said he saw her once, too."

"Oh, please." Daisy jerks the wheel as she steers around a corner. "Let me guess. She's a bloodthirsty hag out to destroy a good boy's virtue?"

"No," I say, annoyed. "He saw what I saw. The same thing. Do you know what this means?" I pause, waiting for her to fill in the blank. "She's real, right? She is."

"Well, duh! Welcome to the club, Captain Obvious."

Malice was right—the ghost bride is real. But does that mean she was right about the curse too? I think about the statue, falling so close to where I was standing. And I shiver.

"So what do we do now?"

Daisy pulls into the driveway and shifts to park, engine running. "Now I think we focus on Nell. Either the ghost was trying to hurt you, or she was trying to tell you something. Either way, there has to be a reason she used Nell to do it. She's the key. We have to figure out who she is. Or was. And what her connection is to the ghost bride."

I let out a breath.

"Roots." The word just springs into my head. "That's the word the ghost bride traced in the dirt. I didn't understand at first, but maybe she meant I need to find her family."

"Yes!" Daisy pounds the steering wheel. "Of course! So how do we do that?"

"Actually," I say, "I might know someone who can help."

After a week of working at Atwater, I'm starting to get the hang of it. But Sundays are a whole different animal. I was told I could come in early, "in case" some of the guests leave before checkout, but when I get to work, it's clear that what I thought was an offhand suggestion is actually the norm. My plan to catch Peggy alone and pick her brain about Nell Whitley Dunlap dissolves like an ice cube in June.

The washers and dryers are all running when I push open the

door, and it's a toss-up whether it's more humid outside or in. Sadie is sitting at one of the folding tables, typing furiously on her phone. She lifts her fingers at me as I walk in, but I'm not sure if it's a greeting or a brush-off.

Jen is talking, her voice raised so Peggy can hear her over the noise of the machines. "—never shuts up. It's like, from midnight to three a.m., she's screaming. And do you think Kurt gets up with her?"

Peggy snorts and shakes her head.

Jen's face is pale and puffy, too little sleep and too little sunlight. She's reached the place I'm headed—the nirvana I've been told is adulthood. And I wonder, is this what Jen saw for herself when she looked into her future? Doing laundry and complaining about her husband, still living in the town where she grew up? I know I want more, but maybe Jen did too, and still, she ended up here.

"I'm so frickin' tired, I want to cry myself!" Jen catches sight of me then. "Hey, Rena Faye. Look at you, all bright-eyed and rested." She sighs heavily and lays her head on the table. "God, I miss sleep."

I look rested? I haven't slept in days. Every time my head hits the pillow, I start replaying conversations in my head. My argument with Momma, the coolness between me and Chance. Knox and his not-so-subtle insinuations. What I should have said differently, how I might have changed things.

And then there are the imaginary conversations I've been having with Arden. Those leave me with butterflies in my stomach and a lump in my throat.

But I'm hiding it well. At least according to Jen. Though she's probably not the best judge at this point. A soft snore sounds.

"Is she . . . ?"

"Leave her be," Peggy whispers.

I follow her outside when she leaves for her smoke break. Sadie doesn't bother to look up from her phone as we pass. When we reach the patio, Peggy shakes out a cigarette and tucks it into the corner of her mouth. "Didn't peg you for a smoker."

"I'm not." I wave off the pack she offers. "I was just curious about your hobby. Not smoking. Your historical research."

Peggy takes a long drag on her cigarette. "No one your age is curious about historical research. Unless you're trying to prove you're somehow related to George Clooney, I don't buy it."

"No, I'm just—I have a . . . theory. About someone's ancestry. But I need to know how to prove it."

"A theory. About who?"

Now that I have her attention, I hesitate. The idea sounded solid last night, when Daisy and I were talking. Even after Knox's ridiculous story. Maybe more so. But what if Peggy thinks I'm an idiot?

Maybe she already does.

I lean my arms on the railing. "I was up at the cemetery the other night," I say. "There's a grave marker. Or there was." I pause. Are we going to get in trouble for vandalizing Nell's grave?

"There's a lot of 'em there. It's a cemetery?" she says, smirking, as she exhales another plume of smoke.

I move my head to avoid it.

"Nell Whitley Dunlap."

Peggy squints through the smoke hanging in the air between us. "What about her?" A smudgy O rings her filter, an imprint of her petunia pink lipstick. "If you're about to tell me you think she's the ghost bride, you're way off base. She's one of the matriarchs of the whole clan. She didn't die on her wedding day and she certainly didn't fall off no cliff."

"I know that. But it got me thinking. Could the ghost bride have been a Dunlap?" I ask. "Related to Nell somehow? That's possible, right?"

Her shoulders twitch as she processes what I've said. "Anything's possible. But like I said the other day, there's nothing in the archives about any dead bride, ghost or no."

"No, I remember what you said. I just wondered how you knew. How did you go about looking for her, I mean?"

"Usual ways."

I don't know what that means, but I plow ahead. "Sure. Of course. But what if you were to go about it in the non-usual way? Like, from the back end?"

She tilts her head slowly to the side, which I take as an invitation to continue.

"What if instead of looking for a dead bride, you researched the Dunlaps? Start with Nell and branch out. See if anything . . . unusual jumps out at you."

Peggy pauses. "It's an interesting idea," she finally says. "Tell you what. I'll do a little research, next time I'm in the office. Just a general search. And I'll let you know if I find anything."

"Perfect. You're a peach," I say.

"Yeah, don't get too excited," she says gruffly, stubbing out her butt against the railing. "Nine times outta ten, nothing comes up."

"And what about the tenth time?" I ask.

The gleam in her eye lights up the whole patio. "It's the promise of the tenth that keeps you going."

CHAPTER 21

I've ridden with Daisy the past two days. Between the revelations at the cemetery and my awkwardness around Arden, it's just easier.

Tonight, she's still working when I clock out, so I duck into the library to wait for her in the air conditioning.

I walk along the back wall slowly, studying the photos under glass. The invention of photography was considered by many to be a modern miracle: the ability to capture a moment in time, a memory, before it was lost forever. A concrete depiction of history, one you could hold in your hand.

But of course, there were deniers. People who didn't understand the technology, who feared it would harm them. The big lens pointed at them as they were told to stand, frozen. The bright flash of the bulb. There were some who said to take a photograph was to take a piece of your soul. There were others who believed giving someone the ability to hold your likeness, to carry it around, gave them control over you in some way. To them, photography was a sort of dark magic. A curse.

I think about this as I scan the pictures of the older generations who came to Atwater.

If I accept that the ghost bride is real, do I have to accept the curse as well?

Or am I falling into the trap of hysteria—the fear of the unknown? Just like those early photography skeptics?

Just because I saw a ghost, it doesn't mean I'm cursed.

Except. Except except except.

My phone did break.

And the truck overheated on basically the one day I've driven it all summer.

And I almost got crushed by a falling angel.

On the wall next to the fireplace, I find the photos of the big fire of 1917. In black and white, it's hard to fully capture the devastation, but someone gave it a good effort. One grainy photo shows smoke billowing from the house, while several depict the charred ruins that remained after it had been doused.

As I'm studying these, I get a strange tingling at the base of my skull. An itch in my brain I can't quite seem to scratch.

There's a fire in the story. The bride watches from the cliff as the house burns. Or she sets it, depending on whose version you believe. But whichever the version, there's always a fire.

"This is a surprise. Other than guests, this place is almost always empty."

I jump at the sound of Kezia's voice. When I turn, she's standing outside her office door, dressed in a mint-green sundress and lightweight cardigan, her arms folded across her chest.

"Am I not supposed to be here?" I ask. "I was just waiting

for my ride and looking at some of these old pictures. They're fascinating."

She moves toward me and I get a whiff of her perfume, subtle and smoky, with a hint of vanilla.

"Aren't they? Atwater certainly has been through a lot."

"The fire." I touch the glass. "How did it start?"

"Ah, yes. Lightning strike. Back then, the manor was all wood. It went up like tinder. You'd think being so close to all that water, they could've saved it. But it burned too quickly." She shakes her head. "Such a tragedy. But Silas Dunlap was not deterred. He promptly rebuilt." She moves to the next photo. "Stone, this time. Much safer. And more expensive. But it paid off." She spreads her hands. "It's still standing today."

"A tragedy," I say, echoing Kezia's earlier words. "How many people died?"

"Luckily, no one."

What? That can't be right. I know Malice's story by heart. *Everyone inside—gone.* Including the bride's lover.

"You look disappointed. I suppose you prefer the gothic and tragic version. All fiction, I'm afraid."

"It's not that. I just thought . . ." I take a deep breath and plunge ahead. "The ghost bride legend mentions the fire. As you know."

"I hardly think that story is an accurate historical record." She manages a brittle laugh. "As I said, there were no casualties."

"But you know it's more than just a story." Arden told me she was with him when he saw the bride. This is an experience we've shared.

Only her smile shrinks, becoming too small for her face, like a piece of clothing she's outgrown.

"I don't know what my son has told you, but that ghost story is an urban legend. Nothing more."

So she isn't going to admit it. Fair enough. I haven't been anxious to talk about it, either, and Kezia has more to lose than I do. She's a prominent member of the community.

"So why the painting?" I ask. "And the story in your brochure? If you don't even believe it?"

"The brochures are new. All my son's idea," she says.

"Sure. But the painting isn't. Someone in your family must have believed, once."

"That painting was a business decision," she says, her mouth twisting as if the words are sour.

"So then why hide it away? Because you felt guilty, promoting a lie?"

It comes out sharper and more accusatory than I intend, but Kezia is unfazed. "Who says it's a lie? Could a woman have fallen from the falls and died? Definitely. But that's a little different than telling people some crazy girl set fire to Atwater."

So she's heard Knox's version. Interesting.

"See, one of those is a total fabrication," she continues. "The other is just good business sense. Warning our guests away from danger." She studies my face, as if searching for a clue of some kind. To what mystery, I'm not sure. "Arden is very enamored of this new promotion. His brand-new advertising campaign and his ghost tours. And I understand where he's coming from. That kind of thing is very popular these days. People love a good ghost story.

A palatable one, of course. Sweet. Tragic. Avoidable."

I shudder. Is she suggesting what I think? Arden wants to lead tours to look for the bride? Because there's no way they should be taking groups of innocent tourists into the woods. Not while she's out there, wandering. Angry.

I fiddle with my hair. Arden can't do this. I need to stop him.

Kezia's gaze follows my hands, her face going rigid. "At any rate, it's late," she says suddenly, pulling her sweater tight. "You'd best be getting home. You should think about what I've said, though."

She ushers me to the door so quickly, I can't help but wonder what it is she's trying to hide.

CHAPTER 22

With Kezia's gaze pressing against my back, I walk through the foyer and straight out the front door without bothering to check the lobby for Daisy. It's clear Kezia doesn't want me hanging around her hotel. Whether it's because I'm the hired help or there's another more personal reason, I can't tell.

I lean against the low stone railing that encircles the veranda, wishing for the hundredth time that I had a working phone. At least it's peaceful out here, with the sun setting and the soft floodlights blurring the shadows around the lodge. Or it would be, if it weren't for the rumble of the truck engine out front.

I squint into the gloom. Is that . . .

"Daddy?"

I walk over to the truck idling at the curb and peer into the passenger-side window. "What are you doing here?"

"Daisy had to run home, so Uncle Ford texted and asked me to pick you up," Daddy says, tapping his fingers on the steering wheel as he stares straight ahead.

"Everything okay with them?"

Daddy waits for me to climb in and click my seat belt. "As well as can be, I guess, what with their daughter runnin' around at all hours doing lord knows what, instead of helping out her family like a good girl should."

I press my lips together. That dig is meant for me as much as it is for Daisy. "She's an adult," I say.

"Doesn't mean she isn't still a member of the family."

My temper simmers. I don't know if we're talking about Daisy now, or me. Either way, he's wrong. Neither one of us has done anything to hurt our families. If anything, he's the one pushing me away.

I study the play of passing headlights over the planes of his face. "Is there something you want to say to me?"

Half his mouth curves up. "Baby girl, if I had something to say, I'd say it."

This I don't doubt. I slouch back against the seat, suddenly exhausted. I'm tired of his veiled comments and his punishing silence and his *baby girl*s. I haven't done anything wrong. All I wanted was the chance to make my own decisions. It wasn't meant as some kind of personal betrayal.

He gestures at a small bouquet of flowers wrapped in paper, which I'd mistaken for groceries. "Those are for you."

I pick them up. "What's the occasion?"

He lifts a shoulder. "For that, you'll need to ask your young man."

I pull out the card from in between the carnations. *Miss you tons. Love, Chance.*

My chest tightens, but I shouldn't feel guilty. I've been busy.

Working. Trying to earn my own way, for the first time in my life. I lift the flowers to my nose and take a deep breath, but all I get is a whiff of Daddy's truck—gasoline and Kentucky mud.

I drop the bouquet in my lap as he passes the turnoff to our road. "Where are we going?"

"Just taking a drive. Give us some time to talk."

So *now* he wants to talk? I bite my tongue and hold back the sarcastic comment. They never get me anywhere with Daddy. When he says he wants to talk, what he really means is he wants me to listen.

He nods at the flowers. "So how are things with you and Chance?"

I shift in my seat and wince as the back of my thigh sticks to the vinyl. "Fine," I say cautiously. I actually haven't spoken to him in almost a week, not since the day we went looking for the ghost bride in the clearing. He's texted Daisy, and I've used her phone to text him back a few times, mostly quick replies. **Love you too. Xoxo.** ☺

Like I said, I've been busy working.

And hanging out with Arden.

As if reading my mind, Daddy says, "That's good. I was worried the Dunlap kid was causing some problems."

"Why would Arden be causing problems?" I snap.

"Knox was talking to Graham about it. He seemed pretty convinced there's something going on between the two of you."

Knox. That bastard. I clench my hands so hard, my nails bite into my palms. "It's none of Knox's business," I say. Daddy's either, but that never stopped him.

"Knox is worried about you. You know he thinks of you like a sister. And Arden is a good-looking kid."

Ew. What is happening? Am I really having this conversation? With my dad?

"Knox is worse than an old lady when it comes to gossip. And Arden and I are just friends," I say, skipping over the whole looks thing. Arden is good-looking—it's pointless to deny that. But a lot of people are attractive. It doesn't mean anything.

"I hope so." Daddy reaches over to pat my arm, giving my elbow a hard squeeze. "Because Chance is a decent young man. And he deserves better than that."

I shift out of reach. "Better than what?" Better than me? It shouldn't surprise me that Daddy is taking Chance's side, but it does. Worse, it hurts. I'm his daughter. What if we *were* having problems? What if I were having second thoughts about our relationship? What would Daddy's advice be then?

"Better than having a partner who's unfaithful."

I snap my head back, knocking it against the back window. "Whoa. Who said anything about me being unfaithful? And *partner*? What are we, business associates?" I rub the knot at the back of my head. "If Chance is worried, he can talk to me himself. Sending my dad in to pitch for him is just wrong." Not to mention the exact thing I made him promise he wouldn't do.

Daddy pulls into the parking lot of the Hamburger Hut. After shifting into park, he holds up his hands in mock surrender. "Okay, okay. Maybe you don't want my advice. But there's such a thing as being faithful to a relationship. Supporting the person you're with. Or at least not hurting them. It's called loyalty. And it's how I raised you."

LOYALTY HAS ROOTS.

It's as if someone has whispered the words on the soft night breeze, and my skin prickles. "I am loyal. Why would you even say that?"

But he's already out of the truck, and by the time I make my way to the open window at the counter, he's ordering. "—extra bacon and a side of mayo. You don't have Diet Mountain Dew, do you?"

Wade Dawson is leaning through the order window, scribbling on a pad. "Sure do." He looks up with a fake smile that vanishes when he sees me. "Hey, Rena Faye." He peers past me with a smirk. "Where's Daisy?"

It's common knowledge that Wade's had a crush on Daisy since middle school. Maybe longer. But that doesn't stop him from hitting on everyone else.

"Not here." He waits for me to say more, but I've got nothing. My mind is spinning, and even though I'm hungry enough to chew on Wade's order pad, I can't focus on ordering.

What is going on with Daddy? Was Daisy really needed at home? Or is this some scheme cooked up by Chance and Daddy to get me alone so he could lecture me?

"The usual?" Wade finally prompts, and I nod, grateful that someone understands me.

Daddy waves me over to a picnic table on the lawn and I slide in across from him. I jab my straw through the plastic lid of my Coke and take a long sip before asking, "What are we doing here?"

"I thought you might be hungry. Long day at work and all that. And there's no food in the house." He winks, his good humor too forced to be real. "Don't tell your momma I said that."

He breaks off as Wade brings our tray over, pressing his lips together and smiling tightly until he's out of earshot.

I am hungry. Starving, actually. The scent of the grilled beef sets my stomach rumbling. But something about this feels off. Are we really going to pretend like the last week hasn't happened? Like we're a normal father and daughter, out for dinner? Completely ignoring the fact that he banned me from my darkroom and refused to speak to me after I quit?

Maybe this is his way of apologizing.

I take the top off my burger to add the extra pickles Wade has heaped along the side of my basket and squeeze out a glob of ketchup.

The first bite is heavenly, but Daddy barely lets me swallow before he drops the other shoe.

"The motel isn't doing so hot this summer," he says, snagging a fry from my red basket and dipping it in mayonnaise.

My chewing slows, the meat and bun like glue in my mouth. Whatever is happening at the motel, it has nothing to do with me.

"As you probably already know, Atwater has upped their game this year. Added some tours, things we can't compete with. Like ghost hikes. And moonlight rafting trips."

Clearly, Daddy's not here to apologize. And now this is starting to feel more like a trap.

I take a sip of soda and choke, the carbonation burning my nostrils and throat. I can't speak even if I wanted to, but Daddy doesn't notice. He's used to his voice being the only one in the room.

"Who would've thought guests would want to go rafting in the middle of the night?" he asks, shaking his head.

Me. I thought that. I gave Knox the idea, and he gave it to Arden. But again, I say nothing. It won't help, and Daddy probably already knows.

"They are raking in money over there. Meanwhile, we've had three cancellations just this week, after the guests figured out we weren't the ones with the rafts."

"We've never tried to compete with Atwater," I say after another drink. "We're a budget motel. People stay with us for convenience and savings. Not for our amenities." I choose my words carefully, but I'm not telling him anything he doesn't know; I'm just repeating what he and Momma have said a thousand times. "What's any different about this?" I catch a stray pickle as it slides off the bun.

"What's different this time is I honestly don't know if we can make it another summer." Daddy wipes his mouth, balls up his napkin, and tosses it onto our tray. "It's time for you to prove where your loyalties lie."

I set down my burger, my appetite gone. "What does that mean?"

"It means either you're with us, or you're against us. Atwater Lodge is a bad place," he says. "Run by ruthless people. Look, I don't know how else to say this. I've tried to give you some space, to figure it out on your own, but enough is enough."

Really? He's tried to give me space? I guess that's one way to interpret his cold shoulder and stony silence.

"Aren't you the one who's always telling me I have to stick with what I start? Whitakers aren't quitters. That's what you always say."

"Don't throw my words back at me," he says, and I flinch at the coldness in his voice. "This is different. It's upsetting your momma and I won't have it." He folds his hands on the table, as if the matter is settled.

But I'm not convinced. I may not talk back to my daddy, but I also never walk away from a secret. If he wants me to quit Atwater, he's going to need to give me a reason.

"Why? Because of whatever happened between Momma and Kezia? What's the big mystery there?"

Daddy turns his head. "They took something from us."

I knew it. Now we're getting somewhere. "Took what?"

He rubs at the scar on his jaw for a long moment. "Business, for one. Money. The usual."

But I know there's more. Something he's keeping from me. "That's it? We undercut their prices all the time. How is that different?"

"Damn it, Rena Faye!" He slaps the picnic table and I jump. Wade leans out of the hut, frowning, and I hang my head to avoid his gaze.

Daddy lowers his voice. "This has gone on long enough," he says, leaning forward to jab a finger at the table in front of me. "You are going to quit. As soon as possible. Do you understand me?"

"Or what?" I say softy.

He stares at me for a long moment, as if trying to decide if the question is an honest one. Then he slowly lifts one shoulder and lets it fall.

I turn my face as he gathers up our garbage, unwilling to let him see the tears in my eyes. Somehow, the fact that he can't—or won't—articulate my consequences is scarier than if he'd made an actual threat.

CHAPTER 23

We drive home in complete silence, which I finally break when he pulls into the driveway. "Can I borrow the truck?"

He looks over at me, one eyebrow cocked. "For what?"

"To drive over to Atwater."

We stare at each other, the cicadas drowning out the thrum of my heartbeat.

"I won't break it," I say, holding my breath as I wait for his answer.

"Don't take no for an answer," Daddy finally says, climbing out of the cab and leaving the keys in the ignition. "And remember"—he points at me through the window—"you don't owe them anything."

Technically, this is far from true. I owe them two weeks' notice, at the very least. Not to mention an explanation. And employee loyalty.

But I don't argue.

I wait for Daddy to walk up the drive before I slide over into the driver's seat.

I let my hair down, tossing Malice's hair clip onto the dash, and drive with the window open, trying to enjoy this little taste of freedom. Will it be my last?

True, I didn't actually say I was quitting, but I let Daddy think it.

If I don't, what will he do?

But if I do, then what does that mean for me?

It's just a job, and not even one I particularly enjoy. Is it worth all of this struggle? I never wanted to hurt anyone. All I wanted was a chance to make my own decisions. But how far has that gotten me? It's taking me further from my family; it's caused problems with Chance.

Unless those problems were already there. And this has nothing to do with Atwater. I glance over at the dying flowers on the seat beside me. I used to live for his attention, one heart emoji the difference between a sunny day and a dreary one. Now his gestures feel a little clingy and annoying. Like they come with strings, tying me to a future I can't clearly picture.

Or maybe I'm just trying not to think about the real reason I don't want to quit Atwater.

But no. This isn't about Arden. I mean, sure, I'd miss seeing him, but if I quit, I'll never solve the mystery about what happened between Momma and Kezia. And I'll never hear what Peggy discovers about the ghost bride.

I make the turn into the parking lot and slam on the brakes. The ghost bride. Is that what this is about? Could this all be related to the curse?

She takes what you value most.

Daddy kept going on and on tonight about loyalty. So did the ghost bride. If she's real, those notes are real. No matter that I'm the only one who saw them.

BETRAYAL HAS LEGS. LOYALTY HAS ROOTS.

What if the curse is the reason Daddy is making me quit Atwater? To give up my independence?

I pound my hand on the steering wheel. Quitting feels like giving up. It *is* giving up. But what choice do I have? Go back and tell Daddy I refuse?

I can't imagine that will go over well.

On the other hand, quitting means letting the bride take from me what she wants—my freedom. Earlier this summer, I told Daisy I was tired of making decisions based on what I was trying to avoid. But here I am—right back where I started.

When the passenger door opens, I yelp and slam the truck into drive.

Which doesn't do anything, because the parking brake is on.

"Hey. Sorry!" Arden climbs in and reaches for my arm. "I didn't mean to scare you. Are you all right?"

I flop back against the seat and close my eyes. "No! What are you doing out here?"

"I was going to ask you the same thing," he says. "I just got back from town, and I saw your truck. I thought maybe . . ." He trails off. "Anyway, I've been wanting to talk to you. See if you're okay. After the other night. You guys left so fast, and I haven't seen you since."

He isn't looking at me as he speaks, just drumming his fingers on his jeans and frowning down at them. "I mean, I'm sure you've been busy. And not avoiding me." His laugh falls flat.

I have been avoiding him. Because what is there to say? *I'm attracted to you? I can't stop thinking about you? Being with you makes me question everything?*

But that's not fair to him. I was questioning a lot of things before he came along. Besides, even if this attraction were mutual, it could never work between us. We may have both grown up in Corbin, but we don't move in the same circles. The Dunlaps are all business and board meetings and charity dinners that cost more than my paycheck. My people are the ones serving at those dinners, or cleaning up afterward. We may both technically be in the hospitality industry, but around here, Arden's family is royalty. And I'm just a working peasant.

"I have been pretty busy," I say.

"I'm glad you're not busy tonight. Even if sitting in your truck long after your shift does seem a little overeager." He's teasing, even flirting maybe, his grin easing those dimples into place as he tilts his head toward me. Then he catches sight of the hair clip on the dashboard. "Weird." He grabs it. "This looks like the one in the painting."

"That's because it is." I run my fingers through a tangle of wind-blown hair. "It belonged to the ghost bride. Or so the legend goes." But I'm less certain now.

"Is it part of that curse you guys were talking about?" he asks as he hands it back to me.

I smile nervously and wipe a sweaty hand across my forehead. "No. It's—" I stop and stare at the piece of jewelry.

It's so obvious, I want to slap myself. I wore it into the woods, the first time we went. When Daisy and I played the wedding game. And when Chance dropped it, I left it there.

Like an offering.

Until I took it back.

"You're right," I whisper. "It's the hair clip. That must be why she appeared to me."

"Wow. Okay. So now what? Do we give it back, or . . . ?"

"Yes." No. I can't go back there, especially not in the dark. But maybe if I break the curse, everything will go back to normal. My world will make sense again and I won't have to make these hard choices. But even as I'm questioning whether it could really be that easy, Arden already has my door open.

"Come on."

"Come where?"

"To the old mill. That's where you saw her, right?"

"Yes, but this isn't the way—"

"There's a path. From the beach."

Despite the warning signal sounding in my brain, my body has other plans. I take his hand and let him help me from the truck.

Arden leads the way down the path to the beach, glancing back to make sure I'm following. "So I'm almost afraid to ask, but what exactly is the curse?" When I don't answer right away, he adds, "Does it have something to do with what happened in the cemetery?"

I step on some loose gravel and my foot slides, but before I even have a chance to worry, he's there to catch me. When I'm steady on my feet, he takes my hand. And I let him.

"The statue, you mean?" My voice echoes off the canyon wall, sounding low and breathy. "Not exactly." I try to recall the sequence of events, but everything after the angel falling is jumbled in my head. The smell of fire, Knox accusing me of cheating. Had Arden heard that? And then the discussion about the bride being a Dunlap. Followed by Knox's ridiculous version of the story. "I'm sorry we took off so abruptly. Daisy gets a little emotional when it comes to her ghost stories."

"Well, sure. Who doesn't?"

I smile in the darkness, though he can't see me.

"Where'd you get the hair clip, anyway?"

"My mawmaw gave it to me."

"But she didn't tell you it was cursed?"

"I don't think she knows. She told me there was *a* curse. And she said it was connected to our family. But I guess she never put it all together." And why would she? I'm not even one hundred percent sure I'm right. All I know is I went back for the hair clip, saw the bride, and since then, a bunch of inexplicable stuff has happened.

Arden jumps down the last step and turns to lift and lower me gently onto the sand. "Hey. Where'd you go just now?" he asks, his hands still resting lightly on my waist.

"Nowhere," I say.

"I don't believe you. You get this look sometimes, like you're seeing something no one else can."

Like a ghost? I swallow down a hot surge of fear and force myself to smile. "I'm right here. With you."

Immediately, I regret my words. *With you?* We're not together;

we're not a couple. Did that sound like an invitation? Like I want us to be one?

We're standing close together, too close. Close enough to kiss, if we wanted.

Which of course he doesn't. And neither do I. Because I have a boyfriend.

I force myself to step away from him, making a show of surveying the beach. I'm not great with directions, but it's possible he's right, and we're closer to the mill than I ever realized. The reason this all looks so familiar is because the riverbank where Daisy and the guys and I celebrated the last moonbow is just around the rocky outcropping at the far end of the beach.

"So where's this path?" I ask.

He comes up behind me, near enough to rest his chin on my shoulder. His breath is hot on the back of my neck and my heart somersaults in my chest. I have an insane urge to giggle. Either that or turn and press my mouth to his.

"This way," he says, pointing over my shoulder.

I move forward so quickly he stumbles, and I pretend not to notice.

"Wait," he says.

I turn, my face flaming. Is he going to say something about how ridiculous I'm acting? Or ask me about Chance? Am I going to tell him?

But he isn't looking at me at all. He's facing the thick tree line behind us, pointing at a tiny break in the corner, on the opposite side of the beach from the rock wall of Lover's Leap. "I'm wrong. I think the path is over here."

Before, I was nervous. Now, staring at the dark gap in the trees, I'm terrified. "Are you sure?"

"I've only been down there one time." He talks slowly as he stares into the distance, like he's remembering as he goes. "But yeah. Pretty sure."

I go cold. Pretty sure isn't much. And I don't want to be wandering the forest in the middle of the night. Not when I know what other things are in there.

"I was young," Arden continues. "But this looks right."

I follow him. It's clear there used to be a path here, although it's grown over with foliage—mostly kudzu. It appears shorter than the trek Daisy and I usually make, but it's slow going picking our way through all the vines. The night is warm, the air heavy with moisture and secrets, and though I'm not eager to draw any attention to ourselves, I make myself talk so the silence doesn't smother us.

"I started to mention this to your mom," I say, "but I got the impression she didn't want to talk about the bride. I'm sorry. I didn't realize it was supposed to be a secret."

"It's not." He grimaces. "But she doesn't like to talk about it. I think that whole time is painful for her to think about. She and Dad were fighting a lot back then. I thought they were going to get a divorce. They had a big fight the day she brought me down here, actually."

He shakes his head.

"Sorry," he says. "I can't believe I'd forgotten all of that."

I'd been afraid to tell him all the details about my story, scared that giving away the ghost bride's secrets might anger her, or that sharing my story with Arden will make him question my sanity.

But it turns out Arden has his own ghosts.

"I'm sorry about your parents," I say. "Almost splitting up, I mean. I didn't know." Although the time frame he's describing is back when we were classmates. When he used to cry all the time.

"How would you?" he asks. "Besides, whatever it was, they worked it out. Who knows, maybe sending me away saved their marriage." He makes a face, but it could just be concentration.

"I'm sure that's not true," I say, although what do I know about marriage?

He pushes aside a branch and waves me under. "It's all in the past, anyway. Nothing I can do about it now. I just regret the time I missed with my dad."

"What was he like?"

Arden thinks for a minute. "Looser than my mom, for sure. Easygoing. We at least had painting in common."

"Did he do those paintings in the cabins?"

His lips twitch into a half smile. "He did the big mural on the dining room wall. But the cabin ones are mostly mine."

He's better than I thought. At nearly everything. He is clearly so out of my league. And why am I even thinking like this? It doesn't matter, because I have a—

"Holy hell." Arden's voice is awestruck.

Actually, it's a good description. Daisy and I usually hike in from the east. Coming at it from this southern trail, the ruins seem to rise up out of the earth like some kind of ancient temple. Or a cursed one.

Arden holds up the flashlight on his phone. "It's smaller than

I remember," he whispers. "And more . . . broken. But somehow more impressive at the same time."

I need to get this over with quickly. Before the bride shows up and does god knows what to us.

"Stand here," I say, my voice trembling. "Right here. Don't move."

He furrows his brow.

"Promise me. I don't want to make her angry."

Understanding bathes his face like moonlight. "Oh. So this is where . . ." He trails off and I nod.

My heart is pounding so fast I'm dizzy, and my hands are sweating and slippery and for once I'm grateful there's no moon, because if the bride is nearby, I don't want to see her.

I pull the hair clip from my pocket and press it tight, the metal biting into my palm.

I keep my eyes down, looking only at my feet as I pick my way over to the flat, unmarked stone, where I lay the hair clip in the middle, gently, and slowly back away.

"Loyalty has roots," I whisper, and lift my face to the sky for the briefest moment.

A gust of wind slaps me then, cold and hard and unforgiving.

I don't wait for what comes next; instead, I grab Arden by the hand. "Run!"

We crash through the trees and out onto the beach, breathless and shaking. The air is pure, the night is clear, and the stars are bright. I collapse onto my knees in the sand, overcome with the sudden urge to giggle. I feel lighter, giddy, free.

Because I am.

I did it. I freed us all from the curse.

I run the cold, silky sand through my fingers as Arden plops down beside me.

"Were you really going to do that all by yourself? Go into the woods alone in the middle of the night?" His voice holds equal amounts of admiration and disbelief. In Arden's eyes, I am invincible.

I laugh out loud. "Actually, before you got into my truck, I was thinking about quitting."

"What? Why?"

I draw my knees up to my chin. "My daddy, mostly. He had me convinced it was the right thing to do. And I almost believed him." I turn my head to look at him. "Until you came along."

He smiles and I blush and flop onto my back, staring up at the Little Dipper above us. I raise my arm to trace the constellation with my finger, toward the North Star. As my heartbeat slows to normal, Arden reaches up and grabs my hand, stealing my breath again.

Only this time for a different reason.

He rolls onto his side to face me, so close that I know all I have to do is turn my head and our lips will touch.

"I'm glad you decided not to quit," he says, his breath tickling my cheek.

I have a boyfriend.

It's what I should say.

Instead, I kiss him.

CHAPTER 24

"**I** have a boyfriend."

This time I say it out loud. Too bad it's much too late.

Arden reaches for me as I pull away. "Wait."

But I don't. I can't. Waiting is what got me into this mess in the first place. Waiting and wanting. Waiting to speak up. Waiting for my real life to start; wanting more than I deserve.

"Please don't follow me." I manage to choke out the words and push myself up off the sand. When I reach the top of the stairs, I sneak a glance back at the beach through the tree branches, afraid he might be right behind me, and equally afraid he won't be. But he's still sitting where I left him, his back to me. As he picks up a chunk of driftwood and hurls it into the river, I turn and run for the truck, tears streaming down my face.

The drive home is endless, and even blaring Carrie Underwood does nothing to quiet my mind, because it isn't words I need to drown out. It's the memory of Arden's lips on mine, soft and insistent. The rush of heat that felt electric, like we weren't just kissing, but connecting. The wrench of pain when I pulled away, this feeling of loss I can't think about but have to shove down deep, because it doesn't make sense and I barely know him and the only thing I've lost is my self-respect.

There's nothing between us. It's just different because it's new. It's been a long time since I've kissed anyone besides Chance.

It's also been a long time since I've kissed Chance.

Thinking about Chance is like pressing on a bruise, but I deserve this pain. I've earned it, with my selfishness and my betrayal.

Betrayal.

I nearly swerve off the road.

If giving back the hair clip is supposed to break the curse, then why am I still hurting the people I love? Why does it feel like so much is falling apart around me?

When I pull up to the house, I park down the hill so the noise from the engine won't wake anyone and slip in quietly through the back door.

But Momma is standing at the sink, staring out through the darkened window. In the harsh light of the single bare bulb, her messy bun is grayer than usual.

"You stole the truck," she says without turning around.

I brace myself on the doorframe as I pull off my shoes, bristling at her tone. "I didn't steal anything. Daddy let me take it."

I'm so tired. Of this night and of this argument. Of my life. I've cried myself out, and now I just want to crawl into bed and pull the covers over my head and go to sleep. To not have to think. To not have to argue. To not have to feel guilty for two goddamn seconds.

Is that too much to ask?

She sets her water glass on the counter with a bang and leans back, arms crossed over her chest. "So where were you?"

I hesitate. "Atwater." Does she know about Daddy's ultimatum? Ironically, it's looking more than ever like he might get his way. No way can I work with Arden after tonight.

"I thought I made it clear how I felt about those people."

I flinch. "When you say 'those people,' do you mean Kezia Dunlap?" I don't want to look at her, but I need to see her face. "Because I know you were friends. Why didn't you ever tell me that?"

She makes an angry face, pressing her lips tightly together. But not for long. "What are you talking about?"

"You and Kezia. All your talk about how the Dunlaps are our competition. About how Atwater Lodge is the enemy. But you never once mentioned the fact that you were friends. Best friends."

"Who told you that?"

"Kezia did." Sort of. Really it was Peggy and then Malice, but I don't say that, because clearly I've hit a nerve.

"Kezia Dunlap is a flaming bitch," Momma says through gritted teeth. "You can't trust a word she says. And yes, I'll admit it. She's one of the reasons I don't want you working over there."

"But you were close once," I say again. I'm not disputing the bitch part—I've seen Kezia in action—but I'm struggling to match up the smiling, hugging girls in the yearbook to the cold, angry women they've become. Is this what Daisy and I have to look forward to? "I want to know what happened."

"It was a long time ago. People change." As she shrugs, her

shoulders hitch a little. Like she's crying. But her voice is like ice when she says, "Life happens."

Oh, come on. "What does that even mean? Of course life happens. You may as well say flowers wilt and die." I squeeze my fist tight. "It doesn't explain anything!"

"Sometimes friendships end. There's no big mystery to be solved, all right? Not everything is a story. Sometimes you remind me so much of . . ." She pounds her fist against the sink.

"Of who? Malice? Heaven forbid I be like your mother."

"You are exactly like my mother. That's why I worry."

"That's a terrible thing to say."

"She was a terrible mother. She spent most of my childhood telling me my life was going to be some goddamned dream come true. And she was wrong!" She slaps the counter. "It wasn't her job to spoon-feed me fantasies. She was supposed to be teaching me how to grow up! How to be a responsible adult, and a mother to my own children. But no—I had to figure that all out on my own. About the only thing she *did* teach me was how I didn't want to be. I begged her not to tell you those stories. Not to fill your head with lies. But here you are, traipsing around at all hours, sand in your hair." She swats at my shoulder.

"The Dunlaps aren't like us," she continues. But the fight has left her voice now. "They will use you, and they will toss you aside, and if you're lucky, they'll do it before you've burned all the rest of your bridges. You're too close to see it now, but trust me. For once in your life, just listen to your momma."

She sounds so earnest, so weary, I waver. And she's right. Arden is not like me. In the fall, he'll go back to boarding school.

Whatever this is between us, it doesn't mean anything. A summer fling. Am I willing to throw my whole future away over that?

"Loyalty has roots, Rena Faye. And betrayal has legs."

My whole body goes still.

"Do you understand what that means?"

"Wait. What did you say?" I never told Momma about my vision, or my curse. Or whatever the hell it is. "Where did you hear that?"

"You yelled that at me the day you quit. Don't you remember?" She shakes her head slowly back and forth. "The moment I heard those words, I knew you'd been up to Atwater Lodge."

"But . . . how? That's not—"

"I'm sorry, baby. I know you want to believe in romance and fairy tales. A dead bride who needs you to be her savior. A knight in shining armor to sweep you off your feet. But that is just not the way life works. Betrayal has legs, because it carries you away from the ones you love. Family is what matters. Even when it's messy and complicated and hard, your roots are where your loyalties should lie."

I stare at her as I turn the words over in my head. What exactly is she trying to say? "Are you accusing me of being disloyal?"

Momma holds her arms wide. "If the shoe fits."

And just like that, we're talking about the motel. Again.

"And what about you?" I hurl the words. "You're the one who just told me how much you hate your own momma. Isn't that a betrayal?"

"I don't hate her! She just wasn't the momma I needed."

"And you think you're the momma I need?"

Her face crumples, but I keep going. "I need a momma who listens to me! Who shares things, real things. About herself. About her life. And who lets me know that I matter! More than some stupid rules and some stupid motel."

"That's only what you *think* you need." She reaches out, as if to touch me. Instead, she drops her hand to the counter, picking up her glass and pressing it down again, making rings on the countertop. "I was just like you, you know. I thought I was invincible. That my future was Technicolor, filled with rainbows and promises, too." Her voice hardens. "It wasn't, and I adjusted."

There's a lifetime in between those words, and it infuriates me that she won't share any of it. "What do you want?" I ask. "A medal for being cynical?"

"I want you to listen to me! To trust that I have your best interests at heart. I want you to grow up and acknowledge, just once, that I might know a little bit more than you."

How many times has she said that to me? Here, in this house. How many times have we had this exact same argument? We know all the lines by heart, and I'm not even sure why we're bothering anymore.

"You don't want me to grow up," I say. "You want me to grow into you."

"Don't be ridiculous. That isn't what I want." She heaves a sigh. "This is probably a better conversation to have when you're not so emotional." She flips off the light and I turn my head as she walks past so she can't see my tears.

Don't be ridiculous. Another of her favorite empty phrases. It's not a command, or even a warning. What she means is that whatever I have to say is too stupid to be acknowledged. That my words don't matter.

I don't matter.

Sometimes I wonder if she's even heard me at all.

Maybe I'm the ghost.

CHAPTER 25

I wake the next day with the bride's words—and Momma's—in my head.

BETRAYAL HAS LEGS. LOYALTY HAS ROOTS.

I kissed Arden. I'm the betrayer. And as soon as I confess, Chance is going to run, as fast as his legs will carry him.

Momma says I must be loyal to my family, which will keep me in Corbin forever.

So Malice was right all along. The curse is taking my freedom. No matter what I do, I'm stuck here. Bound. Rooted.

I shift uncomfortably; my skin screams out in protest. I throw off the thin bedsheet and gasp. Red welts cover my body—my arms, my legs, the spaces between my fingers.

It's the most literal interpretation of a curse yet—*a pox on you!* It would be almost comical, if I didn't itch so much. I work my fingers slowly up to my face, to the unfamiliar bumpy terrain of my skin. A tear leaks from my eye, salt burning the blisters as it falls.

My attempt to lift the curse has clearly failed.

Plus, I still have to face Daddy and tell him that I didn't quit Atwater.

And after that, I have to find the courage to tell Chance about Arden.

I manage to get dressed in the loosest clothes I can find—one of Chance's old T-shirts and a pair of cut-off sweatpants I last wore to help paint the diner.

As I'm raiding the medicine cabinet in the bathroom, I hear Daddy in the hallway. Whistling. Like he doesn't have a care in the world.

Meanwhile, I'm covered in a rash and I cheated on my boyfriend, and if ever there were a clear indication that I'm still cursed, this is it.

I can't bring myself to tell him the truth and face his anger, or Momma's disappointment.

Instead, I head for the only person I can think of who might be able to help me.

She cracks open the door so quickly, it's as if she's been waiting for the knock.

"What happened to you?" Malice says.

I step around the door so she can see me. "Poison ivy." My skin itches beneath a layer of calamine lotion and the hot sun.

"Who told you to strip down and roll around in it?" She sighs and opens the door the rest of the way. "Come on in. I've got some nettle tea around here somewhere."

She hugs me gently when I get inside, and I breathe in her

scent—lemons and dust and a hint of whiskey. Her house looks different today. Cleaner. Less cluttered. A lot of the knickknacks cleared off her shelf, which is surprising, but seems like a good sign.

"You've been busy," I say. "Organizing?"

"Packing." She gives me a firm pat on the back and releases me.

"What?" I follow her to the kitchen as she pulls her tea set from a box on the counter.

"Didn't your momma tell you?" She doesn't look at me, and I can tell it's because she doesn't want me to see she's upset. She fills the teapot at the sink and shuffles over to the stove. "I'm selling the cabin. I found an apartment in town."

"*You* found?" I ask suspiciously.

"Tallulah found it," Malice admits, folding some napkins and tucking them onto her tea tray. "But it'll be easier on everyone. This way, your momma doesn't have to keep coming out here to clean and such."

"Here, let me do that."

But she waves me off. "I'm not an invalid!"

"I know that. And you're not moving into any apartment."

She sinks into a chair. "It's a done deal. Your uncles all agree it's for the best too."

My uncles have never lifted a finger to help out with Malice, preferring to saddle Momma with what they see as "daughter duty." Their opinion matters as much to me as the rear end of a horse's.

"No. No! I've been working hard this summer, at Atwater." I pull out some of the cash from my tip money. "Look! I've got money.

We'll use it to hire a nurse. Or a lawyer. Or whatever we need."

Malice wears a bemused smile on her face as I sit down beside her and take her hands.

"I've just got one year left of school," I say. "Then we'll go somewhere. Away from here. Get a place together. Or we can travel! You know I've always wanted to travel."

"I forget what a flair for the dramatic you have. Daisy gets most of the spotlight, but sometimes you put her to shame." She pats my hand. The teapot rattles on the stove, and she gets up to check it, leaving me gaping after her. "Anyway, it's between me and your momma. Let it be. I want to hear about the curse. Have you and Daisy made progress?" She eyes the pink patches of dried calamine. "It doesn't appear so."

I sigh. I'm not ready to let this topic go, but Malice's question reminds me why I came here in the first place. "We went back to the clearing last week. Where I saw her. And she . . . warned us away." I tell her about the tree and the ghost bride's ominous message carved into the bark.

She sets a cup in front of me, a tea infuser filled with dried nettle leaves balanced on top. "I have a feeling there's more to this story," she says as she pours the water.

I wrap my hands around the hot mug as Malice snags a bottle of whiskey from the cabinet and adds a heavy dollop to her own mug.

"Spill."

I can't help but smile as I stir a spoonful of honey into my cup. "You sound like Daisy." I sip my tea. "That's what she calls gossip. Spilling tea." I wince.

"What is it? Too hot?"

"No." I set my cup down. "I just can't help but think we could have avoided all this by going on our trip. Instead, this summer has been awful."

Malice takes a sip of her own tea, makes a face, and adds more whiskey. "I suppose that's what happens when you let someone else take control of your destiny."

"You mean Momma?"

Malice's mouth sags at the corners. "We all turn into our mothers, eventually. Trust me, it's not all bad. Sometimes you even realize she was right. About some things."

"I don't want to be anything like her," I say, sloshing the tea in my cup.

"You don't want to be strong? Hardworking? Fiercely loyal?"

"Loyal to *who*? And how can you say that? She's taking you from your home!"

Malice's eyes cloud over. "The truth is, she's right. I can't take care of this place myself anymore. And it isn't fair to ask her to come out here and clean when she's got so much else to worry about. Plus, all these things I've collected over the years?" She coughs a little and slurps some whiskey tea. "They used to bring me joy. But now they just make me sad. So maybe it's time we all move on. Make a fresh start."

My heart is shredding. "But . . . but you love these things," I whisper. "They're your stories."

"My stories are here," Malice says, tapping her head. "And here." Her heart. "The rest is just . . . stuff." She leans over to scrub my cheeks with her napkin. "Don't worry. I'm not giving away everything. And you can pick your favorites. You've already got the hair clip."

The back of my neck tingles and I rub it, breaking open one of my scabs. "Actually, I don't."

Malice tilts her head and narrows her eyes.

"It's not lost," I continue hastily, dabbing at the blood with a napkin. "I gave it back to the bride. Or, I tried to, anyway."

Malice pushes herself up from the table, grabbing her cup and her bottle. "I need to get more comfortable for this. You'd better start at the beginning."

I trail her into the living room. "Everything is a mess. Momma and Daddy hate me. And I've been a terrible girlfriend to Chance." I almost tell her about Arden, but chicken out at the last minute.

"And then I got to thinking yesterday, what if we were wrong? What if she isn't asking us for help? What if she just wants her hair clip back?" I ask. "I was wearing it that night in the forest. Daisy and I . . . we were joking around. Playing brides." I rush on before she can admonish me for my foolishness. "And I accidentally left the clip there. So I went back the next day to get it. But now I think maybe that's what made her mad. Maybe she wanted it back all along. And I took it."

Malice rocks in her chair slowly, staring down at the poison ivy welts on my arm. "The hair clip," she whispers. "Can it be?" She shakes her head quickly. "No. no. I *gave* you the hair clip. Did I put you in danger?" Her hand trembles as she presses it to her throat. "All this time, all I wanted was to break the curse. But maybe I was the one continuing it."

"No! Of course not." I shake my head, wishing I could take

the words back. "It was just a dumb theory. I was wrong." I hold out my blistered arms as proof. "This is what happened after I gave the clip back."

Malice sighs. "I told you to be careful." She's shaking so badly her tea spills in her lap. But she doesn't notice. "Don't take chances. Don't anger her."

I kneel down beside her. "I won't. I promise. And I didn't go alone. Arden came with me."

"Arden Dunlap?" She arches an eyebrow.

My face gets hot and my blisters tingle. "It wasn't like that."

Except it kind of was.

Malice leans forward in her chair and grips my hands. "Do you know why we must tell her story?"

I shake my head.

"Because keeping her story—keeping any woman's story—is our legacy. And our burden. It's the emotional labor that always falls to the women. We have always been the storytellers. We couldn't always read and write, but we could hold the oral traditions and pass them along. Men didn't want to bother with 'women's work.' But we knew better. And we committed our stories to memory, and we shared them. In the hopes that someday, we could avoid passing on the pain." Her eyes cloud over. "But now all I've done is pass that pain—and our curse—on to you. And after I promised Tallulah I wouldn't."

"What do you mean? You promised Momma what?" I ask sharply.

But Malice doesn't answer, just twists the edge of her cardigan and mutters something to herself, over and over.

"Malice," I say gently, prying the wool from her hand. "What did you promise Momma?"

Her eyes are bright and glassy and they skitter away when I try to hold her gaze. "That's why she agreed that we could go away."

"Are you talking about the trip? I don't think Momma ever wanted—"

"She was afraid. She knew it would be this year. Your last summer of high school. That's the summer the curse takes hold. That's when my sister drowned. And it's when Tallulah and Kezia . . ."

"When Tallulah and Kezia what?" I ask. But Malice doesn't finish. "What happened between them?"

Malice just shakes her head. "She was so insistent. *Take her on vacation*, she said. As long as I didn't fill your head with nonsense. She said the stories were the problem." Her face clears. "But she was wrong. Don't you see? The story is the key."

CHAPTER 26

I can't get any more out of Malice—not about the curse, or about Momma and Kezia. Something clearly spooked her, but I don't know what exactly.

I think about what I do know: returning the hair clip didn't lift the curse. So maybe Malice was right; I need to figure out how to put the ghost to rest. She said the story holds the key. And the story leads back to the falls, and to Atwater Lodge. Who knows, maybe that's why the bride appeared to me when she did—right after I'd taken the job.

I can't quit Atwater, not when I'm so close.

Later at home, I'm eating a bowl of Cinnamon Toast Crunch over the sink when Momma comes up behind me. "Why the hurry?"

I mop spilled milk off my chin with the back of my hand. "Work," I say. "Why aren't you at the diner? Is something wrong?"

Momma waves off my concern and squints at my arm, which

is still inflamed, though cleverly masked with a layer of calamine so thick, it looks like I put it on with a paint roller.

"Just a slow morning. I thought Daddy told me you quit."

Shit. "I . . . he did. I went there . . . But I couldn't just . . . quit." I stumble over the words.

"So you gave them notice?" Her gaze is scrutinizing, as if she's got some kind of built-in lie detector and she's scanning me for untruths.

I bob my head and make a production out of rinsing my bowl. "Yup."

"Two weeks?"

"That's the standard, right?"

She squints at me a beat longer, then sighs. "I have to say, I'm relieved. I'm anxious for everything to go back to normal."

Normal. Right. Has she seen my face? Does she realize I'm cursed? Or does she just not care?

"Anyway, I just wanted to say I'm proud of you."

"What?" Her words are so unexpected, I practically spit in her face.

"I know it can't have been easy. And that's why . . ." She pauses awkwardly. "I got you something." She pulls a phone out of her pocket and hands it to me. "Truce?"

I don't move. Is this some kind of reverse psychology thing? Does she know I'm lying and is testing how far I'll go? But her expression is contrite. Hopeful, almost.

"Sure," I say, reaching for the phone. Our fingers touch briefly before she lets go. "Thanks," I add, forcing a smile and ignoring my conscience yet again.

But why should I feel guilty? It's not like I told an outright lie. She jumped to conclusions. All I did was agree with them. Besides, she's keeping things from me, too.

"I've gotta go. Daisy's probably waiting."

Momma nods and looks like she wants to say something more, but doesn't. After a few more seconds of silence, I give her a half-hearted wave and head for the door.

I may have bought myself some time with my parents, but that doesn't help solve my other problems.

Not quitting means I have to face Arden.

I debated calling out sick, but hiding isn't going to solve any-thing. And it won't help me track the ghost. But when I walk into the laundry cabin, any ideas I had are gone.

Peggy takes one look at me and her face goes slack, her mouth falling open.

"Take a picture. It'll last longer," I snap. Not particularly original, but I figure Peggy might appreciate the callback to her own generation.

I store my purse and my sweatshirt in my cubby and turn to find her and Sadie still staring at me. "It's just poison ivy," I say. "Don't worry. I'm not contagious."

"Been doing some weeding?" Peggy asks.

Behind her, Sadie snorts a laugh.

"What's that supposed to mean?"

Peggy circles her hand around her face. "Just wondered where you got that, is all."

"The woods," I say.

She gives a curt nod. "Makes sense."

Sadie chuckles again, then ducks her head when I glare at her.

"Can we just get to work?"

"Sure." Peggy hands me my daily sheet. "Light day today. I'm not so sure Kezia's going to want your help inside, looking like you do. So maybe just finish up your cabins and you can go."

I consider arguing, but what's the point? It's probably better if I don't talk to Kezia right now anyway. I've got so many questions about her and Momma and the curse, but I need to do some more research before I ask them. "Fine."

I'm also dying to ask Peggy if she's found out anything, but I don't want to bring it up with Sadie there, staring at me like I'm some alien beamed down from another planet. So we finish loading our carts in silence, and I watch as Peggy and Sadie drive off ahead of me.

I'm still organizing my supplies when Arden comes up behind me. "I'm surprised to see you here," he says, and my heart sinks. Was he hoping I'd quit?

I turn.

Whatever secret thrill I'd felt at the sound of his voice drains the moment I see his face.

"Oh no."

He points at the red blotches on his face. "You too? I was hoping maybe you weren't as bad off as me."

"Crap," I say. I can feel my welts flare up as my embarrassment deepens. "No wonder Peggy and Sadie were laughing. They must have realized . . ." I swallow hard, unable to finish the thought. "I've got to go. I'm going to be late."

I take a step forward, but Arden doesn't move, and I don't want to push him out of the way, less because of how rude it would be and more because I don't trust myself to touch him.

So far I've chickened out of telling Chance what we did. Instead, I texted him from my new phone and told him I was sorry, but I couldn't see him until my poison ivy rash healed. It wasn't a lie, and since the kiss between Arden and me was a one-time thing, a ridiculous fluke that only happened because I was so relieved to be rid of my curse, Chance doesn't need to know. At least that's what I tell myself.

I tell myself a lot of things. It doesn't make them true.

Arden rubs the back of his neck. "I need to talk to you about something," he says.

I'd been hoping to avoid any awkwardness, but this is even more excruciating than I could ever have imagined. Maybe it's better to get it over with. Just not out here in the open.

"I've got the far cabins today," I say, holding my breath as I slip past him. "Can we talk on the way?"

Arden climbs into the cart on the driver's side, leaving me to climb in beside him, annoyed and silent. Driving the golf cart is one of the only parts of the job I actually like. But technically he's my boss, so I don't say anything.

"So," he says, after a long, tense minute. "Did it work?"

For a second, I think he's asking if kissing me made me break up with Chance.

"The curse. Is it lifted?"

I hold out my hands in front of me. "What do you think?"

He laughs. "Yeah, but this isn't part of it. This is just because we . . ." He stops. Tries again. "I mean, if poison ivy were the curse, that would mean I'm cursed, too."

Fair point.

"My mawmaw seems to think the curse is confined to my family." I study the side of his face as he drives. "But she did mention your mom. Plus, the angel statue was in the Dunlap section." I shrug. "So I don't know. Do you feel cursed?"

"I didn't," he says, and though it sounds like he might go on, he doesn't. Instead, he parks the cart outside my first cabin and turns toward me. "It sounds like you really want to believe my family is involved with this ghost bride," he says. "Like maybe you think we're guilty of something."

"I'm not saying that." I slide off the seat. "But the bride does have something to do with Atwater. The story says so."

"Which story? Knox's story? That was a bunch of bullshit."

"At least we agree on something."

I expect to get at least a smile, but Arden's expression hardens. "Are you trying to manufacture a reason to avoid me?"

And there it is. My face goes hot; the angry blotches begin to throb. "I don't need a reason," I say. "You know why."

"Because we kissed?"

I look up and down the path, certain his mother is lurking somewhere nearby. "Why would you announce it like that? Have you told anyone?"

"No, but . . ." And he waves a hand that encompasses both of us and I know exactly what he means. As soon as people see us it'll be as obvious to everyone else as it was to Peggy and Sadie—if word hasn't already spread.

I take out my passkey and knock on the door, calling "Housekeeping" before opening it, while he grabs my tote and follows me into the empty cabin.

He slams the tote down on the nearest table. "I didn't realize you were so ashamed of it."

"No . . . it's not . . . it's complicated," I stutter, my heart beating so loudly not even the thick draperies or the mound of pillows on the pulled-out sofa bed can muffle it. We are completely alone. Just me, Arden, and that big bed. "I have—"

"A boyfriend. I know. You said." He leans against the door. "And if you're happy with him, then fine."

It is fine. Everything's fine.

Arden is fine.

"But I like you," he continues. "And I thought you liked me too. I mean, the other night—"

"I do like you," I blurt. It's not what I mean to say, but I need him to stop talking about it. It's bad enough I can't stop thinking about it. About him. "It's just . . ." I raise my hands.

"Complicated?"

"Yeah."

"I'm not trying to complicate your life. But you're the one who kissed me," he says. "So I thought maybe I had a shot. That maybe you want the same thing I do."

Don't say it, don't say it, don't say it. "What do you want?" I whisper.

His smile is crooked. "Do you remember that day under the monkey bars? When we kissed? I had such a crush on you. I think maybe I still do."

I'm speechless. And breathless. And every other romantic movie cliché I've ever seen. Which makes sense. Because this is all just some kind of dream.

"I'm not trying to pressure you," Arden says. "I'll leave you alone, if that's what you want."

It is what I want. Isn't it? Or is that just what's easiest?

"I need some time," I finally say.

He nods. "Okay. Sure. But before I go, there's something I need to show you."

He reaches for his pocket.

"This was on my phone," he says. "After we went into the woods." He scrolls through some photos before landing on one, using his fingers to enlarge the image.

He turns the screen toward me and the hairs go up on my arms. It's a photo of the ash trees to the left of the ruins. And standing between them, a hazy figure. But there's no mistaking that it's a woman. In white.

"You saw her," I whisper. I take the phone from his hands and my mouth goes dry. "Why didn't you say anything?"

"I didn't see her," he says. "I was using the phone as a flashlight. I didn't mean to take the photo."

"But here it is," I say. "On your phone."

"There it is," he echoes.

"Right," I say. "So tell me again how the ghost bride has nothing to do with your family?"

THE LEGEND OF THE CUMBERLAND GHOST BRIDE

according to GhosthuntingKY.com

Venturing further into Southern Kentucky, we offer you a terrifying tale of a woman scorned and her decades-long crusade for revenge. Known as the Cumberland Bride, this vengeful ghost is the spirit of a woman who was murdered by her husband on their honeymoon. Legend has it, they were vacationing at Cumberland Falls in the days following their wedding. While on a visit to the area known to locals as Lover's Leap, the murderous mate pushed his wife over the edge of the cliff and into the river below. Was his motive greed? Jealousy? Or just a marital spat gone horribly wrong? We can't tell you, because out of the two people there, he's not talking and she's dead.

What we do know is that the angry bride still haunts that very spot, hunting for the man who wronged her. It's said that newlyweds are particularly vulnerable to her wrath, as she feeds off their joy and love. If she can't have her happily-ever-after, why should they??

While we've never seen the bloodthirsty bride ourselves, she's an apparition well known by the locals, as is her haunting ground. Over a dozen people have drowned in that stretch of river over the years. Coincidence??? We think not.

IF YOU GO:

Go with a group.

Popular spot, especially in summer. Heavily trafficked during full moon nights, when a moonbow can be viewed in the mist coming off the falls. It's a great photo op, but watch your backs. And check your photos when you get home. You may just snap a shot of someone not on your guest list!

Cumberland Falls Park is a county park off Route 9. Follow the road past the imposing and privately owned Atwater Lodge, and take the first turnoff to your left.

Pets allowed on leash. No restroom facilities on site. Ample parking available.

CHAPTER 27

I spend the next few days reading everything I can find online about the ghost bride of Cumberland Falls. But all too soon, I'm overwhelmed with information. Worse, none of it matches up with the story I know.

"Do you know how many ghost brides there are?" I ask Daisy when she plops down across from me at a picnic table in the staff break area behind the parking lot. I can tell she's pondering the question by the way her face lights up, but I don't wait for her answer. "Hundreds. Literally. Around the world. They jump, they fall, they get pushed. They're angry, they're sad. They're haunted. They're hunters."

I show her the site I've pulled up—GhosthuntingKY.com— run by a dude who calls himself Boograss87. How does he expect anyone to take his information seriously?

Daisy stares at the screen for a minute while she chews her sandwich. "Ample parking. Good to know."

I lay my phone facedown on the table. "None of this is helpful!"

"Did you think it would be?"

"Malice said the story was the key. But I don't know which story is true."

She turns her bag of chips toward me. "I told you—mine. The ghost bride is clearly pissed off because of her shitty boyfriend."

I think about Daisy's story again, about the poor young woman whose only mistake was trusting the boy she loved. "I guess it's possible. I mean, the notes? About loyalty? And betrayal? Maybe he betrayed her." I lean closer and lower my voice. "Just like I betrayed Chance."

Daisy knows this already; I told her all the sordid details in the car on the way to work the morning after Arden and I kissed. Her reaction was less shock and more solidarity.

"Please," she says now. "Do you really think this is some kind of punishment? For what? Not pledging your complete and everlasting devotion to the one and only boyfriend you've ever had?" She rolls her eyes. "I mean, the ghost bride is old, but she's not *ancient*."

"So what does it mean? 'Betrayal has legs'?"

"How do I know? The dead are inscrutable."

"Come on. Help me."

"I can tell you you're not going to find an answer here," Daisy says, waving her hand at my phone. "This is all sensationalized clickbait. It has nothing to do with the curse. These kinds of stories aren't even about real spirits. They're more about the teller than the ghost."

I pull a sour cream and onion chip from the bag. "Explain."

"Storytelling is a ritual, right? A way to connect, or to pass along information. Ghost stories, specifically, are about our fears. Think about it. What do most people fear? Getting older? Never having true love? Being alone? Enter a lonely ghost bride. She jumped because of A, B, or C. Or all of the above."

I consider arguing, but what she's saying makes a certain amount of sense. It explains the differences in all the legends, at least.

And Daisy's not done. "The most common ghost stories have to do with women, right? Ever notice there aren't a lot of dead celibate men wandering the countryside? It's all girls in prom dresses or wedding gowns. Because that's what we're afraid of! Or, at least, it's what men *think* we should be afraid of. Getting murdered. Or worse, deflowered!" She snarls as she hooks her finger and swipes it at me.

"I see your point, but so what? I mean, I saw her. She's definitely dead, and she definitely drowned. That part I know. Beyond that, how do I separate the truth from the rest of this crap? And more importantly, how do I lift the curse?"

"Who's cursed?" Peggy plops down beside Daisy at the table and fans her face. "Are you talking about the weather? 'Cause, damn, it's a scorcher today."

"We were talking about ghost stories."

"And men," adds Daisy.

"Well, sure." Peggy nods, unfazed. "Men suck. And everyone loves a good ghost story," she adds. "Speaking of which . . ." She leans forward. "I checked into that grave you asked about."

"Nell?" Daisy practically squeals, scooting forward on her bench.

Peggy pulls out a cigarette and tucks it into the corner of her mouth. "Like I told you before, all the Dunlaps are accounted for. Nell included." She hands me a piece of paper, then lights up.

"Nell Whitley, born 1856," she says, blowing smoke sideways, away from us. "Daughter of a prominent landowning family. Her marriage to Silas Dunlap in 1875 netted the Dunlaps a huge section of land they mined for the next century. In return, Nell got all this." Peggy waves a hand in the air, encompassing the lodge and everything around us. "A successful marriage, by all accounts. They had four kids. The oldest and only son, Luther, inherited Atwater Manor as well as the Black River Mining Company. And before you ask, he and his sisters all married, but they all lived well past their wedding days. Nell was well known as a philanthropist and patron of the arts. She helped organize a letter-writing campaign to get a Carnegie library here in Corbin, among other projects. Died in 1947, at the ripe old age of ninety-one. So, like I said. No dead brides."

Every time I think I'm getting close to the truth, it disappears like a puff of smoke. Or a ghost. It would be ironic if it wasn't so frustrating.

I ball up the paper. "Everyone talks about the bride, but I start asking questions and all of a sudden everyone's all, 'It never happened. That's just a legend.' Well, guess what? I used to think that, too, but now I know the truth. She's real! And she deserves justice. Or, at the very least, a name!"

Daisy and Peggy exchange a look.

"I saw that! I am so sick of everyone acting like I'm nuts. I'm not crazy!"

Peggy smokes calmly through my outburst. When I wind down, she crosses her arms. "You've seen her."

"I didn't say that." I clamp my mouth shut.

"Honey, you don't have to be embarrassed. I'm not judging you. I've seen a lot of things through my years."

"Like a ghost?" I ask.

"No." Peggy shakes her head. "But nothing surprises me anymore."

It sounds like a challenge. So I tell her my story.

When I finish, she says, "Huh."

"That's it? 'Huh'? That's all you've got?"

"I'm not saying I don't believe you. Clearly, you saw . . . something. Something that freaked you out. But—and I'm just playin' devil's advocate now—if this bride is able to communicate, and clearly she can write, why not just tell us what she wants us to know?"

"Maybe that's all she can manage," I say. "Those few words. Maybe that's her curse."

Daisy shakes her finger at me. "This is what I was saying the other day about paranormal phenomena. You need independent evidence. Otherwise, it gets discredited because of things like this. Faulty logic. You're using your own conclusion to construct the hypothesis."

"I don't know about that, but I'm saying if she can write sentences, she should be able to write her killer's name," Peggy says.

"Or her own, for that matter," Daisy adds.

"You're assuming she was murdered," I say. "*That's* faulty logic." I hold my head in my hands and groan. "Can we please focus? This isn't about gathering evidence. It's about figuring out the bride's identity."

"Fine." Daisy dusts the chip powder off her hands. "What do we know for sure? What do all the stories have in common?"

She holds up fingers as I list the similarities off. "She was a bride. She had a lover. She drowned. He died in the fire. One of them had some connection to the Dunlaps."

"Slow down," Peggy says, staring at Daisy's five fingers. "I think you skipped a couple steps there."

"Such as? The story clearly talks about Atwater. And"—I pull up the photo Arden took and then sent me—"this photo appeared on Arden's phone the other night. When we were in the forest. He's a Dunlap. That can't be a coincidence."

Peggy puckers her lips. "O-kay, then. Carry on."

Daisy snaps her fingers and jumps to her feet. "That's right! And we already know the connection to Atwater, don't we? Her lover died in the fire. So we should be able to—"

But I shake my head. I know what she's suggesting—that we can look up the historical records and see who died when. "I thought of that, too, but we won't be able to find him that way. Apparently, that part of the story is wrong. I was talking to Kezia the other day, and she told me no one died in the fire."

"Damn." Daisy spreads her hands on the table and sinks slowly back to her seat. "So close."

"Hold on," Peggy says. "Are you talking about the fire of 1917? Because it's true no one died in *that* fire. But what about the ear-lier one?"

CHAPTER 28

Daisy and I wait until we're certain Kezia is at dinner before heading to the library. Without any sunlight streaming through the stained-glass windows, the room is dark and gloomy, the corners shrouded in long shadows. Someone's lit a fire in the massive fireplace, maybe to offset this effect, but if anything, the flickering light makes it worse. If the ghost bride or her lover did die on the premises, what's to stop them from haunting this place? There are plenty of places to hide.

I shiver, and Daisy punches me in the shoulder.

"Ow!"

"This was your idea. No chickening out now."

"I'm not chickening out," I say, rubbing the bruise. "I'm thinking."

"Yeah, well, think faster. I hate this place. It's creepy."

"It's not creepy. It's just quiet." I stop in front of the large portraits hanging over the fireplace. Silas Dunlap and Nell Whitley Dunlap. "Look. Here's Nell."

Daisy stares up at the imposing older woman, her head cocked haughtily to the side as she stares off into the distance at something we can't see.

"She was okay-looking. I guess I expected more."

"Looks aren't everything. Besides, she had to put up with him." Silas's portrait is done in dark oils, the contours of his face lost beneath his thick beard and eyebrows.

Daisy shudders. "He's terrifying. Good thing he was rich."

"This must have been painted when he was in his sixties at least. Maybe he was cuter when he was younger."

I move slowly down the wall, snapping the occasional photo with my phone. "If there's any evidence her lover lived or worked here, this is where it would be. If you'd stop panicking, you'd see these are fascinating." I stop in front of the photos Kezia and I had been admiring the other day. "Like these. This is from the second fire. Atwater was built out of wood at one point. Can you believe that?"

"Yeah, yeah. Wood. Fascinating." Daisy makes a rolling motion with her hand. "What about the lover?"

"This was actually fire number two." I step back and glance over at the other wall. "Which means if we're right about lover boy, any evidence would be over . . ."

But the wall is empty. Instead of photos, a single piece of paper has been taped to the inside of the glass: Display in Progress.

I press my hand against it. "That's weird. There was a display here before."

"Are you sure?"

"Yes, I'm sure. I saw it my first day. I remember thinking the photos had to be some of the earliest taken. There was a staff photo . . ." I turn slowly, studying the rest of the room. Maybe things are being rearranged. "Kezia found me in here last week. And she was talking about this fire, and how no one died. She was acting squirrely . . ." I trail off. "Do you think she deliberately misled me? So she could buy herself enough time to hide the other photos?" I ask.

"It seems like a lot of work," Daisy says. "And for what?"

"I'm not sure. But I do know there's some kind of big secret between her and Momma. Something happened that they won't talk about."

"Whatever it was, it didn't happen way back then," Daisy says, waving at the empty wall.

"There's one way to prove it." I take a step toward Kezia's office door, tucked between two bookshelves on the far wall.

"Oh. No." Daisy shakes her head. "I can't. No offense." She chews her lower lip. "I know you want answers. But I can't break into my boss's office. I need this job."

I wave her off. "It's fine. It's probably quicker if I go in alone anyway. Can you watch from the front desk and text me a heads-up if you see anyone coming?"

She nods and is goné in an instant, as if one more second in this room might curse her, too.

Should I close the library door? It's usually open, and being closed might be a red flag to Kezia or any other staff who notice. On the other hand, it could buy me a few seconds. The difference between being caught in the library outside Kezia's office versus inside could mean the difference between getting reprimanded and fired.

I close it.

Daisy's right. This room is creepy—even more so without the ambient sounds of the hotel around me.

A log shifts in the fireplace and I almost sprint for the door.

I need to get a grip. I slip into Kezia's office and click on a small lamp beside the door. Bookshelves make up the wall to my left, while the right is lined with tall dormer windows and a padded bench beneath. Kezia's long, mahogany desk takes up the majority of the back wall, with a couple of buttery leather chairs in front for seating.

The desk is the logical place to start, but most of the drawers are locked, so I move on to the bookshelf. The books are in no kind of order I can determine, and I scan the spines in frustration. I don't even know what I should be looking for. Maybe I should just ask Kezia what she's trying to hide.

But then I find them. On the lowest shelf, tucked into the far corner. The photos from the display, stacked haphazardly in their frames.

In progress, my ass.

I kneel on the plush carpet and spread them out in what I think is chronological order. There are some faded black-and-white shots of the old manor, as well as the falls, and I photograph these with my phone. There's also the staff photo I'd admired, mostly because of how rare it would have been back then, what with the difficulty involved in gathering everyone from their midday chores and the expense of hiring the photographer.

I'd been hoping for names. Why else would Kezia be so secretive about it? But there isn't anything to identify anyone in the group.

I turn the frame over, but hesitate before I open it. It's ancient. The frame itself looks fragile, never mind how delicate the photo will be. I want answers, but not badly enough to damage a historical artifact. I'll have to settle for another photograph and hope Peggy can help me with identification later. Because who knows? The bride's lover could well be one of the unsmiling men standing in that back row.

Or he could be a Dunlap. There are also portraits of all the early ancestors, and I get those, too.

I check my phone for a text from Daisy, but there's nothing. Hopefully Kezia is a slow eater.

Besides the photographs, she's stashed a set of leather-bound scrapbooks on this shelf as well. I pull one out at random and open it, half expecting baby pictures of Arden. But it's much older than that. I turn the pages carefully, trying not to disturb the brittle, browning paper inside. The front is full of ledger paper, a handwritten accounting of all the expenditures of Atwater House. I run my finger down one of the columns labeled *Staff Wages*. The housemaids were making between five and ten dollars a week, depending on their length of service.

And I thought my parents paid crap wages.

While it's an interesting look into the past, it doesn't help answer my questions.

I open a second, thicker book, this one bulging with newspaper clippings and photos, as well as a padded envelope labeled *Promotional Materials*. As I set that aside, a loose clipping flutters to the ground. It's a story from the *Corbin Times Tribune*, dated June 1875.

FIRE DESTROYS ATWATER MANOR.
Silas Dunlap Missing, Presumed Dead!

My heart stutters in my chest. But there's no way he could have been the lover. And he didn't die in that fire. He married Nell, and went on to build the present building, which would eventually become the lodge. After the second fire. Where no one died.

So who were the casualties from the first?

My phone chirps.

Kezia's done eating. Chatting with guests in front lobby.
GET OUT OF THERE.

I hurry to put the books back, checking I haven't left any fingerprints in the dust. I grab the padded envelope and hesitate. It has the Atwater Lodge symbol stamped on the front, so it's clearly hotel information. It won't have anything to do with the bride.

Except. My welcome packet contained an abbreviated version of her story. And what had Kezia told me? The bride made good business sense.

I text Daisy back—**Stall her**—and pry open the flap on the envelope.

It's filled with old brochures, along with typed and printed pages that are clearly early versions of the same packet they are still distributing. Which doesn't make any sense, since Kezia told me those brochures were "brand new."

I pull everything out, dumping it onto the chair. But there's nothing else here. No story. No secrets.

What did I expect?

I sift through an old set of photographs as I put everything back. At first glance, the woman, a bride, looks like she's straight out of the 1950s, decked out in a tea-length ball gown and lacy veil. It's not until one of the last photos, near the bottom of the pile, when the bride finally turns her head to face the camera, that I realize I've been wrong about everything.

This isn't from 1950. And it isn't just any bride.

It's my mother.

CHAPTER 29

This makes no sense. I've seen Momma and Daddy's wedding photos. This isn't one of them.

Was Momma married before?

I stare at the photo, as if I can will it to speak. There's something eerily familiar about her pose. And her dress. And the hair clip above her ear.

It's nearly identical to the painting of the ghost bride—the one that hangs above the fireplace in the lobby.

So what the hell does that mean?

The grandfather clock in the corner whirs to life, bonging out the hour. I shove the photo into the pocket of my apron and everything else back into the envelope.

My phone buzzes.

Where are you??

I need to get out of here.

But I'm rooted to the spot.

As always, the ghost bride's words come readily to mind. LOYALTY HAS ROOTS.

But this feels more like a betrayal. Of epic proportions.

My own momma posed for the painting of the ghost bride? What does that even mean? Jackson must have painted it, which makes sense. He did the other big paintings in the lodge. But why ask Momma to pose for it? Because Kezia would be too recognizable? I can almost imagine a scenario in which that works: Jackson wants to promote the story, but his wife—or girlfriend?—is too obvious a choice. So who does he pick?

Kezia's best friend.

I think of Arden telling me how much his mother hated the painting. Hated the whole idea of the ghost bride as a publicity gimmick. And I think it's a little weird too. But it's not like they did anything illegal.

So why all the secrecy?

At the creak of the library door, I take one last, frantic look around. Have I left anything incriminating?

I don't think so, but I don't have time to worry about it.

I hold my breath and crack open the office door, slipping out and sliding behind the baby grand piano as the door shuts quietly behind me.

I lean against the wall and close my eyes, willing my heartbeat to slow.

I should be happy. I found whatever Kezia was hiding, and I didn't get caught. Instead, I'm sick to my stomach and sick at heart, and filled with a million questions.

At the squeak of a shoe against the floor, my eyes fly open.

"Did you need something?"

Oh no.

Arden—not Kezia—looks pointedly from me to the door.

"Ah, um. No. I was just . . . looking at the photos," I say, gesturing vaguely toward the wall.

"With your eyes shut?"

I step out from behind the piano, my face flaming. We stare at each other for a full minute without speaking, me watching the expressions on his face change as he struggles with whether or not to accuse me of what I was clearly doing.

But I've got nothing. I can't explain my way out of this.

I clear my throat. "I know you probably don't want to hear this, but—"

He holds up a hand. "Please don't. I know what you were doing. I just can't believe it. I told you how I felt. I laid everything out there. And I thought maybe . . ." His Adam's apple bobs as he swallows convulsively, like he's trying to choke down whatever lie he thinks I'm going to offer. "But none of it meant anything to you, did it? It's always been about the stupid bride. What about our kiss? Was that real?"

"Arden. Don't. Of course it was. I like you." I hate that I'm hurting him, but I don't have time for this now. "I just . . . it's—"

"Do *not* say 'It's complicated' to me again! This is not normal. You realize that? It's like you're obsessed with this dead girl or something. But take it from me. You can search for meaning or answers or whatever it is you're looking for, but you are never going to find it. Ghosts can't give you what you want. They aren't capable of it. Trust me." His voice cracks.

"I know that," I whisper. "But you're wrong. I'm not obsessed." I'm cursed. There's a difference. "I'm sure your dad would send you some kind of message or sign if he could. But that isn't how they work."

Like Daisy said, the dead are inscrutable. We have to puzzle out the message ourselves. Even if it's not the one we want to hear.

"God, can you hear yourself? 'How they work'? What, you think you're some kind of expert? They don't 'work' at all. They're dead. Gone."

"That's not—" I cut my denial short. "Would you just listen to me for a minute? Let me explain?"

"What is there to explain? You're just like everyone else. You don't see me; all you see is Atwater."

"That's not fair! If anyone knows what it's like to be overshadowed by their family, it's me." I take the photo of my mother from my apron pocket and hold it up. "That's what I've been trying to tell you."

Arden crosses his arms over his chest.

"I found this. In your mom's office. Do you know what it means?" My hand trembles. "It means your mom and my mom have a secret. A big one. Your dad, maybe, too—"

I break off as Kezia steps into the room.

"Don't stop on my account. What is it you think we did, exactly?"

She waits bathed in the light of the fire, arms folded, chin tilted expectantly. When I press my lips closed, she moves to stand beside Arden.

"As far as I can tell, the only person that photo implicates is your mother. Well, and you, of course." She pulls out her phone, dials, then speaks. "I need an escort off the property for a termi-nated employee."

Arden rears back. "Mom. Wait—"

Kezia ignores him as she ends the call without taking her eyes off me.

"Fine," I say. "I don't need an escort. I'll go. But at least tell me what this means." I show her the photo.

Kezia takes two steps toward me, so we're close enough that I can hear everything she says through gritted teeth. "Your mother took those photos. Ask her."

"But Momma doesn't believe in the ghost bride."

Kezia flashes a brittle smile. "Oh, I think we both know that's not true. I know all about the curse, Rena Faye. And if Lou thinks for one second that she can try to offer up my son instead? She's wrong. Dead wrong. So you go back and tell her that." She takes another step forward, and I take another back.

Kezia continues, "She could've just asked for the photos back, you know. Instead of sending you to get a job here. To do her dirty work."

"She didn't send me here. She never wanted me to . . ." My head is spinning and I can't grasp on to more than a few words at a time. None of what Kezia is saying makes any sense. And yet. Momma is in the photos. Momma is—or was—a photographer.

"Never wanted you to what? Discover what she'd done? How she's cursed you? If you're looking for someone to blame, I sug-gest you take your nose out of my business and start looking at the woman who disturbed the ghost bride in the first place." She taps a nail on the photo.

Momma's face stares up at us from the glossy image. "I don't believe you," I manage to say.

Kezia's green eyes search mine for a long moment. "You don't have to believe it," she finally says, "but you do have to leave. Because you no longer work here. Get off my property. Before I have you thrown off."

CHAPTER 30

I don't wait for Kezia's escort, and I don't listen to Arden calling me back.

Instead, I run, out the door and down the walkway, past the parking lot and onto the public path leading to the falls. It's crowded tonight, and I try to lose myself in the mass. People lying on blankets, their picnic suppers spread out on the rocky outcropping as they watch the sunset.

I walk to the railing and stare down at the water, letting the spray mingle with my tears.

The way Kezia looked at me when she accused me of working with Momma. As if I'd betrayed her.

But Momma doesn't have anything to do with the ghost. Or the curse.

Kezia is wrong.

She has to be.

Otherwise, every single thing I know to be true is a lie.

Because if any of what she's saying is right, this story was written long before I ever got here. I never had a chance at any kind of happy ending. All this time, I thought maybe Arden and I were heading for some kind of star-crossed romance. But it turns out he's just like the others. Refusing to listen to me, telling me what to believe.

Once again, I'm just a minor character in someone else's drama. A shadow of someone else.

My mother.

Is this how the bride felt? She thought she was living her very own romance, but it turned out her lover had been crafting a different story all along. And he'd written her out.

Maybe that's why she jumped. Because at least then she'd get to write her own ending.

"Are you okay, miss?" An elderly woman touches my sleeve. She and her husband stand beside me, matching worried expressions on their faces. "You look so sad."

She shifts her gaze from me to the railing and back, as if trying to gauge the distance.

I wipe my tears and force myself to smile. "I'm fine. Just, you know, teenage drama. Thanks."

I turn around and look up at the lodge, rising from the mountain behind us. For a short time, I thought I might be able to write my own story. But that's over now.

I move away from the couple and pull out my phone. I need to get out of here, away from the lies and broken fantasies. Momma is right about that, at least. Fantasy only brings you heartbreak.

I text Daddy for a ride, against my better judgment.

The whole way home, I keep my mouth pressed shut, afraid

of what I'll say if I give myself the chance. Momma's photo burns in my pocket, daring me to ask him what he knew and when he knew it.

But maybe Daddy is as innocent in all of this as I am. He doesn't believe in ghosts or curses, after all. And I can't imagine Momma telling him any of this.

Still, things don't add up. She's young in the photo. My age, maybe. And she and Daddy were high school sweethearts. So wouldn't he have known if Jackson were painting her?

Someone is lying. But who? Kezia clearly hates Momma. And what did Momma call Kezia? A flaming bitch?

Daddy idles the truck in front of our lobby. "Your momma said you gave your notice."

I don't wait for the rest of whatever he's gearing up to say. "Yeah, but I'm done. As of tonight. I guess they don't need me any longer." My voice catches, and I shove the door open before he can ask any more questions.

"I'm heading over to Malice's. Help her and your momma with the packing. You gonna be all right?"

I manage a nod.

"It's for the best," Daddy calls after me as I head up the driveway.

The best what? I want to ask. Everyone keeps saying that to me. But they never tell me why.

Inside I'm greeted by silence.

Graham's manning the front desk down at the motel, and Daddy said Momma's with Malice, so I'm alone.

Good.

I take a hammer from Daddy's workroom, savoring the heft of it in my hand as I slam it down on the handle of the darkroom.

There are probably easier ways to pick a lock, but I want to destroy all of it. Every bit of Momma that's left in me, every single thing we have in common. All of the hopes I had that are packed into this room. That one day, she'd understand me. One day, we'd be close. But those dreams are dead now, buried beneath the secrets and lies.

Maybe it's like Malice said. As many stories as we may tell to try, as much as we want to avoid passing on our pain, it's a cycle we can't break. Malice disappointed Momma, Momma disappoints me. One day, I'll probably have a daughter whom I'll disappoint as well.

Except I'll know better.

Momma may not use this room anymore, but she's still everywhere, in her photos on the wall, her fingerprints in every dusty corner. But right now, it's her negatives I'm after. Stored in boxes on a high shelf that borders the room. I pull them down and dump them on the floor, one after another, the sheets sticking together until I peel them loose and shuffle them around.

Eventually, I find something.

I hold the negatives to the light. It looks like Momma shot a whole series by herself, since it's evident it took her a while to get the timing right. In the first few frames, she appears only as a blur, running toward the camera or away.

In these shots, the backdrop is easily recognizable. It's the wall from the ruins.

Momma knows about the clearing.

Mine and Daisy's special place.

I lean my back against the wall, my feet sliding against the slick negatives.

Malice said Momma shirked her responsibility to the ghost bride because she didn't want to believe. But that wasn't true. Instead, Momma went to the clearing, *dressed* as the bride. She conjured her, just like Daisy tried to do. And if Kezia's telling the truth, it worked.

Is that why the bride appeared to me? Not because of the clip, but because Momma had called her forth?

BETRAYAL HAS LEGS. LOYALTY HAS ROOTS.

This time, I hear the words in Momma's voice. She said she knew the minute I'd said them that I'd heard them at Atwater. Because she thought Kezia had told me.

Which means this is the same warning the ghost gave her. It has to be.

I pound the back of my head against the wall.

Momma knew about the ghost all along—knew that she was real—and she never even tried to warn me. Worse, she acted like Malice and I were the crazy ones. Sweet Malice, who was so worried when I told her about the hair clip. She thought she'd done something to hurt me. But maybe Momma wanted me to be scared. She always says that Malice and I feed off each other. Maybe she needed Malice to sound as off her rocker as possible, so her brothers would go along with moving her out of her cabin and into town.

Or maybe this isn't about Malice at all. Maybe it's some elaborate punishment. Because I quit the family business.

BETRAYAL HAS LEGS.

Was Momma trying to teach me a lesson?

My head hurts and I can't tell which connections are real, and which ones are all in my head. What's true and what's a lie.

I know only one thing for certain—Momma knows about the bride and the clearing, because she took these photos.

Daisy keeps telling me to find evidence, and I'm literally holding proof of Momma's lies in my hands.

But I'm going to need more than this to figure out the truth.

CHAPTER 31

I have a plan. Or at least the start of one.

But I need a ride, and Daisy's still at work. My fingers itch to text Arden, to try to apologize and explain once more what I was doing in his mother's office. But our argument is too fresh and there's still the awkwardness between us because of the kiss.

That *amazing* kiss.

Stop it.

Chance is probably the last person I should be seeing right now, next to Momma. Poison ivy was a good excuse the past few days, but tonight his text—**You busy?**—is perfectly timed, like the knight in shining armor he believes himself to be.

I grab my camera and wait for him near the pool gate. He brakes right in the middle of the driveway, and his thoughtfulness catches in my throat like a sob.

Why have I been so hard on him these past few weeks? Why have I worked so hard to push him away? Clearly he cares about me. He's the one who's here for me when I'm at my lowest.

He jumps out and runs around to open my door, leaving the engine running. Always the gentleman.

When he gets back in, he smiles at me. "You look . . . itchy. Are you feeling any better?"

I shake my head, afraid if I speak, I'll burst into tears.

He doesn't seem to notice as he pulls forward into the parking lot to turn around. "I'm glad you texted me back. I was wondering if you wanted—"

"I got fired," I blurt out, staring down at my hands.

"Wow. I'm . . . sorry." His pause is long enough that I know it wasn't what he was originally going to say. "What happened?"

As his headlights sweep across the motel, I see Graham standing by the lobby door. We lock eyes for a moment as the truck glides past. I can't read the expression on his face, and I look away before he does.

Chance is watching me, waiting.

"I . . ." I lose my voice, swallow, try again. "I did something. Something I shouldn't have." *Now is the time to tell him*, I think. *Tell him about Arden, about how foolish I've been. Rip off the Band-Aid.* "I broke into my boss's office," I say instead.

He jerks his head back. This is not what he's expecting to hear. Chance's moral compass is strong. He isn't prepared to deal with my weakness.

"Why don't we go somewhere to talk? I've been wanting to spend some time alone together. And this seems like the perfect chance."

Perfect? I shake my head. "I don't want to talk. I need to go to the clearing." I need to try to see the bride one more time. To figure out what's the truth and what's a lie. But I promised Malice I wouldn't go alone. Chance seems like my best bet for a body-guard at this point.

I also sent Momma a text, telling her I was going to the woods, but not why. Whether she shows up will give me at least some of the answers I'm looking for. Like, has she known all along what kind of danger I'm in? Even as she was telling me to "grow up" and to stop believing in fairy tales? Or worse, is Kezia right? And is Momma the reason I'm cursed in the first place?

"Okay." He veers off the road and kills the engine. "What's going on?"

I slip the photo of Momma from my pocket. "I found this. In my boss's office."

He takes the picture from me. "Is that . . . was your mom married before?"

"No. At least . . . I don't think so," I say, less convincingly the second time. "I think she was posing for a painting. But there were other photos, too."

"In your boss's office," he says, sounding doubtful.

"Yes! She and Momma used to be friends. Malice told me."

"Is that why you broke in? To find this?"

"No." I take the photo back. "No, this was a total surprise. I was searching for evidence—historical evidence—of the ghost bride."

"Of the what?"

"You know," I say impatiently. "That's why I need to go to the clearing. Because now *I* need to know. If the curse is on me. Or if Momma—"

"I thought you were done with this," he says, trying to take my hand. "We agreed. Remember?"

We agreed. The echo of so many other conversations reverberates in his words, and though they're familiar, I truly can't recall the agreement part.

I shake my head. "It's not over." I swallow around the lump in my throat at the look of disbelief on his face. "I'm still cursed. I went looking for the bride, to try to end this. But what I found was Momma."

I tap the corner of the photo softly against my knee as I stare out the window. We're pulled over just past the bridge, and I can hear the shush of the river below, but I can't see it from this angle. Just the rock wall of the cliffs, boxing me in. I've lived my whole life inside this box. How foolish to think that somehow Atwater was my way out.

My phone vibrates. Don't even think about it, missy.

I delete the text from Momma and turn off my phone.

Chance starts the car and steers us into the parking lot of the Leap.

"What are we doing here? I said—"

"Not everything is about you," he says, trying to soften the words with a smile. "I had a sur—something . . . in mind. Before I knew how upset you were. I thought maybe we could spend some time together. Take your mind off things."

I don't need to take my mind off things. I need to get to the clearing. Preferably ahead of Momma.

"I didn't expect it to be so crowded," he says.

It may not be moonbow, but it's Friday night—of course it's

crowded. And this is the last thing I want to be doing.

"I don't want to see anyone right now," I say. "Can we go—"

"That's fine. We can stay in here." He turns off the car and takes off his seat belt, turning to face me, resting his back against the door. "I've missed you," he says. "We haven't done this in a while."

I don't know what *this* is, but I don't say that out loud.

"Be alone together, I mean," he adds.

"It's been a weird month," I say, which might be the biggest understatement ever.

"Yeah. So maybe this is for the best," he says. "You getting . . . being done at Atwater, I mean. Now we can spend more time together."

Is that the silver lining? If so, shouldn't I feel some kind of happiness? And not this deep sense of loss, this heaviness weighing me down?

"Yeah." I shove that stupid lump down down down into the pit of my stomach. "Yes," I say, more firmly. "Sure. At least until I find another job."

He clears his throat. "I mean, there's always the ranch. We'd be happy to have you."

I gape at him. "Happy to have me? I thought we *agreed*. The ranch is not for me." Then again, that argument was so long ago, it feels like it happened to someone else, in another lifetime.

"No, I know. Because of your allergies. And of course I want you to be safe. But there's got to be, like, something you can do, right? A pill you can take or something?"

"Yes, there's something I can do. Avoid horses."

I can tell by the way he furrows his brow and looks away that he doesn't like my answer. I wait for more of an argument, but none comes. Instead he says, "Let's take a walk," and gets out of the truck without waiting for my answer.

As he opens my door, I protest. "Chance. I really don't feel like—"

"Come on. The fresh air will do you good."

I give in and get out because it's easier than arguing, and what am I going to do, anyway? Sit in his truck alone?

I let him lead, and he grabs my hand as we near the Leap. But instead of walking out onto the platform, he pulls me down a side path, into the trees. "This isn't the safest path at night," I warn him. But since no one else is foolish enough to be down here, at least it means I won't run into anyone I know.

He stops abruptly and turns to me.

"What is it?" I ask.

"There's been something I've been wanting to talk to you about. Something I want to ask you." He runs a hand through his hair.

"Please do not ask me about the ranch again. Because I don't want to keep arguing about it. We're never going to see eye to eye on that."

"That's the thing, though. I need us to."

"You *need* us to?"

He drops to one knee in the dirt.

"What the . . . oh my god."

"Rena Faye, I love you. And I want you to be my wife. Eventually. And I think that's what you want too. For us to be together. Because it's always been us. And I know you think the ranch is a deal-breaker, but it's not: we can work that out. What's important is that we belong together."

I am frozen with shock, so before I can even process what he's said—and what *I* want—Chance has slipped the promise ring on my finger and he's standing and kissing me and it's clear he thinks I've agreed, though I haven't said a word.

CHAPTER 32

I look down at the ring on my blotchy hand—a tiny round stone on a plain gold band—and back up to Chance's beaming face.

I am not engaged. That would be ridiculous. I'm seventeen. Still in high school.

Still. A promise ring means you're at least *pre*-engaged. Right? No. This is a mistake.

Chance looks so happy, and I do feel like I'm floating, just like all the books describe. But not on a cloud. More like I've gone invisible and ceased to exist. Because the love that shines in his eyes, it's not for me. It's for some other girl. A different Rena Faye. One Chance has constructed in his mind—a perfect woman who fits into the slot he's so carefully carved for his future.

And me, I'm nothing. A nonentity. A ghost.

But I'm to blame, at least for part of it. I stopped paying attention and I lost control of my own life. Even after all the things that used to come naturally started to feel unnatural, I didn't dare question them because anything was easier and a lot less scary than saying the words that might change everything. But deep down, I've known for a while now that Chance and I aren't destined for some fairy-tale ending. I've been holding on to the ghost of this relationship for far too long, hoping to resurrect it out of some kind of loyalty, or maybe nostalgia. Because that's all that's left between us now. The rest of it is dead.

Malice is right—stories are easy; the truth is harder.

I twist the ring, slowly at first, then more determined, yanking it from my finger.

Chance grabs my hand. "Doesn't it fit?"

"I can't do this," I say. I push the ring into his palm and take a step back.

"Why not?" A dozen emotions flutter across his face, and I can name them all. That's how well I know him. Fear, anger, embarrassment, confusion. Understanding, with a splash of condescension.

"If you're afraid of what your family will say, you don't have to worry," he says. "I already talked to your daddy."

Of course he did. I'm not even the slightest bit surprised. They probably picked out the ring together.

See, I know Chance so well. But he doesn't know me at all.

"I cheated on you." It just comes out. All this time I've spent agonizing over what to say and how to say it, and now, when I'm angry and sad and tired of pretending, the words come easy. "And I didn't tell you when it happened. Which is basically like a lie. So"—I nod at the ring—"I'm sure you'll want to hang on to that, now that you know."

He clenches his hand around it, his knuckles going white. "With Arden." It isn't a question. "I will kill him."

I always knew he had a jealous side. I may have underestimated his temper.

"Nobody is killing anyone. It's not his fault. I kissed him. And I didn't tell him about you."

He works his jaw. "How long?"

"It's not . . . we're not—"

"How. Long?"

"It was just that one time. After we . . ." I trail off and press my lips together. Details aren't going to help the situation.

"Okay." He walks in a small circle, kicking up leaves. "Okay. So you had doubts. You got scared. It's understandable."

It's as if he's talking to himself and not to me.

"And you were honest. I have to give you credit for that."

"You really don't," I say.

"I forgive you," he says, as if I haven't spoken. "Or I guess I'll learn to forgive you. But I can do it." He nods. "Yes, I know I can."

The final shards of guilt fall away; he hasn't heard a word I've said. "I'm not asking you to forgive me," I say, my voice rising. "I'm telling you I'm not in love with you anymore. I have feelings for someone else."

"But you said it was one time." He barks the words, and I take another step back, until I'm nearly in the bushes. "So this whole time, while you've been working with him and kissing him and lusting after him, you've been—what? Pretending with me? After you told me I had to 'let you make your own decisions.' Now you choose to be with him?"

"That's not how it was," I say quietly. "I was trying to ignore my feelings for him. And I was trying to make it work with you. I really was."

But we both know I'm protesting too much.

"Yeah, well, you don't need to do me any favors." He flings the ring—at me or past me, I can't be sure—and it bounces off my cheek and into the bushes.

He doesn't wait to see it land; instead, he takes off up the trail, his muffled curses lingering long after he's gone. I debate following him or searching for the ring, but I decide to do neither. Let him crawl around in the dirt for a hot minute while he questions his life choices. I've done enough of that already this summer.

I sink to the ground with a small sob. I needed to lay my heart bare, but now that I have, I'm cold and shaking.

I've lost everything. My job, my relationship with Chance. Arden and whatever we had. Friendship? Something more? Telling Chance my true feelings is the closest I've gotten to honesty in weeks. But any relief is far outweighed by the guilt at the things I said to both of them.

I should never have showed Arden that picture of my mom. Or said what I did about ghosts. His dad died not that long ago. What kind of monster am I, ruining his memories of his father? He's right; I'm no expert. I hurt Chance, too. And though I needed to come clean with him, it doesn't make me feel better. I should have been honest with him from the beginning. After a lifetime of friendship, I owe him at least that much.

I need to make all of this right, but I have no idea how.

• • • •

After what feels like hours of crying in the dark, I pull myself up and make my way to the parking lot. I don't expect that Chance has waited for me, but I look for his truck anyway. When I see that it's gone, I can't tell if I'm relieved or pissed off.

But I think I have a plan.

Unfortunately, Chance has my camera, which is going to make the next step much more difficult.

"Well, well, well. Rena Faye Whitaker. What are you doing out here all by yourself?" Wade Dawson leans out of a pickup truck window a few parking spots over, still wearing his Hamburger Hut T-shirt. At least he ditched the stupid paper hat.

I realize, belatedly, that I've been staring in his direction while contemplating the dark pit my life has become.

"Hey, Wade." I raise a weary hand, then pretend to study my phone.

"So what do you think?" he says loudly, speaking to someone in the passenger seat. "Did Chance finally cut her loose? And she's come out here to end it all? Just like that crazy ghost chick?"

"Actually, I cut him loose," I say, and immediately regret it. This story is going to be all over town in about twenty minutes.

"You don't say?" He raises an eyebrow to leer at me.

I shrug. "We had a fight. It's no big deal." I take a step closer to the truck and now I can make out his passenger. Benjamin King. He's a decent guy. They have a truck and I need a ride and it's not like I have other options at the moment. So I ask, "Hey, do you think you guys could give me a lift?"

"Well, that's gonna cost you," Wade says.

Benjamin knocks his shoulder. "Hop in," he says.

I climb in the back, kicking aside the beer bottles that roll at my feet. "Thanks."

Wade looks at me in the rearview. "Caudell really left you stranded? Must've been some fight."

I look away and Wade pulls out onto the road. "Like I was saying, a ride'll cost you."

"I've got five dollars," I say.

"I was thinking more like something in trade," he says, pulling off suddenly into a dark driveway and killing the engine. "Ben and I don't mind sharing."

I feel my pulse quicken.

Wade has said some skeezy things in the past, but I figured they were just words. I didn't think he might be an actual creep.

"Nice try, jackass," I say.

His eyes find mine in the rearview mirror. "I'd watch that tone if I were you. No one knows you're with us. They won't know where to look for you."

I wait for him to say he's just messing with me, but he doesn't. There's not a trace of laughter in his voice.

My blood goes cold.

What the hell was I thinking getting into this truck? This is exactly the kind of thing my momma has been warning me about my whole life. This is how girls go missing, and it has nothing to do with a curse. No, it's men and their need to dominate women so they can feel better about themselves.

Between Chance acting like he owns me—like our future together is a done deal—and Daddy's condescending insistence that losing my job is for the best, I am about fed up with boys and their fragile egos. Which is too bad for Wade Dawson. Because he picked the wrong girl to mess with tonight.

"Say cheese, asshole." I hold up my phone and click the picture as Wade's head snaps around. "Guess who just threatened to rape and murder me when I asked him for a ride?" I say out loud as I type. "Post photo? Yes, please."

Wade grabs for my phone, but I hold it out of reach.

"Delete that. Now."

"Sure. Just as soon as you drop me off. Atwater parking lot is fine. I left my car there," I lie.

Benjamin breaks the awkward silence. "He was just joking. He always takes everything too far," he tells me. "Jesus, Wade, she's right," he says, lowering his voice. "Knock it off. You sound like a serial killer."

Wade swears as he backs out of the driveway. "I guess the bitch can't take a joke."

"Guess not," I say.

The second we pull into the lot at Atwater, my door is open and I can't get out of the truck fast enough. My legs barely hold as I stagger away.

"Hey," Wade yells. "Aren't you forgetting something?" When I turn back, he rubs his fingers together. "You said five dollars, right?"

I pull my hand from my pocket and give him the middle finger.

His engine drowns out whatever he calls me as he roars away.

I'm shaking with fury and fear, but also a strange sense of justice. I'm not deleting that photo. Let Wade try to explain himself to his friends. It's not the kind of joke that gets funnier with the retelling.

I'm too chicken to head inside to look for Daisy, so I text her from one of the picnic tables in the back of the lot.

Still at work?
Sorry. Home already. WHAT THE HELL HAPPENED??
Long story. And Wade Dawson is a dick, FYI
Old news. I was talking about your job??
What job? 😦

I watch the dots jump as she types a reply, drumming my fingers on the table.

SPILL
Later.

I really don't want to go into the woods by myself. But if I'm right, Momma will meet me there. Because despite all the things I don't know about her past, I do know how she feels about the woods. And there is no way she's going to let me go there alone at night.

And now I know why. I've been trying so hard these past few days to figure out how to lift this stupid curse, when it turns out all I had to do was ask my own momma.

CHAPTER 33

I use my phone as a flashlight and make my way down the path to the beach. These steps are definitely not intended for nighttime use, but I'm committed and I'm not going back.

Not until I see the clearing and get some answers—either from Momma or from her ghost bride.

The beach is deserted. The sand shines silver in the moonlight, the washed-up driftwood casting brittle, stretching shadows that grasp at my ankles.

I keep my head down, concentrating on my feet and the small beam of light as I move forward. I'm scared. No question. But I'm also sick of feeling this way. I'm sick of feeling cursed, of doubting myself. I'm so tired of questioning everything, of waiting for someone to tell me I'm doing the right thing. Or worse, letting people push me around, in the hopes that eventually they'll push me into a version of myself that will appease everyone else.

I don't want to be that girl anymore.

For a while, this summer, I thought I'd banished that Rena Faye. The curse actually helped with that—once I let myself believe in the bride, I started trusting my instincts. I was growing up and making my own choices, just like Momma keeps ordering me to do. But now here I am, in the middle of a goddamn haunted forest, waiting for someone—Momma or a dead girl—all so that I can prove . . . what? That I'm smart? That I don't deserve to be fucked with like this? That I matter?

No more.

Tonight, they're the ones who are going to have to answer to me.

I stop just shy of the clearing, trying to keep my movements as quiet as possible. I walk the perimeter slowly, searching for any sign that I'm not alone. But there's nothing. The ruins are as empty and forlorn as ever. The tumbled stones form their own kind of monsters in the darkness and these are my only companions. Unease puckers my skin. It's cool, but not the biting cold that accompanied the bride last time.

I wait in the silence and the stillness, unsure what to do next. I thought Momma would be here already. The thought of having to confront the bride by myself might take courage I don't possess.

"Momma?" I say, but my voice is swallowed by the trees. "Are you out there?"

I wait; the branches above creak softly. Is that a breeze? Or my imagination?

I hold out my arms. "I know you wouldn't let me come out here alone. Because you know the danger, don't you? You've seen her. Kezia told me."

This time, there's a definite brush of air through the leaves, like a soft breath. Or a sigh.

I wait, but nothing happens.

I'm tired and cold and hungry and nervous and now out of patience. It's been such a long day and I just want to go home and crawl into bed.

"Why? Why would you do this to me? You just let her haunt me? Without any warning? Or help? Is this supposed to be some kind of sick punishment?" I cry. "You *knew* she was out here. You knew I would be cursed. But you lied to me and then just . . . walked away. Like it didn't matter. Like *I* don't matter."

I wait, for an answer. For confirmation. But nothing comes. So I keep going. "Just because I don't want the same things you do, that doesn't make me disloyal. And trying to live my own life isn't a betrayal." My voice rises with each sentence, until I'm yelling into the treetops, the echo of my words calling back at me like an accusation.

"She wrote those words to you, too, didn't she?" I snatch up one of the pieces of paper lying on the ground, but it's blank. "And you used them against me! But just because I want to go to college doesn't mean I'm running away. I'm just trying to live my life. You keep telling me to grow up, remember? Well, guess what. You can't have it both ways. You can't tell me to be independent and think for myself and then accuse me of running away and turning my back on family when I do it." I take an icy breath.

"You know what else has legs? Secrets. The longer you keep one and feed it, the bigger and stronger it grows. Until it becomes its own monster. And *that* can carry you away from the people you love too."

Still nothing. I shiver and blow on my hands. "Why can't we both just be honest?"

The forest is still, like it's holding a breath. Or maybe that's Momma, waiting for me to say more.

"Look, I've tried to be loyal. To you, to our family. But you can't just *demand* it. It has to be earned. Planted. Loyalty has roots, remember? My roots will always be here," I tell her. "College won't change that. You and Daddy don't have to try to force me into some broken relationship with Chance just to keep me home."

The hair goes up on the back of my neck then, as if pulled by a string. I'm chilled, and not just because these truths have drained me. The temperature has dropped, the humidity of the summer evening gone.

I turn, and she's behind me.

Not Momma.

The ghost bride.

Standing in a sliver of moonlight. Motionless. Her hair and dress are soaking wet, and the forest is so still I can hear the *drip drip drip* of water as it splatters on the leaves beneath her. She tilts her head to the side, as if I'm the anomaly. Her eyes are dark pits, devoid of emotion or life.

Frosty air burns my lungs.

"Momma? Are you here?"

The bride slowly shakes her head back and forth.

Why on earth did this seem like a good idea? The only thought in my head right now is *Run!*

But I can't. I'm frozen in place while the wind picks up around me, pine needles stinging my ankles while my hair whips my cheeks. She remains deadly still, wet hair clinging to her pale face.

I force my uncooperative mouth to form words. "Who are you? What do you want?"

She doesn't move.

"Are *you* cursed? Because . . . because I want to help you. Lift it. Just tell me what I need to do."

Her dark eyes lock with mine, and I can't remember if we've been standing here for seconds or for days.

Finally, she stretches out an arm, slowly scratching ROOTS into the dirt once again.

"I don't understand what you mean. Help me understand." I clench my numb fingers together. The more I talk, the more unreal this becomes. Maybe she can't hear me. Maybe ghosts are nothing more than a memory, stuck on a loop in this one place, doomed to repeat some specific moment for all eternity.

"'Loyalty has roots'?" I scream this with so much force it should move her on her feet. "Did someone betray you? Was it your lover?"

She flickers, like an old film getting caught in a projector, and for a moment time seems to freeze as she stands before me, whole and smiling, as she must have looked on her wedding day. Her hair pinned back in Malice's clip, her nightgown white and silky and new.

Nightgown?

I blink, and the image dissolves.

What the hell was that?

Is it because I mentioned her lover? "I tried to find him," I say, "but I need your help. What was his name?"

She flickers again, the image holding longer this time, which only makes the drowned version that much more chilling when it reappears.

"I think I understand. You can't speak. But if you could write it down . . . We could use one of the notes—"

As I move toward the wall, she slashes a hand through the air, so quickly it's a blur, and the wall collapses in a thundering crush of stone.

I stumble backward, away from the cloud of dust and debris.

So, no on the notes.

I'm dizzy and confused. If I had been any closer to that wall, she could have killed me.

Just like with the statue from Nell's grave.

"I don't know what you want from me," I whisper.

She moves then, finally, swiftly. Skimming across the forest floor so impossibly fast that I scramble backward once more. I hold out my arms to ward her off.

"Don't! Nell!" I scream the first name that comes to mind.

She rears back as if jerked by a leash.

We stare at each other, the dark hollows of her eyes boring into me, barely a foot between us. And that's when the humming starts, softly at first, then louder and more insistent. A crazy tune that hurts my ears as it blends into a shriek.

I cover my ears as her eyes begin to burn with a blue fury.

"Please stop. Please. Stop. No. No. No!"

I trip on the fallen rocks beneath my feet and suddenly I'm on my back.

The trees above me are fuzzy and soft, swaying back and forth in rhythm with the one remaining wall. The sharp pain in my head is making it hard to concentrate, but I manage to bring the world back into focus.

The ghost bride kneels over me, her hair dripping cold, fetid water onto my face. Her gaping mouth is a dark portal to hell, drawing closer and closer, stealing my breath.

Until it swallows me whole.

CHAPTER 34

I'm standing on a ledge overlooking the falls. It's night, but the moon gives the water a silvery shine. As I watch, the moonbow arcs up out of the darkness, toward me, as if forming a bridge.

The Leap. How did I get here?

The roar of the falls makes it hard to concentrate, and the rushing water has taken on an oddly rhythmic tone, pulsing and stopping.

Stopping? I wince and grab my head as a wave of pure pain washes over me.

Stay with me. You're going to be okay. The words seem to come from somewhere outside myself, but they are strangely comforting.

I turn away from the bow and there she is—the bride. Only she's not scary like before. Instead, I see her as she was before she died, radiant in the glow of the moon as the nightgown of creamy lace billows out around her. Her auburn hair is braided and threaded with violets.

She smiles at me, and I smile back. "Are you okay?" I ask.

She gives a little shake of her head and motions toward the bridge.

"No!" I reach for her, but my hand touches only air.

Her smile is sadder this time, and as she steps forward, I hold my breath. I'm not ready to follow her, but I don't want to watch her die, either.

Then she turns suddenly, neck straining, her attention caught by a sound behind us. It's coming from the ruins. Another rushing noise, but this time, it isn't running water. Instead, it sounds like . . . arguing.

A letter? Really? You couldn't tell me to my face?

The voice is tinny, like an old recording. Or an echo. It sounds like . . . Kezia? Who is she talking to?

This is about Harlan, isn't it? I should have known you'd give in to him.

No! He has no idea that I—

"Momma?"

That you what? Sold him out? Look at you, dressed like your dead bride. You're a hypocrite, you know that.

And then I see them, silhouetted in the moonlight spilling over the ruins. More shadow than light. Momma, dressed in the wedding gown, hair pinned back. Kezia, younger and wilder, her hair long, her jeans and Muckrakers T-shirt both torn.

We agreed . . . the legend will help both our businesses. You can't just quit now.

I have to. My mother was right.

I look at the bride, wondering if she's as surprised as I am to hear these words from Momma's mouth. But she's watching

Kezia, who waves something in the air—a piece of paper—before she shreds it, letting the pieces scatter. One lands near my feet, and I bend down to pick it up.

I read silently, as Kezia screams the words along with me: *BETRAYAL HAS LEGS. LOYALTY HAS ROOTS.*

"Did Momma write that?" I ask my bride.

But she's gone, obscured by the cloud of smoke that suddenly engulfs us. I cough, trying to wave it away. The ruins have gone cold and dark. Momma and Kezia have vanished.

I am alone.

No. Wait.

The bride stands beside a tree at the far end of the clearing. She motions for me to follow, and I have no choice. This is why I came here tonight. To get answers.

So I run.

We go deep into the woods, where it's cold and dark and the ground is littered with hazards I can't see. I trip and stumble, every jar causing my head to pound harder. Something sharp pinches my wrist, and I cry out. A branch, maybe. But still we're running, and I don't look back.

Finally, the bride slows. I hardly recognize the building, but somehow, I know it's Atwater Manor. It's big, but not nearly as massive as it will be someday. Constructed of wide logs, with porches that wrap around both stories and soft light flickering in the windows.

Fire?

No—it's only candlelight.

The bride climbs the steps and waves me forward. I grab the

doorknob, but it's hot to the touch and I burn my hand, the searing pain almost enough to wake me. Because I must be dreaming. I'm wearing a nightgown, too.

"What happened to your wedding gown?" I ask, following her through the front door and down a narrow hallway as it fills with smoke. There are other people here, but they don't see us; they shriek and run, pressing towels against their faces and hurrying away from the heat and the flame.

Only me and my ghost are heading toward it, to a bedroom in the back. To a man who looks like he's stepped out of one of the library photos. He's dressed in pajamas; a pressed tuxedo hangs from the armoire behind him.

The bride rushes forward to embrace him, then steps back. Emotions ripple across her beautiful face like waves of heat as she catches sight of the suit—happiness, then confusion. Pain. She slaps him, hard, and he recoils. And in the moment that he looks away, she snatches something from his dresser.

Betrayal has legs. It carries you away from the people you love.

It sounds like Momma's voice.

"I didn't betray you!" I say, the man's voice behind mine, like an echo.

The bride rears back, fury twisting her face. She raises her hands and presses the hair clip into her braid, the large center stone casting shards of light as the walls burst into flame. The blaze eats away at everything around me; all these fates destroyed. My throat burns with the loss.

Tongues of fire lick at my feet and creep closer to where we stand.

"We have to get out of here," I say. I hold out my hand and she tries to take it, but she can't. She can't hold anything. Because she's only a dream, my bride.

You need to go. I have to try to save the house, the man tells us.

But he's much too late. The house will burn to the ground tonight. People will die.

I blink, and once again I'm standing outside, on the cold, rocky cliff. Instead of the house in front of me, there is only rubble, cold and charred and dark. But I can still hear the bride's voice, the memory of some long-forgotten argument.

You said you loved me.

And I do. But it's complicated. This marriage is important to my family.

"Whose marriage?" I ask.

But the bride can't answer. She's weeping, her face in her hands as her shoulders heave with the effort. Tears drip down her face, choking her, soaking the bodice. She shakes as she runs, mindlessly, closer and closer to the cliff. I'm afraid, suddenly. This is how it ends. She's going to die, right here in front of me.

Unless I can stop her.

"Stop! Watch out!" I squeeze my eyes shut so I don't have to see.

I will not let you ruin my reputation, after all I've done to build it. Over my dead body.

The words echo in my head, and I scream them away.

Then it all goes quiet. I open my eyes.

The bride is the ghost I know again. Soaked and dead and sad. I should be scared, but I'm not. At least the voices have stopped.

I follow her back through the forest, back to the clearing and the river. The moon is high and bright, and I lift my face to the cool light, letting it bathe my forehead like a wet cloth.

When we reach the ash tree, the bride falls to her knees, her grief so palpable I can taste the coppery blood of it in the back of my throat. She clutches at the trunk and wails soundlessly as her torn gown soaks the dirt beneath her.

Her dirty, broken nails scrape at the bark. At the word she carves—fresh and raw.

GO.

I can't, I try to say. *I don't know how. Let me help you.* But the words stick in my throat.

And I reach for the weeping ghost just as everything goes black.

CHAPTER 35

There's something binding my hands. I'm tied down. The bride has tied me to her tree . . .

The dream fades away as I blink, slow and woozy. White walls come into focus and then slide away.

Where am I?

I look down at my hands. It's not rope that holds me, but tubes. An IV taped to one hand; another running to—I touch my face—my nose.

The hospital. I'm in the hospital. What am I doing in the hospital?

How did I get here? The last thing I remember, I was in the woods. And at Atwater Lodge? Or was that all a dream?

I try to rewind the night, back to the argument with Chance, but the throbbing in my head makes it hard to concentrate.

I let my head roll on the pillow. There's an empty chair pulled up to the bed beside me. And a table, with a phone on top. I reach out a hand, but quickly snatch it back when I see what's lying next to it.

The bride's hair clip.

Arden and I gave it back to her. She was wearing it last night. So how did it get here?

I struggle to sit up, accidentally yanking the tube from my nose. I fumble and try to pat it back into place as an alarm beeps from one of the machines beside the bed.

The door swings wide. It's a nurse, dressed in baby blue scrubs and matching Crocs.

"Look who's finally awake," she says, pushing some buttons to quiet the machine and then tucking the oxygen back into my nose with a practiced hand. "Settle down, sweetie. You're safe. I'm Ruby. Anything hurt?"

My hand flutters near my forehead. "I have a terrible head-ache. And my feet . . ." I shift them; the pain makes me suck in a breath. They're bandaged tight, so I can't see the damage.

"I imagine so. Sounds like you were out there for a long time. Barefoot. Took a nasty tumble, too."

Barefoot?

Images flash through my mind. The falling rocks, the angry bride. The drip of her hair.

The machine beeps loudly.

"Relax," Ruby murmurs, rubbing my arm. "You've got quite a bump on your head. You need rest." She checks my wristband. "Why don't I get you something for the pain?"

I nod. Just the slight movement loosens tears down my cheeks. "How did I get here? I don't remember anything." My voice is raspy, as if the words have to climb through sand to get out.

Ruby holds a straw to my mouth and I suck in cold, sweet

water. "Your momma found you," she says. "Sleepwalking, or some such nonsense. Wandering pretty close to the falls, too, from what I hear. You're a lucky girl."

I jolt, jostling the water cup. Close to the falls? That's not right. I was at the bottom of the falls, by the river. The rest was all a dream.

Wasn't it?

"Your daddy was speculating on what you could've been doing out there," Ruby says, shaking her head. She presses her finger to her lips. "I didn't say a word. Though I suspect it had something to do with a certain legend." She lowers one eyelid in a long wink.

"Something like that," I mumble. Momma probably should've left me in the woods. It would've been less painful than whatever Daddy's going to do to me. I point at the hair clip. "Do you know where that came from?"

Ruby tilts her head and frowns. "It was in your hair when they brought you in."

In my hair.

As she leans down to shine a light in my eyes, one at a time, my heart skips a beat. I know because it shows up on the monitor.

"Easy," Ruby says. "It's fine. Nothing broken. I'll just put it with the rest of your personal items." She opens a tall cupboard in the corner of the room.

My personal items. What personal items? My phone?

"Is my family here?" I ask instead.

"Lou was here most of the night. She just went home to shower. I told her I'd look after you. She was a bit of a mess," she shakes her head. "Sick with worry. And who could blame her?"

"You . . . know my momma?"

"We went to high school together."

"So you must know Kezia Dunlap, too."

She clucks her tongue. "Those two. Like this." She twists her fingers together. "Back in the day."

"Yeah." I try to nod, but the pain stops me. "Do you know what happened between them?"

The pain in my head is so intense, my vision goes dark and sparkly, and I press my fingers to my temples.

"You need to rest," she says again, pressing me down and tucking the blankets around me. "I mean it. You've got to quiet that brain of yours."

I turn my head away as more hot tears slip down my cheeks. What happened out there? Was the bride trying to hurt me? Kill me?

Or was she trying to tell me something?

I let my eyes drift shut, to rest them, just for a second.

When I open them again, the sky is another color and Momma's here.

She's been crying, her face pale and puffy, purple smudges under her eyes. But they light up when she's sees I'm awake. "Hey, baby. There you are. You were out for a long time." She presses a cool hand to my forehead. "I left Daddy and Graham at home. I didn't know if you'd be up for seeing them yet." She stares into my eyes, as if trying to read something there. Maybe she can see everything. Maybe she can still help me find the answers . . .

"Momma?" I whisper.

"Yes, baby?"

"Why didn't you tell me the ghost bride was real?"

CHAPTER 36

"What?" She pulls away and busies herself with straightening my sheets. "What on earth are you talking about?"

"Momma, I know you're lying," I say sharply. "Can't you be honest? For once? I almost died out there trying to figure it out. Why didn't you just tell me the truth?"

She chews her lip. "I was only trying to protect you."

But I know that look. I've seen it a thousand times. She's working to pull herself together, struggling to make up some excuse or lie to cover up whatever truth she thinks I can't handle. All this time she's been urging me to grow up, and I've been listening. I've been trying.

She's the one who hasn't been paying attention.

I throw aside the covers and try to swing my legs out of the bed.

"What do you think you're doing?" She jumps forward to stop me.

"I need to get something. To show you."

"You need to rest. Doctor's orders." She pushes me back against the pillows, less gently than the nurse, and tightens the blankets around me.

"Can you bring it to me, then? Ruby said it's in the cupboard. In my sweatshirt pocket."

She hands me the sweatshirt and I pull out the photo of Momma in her full bride getup and lay it on the tray in front of me, turning it with one finger so it's facing her.

Momma's hand trembles as she presses it to her mouth. "Damn Kezia," she says, under her breath.

"You came looking for me," I say. "I knew you would. Once Kezia told me you believed in the ghost bride, I knew everything you told me was a lie. You said she wasn't real. But she is, and you know it."

"I was worried sick," Momma says, flipping the photo over as if she can't bear to see it. "I didn't know what you were thinking. It took me hours, but I finally found you. Out near the overlook. Though what you were doing out there . . ."

What *was* I doing out there? I must have walked, in my fever dream, all the way back to the lodge from the clearing. Barefoot, apparently.

"I was looking for answers. Since you wouldn't help me." I touch the bandage on my head. "What do those photos have to do with anything? And why does Kezia have them?"

"Whatever happened between me and Kezia was a long time ago."

"Whatever happened?" I echo. "You mean like you guys using the ghost bride story for publicity?"

She flinches. "We were going to do that," she corrects me. "And then I . . . changed my mind. Something happened. And I couldn't go through with it."

"Tell me," I beg, so softly I think she may not hear.

But she sinks down in the chair beside me and begins to talk. "It all started the summer before graduation. Harlan—Daddy—and I had dated all through high school, on and off. But we had a big fight after he enlisted." She twists at her wedding band, hard, as if she's trying to open a jar. "I thought the war was stupid—I thought he was stupid, for wanting to fight in some far-off country I'd never even heard of. After he was gone, I was sorry. I was working for his family by then, at the motel. And I wanted to make it up to him. I grew up with Malice and her stories, remember. And so I had this crazy idea to reinvent the story about the bride. Make it romantic. Take some photos, spread some rumors. Hint at some ghost sightings. I thought it would be a good promotional tool. I thought we could do haunted tours, maybe even hint that the bride stayed with us on her honeymoon. We'd bring in droves of people and make the motel a success. And I'd make your daddy proud."

A good promotional tool. Kezia used almost this exact phrase. It's as if my mother is pulling forth an echo from decades past.

"But it didn't work, did it? You helped Atwater Lodge, not the motel."

Momma grimaces, as if the taste of the memory is still too bitter to swallow. "Kezia had started seeing Jackson by then, and we were young and foolish. Somehow, we thought we could make the story work for both of us. Until." She pauses and bites her lip. "She and I went to the clearing one night, to take some more photos. I'd done some alone, but I'd had a hard time. I needed help setting up the shot. And I wanted to get some on a moonbow night." She presses a hand against her chest. "And that's when we saw her. Well, I saw her. We'd been drinking, and Kezia was pretty gone at that point, and so she claimed not to have seen anything at all."

I shift in the hospital bed and bite the inside of my cheek so Momma won't see me wince. My pain medication is wearing off, and I ache all over. But I can't let her stop yet.

"What did she do?" I ask.

"Kezia?"

"The bride."

"Not much." Momma has gone pale. "It was more the way she looked. And felt."

I shiver and pull the blankets tighter. I know that feeling.

"You have to understand, I'd never really believed. To me, ghosts were no different than . . . than Malice's pirates or unicorns. All my life, I'd thought it was just a story."

"Me too," I whisper.

"And then there she was." Momma stares at the wall behind me as she replays the memory in her head. "But she wasn't sad or lost or searching for her lover, like Malice said. No, she was pissed off."

I try to sit up. "And then what happened?"

She blinks, the spell broken. "Your daddy came home."

"No, I mean with the—"

"He was injured," Momma continues, as if I haven't spoken. "There he'd been, fighting a war, while I was playing make-believe in the forest." She closes her eyes and shakes her head. "He hated the whole idea of trying to bring in business with a ghost story. He'd seen his fair share of death overseas and said the dead deserve our respect—not to be the subject of our games. Called me foolish, and I didn't disagree. Kezia blamed him, of course. Said I was 'giving in to the patriarchy.' That I'd lose myself if I married him.

"At any rate, she was wrong. Yes, your daddy can be stubborn. And maybe a tad bit too tied to his ideals. But he's a good man. He believes in God and family. Not ghosts. And certainly not curses. And I couldn't ask him to compromise those beliefs for some stupid publicity stunt. Besides, after I saw that poor girl, I knew I couldn't do it. I couldn't exploit her, or capitalize on her story. Not after I'd felt her pain and her anger.

"Don't you see? It was my fault. I . . . provoked her. Or called her forth. Dressing up like her, taunting her." Momma shudders. "I was so ashamed of myself. Malice had given me the hair clip that summer, and I gave it right back. Said I wouldn't participate in whatever fairy tales she was peddling. I needed to put the ghost bride and the curse as far away from me as possible. And Daddy needed someone to help run the motel. The engagement ring and the life together he offered—that was solid and real. About as far from the bride as I was going to get."

"But didn't you at least try to break the curse?"

Momma leans over and cups my cheek. "Don't you see, baby? There is no curse. That's just made-up nonsense. We blame this poor girl for all our troubles, but she's not responsible. She's dead. And there's nothing we can do to change that. The only decent thing is to let her rest in peace."

"But she's not resting," I say, my body trembling.

Momma blinks away a tear. "I did the best I could," she whispers. "I vowed never to speak of it again. I hid the negatives and closed up the darkroom. I wrote Kezia a letter, trying to explain myself."

I shake harder, and clench my hands beneath my blankets to try to still them. This was the fight I saw in the forest—the one the ghost bride showed me. "Betrayal has legs. Loyalty has roots," I say.

Momma nods. "She didn't take it well. She was angry. She called me a hypocrite and told me it would be a crime to waste all the work we'd put into it. She stole the photos. I told her to burn them." She dashes a tear with the back of her hand, then reaches for a tissue. "She didn't, obviously."

"But something must have happened to change her mind. Because she believes now."

"She went back. Years later. With Arden. Why, I have no idea. But I think she saw the bride herself, because she called me up, ranting and raving. Accused me of trying to scare her, or sabotage her business. I told her the same thing I'd been saying all along. Clearly, we'd angered the bride. The best thing to do was to stay away." She mops at her face. "They closed down the swimming beach after that. Sent Arden away to boarding school. And I guess mostly forgot about the ghost. Until you started working for her."

My head is spinning. Ruby warned me not to use my brain, and maybe she was right, because I can't process any of this. Momma, who lacks any ounce of imagination. Who denounces any kind of magic so strongly she may as well be flipping off the devil himself.

Momma summoned the ghost bride.

"Is that why you called off our trip? Because you knew Malice was going to tell me the truth?"

"I called off your trip because Malice isn't capable of going. And you're not old enough to care for her the way she would have needed. Believe me, if it were safe, I would have sent you off in a shower of balloons and confetti."

"So somehow this is my fault? When you're the one who put me in danger all those years ago? And never, ever tried to warn me? Maybe if you'd been honest—"

"If I'd been honest, you would have beelined it into those woods, first chance you got. Trust me. It was safer if you never heard about any of it. That's why I told Malice I wouldn't take you to visit if she so much as mentioned the curse. Don't you see? It was her fault for putting the idea in my head in the first place. I wasn't about to let her do that to you."

We're back to this again—me blaming her, her blaming Malice. Maybe this cycle is the real curse. "It's not her fault! At least she was honest. She told you because she was trying to protect us! Unlike you—"

"I didn't know how to protect you!" Momma hardly ever raises her voice, and when she does, it's terrifying. As if witnessing the queen losing her head. She takes a ragged breath. "I did the best I could."

"That's always your excuse. You've spent my whole life saying you wanted to protect me, when really all you were doing was controlling me. Telling me what to do, where to go, who to be. 'Grow up, Rena Faye.'" I spit the words at her. "How am I supposed to do that, when you're constantly looking over my shoulder? Judging me? No wonder Kezia hates you. 'Loyalty has roots'? What the hell is that, even?"

A half laugh, half sob escapes her mouth. "It's not a curse, Rena Faye."

Isn't it? Then why are we still stuck in Corbin, playing out this same scenario over and over again, generation after generation?

All this time, and all we've managed to do is pass on our pain.

The only thing that's changed is which girl has to bear it.

CHAPTER 37

The knocking wakes me and I sit up with a great gulp of air, as if I've been underwater. The door swings open and Daisy sticks her head into the room.

"Hello?" she calls. "Oh no. Did I wake you?" She's holding a teddy bear nearly twice her size, and she spins in a sort of half circle. "I'll just leave this and come back."

"Stop being a drama queen and help me get my ass out of bed," I say.

"I would. But"—she pulls her sunglasses down her nose—"you look like shit." Her face scrunches up as she tries to hug me in between the mess of tubing and bandages. Finally, she gives up and shoves the bear at me. "Here. Take the damn thing. I was worried sick. Don't ever do anything like that again!"

I laugh and it comes out on a sob. "No promises," I say, smoothing the bear's pink bow tie. I try to hang on to his silky fur, but he's too big and bulky, and he slides off the bed and onto the floor. "How did you even get that into your Jeep? Strap it to the luggage rack?"

"Maybe." She pulls off her glasses and nibbles on one of the arms as she perches on the edge of the bed. "Seriously. How bad is it?"

I shrug. "Probably better than it looks. I'm okay, other than my head and my feet."

She studies my face, her lips pursed as her eyes well up with new tears. "Shit. This is my fault. I should have come with you. Why didn't you tell me what you were planning?"

"Quit crying, would you? It's freaking me out." I shove her half-off the bed so I can move my bandaged feet and straighten the sheet. "It's not your fault. I don't know what I was thinking. I was mostly pissed at Momma. I saw that photo and I . . . I lost it." I wave a hand at the photo on the table, and Daisy flips it over. "I needed to make her listen to me."

"This was with Kezia's stuff? I knew I should've come with you to search her office. I'm kicking myself."

"Nah. We just both would've gotten fired."

"Fired, right. I almost forgot about that. You definitely had one shitty night."

"I haven't even told you about Chance. He tried to give me a promise ring."

Daisy's mouth is a round O of surprise. "Tried?"

"I told him about Arden. He said he could 'learn to forgive me.'" I snort. "And I told him I didn't want him to. That I wasn't in love with him anymore. Then he threw the ring at my head and ran off."

"Holy. Shit."

"I know, right? I've screwed everything up so badly, I'm not sure I can fix it."

"Look, far be it from me to tell you what to do—"

I can't help but smile.

"What?"

"Nothing. I should have known even being half-dead in a hospital bed wouldn't save me from your advice."

"Half-dead? Who's the drama queen now?" She hits me with a pillow. "So? Are you going to tell me, or do I have to ask?" She lowers her voice. "What exactly happened? With the bride?"

I give her an abbreviated version of the story as she studies the photo of my mom.

"This is pretty unbelievable."

"Which part? The ghost? Or my dream?"

She flaps the photo. "You're telling me *Aunt Lou* conjured the ghost bride?"

"Yep. Is it any wonder I'm cursed? I mean, if Momma had just told me—"

"Then what?" Daisy interrupts. "You would've been a good girl and stayed out of the woods?"

"Maybe."

"Hell no, you wouldn't have. What's the first thing you did after Malice told you the truth?"

"That's not fair," I protest. "You dragged me there!"

"How much dragging did I have to do? And be honest! If you had known about it any sooner, if Aunt Lou had spent your whole childhood warning you away from the woods—"

"She did do that, actually."

"See? And what did you do?"

"So you're saying this was all inevitable?"

Daisy shrugs. "I don't know. But it isn't doing us any good crying over something that didn't happen. What we need to do is figure out our next move."

"What do you mean?" My body trembles. "I'm not going back there. I can't. I almost die—"

"But you didn't." Daisy leans forward, a gleam in her eye. "She could have killed you, yes? Pushed you off a cliff, or, I don't know, made a tree fall on you? But she didn't!"

"Great. Let's give her another chance."

She swats my shoulder. "Put on your big-girl panties, sister cuz. Because we are going to figure this out and banish your curse. Once and for all."

I groan. "I should have known the tears and teddy bears weren't going to last."

"You want coddling, go to Malice."

But I can't go to Malice until this is right. I don't want to even think about what she'll say. Or how upset she'll be. I sit up and shove another pillow behind me. "You're right," I tell Daisy. "She didn't kill me. Actually, it felt more like she was trying to show me something. What happened to her, maybe. But I don't know what was real and what was me, dreaming or hallucinating from the pain meds or whatever."

And then I remember—

The hair clip.

"Wait." I lean forward. "In the cupboard," I say, pointing and snapping my fingers.

Daisy opens the door. "It's just your clothes," she says. "And your mawmaw's hair clip."

"Yes! Bring that here."

She hands it over and I wave it under her nose. "This is proof!" I turn it over in my hands. It's definitely worse for wear. Like it's been outside for days.

"Of the curse?" Daisy asks.

"I gave it back to her, remember? Last week. I took it into the woods. With Arden. That's when we kissed. Well, afterward—anyway, that part's not important. The point is I left it there for her. So she'd leave me alone. But this was in my hair. When they found me last night."

"So you're saying the hair clip is haunted." Daisy doesn't sound skeptical, exactly, but she's not on board yet either.

I turn it over in my hands, touching each pearl. "Momma wore it into the woods," I say, thinking out loud. "When she took the photos. And I had it in my hair the night we met the boys there."

"And the night you went with Arden."

"Right. So maybe the bride is using it to try to tell me something. Because she doesn't speak to me. Not even in my dream."

"So instead, she leaves notes. And hair clips."

"And photos! Arden had that photo on his phone," I remind her.

"Let me see that again." Daisy holds out her hand.

I give her my phone and continue to think out loud as she scrolls.

"Betrayal has legs . . . I think her lover betrayed her. When she took me to Atwater, I overheard an argument between them." I frown. "But I didn't recognize him."

Daisy's voice is oddly high as she says, "Hold on. I don't think it matters who he was. Because I think I've found her."

She holds up Arden's photo, where she's zoomed in on the ghost's face.

I wave an impatient hand. "I already know what she looks like. That still doesn't help us identify her."

"This isn't Arden's photo." She pinches the screen to make it smaller, and as she zooms out, it's the staff photo from Kezia's office. I took a picture of it when I snuck in.

Daisy flips back to Arden's photo.

There's no question. It's the same woman.

CHAPTER 38

They don't keep me long at the hospital. Aside from the headache and a few scratches, there's really nothing wrong with me. Other than the fact that I can see ghosts.

I'm dying to talk to Peggy, but since I was fired, it doesn't seem like the best idea to go looking for her at Atwater, so Daisy and I arrange to meet her at the Historical Society on Monday. By then, even Momma's had enough of me being underfoot and is ready to cut me loose.

With a bit of effort and after a botched GPS search, we find the address tucked into a cul-de-sac behind the highway, in an old shotgun-style cabin similar to Malice's.

Peggy meets us on the front porch.

"What the hell happened to you?"

"Ghost attack," I tell her.

She nods once and I'm strangely comforted by the fact that she doesn't seemed the least bit fazed. Because we're about to lay a lot weirder on her.

"I've got some information and we need help sorting it out," I say.

"Let's see it, then." She waves us into the little house. Inside, the layout is similar to Malice's, but most of these rooms contain endless rows of filing cabinets and nearly every surface is covered in stacks of paper. The front room has a long desk, as well as several tables piled with various binders and clipboards. Peggy gestures to one that's relatively clear, and we all sit down.

I pull up the photos on my phone, giving her an abbreviated version of how I got them.

She cuts me off. "So you broke into Kezia's office." She shakes her head. "I wondered what you did to get yourself fired."

"You know about that?" My face goes hot with embarrassment.

"Relax. I had money on fraternization, so I guess I'm out twenty bucks."

"Oh, she did that, too," Daisy says.

"Could we focus on the bride here?" I ask. "And not which rules I've violated?"

"Was it worth it?" Peggy asks, and for a crazy moment, I think she means the kiss.

"You mean the breaking and entering? Yes. Look what I got." I turn my phone so she can see the two photos side by side— Arden's ghost and the staff photo.

"Email that to me," she barks, standing up and hurrying over to the computer on the desk. "In fact, email them all." She rattles off the address and I type it in.

"Do you really think you can find the bride?" Daisy asks.

"We should probably stop calling her the bride," I say. "When

I saw her, she wasn't wearing a bridal gown. It was a nightgown."

Daisy raises an eyebrow. "When you saw her in your dream, you mean."

"Well, yeah. But what if that's what we've been getting wrong? Everyone always searches for wedding records. But if she was betrayed by her lover and not her husband, maybe there aren't any."

Peggy brings over a scrapbook and drops it to the table with a loud bang. "Nightgown makes more sense," she says, "if she died in the fire. This is everything we've got from 1875," she adds. "There were a few casualties. Mostly staff. They were all buried behind the Dunlap plot in Hillcrest Cemetery."

Daisy gives me a look. "Told you the Dunlaps were involved."

I flip open the scrapbook. On top is a clipping from the same newspaper I saw in Kezia's office.

"They thought Silas was dead," I say. "What was that all about?"

"He was missing. For almost two days. It must have been mass chaos," Peggy says. "Can you imagine? No fire trucks could get out there. Just people trying to scoop water from the river, which was more dangerous than it sounds. The current was much stronger then, before all the years of drought and climate change. Back then, it was easy to get carried away and over the falls, especially in the dark." She taps the article. "I s'pose they thought that's what happened to Silas."

"So what did happen?"

She flips back and forth, but there isn't any follow-up. "I guess we'll never know."

"Silas didn't die in the fire," I say. "But who did?"

"Mamie Lewis. Irene Chesney. Esther Price. And Georgianne Owens," Peggy says.

"What? How do you know that?"

"I told you, death certificates are easy. They're all in the database. If you know where to search. Better yet, that staff photo was archived and digitized. So"—a few more keystrokes—"if we cross-reference it with those names, voila!" Peggy turns the screen. "There's the girl from your photo. Georgianne Owens."

"Georgianne," I say. "Why does that sound familiar?"

"Because of the cemetery," Peggy says, jumping over to another desk. "The grave across from Nell's. Georgianne. No surname."

"Yes! We saw her gravestone. I can't believe you remembered that."

"It came up when I was doing the research for you on Nell. It stuck in my head because it was so unusual."

"Her name, you mean?" Daisy asks.

Peggy shakes her head. "The grave. Whoever Georgianne was, she's not actually buried there. Nobody is."

Something tickles the back of my neck. "What do you mean?"

"There's nobody in that grave. No. Body." She unfolds a piece of paper on the table between us.

"That must be a clerical error or something," I say.

Peggy shakes her head. "They did this study a few years back. Used ground-penetrating radar to map all the cemeteries in the county. You might have heard about it? It was kind of a big deal."

I think she's waiting for us to be impressed, but all I can see is a bunch of squiggly lines on inked-up paper. I lift a shoulder. "Okay?"

"It's a pretty neat idea," Peggy says. "They take this big machine. Looks like a cross between a lawn mower and a floor polisher. And they run it over the graves. You get a cross-section readout like this one here."

It reminds me of the art projects we used to do in primary school, where we'd color the page, then completely cover it with black crayon so we could scratch out designs in the wax.

"They've discovered quite a few old cemeteries on plantations using this technology. As you might imagine, slave owners didn't always mark graves properly. Bastards." She spits the last word.

"These red lines are the radar waves. The white ones tell you if something's buried below." She traces some of the lines. "The younger the grave, the better the image. The newer coffins are much easier to pick up. But even the older ones will show any major disturbances in the soil. Take Nell, for instance. These lines here? Means there's a body."

She moves her hand to Georgianne's grave—or, at least, where the stone marker is. In the blank space, she's drawn a question mark. "Here? Nothing."

I squint until my eyes water. "And you're sure."

"I'm sure."

"So we've got a dead bride—or woman, sorry," Daisy says. "And an empty grave. That can't be a coincidence."

"It's her," I say. "It has to be. I can feel it. She drowned. Maybe they never recovered her body. That makes sense, right?"

"What else do we know about Georgianne?" Daisy asks.

Peggy pecks away at the computer. "Born in London, Kentucky, 1858."

"She was only seventeen when she died?" Daisy asks, doing the math on her fingers. "That's horrible."

"Parents were Welsh immigrants. Both were employed by the Dunlaps in some capacity. Father was a coal miner. Mother was a housemaid. Georgianne started working at Atwater Manor when she was twelve."

"Wait," Daisy says. "There's a flaw in our logic."

"Only one?" Peggy asks, eyebrow raised.

"Read that list of casualties again. None of them were men, right?"

Peggy rattles them off. "Nope. No men. So?"

"So who was her lover? She jumped because he died, right? At least that's what the story says."

I page through the scrapbook. Midway through, there's a wedding photo, along with another newspaper clipping. The headline on this one reads:

Silas Dunlap and Nell Whitley— Finally Wed!

An electric tingle runs through me.

"This is him," I say. "Silas. He was her lover."

"Of course!" Daisy cries. "She thought he was dead. That's why she jumped!"

But something doesn't feel completely right to me. In the vision I saw, or whatever it was, Silas was still alive when we left him. And why did she slap him?

My head aches as I try to remember. The bride and her pain. Her fury. But everything from that night is jumbled in my mind. One minute the house was burning: the next it was gone. I can't trust what I think I saw. I have to rely on the evidence we have in front of us.

"So that's it?" Daisy says. "We solved it? It's a bit . . . anti-climactic."

Peggy leans over my shoulder to peer at the photo. "He didn't waste much time, did he? The fire was in June. Wedding in November."

You said you loved me.

I do love you. But it's complicated. This marriage is important to my family.

The words sear into my memory. "We're not done yet. We might know what happened to Silas," I say, "but she doesn't. We have to tell her. Maybe then she'll finally be able to rest."

CHAPTER 39

Daisy and I decide to tell the bride—Georgianne—what we've learned on the next moonbow night. It seems like our chances to reach her might be easier then. After all, it was a moonbow night when she died. And moonbow when Momma and I both called her forth. It's only fitting that it should be moonbow when we try to lay her to rest.

Which gives me a little over a week to stay home and recover and try to repair the mess I've made of my life.

Mostly, I hide in my darkroom.

Neither one of my parents says anything about the destruction, but Momma does install a new lock and gives me the key so I can clean it up myself.

It feels good—right—to be back under the red light, the sickly tang of the developer in my nose. This is where I belong. Not at Atwater, which was just the motel with different trappings. And not working to make someone else happy, though I imagine I'm not quite done with that. Momma has managed to get Daddy to lay off me about working for the time being, but I don't know how long this reprieve will last. For now, I'm taking advantage of the downtime to work on a new photo essay for my college applications.

Since Daddy locked me out of the darkroom before I had the opportunity to develop the photos from the day Daisy, Chance, and I went ghost hunting in the clearing, I decide to start there.

I'm hanging the last of the prints on the line when my phone pings.

It's Arden. Can you talk?

We haven't spoken since the night he watched his mom fire me. What could he possibly have to say now? I almost type this. Instead, I text, **Sure. When?**

I'm on your front porch.

Arden leans against the railing, gazing down toward the motel, but he straightens and runs a hand through his hair when he hears the door. It's strangely adorable. Is he actually still worried about impressing me? After the horrible things we said to each other?

He studies the Band-Aid on my forehead and the healing scrape on my chin as if trying to memorize my imperfections before shoving a bouquet of tulips at me. "I was going to visit you in the hospital, but my mom didn't think it was such a good idea."

I take the flowers. "Thanks," I say. "They're beautiful."

"They're an apology," he says. "Tulips, I mean. And this. I'm apologizing." His face goes pink. "I said some things the other night. That I'm not proud of."

I rub my fingers against one of the waxy petals. "No, I was out of line. You were right—I was obsessed with figuring out who the ghost was." I kick softly at the railing of the porch. "I did it, actually. Well, we did. Me and Daisy and Peggy."

"Daisy told me. So how does it feel, now that you know?"

I lift one shoulder. "Honestly? I thought it would feel more final. Less cursed? Maybe after we go to the woods it will. We're going to have a ceremony for her."

"That's what I heard."

"You and Daisy must have had some conversation."

"You know your cousin. She's not the quiet one in your family, is she? I think you once told me she takes her ghost stories very seriously."

We both crack a smile at that.

"And it turns out you were right about the ghost's lover, too. He really was my ancestor?"

"Yeah, maybe. I mean, that's our guess." I don't want to go into the whole story right now, about my dream or vision or whatever it was.

Arden jams his hands into his jeans pockets and stares down the hill. "I'm still trying to wrap my head around it. I mean, my mom never even hinted that the ghost story might have anything to do with Atwater Lodge. In fact, in my family, there's this whole mythology around Nell and Silas. They were this perfect power couple, you know? 'The union that married two counties' and all that. I was raised on that crap. And maybe it was all a lie. How are we ever supposed to know what is true?"

"We're not. All we've ever got is the stories that survive."

"I suppose you're right." He tilts his head. "Speaking of stories, I heard Chance proposed."

"Ugh." I make a face and bury my nose in the flowers. "No. That's just a rumor."

"So there was no ring?"

For a second, I see the flash of the diamond chip in the ring as Chance throws it.

And the stone in the hair clip as the ghost bride fixes it in her hair.

The hair clip . . .

If my weird night in the forest was really the bride trying to tell me something—then whatever Georgianne has been trying to convey has something to do with that clip. I watched her fix it into her hair, just before she went over the cliff. Which means her death couldn't have happened like the story says. Because if she died wearing it, how did Malice come to own it?

Arden is staring at me with a strange expression on his face.

I shake my head. "I'm sorry, what did you ask? About Chance? He did offer me a promise ring. But I turned it down." I take a deep breath. "I had to tell him the truth. I was an awful girlfriend. I cheated on him. And it wasn't fair. To either of you."

"I wasn't super honest, either." Arden stands up straight and looks me in the eye. "I knew you had a boyfriend. Or at least I'd heard about him. I could've asked you directly. I probably should have. But I didn't really want to know."

"Sometimes it's easier to ignore what's right in front of you," I say.

"I hope that's not always true," he says, reaching for my hand.

"Maybe now that we're both seeing a little clearer, we could try things again."

"What are you suggesting?"

He lifts his shoulders to his ears. "A date? Maybe?"

"Maybe? You don't sound very sure about this," I say.

"I'm sure. About everything except your answer."

"My answer is yes," I say. "I'd love to go on a date with you."

His smile makes me melt inside, as does his uncertainty, which I share.

I don't know what the future holds, and I don't know where Arden and I are going or how this will all turn out. But what I like most of all is that *he* doesn't know, either.

After Arden leaves, I head back to the darkroom, lighter than I've been in weeks. I can't stop smiling, and I'm whistling some nameless tune.

Thank God Daisy isn't here. I'd make her sick.

I carefully remove the dried photos from the clips, lining them up on the counter before turning on the overhead light. I got a few good shots of the trees on our walk in. One shot of Chance's startled face, which I'm tempted to toss straight into the trash can. My shots of the ruins are clear, and there's one or two I can possibly use, but they aren't what I want to see.

Deep down, I was secretly hoping I'd managed to capture photographic evidence.

Like Arden did.

The final pictures are a series of the ash tree. I shot these right after we saw the eerie word *GO* scratched into the bark, and as we fled. In the second to last shot, there's a blur, as if something smudged the lens.

And then—

In the last one, a figure stands beside the tree, her body half-hidden in shadow.

Georgianne.

She's faded to almost a mist, but her form is unmistakable. As is the warning.

In my vision, she'd carved the word with her bare hands before sinking down between the tangled roots at the base of the tree.

I look at the picture more closely. The letters were clearly carved deep into the bark, with something sharp. From what I can tell, the wood beneath is weathered smooth. This doesn't look like a fresh warning. So what could it mean?

GO.

I think back to what I know.

The marker for Georgianne, and the empty grave beneath.

LOYALTY HAS ROOTS.

GO carved into the tree; the ghost, on the ground, hopeless.

LOYALTY HAS ROOTS.

Trees have roots, too.

Georgianne Owens.

G.O.

Something clicks and suddenly I know—

She doesn't want me to find her lover.

She wants me to find her body.

CHAPTER 40

When I was little, Malice told me that the moonbow helped us soak up the magic we lost to everyday life, and I used to stare until I went cross-eyed, willing it to become clear so I could absorb it all at once, in one big gulp. Now I know better. The moonbow is best viewed from the corner of your vision. Like a painfully shy lover—or a ghost—it needs to be lulled and wooed, almost seduced into appearing. Only then does it solidify into something other than its shadow-self. And you hold that ephemeral glimpse as long as possible, but you can never keep it. It slips through your fingers like smoke. Even the best photographers have trouble capturing it. Which is why tourists end up with photos purchased in the gift shop instead of their own, and try to brush aside the subtle, nagging sense of loss at the feeling of something they've missed. It's why we're drawn back here to the falls, month after month after month.

We chase magic because once we've had a taste of the illusion, we can't bear to live without it.

It's why I wanted a reason to believe in the ghost bride, even when I was denying it.

Now that I know she's real, it's my turn to work some magic and try to bring her peace.

I owe her at least that much.

The moonbow is barely visible tonight, as Daisy and I drive past the falls on our way to the turnoff; this early in the cycle, its presence is more faith than foundation. But I can feel it in the heaviness of the air, the way the trees whisper and the night holds its breath in anticipation. The way the mist swirls and spits, parts and finally comes together in an arc of light and darkness.

My cousin is not completely on board with my new plan, at least not at first. "Have you lost your damn mind?" is what she actually says.

"Look at the photos," I repeat. "You know I'm right." In addition to the shot I got of Georgianne, near the tree, I also gave her a copy of Nell and Silas's wedding photo. After making the connection between Georgianne and the hair clip, I went back to Peggy for confirmation. And on closer look, we discovered that Nell was wearing the hair clip at her wedding.

The same hair clip Georgianne was wearing when she died.

The same clip I now hold in my hands.

"So you're saying someone must have found it after her death."

"Not only found it," I say, "but found it and somehow knew it was connected to the legend of the ghost bride."

"I get all that," Daisy says. "What I don't get is why we can't ask Aunt Lou and Kezia to help us. The last time you went alone, you were nearly killed," she says, as if I need reminding. "I think it's safer if we have backup."

"*Nearly* being the important word. Also, I wouldn't say *nearly*. I lost my shoes. I'll do better this time," I say. "I have a theory, and I need to test it."

"Wasn't that what you were doing when you got hurt?"

"I was angry and fed up. This time, I feel like I know what I'm doing. I just hope it doesn't anger Georgianne more."

"So what is your plan?" Daisy asks. "Are we just going to . . . what? Call her name? Show her Silas's wedding photo?"

"Don't be ridiculous," I say, popping open the back so I can hand her a shovel. "We're going to dig up her body."

Daisy gives me a look like I've completely lost it. "Remind me how you figured this all out?"

"It started with the vision," I say. "A lot of it's jumbled, but at least some of it had to be real. We were here, by the river. And the wind was blowing. My mom and Kezia were fighting, only they were younger. And somehow, that got mixed up with Georgianne and her lover—Silas—fighting." I squeeze my eyes shut. "She slapped him. And then she grabbed something off his dresser. I think it was the hair clip, because she was wearing it when she jumped."

"Wow. Busy night. No wonder you looked like shit."

I make a face. "Yes, but don't you see? She was clearly trying to tell me something." I turn and brace myself. "Georgianne!"

There's a rustling off to my right, toward the beach trail. I hold my breath and wait, but nothing happens.

"Well, I guess we start digging." I push the tip of my shovel into the dirt at the base of the ash tree that bears *GO*, using my foot to drive it in. "This is where I saw her. Clawing at the bark. This is where she's buried. I'm sure of it."

"Hold on." Daisy grabs my wrist. "We can't just dig. What if we . . . hit . . . something?"

"So dig slow."

"You know this is crazy, right? First of all, if you're right, he did nothing to preserve her body. Just . . . dumped her in a hole." She waves a hand at the ground. "Which means she would've decomposed by now. We're talking almost a century and a half. There won't be anything left."

"What, are you an archaeologist now?"

"Anthropologist," she corrects me, "but I'm still right. And second, whatever might be left—jewelry, maybe? Or bone fragment? It's going to be small. We can't just start mucking around in here. We're going to need to call in professionals."

"You mean like Peggy?"

Daisy rolls her eyes. "I mean like forensic scientists."

I stab my shovel into the ground and swipe the hair off my forehead as I sink down. "So what are we supposed to do now?"

"I don't know. I thought you'd call her forth. Like you did before."

"I'm not sure how I did it before," I confess. "I think it was by dressing up and imitating her. It seems disrespectful to do it again, now that we know better."

"Maybe if we sit here long enough, she'll appear. And thank us. Or something," Daisy says, sitting down beside me.

A tree branch cracks and Daisy grabs my hand. "She's here."

We both stare into the forest, as the leaves on the birch elms twitch. Suddenly, they part.

Momma and Kezia step into the clearing.

"You have a lot of nerve, young lady," Momma says when she catches sight of me. "Of all the asinine stunts you've pulled, this has got to be top of the list."

"Momma, calm down!"

Kezia nods at me as she steps around us, and I nod back. I know I owe her more—an apology, for starters. But I have to deal with Momma first.

"Why are you here?" I ask.

"We're here to save your necks."

"If you will just give me five minutes—"

Momma looks like she wants to slap me. "Oh, five minutes! You want five minutes to *what*? Run around this death trap one more time? See what else you can break?"

"You're exaggerating," I say. "Look. We think we found her grave."

Momma's face goes white, but before she can respond, Kezia breaks in. "Found whose grave?"

"Georgianne's. She was a maid at Atwater Manor. We think she had an affair with Silas Dunlap. He broke up with her the night of the fire."

"And she killed herself?"

I lift a shoulder. "Maybe? I think she did jump from the cliff. But she didn't bury herself. Or carve her own initials into this tree."

I think about the vision I had and the way she looked at the base of the tree. How lonely she must have been, sitting here year after year as the young girls came and partied. Told her story like it was an anecdote. Or a punch line. Acting out the wedding she never got to have.

"I think I know why she's so angry," I say out loud. "And it's not just about Silas. It's about us, too. Yes, he buried her, and then let everyone forget about her. No one ever got to mourn her properly. Instead, the rest of us, we twisted her story for our own purposes. We mimicked her. And used her."

Kezia and Momma exchange a look.

"Not just you," I say. "Daisy and I did it too. We played 'wedding.' Without any thought to who she really was. Or what had happened to her. How she'd suffered. Malice told me there was a curse," I say. "After that, it was easy to convince myself that all the bad things that happened to me were because of this scorned woman, hell-bent on revenge. When in reality, it was me. It was all of us. We're responsible for our own bad decisions. For getting stuck in this cycle and repeating it, over and over. Repeating the gossip and the rumors."

I look from Daisy to Kezia to Momma. "Don't you see? She isn't trying to kill us. She's just trying to get someone to listen to her!"

And I know how she feels. I've been stuck this summer, tied to my past and my childhood and Chance. Rooted in place and unable to move forward. Trying to get people to take me seriously. Maybe that's why I relate so strongly to this woman.

We've both struggled against someone else's version of our truth, fighting for the right to tell our own stories.

And we have both made choices that felt more like curses.

I even think I understand why Momma did what she did. Why she tried to control me, under the guise of keeping me safe. Because when you love someone, sometimes you hang on too tight. Especially if the only other option is letting go.

It doesn't mean I'm ready to forgive her, but it's something. For the first time, there aren't any secrets between us. Nothing but silence separates us now.

"She needed a woman, someone who would understand. Who would tell her story." I hold up a hand. "Not the legend we all keep repeating. The *real* one. It's a story of betrayal and loyalty." I gesture to the tree. "The story of her roots."

The wind picks up, scattering the last of the paper wishes.

Kezia gasps.

Daisy lets out a strangled scream.

I turn around, and there she is.

Blocking the path.

I've brought her forth once more.

And now it's time to send her home.

Momma steps forward, blocking me with her body.

"It's okay, Momma," I say, gently moving her aside. "I know how to make this right."

I hold out my hand to the bride. "We came to apologize. Isn't that right?"

There are tears running down Momma's cheeks as she slowly nods. "Yes," she whispers. "I'm so sorry. I was wrong to do what I did."

"I was wrong, too," Kezia says. "I manipulated your story for the sake of the hotel. And I covered up a lot of Silas's lies. I didn't know everything," she adds. "But once Rena Faye started asking about the fires, I knew a Dunlap must have been involved. And I hid that. To protect the reputation of the lodge. And my son."

Georgianne flickers, from white to dark and back again. Her long hair *drip drip drip*ping.

"We can't undo what we've done," I say. "But we can try to make this right. We can tell your real story. You won't be forgotten anymore."

Momma takes my other hand, and Daisy my elbow. I can feel Kezia behind us as well. Together, we are strong. We are brave. We are truth tellers.

We are women.

Maybe that's why the bride was drawn to me. She knows I will carry on her story because I come from a long line of storytellers. I also come from Corbin, from the river. And that's what rivers do. We carry on.

Slowly, the wind around us dies. And as we watch, the ghost flickers again, her light growing softer and softer.

Until finally, we see her as she had been, all those years ago. Whole. Hopeful. Happy.

She smiles as she flickers once more and then disappears.

CHAPTER 41

Malice sets a gigantic pitcher of her famous lemonade on the kitchen table. "Can you get the cups, sweetheart?" She raises her voice to be heard over the pounding coming from the living room. "I've got to go make sure your daddy doesn't break anything installing that ridiculous contraption. Though why we need it is anyone's guess," she mutters as she wanders off to yell at Daddy.

"We need it because it's a hundred degrees in here," Daisy says, though not loud enough for Malice to hear. She and Hazel have been put on decorating duty, blowing up balloons and hanging streamers for Momma's surprise party.

I grab the plastic cups from the top cupboard. "Remember the birthday sleepovers I used to have here, chasing fireflies and roasting marshmallows over the firepit? It'll be weird not to visit Malice here anymore." I say, staring out at the back lawn from the window over the sink.

"Not as weird as it will be to visit Hazel here," says Daisy.

Hazel pokes her tongue out at her sister. "At least Bastian and me are kind of keeping it in the family."

Hazel and her boyfriend Bastian are engaged. They're also pregnant and in need of a home of their own. When Momma first suggested the cabin, I balked. But it makes sense for everyone. Malice is happy with her new apartment, which is closer to everything in town. Plus, Hazel and Bastian aren't exactly loaded, so this tiny place is about all they can afford before the baby comes.

"A shotgun cabin for a shotgun wedding," Graham says as he comes in through the back door, where he's been busy moving cars out of sight. He grabs a carrot stick off the veggie tray.

Daisy punches him in the shoulder, hard.

"Ow."

"Say that in front of my daddy, and he'll show you the business end of his shotgun," Daisy says.

A knock at the door cuts the argument short, which is a pity, because Daisy was definitely winning.

"I'll get it," Graham offers.

Like I've always said, my brother knows how to time an exit. Too bad there's no career in that.

"Rena Faye, your *boyfriend* is here," he calls a second later.

I feel my face go red as Daisy laughs and Hazel gives me a moon-eyed, knowing look.

"He's not my boyfriend," I protest weakly, wiping my hands on a napkin. "We've only been on three dates." Three dates and three very hot make-out sessions. But I don't tell them that.

I sense Daisy knows anyway. "Uh-huh." She pops a grape in

her mouth and wiggles her eyebrows at me. "Not buying it."

I leave my cousins to their giggling and go rescue Arden. He and Kezia are waiting on the cabin's front porch. Graham has already disappeared.

"I'm glad you could make it," I say, giving Arden a hug and letting Kezia peck my cheek. Things are still a bit awkward between her and me, but now it's due more to the fact that I'm dating her son than anything else.

"Come on in. We've got food and drinks in the kitchen. And I think Daddy's almost got the air conditioning going."

"Thank heavens." Hazel comes out fanning her face, Daisy trailing behind her with the cake and a handful of balloons.

"All set," Daddy says, and we wait as he clicks the button. A cheer goes up as the motor roars to life, and even Malice manages a smile. "Now, where are Ford and Ellie? They're supposed to be bringing Lou over as soon as she finishes up at the diner."

"They're here," Graham says, pulling aside the curtain. "Everybody hide!"

We look around the room, which has been mostly cleared of Malice's things.

"Where?" Daisy asks.

"Just stand behind me," Daddy says.

Momma opens the door, talking to Aunt Ellie over her shoulder. "—still a few boxes we can fit in your—"

"Surprise!" we yell.

To our credit, she does look surprised. And even a little bit pleased, though it's hard to tell with Momma.

As Momma greets her guests, Malice pulls Arden and me

aside. "This must be the new beau I've been hearing so much about," she says, beaming up at him.

"Pleased to meet you, Mrs. Slocum," he says. "And thank you for inviting us."

"My pleasure. And call me Malice. Everyone else does. Now tell me"—she motions for Arden to bend down—"how do you feel about ghost stories?"

"I love them," he says. "I'm hoping to have one of my own someday. Right now, though, I'll settle for Rena Faye's."

"Yes, well, I'm still waiting to hear the rest of that one myself. Tell you what. Why don't you help me in the kitchen and fill in the blanks?" she asks, linking arms with him.

"Sure thing, Mrs. . . . Malice," he says, winking at me over the top of her head.

I smile after them, then turn to arrange the forks on the small cake table next to the door. Kezia's hovering in the corner, lemonade cup in hand, staring toward the kitchen. When I follow her line of sight, I see she's watching Momma.

"You should go over and say hi," I say. "She won't bite."

It's been nearly a week since we sent Georgianne to her final rest, or the great beyond, or wherever it is that ghosts go to finally find their peace. Not near enough time for me to have processed everything that happened. And definitely not enough time to erase twenty years of resentment.

Kezia shakes her head and sips her drink. "I wouldn't be too sure about that."

"So how was your Fourth of July?" I ask, changing the subject. Atwater always does it up big, with a picnic on the lawn for guests and a firework display at night. Arden invited me, but since yesterday was Momma's actual birthday, I opted to stay home and have dinner with her. We caught a glimpse of some of the fireworks from the living room window, though.

Kezia waves a hand. "It was busy, as usual. Nothing beats a weekend holiday, am I right?"

"You are," I agree. The motel has been booked solid as well, though most of our guests checked out this morning. It's the only reason we were able to swing this party. The fact that we're a day past must have helped with the surprise factor.

"Wait. Fourth of July!" I slap my forehead, and Kezia gives me one of her cold stares. "Arden told me you took him to the clearing once. On Fourth of July. Momma's birthday. That's why you went, isn't it? Because you missed her."

Her eyes unexpectedly fill with tears and she blinks. "I still miss her. She was my best friend."

"You should tell her that."

Kezia uses a finger to wipe condensation from her cup. "It might be too late for us."

I look over at Momma. "I don't know about that. Momma's most prickly when she really cares about someone. If she totally hated you, she'd be polite as can be." Momma looks up and catches my eye then, giving me a tiny smile. "Trust me on this."

"Time for presents!" Daddy's voice is loud in the tiny space. He ushers Momma over to the single chair in the living room, and we all gather round as Momma opens gifts—a gold cross necklace from Daddy, a CD from Graham. Malice gives her a book, and when Momma reads the title, she rolls her eyes.

"*Ghost Stories of Kentucky*? Really, Ma?"

Malice blinks innocently. "I thought you might have acquired a new appreciation for them."

When Momma gets to my gift, she pauses with the paper halfway off and presses her hand to her mouth. "Oh, baby. Where did you find this?"

Momma turns it around to show everyone the black-and-white photo I've had matted and framed. It's the two of us, me and Momma, taken when I was just a toddler. I'm sitting on Momma's lap, eyes wide and finger in my mouth, while she holds me and aims her camera toward a mirror. The flash reflected in the glass shines in the corner of the photo like a star.

"I found the negative in one of the boxes in the darkroom," I say. "I'd never seen it before. But it's such a cool shot. I thought maybe we could hang it up."

She clutches the frame to her chest and squeezes my hand tight. "Yes. I'd like that."

She holds up Kezia's gift next. "You didn't have to get me anything."

Kezia shrugs and fiddles with her bangle bracelets. "It's not much."

Momma tears the paper, pulling out the pair of fuzzy gray socks adorned with glittery white ghosts. Her eyes are shiny with tears as she looks up at her old friend. "Thank you. I love them." She kicks off her flip-flops and pulls them on, wiggling her toes.

Daddy looks from Malice to Kezia. "I'm sensing a theme."

"Relax, Harlan. Just having a little fun. Don't get your tighty-whities in a twist," Malice says.

"Ma." Momma shoots her a warning look.

Daisy says, possibly to change the subject, "Socks? Really? It's hot enough to melt butter in here."

Kezia says, "Her feet were always cold."

"They still are," I say.

After that, it's cake and more lemonade and chitchat, until Daddy finally looks at his watch and claps Graham on the shoulder. "We've got to go, son. Tourists wait for no man."

Graham scowls. "How did Rena Faye end up getting the summer off, while I'm stuck working basically every shift?"

I'm not sure if I should laugh or cry. "Believe it or not, Graham, I used to wonder the exact same thing about you. It doesn't seem fair, does it?" I feign a sympathetic smile. "Maybe you'd rather stay here and help us clean up and finish packing?"

"Happy birthday, Ma!" he calls, already on his way to the door.

Uncle Ford and Aunt Ellie make their departure as well, Hazel trailing behind them and looking ready for a nap. Then it's just me and Daisy, Malice and Momma, and Kezia and Arden. And Peggy, who somehow slipped in without me noticing and is helping herself to cake.

"Finally!" Malice says. "I thought they'd never leave!"

"Be nice, Ma!"

"I am nice. Nice enough I didn't say a single word to your husband about the ghost bride or Rena Faye's midnight trek into the forest. But my patience is wearing thin and I'm about to pop! Now, who's going to tell me the story?"

Daisy nudges me with her shoulder. "Go on."

I tell her everything—my second encounter with the ghost,

the fire and the fight with Silas. When I get to the part about visiting Peggy at the historical research center, Malice leans forward in her chair.

"Get me my Bible."

"You think we should pray?" I'm surprised; that's more Daddy's thing than hers.

"It's over there, on the bookshelf." She points, and Daisy fetches the big leather-bound book.

We crowd around the back of her chair as Malice flips to the family tree in the front, running her finger over the names. Then she lets out a crow of delight. "That's what I thought. Looky here." She taps the page, and Peggy practically shoves me aside to get a view. "My great-grandma Alma. She was an Owens, too, before her marriage."

Peggy pulls off her glasses to peer closer at the page. "Well, I'll be." She looks at me. "Georgianne is in here too."

My scalp tingles as the hair goes up all over my body. "What are you saying?"

"You're related to the ghost bride?" Daisy clutches my arm.

"According to this, Alma and Georgianne were cousins," Peggy says, chewing on the arm of her glasses.

"That must be why you have the hair clip!" Daisy says. "And why you're cursed! Because you're her descendant."

I turn this information over in my head. "But that doesn't make any sense. How would Alma get the hair clip? Silas pulled her body out of the river to get the hair clip back, remember? He buried her by that tree. And then gave it to Nell, who wore it in her wedding. Unless—" I look from Daisy to Momma to Peggy. "Were we wrong?"

Peggy answers first. "You weren't wrong, at least not about Georgianne's body. I've been in contact with the forensic specialists. They've only done a preliminary search of the area near the tree, but from what I've heard, they're pretty certain someone was buried there. They uncovered some human remains. Teeth."

Kezia clears her throat. "Actually, I think I can shed some light on this. The Dunlap family has a story, too. The legend of the missing Dunlap diamond. As the legend goes, Franklin Dunlap found the diamond when he first opened the mine. Underneath these very hills. It was gorgeous, or so I've been told. A three-carat, multifaceted, miner's-cut gem. Fit for a princess. Franklin's bride wore it on her wedding day, and later, so did Nell Whitley when she wed his son, Silas. And that was the last anyone ever saw of it."

"Until now." She gestures to the clip lying on the table beside Malice's chair. I'd given it back to her when I first arrived, with a promise to fill her in on all the details later.

Momma gasps as Malice fumbles with the clip.

"Careful," Daisy says. "That thing has to be worth a fortune."

No. It can't be. I think of all the times I found it tangled among Malice's other costume jewelry. Of Chance, dropping it carelessly in the dirt. And Arden and me, throwing it into the clearing and running away.

A three-carat diamond.

"I think I need to sit down," I say, dropping to the floor.

Kezia continues, "I'd seen the clip before, of course. When I was much younger. Lou and I used to wear it to play bride in the forest. I always assumed it was just a piece of costume jewelry. It wasn't until much later, after I married Jackson, that I heard the tale of the Dunlap diamond. But I never put the two together."

She nods at me. "Not until I saw Rena Faye in the library one night, wearing it in her hair." Her smile is brittle. "I have to admit, my first thought was not so charitable. I assumed someone in her family must have stolen it. So I did a little digging. But for all the upheaval the missing diamond caused the Dunlaps, there were never any accusations of theft."

"So what are you saying?" Momma asks.

"Personally, I think Nell gave it away," Kezia says. "I've no proof, of course. But Alma Owens was Nell's personal maid for years. Nearly all her life. I think somewhere along the way, Nell figured out what Silas had done. Or suspected. At the very least, she must have known that Alma and Georgianne were related. She knew Georgianne was presumed dead, after all. Lost in the fire. It has to be more than just coincidence that the hair clip ended up in her family's hands."

"There's no way we'll ever know for sure," I say.

"That's true," Malice says. "But I think we know enough to make some educated guesses. After all, we have the hair clip. And the story."

"But it wasn't the real story," I say.

"Actually, if you think about it, Malice's story doesn't make Georgianne look so great," Daisy says. "No wonder she hated it. In Malice's version, she just watches the house burn. She never goes for help. She doesn't even try to find out if her lover survived."

"Yeah, well, she doesn't come off so hot in your version either," I say.

"Maybe Nell told multiple stories. You know, to put people off the scent," Peggy suggests.

"People like Georgianne's cousin," Malice adds.

"Yes, her cousin, who might've known about the affair. Or at least known there was a lover," Daisy says.

"It's also possible the diamond was a payoff," Kezia adds. "To keep quiet."

"Maybe that was our curse all along," Malice says. "We weren't burdened with her truth. We were burdened with someone else's lies."

I exchange a look with Momma. We've both come to the conclusion that the curse wasn't real. After generations of carrying on the story, somewhere along the line, it became easy for the women in our family to lay the guilt at the ghost bride's feet. But Georgianne didn't curse us. She was just trying as hard as she could to tell her story, with whatever limited options were available to her—Momma's letter to Kezia, Malice's hair clip.

Malice doesn't completely agree, but then again, she's been carrying Georgianne's story longer than either of us. It makes sense that it will take her longer to set it down.

I take the hair clip from Malice—very gently, a real diamond!— and hold it out to Kezia. "I guess this belongs to you, then. To your family."

Kezia shakes her head. "It's yours. Whatever her motivation might have been, Nell clearly wanted your family to have it."

I stare at the jewel in my hand. Three carats. I shake my head. "I'm not sure I want to wear it anymore," I say. "Knowing what I know."

"Well, three carats should buy you at least a semester at your fancy art school," Malice says, patting my hand.

I take Malice's hand and squeeze. "What do you think Georgianne would want?"

Momma wraps her arm around my shoulder and touches her head to mine. "I think you were right all along. Georgianne just wanted her story told. And she finally found the right girl to tell it."

THE LEGEND OF THE GHOST BRIDE

as told by Rena Faye Whitaker

Let me start by saying that while she may have been a ghost, she was never a bride. That's the problem with these kinds of stories—too often, the truth depends on who's telling the story. And while it's true that around here, most of us knew her as the ghost bride, she had a name.

Georgianne Owens.

By all accounts, Georgianne was very beautiful. And she was just seventeen that fateful summer of 1875, working as a housemaid at the big house at the top of the falls—Atwater Manor. So is it any wonder that this young, vivacious girl caught the wandering eye of Silas Dunlap, notorious playboy and heir to the Dunlap fortune?

(As I've already warned you, the truth depends on the teller. And while I have no proof of Silas's debauchery, I can say I met the man—sort of—and believe me when I tell you he was no prince.)

Despite his obvious flaws, Georgianne fell hard and fast for her smooth-talking Romeo. As my cousin says, there's nothing like love to keep a girl from seeing truth. Maybe that's why Georgianne kept their romance a secret—deep down, she might have known what would be obvious to the rest of her family: that Silas never had any intention of marrying her, despite whatever lies he might have fed her. Had she told someone—her cousin Alma, for instance—Alma might have pointed out that Silas was already betrothed to another. His engagement to Nell Whitley, daughter of wealthy landowner Philip Whitley, had made quite a splash in the local newspaper.

But whatever Georgianne knew, or didn't, about Silas, she loved him deeply. That's why, when Atwater Manor caught fire in the middle of the night one sweltering June evening, Georgianne's first thought was for his safety, not her own. Imagine how she must have felt when she burst into his room, half-sick with fear, only to be confronted with evidence of his wedding preparations.

A wedding she knew nothing about.

He tried to reason with her—I do love you, he said. This marriage is important to my family, he said. But the house was literally on fire, and there wasn't time to argue. With smoke choking them both and flames licking at their feet, Georgianne grabbed what she saw as the concrete piece of evidence of his betrayal—the Dunlap diamond.

Legend has it, Franklin Dunlap, Silas's father, found the

three-carat stone in the mines beneath the very mountain where he built his house. It became an instant family heirloom, a talisman of their luck and good fortune. He'd had the miner's-cut stone set into a gorgeous pearl-clustered hair clip for his new bride, and Silas in turn was expected to give it to Nell as a wedding gift and a promise of their glorious future.

But in one swift move, Georgianne changed all of that.

With that one terrible decision, she sealed her fate.

She took the hair clip, securing it in her braid as she fled the burning building. If she couldn't have Silas, perhaps she was thinking Nell couldn't have the diamond. More likely, she wasn't thinking at all.

You must know what happened next. This part is the same in every version.

Georgianne plunged over the side of the cliff, taking her love and her dreams and Silas's diamond with her.

Silas must have panicked. Can you imagine? He knew the body would wash ashore at some point. If this girl—this beautiful maid who worked for him and flirted with him and lived in his house—if she were to be found with the Dunlap diamond in her hair? People would talk, there was no question. Possibly there were already whispers. Whispers that couldn't get back to Nell. There was too much at stake, too much riding on their union.

Silas had no choice. He had to find Georgianne and get that hair clip back.

She would not ruin his reputation, or his future.

Over his dead body, he said.

But actually, it was hers.

Silas combed the riverbank below the falls, searching for Georgianne's body. According to the newspaper, he was missing for two days. For a time, they presumed he'd perished in the fire. Imagine the relief of his family when he emerged from the forest, dirty and dehydrated. They were so thrilled to see him alive, they never questioned his story about being knocked unconscious and wandering the woods, dazed and disoriented.

At least, most didn't.

Nell may have had her suspicions. But what could she do? She wed him anyway, dressed in satin and lace, that Dunlap diamond in her hair.

How did he get the diamond back, you ask?

Surely you can guess.

After pulling her lifeless body from the water, he pulled that diamond from her hair. And then he buried Georgianne beneath an ash tree on the bank of the river.

Perhaps he had loved her, in his own way. Because he didn't leave her in an unmarked grave. He carved her initials into the bark of the tree.

And what became of poor Georgianne, her life cut so short? Her death all but forgotten?

Years passed, a century, then more. And as time went on, she heard whispers of the story. Her story, but not her story, the variations twisting and spreading, like the flames that consumed the manor. The story of a poor, sad bride and a fatal fire. A jilted lover and an unwanted pregnancy. A murderous husband and a demon hell-bent on revenge.

With each telling, she grew angrier and angrier. Moonbow after moonbow, year after year, she walked. Haunting the forest, in search of someone who would listen. Someone who would search for the truth.

Georgianne couldn't rest until she found this person—this girl—who would tell her real story.

And now, finally, she can.

Acknowledgments

The moonbow phenomenon is real, and Cumberland Falls is one of the few places you can view one on a regular basis. The first time I visited, in 2005, I was mesmerized. I wanted to capture some of the wonder and camaraderie I felt, standing at the top of a waterfall in the middle of the night with a group of strangers, so I returned to my room at Dupont Lodge and wrote a page and a half, a snippet of a story, about a girl who grew up in the mountains nearby and was feeling trapped. I knew she worked at her parents' motel, and I knew the moonbow was an important marker in her life. Then I set that story aside—for fifteen years!—until my brilliant agent, Barbara Poelle, plucked it out of half a dozen other ideas and said, "That's the one." Barbara, if not for you, this book would literally not exist. You are amazing and a rock star of an agent, and I thank you from the bottom of my heart.

Liza Kaplan, my ever-patient editor, also deserves my deepest gratitude. There was a time I thought this book might not happen, but you never wavered. Thank you for the countless phone calls as we tried to wrangle this plot into submission, your thoughtful edit letters, and your words of encouragement. I am so humbled and honored by your dedication to the story and your determination to make it better.

I'd also like to thank my amazing friend, critique partner, and impromptu therapist, Linda Davis. I am grateful to you for so many things—for reading this manuscript eighty-seven times and never complaining, for taking my sobbing phone calls and never once hanging up, for talking me down off numerous ledges and out of too many plot holes to count, and for reading the final pages in a grocery store parking lot when I was minutes away from deadline—just to name a few. What if we hadn't met at that SCBWI retreat all those years ago? That is the kind of horror story that keeps me awake at night!

To the whole Philomel Phamily, including Talia Benamy, Jill Santopolo,

Krista Ahlberg, Katie Bircher, Marinda Valenti, and Monique Sterling, thank you for your dedication and your commitment to excellence. Each time I receive a draft back, I am touched and amazed all over again by all the hard work that goes on behind the scenes to make these stories shine. And a special thanks to Theresa Evangelista for the stunningly gorgeous cover she created, which I love so much that better words escape me.

I owe a debt of gratitude to the staff at Dupont Lodge, the Sheltowee Trace Adventure Resort, and the employees of Cumberland Falls State Park. I have taken many logistical and historical liberties with this story, and as a result, any mistakes are all mine. Cumberland Falls State Park is the best place to view the moonbow, and Dupont Lodge is a fantastic place to stay. But before the land was protected by the state, it was privately owned, and there were a few versions of a hotel that stood on that piece of land above the falls. I've presented a sort of alternative history in the book, a what-if, if you will. What if the land had never been sold, and the lodge continued to be privately owned by a wealthy, fictional family with secrets of their own?

I kicked off the writing of this book with a research trip to view the moonbow in September of 2019. By the time I turned in my first draft, we were in lockdown in the middle of a worldwide pandemic. To all my friends and colleagues who supported me in the writing of this novel, virtually and otherwise, know that I am so very grateful for your friendship and encouragement. I miss you all and cannot wait to hug each and every one of you!

Emma, Ari, and Cameron, you are always and forever my greatest joy and inspiration. Whether we've been locked together or kept apart, know that you will always have all my thanks and all my love.

Josh, you will always have my heart. I'm grateful for far too many things to list here, but I'd be remiss if I didn't mention the cemetery scene. Most of your suggestions are ridiculous (you know it's true!), but that one actually worked and the book is better for it. Boo! I love you.

As for ghost stories, there is a real legend of a ghost bride at Cumberland Falls. The most popular version of the story is similar to the official Atwater Lodge version included in the book. But like all good legends, there are countless variations, with those variations perhaps being more important to the people who tell the story. While researching, I discovered numerous other ghost brides throughout the world, thousands of mysterious women in white, and I started to wonder what it meant. Why do we tell these stories over and over? What are we projecting onto these nameless, ephemeral women? I wrote this book to try to answer those questions, and I am grateful to every single reader who has chosen to pick up this story and join the conversation.